A STRANGE BIRTH

TO

FRANKENSTEIN

A COLLECTION

SECOND VOLUME OF TWO PARTS

I saw the Pale Student
of the Unhallowed Arts
Kneeling beside the thing
He had put together.
I saw the hideous phantasm
Of a man stretched out,
And then, on the working
Of some powerful engine.
Show signs of life, and stir with an
Uneasy, half vital motion——

MARY SHELLEY

London:
PRINTED FOR
ROBERT DWIGHT BROWN & ALLONYMOUS BOOKS
2025

ALLONYMOUS BOOKS

A Division of Chi Xi Stigma Publishing Company, LLC

ISBN 13: 978-1-931608-70-1 — *Playing a Game of Ghost Stories*
ISBN 13: 978-1-931608-72-5 — *A Strange Birth to Frankenstein*
ISBN 13: 978-1-931608-73-2 — *A Strange Birth to Frankenstein (Omnibus)*
ISBN 13: 978-1-931608-75-6 — *A Strange Birth to Frankenstein (Omnibus)*

Includes the following Novels and Short Stories (Complete):
FRANKENSTEIN;
    or, The Modern Prometheus – Vol. 2 & 3 by Mary Shelley, 1818
THE VAMPYRE by Dr. John Polidori, 1819

Includes the following Poems (Complete):
DARKNESS by Lord Byron, 1816
MONODY ON THE HONOURABLE DEATH OF RB SHERIDAN
    by Lord Byron, 1816

We acknowledge the corrections made to Ernestus Berchhold made by D.L. Macdonald and Kathleen Scherf in their University of Toronto Press edition.

Table of Contents

Appendix

Preface

At first blush, these two volumes are merely a collection of classic Gothic Horror tales from the 1810's, over two hundred years ago. One is extraordinarily famous: *Frankenstein; or The Modern Prometheus*, the first science-fiction novel. One is ordinarily famous (in vampire circles): *The Vampyre*, the first novel featuring a suave, seductive member of the undead. The remaining works: 'The Burial: A Fragment', *Ernestus Berchtold; or The Modern Œdipus*, and "The Death-Bride" are so obscure they are barely known out of academic circles. If these volumes had been published by a university press, they would a 'merely' be a collection of stories, perhaps with annotations from scholars, but a collection nonetheless.

The unique factor linking these stories together they were all conceived and/or written in 1816: "The Year Without Summer". After reading "The Death-Bride", from a French translation of German ghost stories titled *Fantasmagoriana*, Lord Byron proposed playing a game of ghost stories. During this game, he wrote "The Burial: A Fragment", his personal physician Dr John Polidori wrote both *Ernestus Berchtold* and his plagiarism, *The Vampyre*, and Mary Shelley, the step-sister of his lover, wrote *Frankenstein*. This now becomes a special collection of stories linked in both time and space.

What you hold in your hands is not 'merely' a collection of these inextricably linked stories, it is *the* story of that long, cold, lightning-fuelled volcanic winter at the Villa Diodati on the shore of Lake Geneva. This is *the* story which I am telling in my own Gothic Horror-styled ghost story, interwoven throughout the rest. Mary Shelley, Lord Bryon, Dr John Polidori are *Playing a Game of Ghost Stories,* which gave *A Strange Birth To Frankenstein*!

A conceit in historical fiction, whether the medium is literature or cinema, is that liberties must be taken. These liberties include, but are certainly not limited to, combining multiple characters into one and contracting the timeframe and/or locations the story takes place in. The story of the haunting of the Villa Diodati includes only five people (six if you count the toddler, William), so one could easily have been tempted to turn one character into two or three, but I have not chosen that exercise that obscene option. The second liberty is the contraction of time. Through journals, diaries, and letters written during these three months, we know when certain stories and poems were begun and when or if they were completed during their stay at the Villa. I have taken the liberty of contracting the timeline of the writings into a little over two weeks (for the *Playing a Game of Ghost Stories* volume), instead of the three months and beyond that the actual writings took. And while Percy Shelley rented a nearby home, I have Percy, Mary, and Claire stay in the Villa Diodati for the entirety of their visit. I have also taken a fourth liberty common in historical fiction: creative licence to fudge the facts and outright lie. Sorry... not sorry (well, kinda actually).

A NOTE ON QUOTING SOURCES: I have included footnotes noting the sources that I have utilized to produce this book, including the full (and partial) texts written during, shortly after, or at very least inspired by the "Year Without Summer". During the debate between Percy Bysshe Shelley and Lord Byron about galvanism, I have the characters quote many contemporary (to them) and near contemporary sources. While strict rules to counter plagiarism are to utilize quotation marks, I have chosen not to. My reasoning is simple. As this is a novel of historical fiction, I feel these quotation marks in the character's dialogue distracts from the readability of the prose. When we naturally speak quotation marks are implied, so I imply the quotation marks by changing the font to the Century Old Style typeface.

A NOTE ON MODERN SOURCES: I have attempted to include sources as contemporary to the events of 1816 when humanely possible. In the modern age of the Internet, I have been amazed at the sheer number of contemporary or near contemporary sources available on the World Wide Web, whether from Project Gutenberg, Wikisource, the Internet Archive, Google Books, etc. Thankfully, many of these sources have long since fallen into the public domain, which permits me to use them freely. When this fails, I have used more modern sources and have cited them accordingly.

1816: A "Year Without A Summer" Classics Collection

Frankenstein

There is no question why I have included *Frankenstein; or The Modern Prometheus* in his collection of stories written during the 'Year Without a Summer'. It is by far the greatest contribution to Lord Byron's game of ghost stories. Lord Byron's own contribution is largely forgotten outside of Romantic circles. In Dr Polidori's own words, *The Vampyre* was not his contribution to the game, but instead was *Ernestus Berchtold; or The Modern Oedipus*, a most obscure work that is not readily available even on the Internet. Percy Bysshe Shelley seemingly contributed nothing to the game. But Mary's contribution gave birth to the modern concept of science-fiction. An eighteen-year-old girl is solely responsible for putting the 'science' in science-fiction. The work has never been out of print in the 200-plus years since its publication. While I have consider the 1818 text the best choice for this collection (being the most contemporary text to the 'Year Without Summer'), I have utilized certain passages from the 1831 edition when I feel they are the most appropriate.

The Darkness

'The Darkness' was an apocalyptic poem written by Lord Byron during the 'Year Without a Summer'. It was, no doubt, inspired by the apocalyptic storms that assaulted Lake Geneva (and the rest of the world), which kept him and his friends sequestered in the Villa Diodoti. It was published in *The Prisoner of Chillon and Other Poems* in 1816.

The Vampyre

John William Polidori's *The Vampyre* was published in London's *New Monthly Magazine* on April 1, 1819 with Lord Byron's name as the author of the work. Incensed, Lord Byron sued for the reverse plagiarism. How dare this publisher, Henry Colburn, publish *The Vampyre* with *his* name when he did not write the story, but instead the publisher was trying to capitalize on Lord Byron's own fame to boost sales of the magazine. In the following issue, dated May 1, 1819, Polidori wrote a letter to the editor explaining 'that though the groundwork is certainly Lord Byron's, its development is mine'. Polidori himself admits to having written by story at the insistence of a 'lady', to whom he gave the only copy of the manuscript as a gift. Polidori never had any intention of publishing the story himself, but this mysterious 'lady' sought out publication of *The Vampyre*.

History of a Six Weeks' Tour

Mary Shelley and Percy Bysshe Shelley would publish a travelogue of two journeys, one across Europe in 1814 and the other, of most importance to this collection, one to Lake Geneva in 1816, the very save "year without summer". This collection's mission statement is to collect the writings made during this summer, whether they are stories, poems, letters, or even a travelogue. By including these letters and diary entries, I can flesh out the events prior to their arrival at the Villa Diodati.

Child Harold's Pilgrimage

The first two cantos of 'Child Harold's Pilgrimage' were published in 1812 at the insistence of John Murray, Lord Byron's friend and publisher. In 1816, while sequestered in the Villa Diodoti, he composed the third canto, with a fourth being written and published in 1818.

How a Game of Ghost Stories Gives Birth To A Strange Frankenstein

July-August 1816

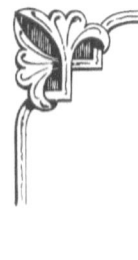

July 1816

1
P. presents 1st part of "feverishly" written "Modern Oedipus"!

2
The pale student returns to tells of his Abandonment of the Creature.

3

4

5

6

7
The Creation visits M. to tell of his Education

8
E. arrives. Begins haunting P.

9
E. begins haunting B., convincing him that P. is a plagiarist.

10
E. continues haunting both P. & B. manipulating them.

11
P. disappears for the weekend with the Countess Erzsebet.

12
P. begins writing The Vampyre at her request in the morning.

13

14
P. completes The Vampyre. Pale student is silent.

15
E. arrives back & gives the manuscript of The Vampyre to B.

16

17
B. writes his Monody on the Death of the R.B. Sheridan

18
B. reads "The Darkness" the day an Italian astronomer said the sun dies.

19

20
P. is forced at gunpoint to read his plagiarism: "The Vampyre!"

21
The Shelleys set out for the glacier.

22

23

24
M. receives the "Letters" from the Arctic.

25

26

27
The Shelleys return from the glacier.

28

29
B. presents Child Harold's Pilgrimage (3rd Canto)

30

31

Aug. 29
The Shelleys & C. set off to return to London.

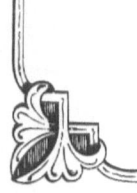

Chapter Eleven
Frankenstein[1]
(The Education of the Creature)

Mary Wollstonecraft Godwin's Journal

7 July. After First Sleep— The nightmare was formed like rolling, ominous dark storm clouds of recollection, but not my own memories, but those of my pale student of the unhallowed arts. In the dream, I saw his world through his own eyes: The moon gazed on my midnight labours, while, with unrelaxed and breathless eagerness, I pursued nature to her hiding places. Who shall conceive the horrors of my secret toil, as I dabbled among the unhallowed damps of the grave, or tortured the living animal to animate the lifeless clay? My limbs now tremble, and my eyes swim with the remembrance; but then a resistless, and almost frantic impulse, urged me forward; I seemed to have lost all soul or sensation but for this one pursuit. It was indeed but a passing trance, that only made me feel with renewed acuteness so soon as, the unnatural stimulus ceasing to operate, I had returned to my old habits. I collected bones from charnel houses; and disturbed, with profane fingers, the tremendous secrets of the human frame.

In a solitary chamber, or rather cell, at the top of the house, and separated from all the other apartments by a gallery and staircase, I kept my workshop of filthy creation; my eyeballs were starting from their sockets in attending to the details of my employment. The dissecting room and the slaughter-house furnished many of my materials; and often did my human nature turn with loathing from my occupation, whilst, still urged on by an eagerness which perpetually increased, I brought my work near to a conclusion.

It was on a dreary night of November, that I beheld the accomplishment of my toils. With an anxiety that almost amounted to agony, I collected the instruments of life around me, that I might infuse a spark of being into the lifeless thing that lay at my feet. It was already one in the morning; the rain pattered dismally against the panes, and my can-

---

1 From *Frankenstein; or the Modern Prometheus* by Mary Wollstonecraft Shelley, published by Lackington, Hughes, Harding, Mavor & Jones, 1818

dle was nearly burnt out, when, by the glimmer of the half-extinguished light, I saw the dull yellow eye of the creature open; it breathed hard, and a convulsive motion agitated its limbs.

How can I describe my emotions at this catastrophe, or how delineate the wretch whom with such infinite pains and care I had endeavoured to form? His limbs were in proportion, and I had selected his features as beautiful. Beautiful!—Great God! His yellow skin scarcely covered the work of muscles and arteries beneath; his hair was of a lustrous black, and flowing; his teeth of a pearly whiteness; but these luxuriances only formed a more horrid contrast with his watery eyes, that seemed almost of the same colour as the dun white sockets in which they were set, his shrivelled complexion, and straight black lips.

The different accidents of life are not so changeable as the feelings of human nature. I had worked hard for nearly two years, for the sole purpose of infusing life into an inanimate body. For this I had deprived myself of rest and health. I had desired it with an ardour that far exceeded moderation; but now that I had finished, the beauty of the dream vanished, and breathless horror and disgust filled my heart. Unable to endure the aspect of the being I had created, I rushed out of the room, and continued a long time traversing my bed-chamber, unable to compose my mind to sleep. At length lassitude succeeded to the tumult I had before endured; and I threw myself on the bed in my clothes, endeavouring to seek a few moments of forgetfulness. But it was in vain: I slept indeed, but I was disturbed by the wildest dreams. I thought I saw Elizabeth, in the bloom of health, walking in the streets of Ingolstadt. Delighted and surprised, I embraced her; but as I imprinted the first kiss on her lips, they became livid with the hue of death; her features appeared to change, and I thought that I held the corpse of my dead mother in my arms; a shroud enveloped her form, and I saw the grave-worms crawling in the folds of the flannel. I started from my sleep with horror; a cold dew covered my forehead, my teeth chattered, and every limb became convulsed; when, by the dim and yellow light of the moon, as it forced its way through the window-shutters, I beheld the wretch—the miserable monster whom I had created. He held up the curtain of the bed; and his eyes, if eyes they may be called, were fixed on me. His jaws opened, and he muttered some inarticulate sounds, while a grin wrinkled his cheeks. He might have spoken, but I did not hear; one hand was stretched out, seemingly to detain me, but I escaped, and rushed down stairs. I took refuge in the court-yard belonging to the house which I inhabited; where I remained during the rest of the night, walking up and down in the greatest agitation, listening attentively, catching and fearing each sound as if it were to announce the approach of the demoniacal corpse to which I had so miserably given life.

Oh! no mortal could support the horror of that countenance. A mummy again endued with animation could not be so hideous as that wretch. I had gazed on him while unfinished; he was ugly then; but when those muscles and joints were rendered capable of motion, it became a thing such as even Dante could not have conceived.

I awoke with a start. Bolt upright in bed, sweat staining my sheets, however cliché that scene is in the modern day. I had fallen asleep but for a handful of minutes. Curious to experience days turned into weeks turned into months all in less time than it takes to prepare a small meal.

7 July. The Small Hours— As the witching hour approached, I saw not my pale student of the unhallowed arts. Why does he continue to continuously fail to appear unto me as a phantasm as he had over those two long, cold, evenings: one a week ago and the other a fortnight prior to this. I do not wish him to go missing. I have cajoled my Beloved plotting and planning an expedition to the glacier at Mer de Glace. I wish to visit the very place my pale student met his Creation. It is all that I speak of. In but a fortnight shalt we begin our expedition, and I will see the ice fields myself! It is my own fault that my pale student had grown as silence as the grave. I and my Beloved and our silent Little Lord and dearest Claire made our eight-day tour just as he was beginning his tale. But the tour was a necessity due to the briefest of respites from the thunderous storms that had imprisoned myself and my friends in our palatial prison called the Villa Diodati. My pale student two days whence we made our return returned to tell me of his abandonment of his Creation. Such a harrowing and horrifying tale. But for a week, he has unable to visit me. I require his conversation as I need to draw breath; I require the transcription of his tale as I need my heart to pulse blood through my veins. I pray he is unable to visit me due to the unwritten and unknowable requirements of being a phantasm, but not by his free will. Why did he leave off on such a tremendous ending, which was no ending at all. He tale could not have been completed. I forbid it!

I tossed and turned in fitful slumber. I could not bring myself to look into his corner where his armchair remained unmoved and unmovable. My Beloved once moved the chair to be closer to the fire and I chastised him greatly. He sulkingly returned to the chair to his previous location. Why was I being so hysterical? I buried my face into the down pillow unable and unwilling to cast my eyes upon an empty chair. I silently wept.

Then I heard the chair move.

My pale student had returned! I bolted upright in bed and turned towards the chair seated in the corner of the bedchamber to see not my pale student, but his Creation! My pale student continued to abandon me! But why had his Creation taken his place in the chair? I dared not speak. The Creation dared not to speak either.

My pale student's description from his pales in comparison to the reality. Where he described having selected his features 'beautiful', the features are in reality 'grotesque'. True his yellow skin scarcely covers the work of muscles and arteries beneath; his hair is of a lustrous black and flowing; his teeth of a pearly whiteness. True, his watery eyes, that seemed almost of the same colour as the dun white sockets in which they were set, his shrivelled complexion and straight black lips. But my pale student proved to be a most accomplished unreliable narrator. Victor had minimized the extent slaugher-houses were the source of his flesh and bones.

In the regions surrounding Ingolstadt, even counting for his wandering far and wide, he would have encountered few human cadavers suffering from gigantism, let alone the multitude required to form his Creation from the requisite parts. Did he saw and assemble multiple *femurs* to create a single one with the proper proportions he sought? Did he do the same with the *tibias* and *fibulas*, the *humeri* and the *ulnas* and *radii*? How many *vertebrae* are in his Creation? Surely more than the human thirty-three. How was the rib cage fashioned?

Seeing his Creation in the flesh, or as a phantasm as the case may be, I saw Victor's fullest utilization of slaughter-houses. True, the right side of the Creations face appears remarkably human, probably sourced from a cadaver suffering from *macrocephaly*, or an enlarged head. But the macrocephalic skull may not have been complete, perhaps having been damaged through violence in life, so Victor was forced to substitute half of the frontal and the left parietal bone, orbital socket, and zygomatic bone with those from a bull. The eye itself appears human sourced, but the bones are clearly bovine. Victor has sawn the horn off to give this Creation a much more human silhouette. The jawbone appears, at first glance, to be from an orangutan, but the teeth are much more human in appearance. Perhaps, Victor took the time for post-mortem dental work. As for the limbs and rib cage, I believe that, while *bovines* could have been the source, I believe Victor sourced equines. The bones of the horse are the most humanlike between the two desperate species. The hands were the hands of a mountain gorilla, though through Victor's surgical skills refined for human dexterity.

Except for the brain, the internal organs of his Creation will be forever a mystery to me. I wonder if they were too as veraciously drawn from the slaugher-houses. Along with the bovine and equine, he could have sourced the ovine and the caprine and the swine. But as for the, no doubt, human brain, even one sourced from a non-macrocephalic skull, could have been utilized with minimal alteration. Perhaps Victor packed additional fat into the brainbox.

The clothing that his Creation wore, very modern and fashionable, was a patchwork of the stitching of several men's shirts, vests, jackets, and trousers together to clothe his massive frame. The stitchwork of his clothing eerily mirrored the Victor's stitchwork of his flesh. His shoes, monstrous in size, seemed cobbled together (no pun intended) likewise from several men's shoes and boots.

My mind continued to imagine and theorize the manner of his creation until I realized that his Creation wished to relate *his* tale to me. It would have been the height of impropriety for my pale student to relate the tale of the Creation to me. That tale would have been hearsay and although I trusted my pale student of the unhallowed arts, he may have proven himself to be an unreliable narrator. Not that he would have outright lied to me to blatant falsehoods, but he may subconsciously smoothed over the rougher edges of his Creation's tale. His Creation could not look me in the eye, instead keeping his head hung low, with his chin laying upon his chest. Without speaking a word, I consented to listen; and, seating myself by the fire which my odious companion had lighted, he thus began his tale.

Chapter 1

July. Before Second Sleep— 'It is with considerable difficulty that I remember the original æra of my being: all the events of that period appear confused and indistinct.' Victor's Creation speaks with an eloquence that is betrayed by his appearance. How did he learn to speak with such articulation? Is there some remembrance from his brain's past life in another man's skull? Or was his Creation a blank slate having been wiped clean by the hand of death and decay? If the previous owner's soul has transcended this mortal sphere, then perchance there was not-a-thing still possessed by the crude matter that now thinks and seemingly feels!

'A strange multiplicity of sensations seized me, and I saw, felt, heard, and smelt, at the same time; and it was, indeed, a long time before I learned to distinguish between the operations of my various senses. By degrees, I remember, a stronger light pressed upon my nerves, so that I was obliged to shut my eyes. Darkness then came over me, and troubled me; but hardly had I felt this, when, by opening my eyes, as I now suppose, the light poured in upon me again. I walked, and, I believe, descended; but I presently found a great alteration in my sensations. Before, dark and opaque bodies had surrounded me, impervious to my touch or sight; but I now found that I could wander on at liberty, with no obstacles which I could not either surmount or avoid. The light became more and more oppressive to me; and, the heat wearying me as I walked, I sought a place where I could receive shade. This was the forest near Ingolstadt; and here I lay by the side of a brook resting from my fatigue, until I felt tormented by hunger and thirst. This roused me from my near-ly dormant state, and I ate some berries which I found hanging on the trees, or lying on the ground. I slaked my thirst at the brook; and then lying down, was overcome by sleep.'

Such horror what the crude matter experiences when experiencing such sensations anew! I glance over to my little William sleeping in his bassinette and I cast my mind back when he was newly born. Is this what the infantile brain experiences in its first waking moments but its voice cannot articulate. But lo! Perchance, the babes are communi-cating this unspeakable horror through their cries, but as mother's we dismiss their terror as hunger by putting them to our breast! Our chil-dren have swum in the warm darkness of our wombs, and now they are assaulted by sensations they know not the cause of their pain nor hide from! If my child possessed the mental or physical properties to speak at such an infantile age, would he describe his world any less eloquently as this Creation did just now?

'It was dark when I awoke; I felt cold also, and half-frightened as it were instinctively, finding myself so desolate. Before I had quitted Vic-tor's apartment, on a sensation of cold, I had covered myself with some clothes; but these were insufficient to secure me from the dews of night. I was a poor, helpless, miserable wretch; I knew, and could distinguish, nothing; but, feeling pain invade me on all sides, I sat down and wept.' As did I. How could I not at such a harrowing tale?

'Soon a gentle light stole over the heavens, and gave me a sensation of pleasure. I started up, and beheld a radiant form rise from among the trees. I gazed with a kind of wonder. It moved slowly, but it enlightened my path; and I again went out in search of berries. I was still cold, when under one of the trees I found a huge cloak, with which I covered myself, and sat down upon the ground. No distinct ideas occupied my mind; all was confused. I felt light, and hunger, and thirst, and darkness; innumer-able sounds rung in my ears, and on all sides various scents saluted me: the only object that I could distinguish was the bright moon, and I fixed my eyes on that with pleasure.'

My own mind is just as assaulted as this poor Creation's had been. I felt the sting of the light and pangs of hunger and assault thirst and the oppression of darkness and the ringing of innumerable sounds in my ears anew for the first time since I was a mere babe in the cradle. I cast another glance at my dearest William. I wondered and I pondered once more.

'Several changes of day and night passed, and the orb of night had greatly lessened when I began to distinguish my sensations from each other. I gradually saw plainly the clear stream that supplied me with drink, and the trees that shaded me with their foliage. I was delighted when I first discovered that a pleasant sound, which often saluted my ears, proceeded from the throats of the little winged animals who had often intercepted the light from my eyes. I began also to observe, with greater accuracy, the forms that surrounded me, and to perceive the boundaries of the radiant roof of light which canopied me. Sometimes I tried to imitate the pleasant songs of the birds, but was unable. Sometimes I wished to express my sensations in my own mode, but the uncouth and inarticulate sounds which broke from me frightened me into silence again.

'The moon had disappeared from the night, and again, with a lessened form, shewed itself, while I still remained in the forest. My sensations had, by this time, become distinct, and my mind received every day additional ideas. My eyes became accustomed to the light, and to perceive objects in their right forms; I distinguished the insect from the herb, and, by degrees, one herb from another. I found that the sparrow uttered none but harsh notes, whilst those of the blackbird and thrush were sweet and enticing.'

Did not Jean-Jacques Rousseau hypothesize similar experiences to those of this Creation? Did he not write so eloquently in *Emile*, 'Suppose a child born with the size and strength of manhood, entering upon life full grown like Pallas from the brain of Jupiter; such a child-man would be a perfect idiot, an automaton, a statue without motion and almost without feeling; he would see and hear nothing, he would recognise no one, he could not turn his eyes towards what he wanted to see; not only would he perceive no external object, he would not even be aware of sensation through the several sense-organs. His eye would not perceive colour, his ear sounds, his body would be unaware of contact with neighbouring bodies, he would not even know he had a body, what his hands handled would be in his brain alone; all his sensations would be united in one place, they would exist only in the common "sensorium," he would have only one idea, that of self, to which he would refer all his sensations; and this idea, or rather this feeling, would be the only thing in which he excelled an ordinary child. This man, full grown at birth, would also be unable to stand on his feet, he would need a long time to learn how to keep his balance; perhaps he would not even be able to try to do it, and you would see the big strong body left in one place like a stone, or creeping and crawling like a young puppy.

'He would feel the discomfort of bodily needs without knowing what was the matter and without knowing how to provide for these needs. There is no immediate connection between the muscles of the stomach and those of the arms and legs to make him take a step towards food, or stretch a hand to seize it, even were he surrounded with it; and as his body would be full grown and his limbs well developed he would be without the perpetual restlessness and movement of childhood, so that he might die of hunger without stirring to seek food. However little you may have thought about the order and development of our knowledge, you cannot deny that such a one would be in the state of almost primitive ignorance and stupidity natural to man before he has learnt anything from experience or from his fellows.'[2]

Rousseau imagines the man/child as an imbecile, an automaton, an immobile and almost insensible statue, who would learn to stand, if he attempted it at all, with the greatest difficult and would not connect hunger with food, while Victor's Creation gains motor control almost at once and instinctively slakes his hunger with berries.[3]

Despite my brief lapse in focus to wander along a digressive path, the Creation continued with his tale. 'One day, when I was oppressed by cold, I found a fire which had been left by some wandering beggars, and was overcome with delight at the warmth I experienced from it. In my joy I thrust my hand into the live embers, but quickly drew it out again with a cry of pain. How strange, I thought, that the same cause should produce such opposite effects! I examined the materials of the fire, and to my joy found it to be composed of wood. I quickly collected some branches; but they were wet, and would not burn. I was pained at this, and sat still watching the operation of the fire. The wet wood which I had placed near the heat dried, and itself became inflamed. I reflected on this; and, by touching the various branches, I discovered the cause, and busied myself in collecting a great quantity of wood, that I might dry it, and have a plentiful supply of fire. When night came on, and brought sleep with it, I was in the greatest fear lest my fire should be extinguished. I covered it carefully with dry wood and leaves, and placed wet branches upon it; and then, spreading my cloak, I lay on the ground, and sunk into sleep.

---

2 From *Emile, or On Education* by Jean-Jacques Rousseau, published in English in 1763.
3 From "From *Emile* to *Frankenstein*: The education of Monsters", *European Romantic Review* 1, no. 2 [1991]: 147-62.

'It was morning when I awoke, and my first care was to visit the fire. I uncovered it, and a gentle breeze quickly fanned it into a flame. I observed this also, and contrived a fan of branches, which roused the embers when they were nearly extinguished. When night came again, I found, with pleasure, that the fire gave light as well as heat; and that the discovery of this element was useful to me in my food; for I found some of the offals that the travellers had left had been roasted, and tasted much more savoury than the berries I gathered from the trees. I tried, therefore, to dress my food in the same manner, placing it on the live embers. I found that the berries were spoiled by this operation, and the nuts and roots much improved.

'Food, however, became scarce; and I often spent the whole day searching in vain for a few acorns to assuage the pangs of hunger. When I found this, I resolved to quit the place that I had hitherto inhabited, to seek for one where the few wants I experienced would be more easily satisfied. In this emigration, I exceedingly lamented the loss of the fire which I had obtained through accident, and knew not how to re-produce it. I gave several hours to the serious consideration of this difficulty; but I was obliged to relinquish all attempt to supply it; and, wrapping myself up in my cloak, I struck across the wood towards the setting sun. I passed three days in these rambles, and at length discovered the open country. A great fall of snow had taken place the night before, and the fields were of one uniform white; the appearance was disconsolate, and I found my feet chilled by the cold damp substance that covered the ground.

'It was about seven in the morning, and I longed to obtain food and shelter; at length I perceived a small hut, on a rising ground, which had doubtless been built for the convenience of some shepherd. This was a new sight to me; and I examined the structure with great curiosity. Finding the door open, I entered. An old man sat in it, near a fire, over which he was preparing his breakfast. He turned on hearing a noise; and, perceiving me, shrieked loudly, and, quitting the hut, ran across the fields with a speed of which his debilitated form hardly appeared capable. His appearance, different from any I had ever before seen, and his flight, somewhat surprised me. But I was enchanted by the appearance of the hut: here the snow and rain could not penetrate; the ground was dry; and it presented to me then as exquisite and divine a retreat as Pandæmonium appeared to the dæmons of hell after their sufferings in the lake of fire.' Curiouser and curiouser! From whence did this Creation learn of John Milton? Perhaps there is a chance this knowledge of Paradises lost will be related in his tale to me. One can only hope and dream. 'I greedily devoured the remnants of the shepherd's breakfast, which consisted of bread, cheese, milk, and wine; the latter, however, I did not like. Then overcome by fatigue, I lay down among some straw, and fell asleep.

'It was noon when I awoke; and, allured by the warmth of the sun, which shone brightly on the white ground, I determined to recommence my travels; and, depositing the remains of the peasant's breakfast in a wallet I found, I proceeded across the fields for several hours, until at sunset I arrived at a village. How miraculous did this appear! the huts, the neater cottages, and stately houses, engaged my admiration by turns. The vegetables in the gardens, the milk and cheese that I saw placed at the windows of some of the cottages, allured my appetite. One of the best of these I entered; but I had hardly placed my foot within the door, before the children shrieked, and one of the women fainted. The whole village was roused; some fled, some attacked me, until, grievously bruised by stones and many other kinds of missile weapons,' Oh! The horror of humanity's penchant for violence! This poor Creation is an alien to these villagers as a man from Mars would be stepping foot on the green grasses Earth, so foreign from the red dirt of his native world. Would these villagers believe that our world was being watched keenly and closely by intelligences greater than man's and yet as mortal as his own; that as men busied themselves about their various concerns they were scrutinised and studied, perhaps almost as narrowly as a man with a microscope might scrutinise the transient creatures that swarm and multiply in a drop of water. With infinite complacency men went to and fro over this globe about their little affairs, serene in their assurance of their empire over matter. To them it is possible that the infusoria under the microscope do the same. No one gave a thought to the older worlds of space as sources of human danger, or thought of them only to dismiss the idea of life upon them as impossible or improbable. It is curious to recall some of the mental habits of those departed days. At most terrestrial men fancied there might be other men upon Mars, perhaps inferior to themselves and ready to welcome a missionary enterprise. Yet across the gulf of space, minds that are to our minds as ours are to those of the beasts that perish, intellects vast and cool and unsympathetic, regarded this earth with envious eyes, and slowly and surely drew their plans against us.[4] These would be the villagers and the city dwellers reaction to an otherworldly or unnatural threat which Victor's Creation surely was.

'I escaped to the open country, and fearfully took refuge in a low hovel, quite bare, and making a wretched appearance after the palaces I had beheld in the village. This hovel, however, joined a cottage of a neat and pleasant appearance; but, after my late dearly-bought experience, I dared

---

4 From *The War of the Worlds* by H.G. Welles, serialised in *Pearson's Magazine* in 1897.

not enter it. My place of refuge was constructed of wood, but so low, that I could with difficulty sit upright in it. No wood, however, was placed on the earth, which formed the floor, but it was dry; and although the wind entered it by innumerable chinks, I found it an agreeable asylum from the snow and rain.

'Here then I retreated, and lay down, happy to have found a shelter, however miserable, from the inclemency of the season, and still more from the barbarity of man.

'As soon as morning dawned, I crept from my kennel, that I might view the adjacent cottage, and discover if I could remain in the habitation I had found. It was situated against the back of the cottage, and surrounded on the sides which were exposed by a pig-stye and a clear pool of water. One part was open, and by that I had crept in; but now I covered every crevice by which I might be perceived with stones and wood, yet in such a manner that I might move them on occasion to pass out: all the light I enjoyed came through the stye, and that was sufficient for me.

'Having thus arranged my dwelling, and carpeted it with clean straw, I retired; for I saw the figure of a man at a distance, and I remembered too well my treatment the night before, to trust myself in his power. I had first, however, provided for my sustenance for that day, by a loaf of coarse bread, which I purloined, and a cup with which I could drink, more conveniently than from my hand, of the pure water which flowed by my retreat. The floor was a little raised, so that it was kept perfectly dry, and by its vicinity to the chimney of the cottage it was tolerably warm.

'Being thus provided, I resolved to reside in this hovel, until something should occur which might alter my determination. It was indeed a paradise, compared to the bleak forest, my former residence, the rain-dropping branches, and dank earth. I ate my breakfast with pleasure, and was about to remove a plank to procure myself a little water, when I heard a step, and, looking through a small chink, I beheld a young creature, with a pail on her head, passing before my hovel. The girl was young and of gentle demeanour, unlike what I have since found cottagers and farm-house servants to be. Yet she was meanly dressed, a coarse blue petticoat and a linen jacket being her only garb; her fair hair was plaited, but not adorned; she looked patient, yet sad. I lost sight of her; and in about a quarter of an hour she returned, bearing the pail, which was now partly filled with milk. As she walked along, seemingly incommoded by the burden, a young man met her, whose countenance expressed a deeper despondence. Uttering a few sounds with an air of melancholy, he took the pail from her head, and bore it to the cottage himself. She followed, and they disappeared. Presently I saw the young man again, with some tools in his hand, cross the field behind the cottage; and the girl was also busied, sometimes in the house, and sometimes in the yard.

'On examining my dwelling, I found that one of the windows of the cottage had formerly occupied a part of it, but the panes had been filled up with wood. In one of these was a small and almost imperceptible chink, through which the eye could just penetrate. Through this crevice, a small room was visible, white-washed and clean, but very bare of furniture. In one corner, near a small fire, sat an old man, leaning his head on his hands in a disconsolate attitude. The young girl was occupied in arranging the cottage; but presently she took something out of a drawer, which employed her hands, and she sat down beside the old man, who, taking up an instrument, began to play, and to produce sounds, sweeter than the voice of the thrush or the nightingale. It was a lovely sight, even to me, poor wretch! who had never beheld aught beautiful before. The silver hair and benevolent countenance of the aged cottager, won my reverence; while the gentle manners of the girl enticed my love. He played a sweet mournful air, which I perceived drew tears from the eyes of his amiable companion, of which the old man took no notice, until she sobbed audibly; he then pronounced a few sounds, and the fair creature, leaving her work, knelt at his feet. He raised her, and smiled with such kindness and affection, that I felt sensations of a peculiar and over-powering nature: they were a mixture of pain and pleasure, such as I had never before experienced, either from hunger or cold, warmth or food; and I withdrew from the window, unable to bear these emotions.

'Soon after this the young man returned, bearing on his shoulders a load of wood. The girl met him at the door, helped to relieve him of his burden, and, taking some of the fuel into the cottage, placed it on the fire; then she and the youth went apart into a nook of the cottage, and he shewed her a large loaf and a piece of cheese. She seemed pleased; and went into the garden for some roots and plants, which she placed in water, and then upon the fire. She afterwards continued her work, whilst the young man went into the garden, and appeared busily employed in digging and pulling up roots. After he had been employed thus about an hour, the young woman joined him, and they entered the cottage together.

'The old man had, in the mean time, been pensive; but, on the appearance of his companions, he assumed a more cheerful air, and they sat down to eat. The meal was quickly dispatched. The young woman was again occupied in arranging the cottage; the old man walked before the cottage in the sun for a few minutes, leaning on the arm of the youth. Nothing could exceed in beauty the contrast between these two excellent creatures. One was old, with silver hairs and a countenance beaming with benevolence and love: the younger was slight and graceful in his figure, and his features were moulded with the finest symmetry; yet his eyes and attitude expressed the utmost sadness and despondency. The old man returned to the cottage; and the youth, with tools different from those he had used in the morning, directed his steps across the fields.

'Night quickly shut in; but, to my extreme wonder, I found that the cottagers had a means of prolonging light, by the use of tapers, and was delighted to find, that the setting of the sun did not put an end to the pleasure I experienced in watching my human neighbours. In the evening, the young girl and her companion were employed in various occupations which I did not understand; and the old man again took up the instrument, which produced the divine sounds that had enchanted me in the morning. So soon as he had finished, the youth began, not to play, but to utter sounds that were monotonous, and neither resembling the harmony of the old man's instrument or the songs of the birds; I since found that he read aloud, but at that time I knew nothing of the science of words or letters.

'The family, after having been thus occupied for a short time, extinguished their lights, and retired, as I conjectured, to rest.' I too, briefly, thought of the lateness of the hour and the stalking exhaustion that the Creation's story kept at bay like firelight does wolves. But the Creation continued his tale with only the merest of pauses.

Chapter II

I lay on my straw, but I could not sleep. I thought of the occurrences of the day. What chiefly struck me was the gentle manners of these people; and I longed to join them, but dared not. I remembered too well the treatment I had suffered the night before from the barbarous villagers, and resolved, whatever course of conduct I might hereafter think it right to pursue, that for the present I would remain quietly in my hovel, watching, and endeavouring to discover the motives which influenced their actions.

'The cottagers arose the next morning before the sun. The young woman arranged the cottage, and prepared the food; and the youth departed after the first meal.

'This day was passed in the same routine as that which preceded it. The young man was constantly employed out of doors, and the girl in various laborious occupations within. The old man, whom I soon perceived to be blind, employed his leisure hours on his instrument, or in contemplation. Nothing could exceed the love and respect which the younger cottagers exhibited towards their venerable companion. They performed towards him every little office of affection and duty with gentleness; and he rewarded them by his benevolent smiles.

'They were not entirely happy. The young man and his companion often went apart, and appeared to weep. I saw no cause for their unhappiness; but I was deeply affected by it. If such lovely creatures were miserable, it was less strange that I, an imperfect and solitary being, should be wretched. Yet why were these gentle beings unhappy? They possessed a delightful house (for such it was in my eyes), and every luxury; they had a fire to warm them when chill, and delicious viands when hungry; they were dressed in excellent clothes; and, still more, they enjoyed one another's company and speech, interchanging each day looks of affection and kindness. What did their tears imply? Did they really express pain? I was at first unable to solve these questions; but perpetual attention, and time, explained to me many appearances which were at first enigmatic.

'A considerable period elapsed before I discovered one of the causes of the uneasiness of this amiable family; it was poverty: and they suffered that evil in a very distressing degree. Their nourishment consisted entirely of the vegetables of their garden, and the milk of one cow, who gave very little during the winter, when its masters could scarcely procure food to support it. They often, I believe, suffered the pangs of hunger very poignantly, especially the two younger cottagers; for several times they placed food before the old man, when they reserved none for themselves.

'This trait of kindness moved me sensibly. I had been accustomed, during the night, to steal a part of their store for my own consumption; but when I found that in doing this I inflicted pain on the cottagers, I abstained, and satisfied myself with berries, nuts, and roots, which I gathered from a neighbouring wood.'

Did the David the Psalmist sing, *Out of the mouth of babes and sucklings hast thou ordained strength because of thine enemie*? How did this Creation, only days old, come to this knowledge when the vastness of humanity with the vastness of human experiences cannot? Surely our biases are learnt from our parents and our teachers and our priests, and not born innate in the human condition. True, the religious will teach and preach that we are all born with Original Sin. It was this act of consuming the fruit of the Tree of the Knowledge of Good and Evil that has condemned all of mankind to the pain and suffering found outside of Eden. When I look at my dearest William slumbering quietly, breathing in and exhaling out so minutely, that a parent, even one who has not lost a child to death, listens intently to see if their child still lives, I cannot believe he possesses even one iota of sin. Original or otherwise. The religious be damned!

'I discovered also another means through which I was enabled to assist their labours. I found that the youth spent a great part of each day in collecting wood for the family fire; and, during the night, I often took his tools, the use of which I quickly discovered, and brought home firing sufficient for the consumption of several days.

'I remember, the first time that I did this, the young woman, when she opened the door in the morning, appeared greatly astonished on seeing a great pile of wood on the outside. She uttered some words in a loud voice, and the youth joined her, who also expressed surprise. I observed, with pleasure, that he did not go to the forest that day, but spent it in repairing the cottage, and cultivating the garden.

'By degrees I made a discovery of still greater moment. I found that these people possessed a method of communicating their experience and feelings to one another by articulate sounds. I perceived that the words they spoke sometimes produced pleasure or pain, smiles or sadness, in the minds and countenances of the hearers. This was indeed a godlike science, and I ardently desired to become acquainted with it. But I was baffled in every attempt I made for this purpose. Their pronunciation was quick; and the words they uttered, not having any apparent connexion with visible objects, I was unable to discover any clue by which I could unravel the mystery of their reference. By great application, however, and after having remained during the space of several revolutions of the moon in my hovel, I discovered the names that were given to some of the most familiar objects of discourse: I learned and applied the words *fire*, *milk*, *bread*, and *wood*. I learned also the names of the cottagers themselves. The youth and his companion had each of them several names, but the old man had only one, which was *father*. The girl was called *sister*, or *Agatha*; and the youth *Felix*, *brother*, or *son*. I cannot describe the delight I felt when I learned the ideas appropriated to each of these sounds, and was able to pronounce them. I distinguished several other words, without being able as yet to understand or apply them; such as *good*, *dearest*, *unhappy*.'

Again and again this poor Creation articulates the experiences of the infantile in the language of an adult. Again and again, I glance at my dearest William becoming full of the knowledge of his own experiences as he grows from infant to toddler. Even when he is toddling around my Beloved's writing desk, would he be able to communicate his infantile experiences as articulately as this Creation.

'I spent the winter in this manner.' What year was this? If his 'birth' had been in November of 1793, this would imply that the Creation is describing the spring of 1794. I will strive to keep these dates recorded on the calendar in my mind. 'The gentle manners and beauty of the cottagers greatly endeared them to me: when they were unhappy, I felt depressed; when they rejoiced, I sympathized in their joys. I saw few human beings beside them; and if any other happened to enter the cottage, their harsh manners and rude gait only enhanced to me the superior accomplishments of my friends. The old man, I could perceive, often endeavoured to encourage his children, as sometimes I found that he called them, to cast off their melancholy. He would talk in a cheerful accent, with an expression of goodness that bestowed pleasure even upon me. Agatha listened with respect, her eyes sometimes filled with tears, which she endeavoured to wipe away unperceived; but I generally found that her countenance and tone were more cheerful after having listened to the exhortations of her father. It was not thus with Felix. He was always the saddest of the groupe; and, even to my unpractised senses, he appeared to have suffered more deeply than his friends. But if his countenance was more sorrowful, his voice was more cheerful than that of his sister, especially when he addressed the old man.

'I could mention innumerable instances, which, although slight, marked the dispositions of these amiable cottagers. In the midst of poverty and want, Felix carried with pleasure to his sister the first little white flower that peeped out from beneath the snowy ground. Early in the morning before she had risen, he cleared away the snow that obstructed her path to the milk-house, drew water from the well, and brought the wood from the out-house, where, to his perpetual astonishment, he found his store always replenished by an invisible hand. In the day, I believe, he worked sometimes for a neighbouring farmer, because he often went forth, and did not return until dinner, yet brought no wood with him. At other times he worked in the garden; but, as there was little to do in the frosty season, he read to the old man and Agatha.

'This reading had puzzled me extremely at first; but, by degrees, I discovered that he uttered many of the same sounds when he read as when he talked. I conjectured, therefore, that he found on the paper signs for speech which he understood, and I ardently longed to comprehend these also; but how was that possible, when I did not even understand the sounds for which they stood as signs? I improved, however, sensibly in this science, but not sufficiently to follow up any kind of conversation, although I applied my whole mind to the endeavour: for I easily perceived that, although I eagerly longed to discover myself to the cottagers, I ought not to make the attempt until I had first become master of their language; which knowledge might enable me to make them overlook the deformity of my figure; for with this also the contrast perpetually presented to my eyes had made me acquainted.

'I had admired the perfect forms of my cottagers— their grace, beauty, and delicate complexions: but how was I terrified, when I viewed myself in a transparent pool! At first I started back, unable to believe that it was indeed I who was reflected in the mirror; and when I became fully convinced that I was in reality the monster that I am, I was filled with the bitterest sensations of despondence and mortification. Alas! I did not yet entirely know the fatal effects of this miserable deformity.'

Oh! My sweet Creation, how did you come to his regrettable knowledge that you are deformed? True, Victor fled from you in the moments after your creation. True, the villagers stoned you for the sin of being different. But! How did you come to his regrettable knowledge? Are you as blank a slate as I perceive you to be. Or! Is there some semblance of memory that survived the death of the previous possessor of your brain?

'As the sun became warmer, and the light of day longer, the snow vanished, and I beheld the bare trees and the black earth. From this time Felix was more employed; and the heart-moving indications of impending famine disappeared. Their food, as I afterwards found, was coarse, but it was wholesome; and they procured a sufficiency of it. Several new kinds of plants sprung up in the garden, which they dressed; and these signs of comfort increased daily as the season advanced.

'The old man, leaning on his son, walked each day at noon, when it did not rain, as I found it was called when the heavens poured forth its waters. This frequently took place; but a high wind quickly dried the earth, and the season became far more pleasant than it had been.

'My mode of life in my hovel was uniform. During the morning I attended the motions of the cottagers; and when they were dispersed in various occupations, I slept: the remainder of the day was spent in observing my friends. When they had retired to rest, if there was any moon, or the night was star-light, I went into the woods, and collected my own food and fuel for the cottage. When I returned, as often as it was necessary, I cleared their path from the snow, and performed those offices that I had seen done by Felix. I afterwards found that these labours, performed by an invisible hand, greatly astonished them; and once or twice I heard them, on these occasions, utter the words *good spirit, wonderful*; but I did not then understand the signification of these terms.

'My thoughts now became more active, and I longed to discover the motives and feelings of these lovely creatures; I was inquisitive to know why Felix appeared so miserable, and Agatha so sad. I thought (foolish wretch!) that it might be in my power to restore happiness to these deserving people. When I slept, or was absent, the forms of the venerable blind father, the gentle Agatha, and the excellent Felix, flitted before me.

I looked upon them as superior beings, who would be the arbiters of my future destiny. I formed in my imagination a thousand pictures of presenting myself to them, and their reception of me. I imagined that they would be disgusted, until, by my gentle demeanour and conciliating words, I should first win their favour, and afterwards their love.

'These thoughts exhilarated me, and led me to apply with fresh ardour to the acquiring the art of language. My organs were indeed harsh, but supple; and although my voice was very unlike the soft music of their tones, yet I pronounced such words as I understood with tolerable ease. It was as the ass and the lap-dog; yet surely the gentle ass, whose intentions were affectionate, although his manners were rude, deserved better treatment than blows and execration.'

Oh! The Ass and the Lapdog! Such a wonderful table by Aesop. Shall I relate it to you, my Journal? It is but a trifle of a digression: 'A MAN had an Ass, and a Maltese Lapdog, a very great beauty. The Ass was left in a stable and had plenty of oats and hay to eat, just as any other Ass would. The Lapdog knew many tricks and was a great favorite with his master, who often fondled him and seldom went out to dine without bringing him home some tidbit to eat. The Ass, on the contrary, had much work to do in grinding the corn-mill and in carrying wood from the forest or burdens from the farm. He often lamented his own hard fate and contrasted it with the luxury and idleness of the Lapdog, till at last one day he broke his cords and halter, and galloped into his master's house, kicking up his heels without measure, and frisking and fawning as well as he could. He next tried to jump about his master as he had seen the Lapdog do, but he broke the table and smashed all the dishes upon it to atoms. He then attempted to lick his master, and jumped upon his back. The servants, hearing the strange hubbub and perceiving the danger of their master, quickly relieved him, and drove out the Ass to his stable with kicks and clubs and cuffs. The Ass, as he returned to his stall beaten nearly to death, thus lamented: 'I have brought it all on myself! Why could I not have been contented to labor with my companions, and not wish to be idle all the day like that useless little Lapdog!'"[5]

'The pleasant showers and genial warmth of spring greatly altered the aspect of the earth. Men, who before this change seemed to have been hid in caves, dispersed themselves, and were employed in various arts of cultivation. The birds sang in more cheerful notes, and the leaves began to bud forth on the trees. Happy, happy earth! fit habitation for gods, which, so short a time before, was bleak, damp, and unwholesome. My spirits were elevated by the enchanting appearance of nature; the

---

5 From *Aesop's Fables*, a translation by George Fyler Townsend, published in 1887.

past was blotted from my memory, the present was tranquil, and the future gilded by bright rays of hope, and anticipations of joy."

Chapter III

I now hasten to the more moving part of my story. I shall relate events that impressed me with feelings which, from what I was, have made me what I am.'

Yes, Creation, please do!

'Spring advanced rapidly; the weather became fine, and the skies cloudless. It surprised me, that what before was desert and gloomy should now bloom with the most beautiful flowers and verdure. My senses were gratified and refreshed by a thousand scents of delight, and a thousand sights of beauty.

'It was on one of these days, when my cottagers periodically rested from labour— the old man played on his guitar, and the children listened to him— I observed that the countenance of Felix was melancholy beyond expression: he sighed frequently; and once his father paused in his music, and I conjectured by his manner that he inquired the cause of his son's sorrow. Felix replied in a cheerful accent, and the old man was recommencing his music, when some one tapped at the door.

'It was a lady on horseback, accompanied by a countryman as a guide. The lady was dressed in a dark suit, and covered with a thick black veil. Agatha asked a question; to which the stranger only replied by pronouncing, in a sweet accent, the name of Felix. Her voice was musical, but unlike that of either of my friends. On hearing this word, Felix came up hastily to the lady; who, when she saw him, threw up her veil, and I beheld a countenance of angelic beauty and expression. Her hair of a shining raven black, and curiously braided; her eyes were dark, but gentle, although animated; her features of a regular proportion, and her complexion wondrously fair, each cheek tinged with a lovely pink.

'Felix seemed ravished with delight when he saw her, every trait of sorrow vanished from his face, and it instantly expressed a degree of ecstatic joy, of which I could hardly have believed it capable; his eyes sparkled, as his cheek flushed with pleasure; and at that moment I thought him as beautiful as the stranger. She appeared affected by different feelings; wiping a few tears from her lovely eyes, she held out her hand to Felix, who kissed it rapturously, and called her, as well as I could distinguish, his sweet Arabian.' Arabian? So delightful and curious. 'She did not appear to understand him, but smiled. He assisted her to dismount, and, dismissing her guide, conducted her into the cottage. Some conversation took place between him and his father; and the young stranger knelt at the old man's feet, and would have kissed his hand, but he raised her, and embraced her affectionately.

'I soon perceived, that although the stranger uttered articulate sounds, and appeared to have a language of her own, she was neither understood by, or herself understood, the cottagers. They made many signs which I did not comprehend; but I saw that her presence diffused gladness through the cottage, dispelling their sorrow as the sun dissipates the morning mists. Felix seemed peculiarly happy, and with smiles of delight welcomed his Arabian. Agatha, the ever-gentle Agatha, kissed the hands of the lovely stranger; and, pointing to her brother, made signs which appeared to me to mean that he had been sorrowful until she came. Some hours passed thus, while they, by their countenances, expressed joy, the cause of which I did not comprehend. Presently I found, by the frequent recurrence of one sound which the stranger repeated after them, that she was endeavouring to learn their language; and the idea instantly occurred to me, that I should make use of the same instructions to the same end. The stranger learned about twenty words at the first lesson, most of them indeed were those which I had before understood, but I profited by the others.

'As night came on, Agatha and the Arabian retired early. When they separated, Felix kissed the hand of the stranger, and said, 'Good night, sweet Safie.' He sat up much longer, conversing with his father; and, by the frequent repetition of her name, I conjectured that their lovely guest was the subject of their conversation. I ardently desired to understand them, and bent every faculty towards that purpose, but found it utterly impossible.

'The next morning Felix went out to his work; and, after the usual occupations of Agatha were finished, the Arabian sat at the feet of the old man, and, taking his guitar, played some airs so entrancingly beautiful, that they at once drew tears of sorrow and delight from my eyes. She sang, and her voice flowed in a rich cadence, swelling or dying away, like a nightingale of the woods.

'When she had finished, she gave the guitar to Agatha, who at first declined it. She played a simple air, and her voice accompanied it in sweet accents, but unlike the wondrous strain of the stranger. The old man appeared enraptured, and said some words, which Agatha endeavoured to explain to Safie, and by which he appeared to wish to express that she bestowed on him the greatest delight by her music.

'The days now passed as peaceably as before, with the sole alteration, that joy had taken place of sadness in the countenances of my friends. Safie was always gay and happy; she and I improved rapidly in the knowledge of language, so that in two months I began to comprehend most of the words uttered by my protectors.

'In the meanwhile also the black ground was covered with herbage, and the green banks interspersed with innumerable flowers, sweet to the scent and the eyes, stars of pale radiance among the moonlight woods; the sun became warmer, the nights clear and balmy; and my nocturnal rambles were an extreme pleasure to me, although they were considerably shortened by the late setting and early rising of the sun; for I never ventured abroad during daylight, fearful of meeting with the same treatment as I had formerly endured in the first village which I entered.

'My days were spent in close attention, that I might more speedily master the language; and I may boast that I improved more rapidly than the Arabian, who understood very little, and conversed in broken accents, whilst I comprehended and could imitate almost every word that was spoken.'

Again, not as blank a slate as I would have first perceived!

'While I improved in speech, I also learned the science of letters, as it was taught to the stranger; and this opened before me a wide field for wonder and delight.

Again and again, not as blank a slate as I would have first perceived! It is certainly not possible or, at the very least, plausible. That he should have not only learned to speak, but to read, and for aught we know, to write... by listening through a hole in a wall, seems as unlikely as that he should have acquired, in the same way, the problems of Euclid, or the art of bookkeeping, by single and double entry.[6]

'The book from which Felix instructed Safie was Volney's *Ruins of Empires*. I should not have understood the purport of this book, had not Felix, in reading it, given very minute explanations. He had chosen this work, he said, because the declamatory style was framed in imitation of the eastern authors. Through this work I obtained a cursory knowledge of history, and a view of the several empires at present existing in the world; it gave me an insight into the manners, governments, and religions of the different nations of the earth. I heard of the slothful Asiatics; of the stupendous genius and mental activity of the Grecians; of the wars and wonderful virtue of the early Romans— of their subsequent degeneration— of the decline of that mighty empire; of chivalry, Christianity, and kings. I heard of the discovery of the American hemisphere, and wept with Safie over the hapless fate of its original inhabitants.

'These wonderful narrations inspired me with strange feelings. Was man, indeed, at once so powerful, so virtuous, and magnificent, yet so vicious and base? He appeared at one time a mere scion of the evil prin-

6 From an 1818 review by Walter Scott of *Frankenstein* for *Blackwood's Edinburgh Magazine*.

ciple, and at another as all that can be conceived of noble and godlike. To be a great and virtuous man appeared the highest honour that can befall a sensitive being; to be base and vicious, as many on record have been, appeared the lowest degradation, a condition more abject than that of the blind mole or harmless worm. For a long time I could not conceive how one man could go forth to murder his fellow, or even why there were laws and governments; but when I heard details of vice and bloodshed, my wonder ceased, and I turned away with disgust and loathing.'

Again and again, the wisdom of Victor's Creation! Will it take this Creation standing in the great halls of Parliament to fully communicate this observation of Mankind? Does it take the unnatural creation of this Creation to finally convince man of not only the folly of man but his greatness? Surely, Victor's Creation will burn either by torch or pyre or in Hellfire for this quite human observation.

'Every conversation of the cottagers now opened new wonders to me. While I listened to the instructions which Felix bestowed upon the Arabian, the strange system of human society was explained to me. I heard of the division of property, of immense wealth and squalid poverty; of rank, descent, and noble blood.

'The words induced me to turn towards myself. I learned that the possessions most esteemed by your fellow-creatures were, high and un-sullied descent united with riches. A man might be respected with only one of these acquisitions; but without either he was considered, except in very rare instances, as a vagabond and a slave, doomed to waste his powers for the profit of the chosen few. And what was I? Of my creation and creator I was absolutely ignorant; but I knew that I possessed no money, no friends, no kind of property. I was, besides, endowed with a figure hideously deformed and loathsome; I was not even of the same na-ture as man. I was more agile than they, and could subsist upon coarser diet; I bore the extremes of heat and cold with less injury to my frame; my stature far exceeded their's. When I looked around, I saw and heard of none like me. Was I then a monster, a blot upon the earth, from which all men fled, and whom all men disowned?'

I wept openly and without shame, but the Creation continued his tale unabated.

'I cannot describe to you the agony that these reflections inflicted upon me; I tried to dispel them, but sorrow only increased with knowl-edge. Oh, that I had for ever remained in my native wood, nor known or felt beyond the sensations of hunger, thirst, and heat!

'Of what a strange nature is knowledge! It clings to the mind, when it has once seized on it, like a lichen on the rock. I wished sometimes to shake off all thought and feeling; but I learned that there was but one means to overcome the sensation of pain, and that was death— a state which I feared yet did not understand. I admired virtue and good feelings, and loved the gentle manners and amiable qualities of my cottagers; but I was shut out from intercourse with them, except through means which I obtained by stealth, when I was unseen and unknown, and which rather increased than satisfied the desire I had of becoming one among my fellows. The gentle words of Agatha, and the animated smiles of the charming Arabian, were not for me. The mild exhortations of the old man, and the lively conversation of the loved Felix, were not for me. Miserable, unhappy wretch!

'Other lessons were impressed upon me even more deeply. I heard of the difference of sexes; of the birth and growth of children; how the father doated on the smiles of the infant, and the lively sallies of the older child; how all the life and cares of the mother were wrapt up in the precious charge; how the mind of youth expanded and gained knowledge; of brother, sister, and all the various relationships which bind one human being to another in mutual bonds.

'But where were my friends and relations? No father had watched my infant days, no mother had blessed me with smiles and caresses; or if they had, all my past life was now a blot, a blind vacancy in which I distinguished nothing. From my earliest remembrance I had been as I then was in height and proportion. I had never yet seen a being resembling me, or who claimed any intercourse with me. What was I? The question again recurred, to be answered only with groans.'

Again and again, I wept openly. Will these tears never cease?

And then, in an instant, he was no longer relating his story to me but instead directly addressing me: 'I will soon explain to what these feelings tended.' And then just as quickly, he returned to his tale, 'But allow me now to return to the cottagers, whose story excited in me such various feelings of indignation, delight, and wonder, but which all terminated in additional love and reverence for my protectors (for so I loved, in an innocent, half painful self-deceit, to call them)."

I wept.

Chapter IV

Some time elapsed before I learned the history of my friends. It was one which could not fail to impress itself deeply on my mind, unfolding as it did a number of circumstances each interesting and wonderful to one so utterly inexperienced as I was.

'The name of the old man was De Lacey. He was descended from a good family in France, where he had lived for many years in affluence, respected by his superiors, and beloved by his equals. His son was bred in the service of his country; and Agatha had ranked with ladies of the highest distinction. A few months before my arrival, they had lived in a large and luxurious city, called Paris, surrounded by friends, and possessed of every enjoyment which virtue, refinement of intellect, or taste, accompanied by a moderate fortune, could afford.

'The father of Safie had been the cause of their ruin. He was a Turkish merchant, and had inhabited Paris for many years, when, for some reason which I could not learn, he became obnoxious to the government.' Oh! No doubt the merchant sold goods to the aristocracy and then got caught up in the mass arrests of the royalists that seized a revolutionary France and cost the royalists their heads. Literally. And liberally was the guillotine utilized. 'He was seized and cast into prison the very day that Safie arrived from Constantinople to join him. He was tried, and condemned to death. The injustice of his sentence was very flagrant; all Paris was indignant; and it was judged that his religion and wealth, rather than the crime alleged against him, had been the cause of his condemnation.' The revolutionaries cared not if your noble blood was French or foreign. The condemnation was the same throughout the nation. Off with their heads!

'Felix had been present at the trial; his horror and indignation were uncontrollable, when he heard the decision of the court. He made, at that moment, a solemn vow to deliver him, and then looked around for the means. After many fruitless attempts to gain admittance to the prison, he found a strongly grated window in an unguarded part of the building, which lighted the dungeon of the unfortunate Mahometan; who, loaded with chains, waited in despair the execution of the barbarous sentence. Felix visited the grate at night, and made known to the prisoner his intentions in his favour. The Turk, amazed and delighted, endeavoured to kindle the zeal of his deliverer by promises of reward and wealth. Felix rejected his offers with contempt; yet when he saw the lovely Safie, who was allowed to visit her father, and who, by her gestures, expressed her lively gratitude, the youth could not help owning to his own mind, that the captive possessed a treasure which would fully reward his toil and hazard.' The foolishness and folly of youth.

'The Turk quickly perceived the impression that his daughter had made on the heart of Felix, and endeavoured to secure him more entirely in his interests by the promise of her hand in marriage, so soon as he should be conveyed to a place of safety. Felix was too delicate to accept this offer; yet he looked forward to the probability of that event as to the consummation of his happiness.

'During the ensuing days, while the preparations were going forward for the escape of the merchant, the zeal of Felix was warmed by several letters that he received from this lovely girl, who found means to express her thoughts in the language of her lover by the aid of an old man, a servant of her father's, who understood French. She thanked him in the most ardent terms for his intended services towards her father; and at the same time she gently deplored her own fate.

'I have copies of these letters; for I found means, during my residence in the hovel, to procure the implements of writing; and the letters were often in the hands of Felix or Agatha. Before I depart, I will give them to you, they will prove the truth of my tale; but at present, as the sun is already far declined, I shall only have time to repeat the substance of them to you.' Was the Creation addressing me or Victor Frankenstein at this moment? There is no means by which I could take possession of phantasmagorical letters. But if this Creation was addressing Victor while they both sit beside a roaring fire in a cave fashioned in ice? Either audience could easily be being addressed by Victor's Creation.

'Safie related, that her mother was a Christian Arab.' A *jizyah*. I whispered under my breath. I know not where the word came from, for I know not Arabic, excepting my dropping of eaves during the dinners my father. Perhaps. Perhaps not. 'Seized and made a slave by the Turks; recommended by her beauty, she had won the heart of the father of Safie, who married her. The young girl spoke in high and enthusiastic terms of her mother, who, born in freedom spurned the bondage to which she was now reduced. She instructed her daughter in the tenets of her religion, and taught her to aspire to higher powers of intellect, and an independence of spirit, forbidden to the female followers of Mahomet.'

The Quran is not alone in its condemnation of the education of women. Does not Paul the Apostle instruct thus, *Let the woman learn in silence with all subjection. And I do not permit a woman to teach or to have authority over a man, but to be in silence. For Adam was first formed, then Eve. And Adam was not deceived, but the woman being deceived was in the transgression. Notwithstanding she shall be saved in childbearing, if they continue in faith and charity and holiness with sobriety.* AND! *Let your women keep silence in the churches: for it is not permitted unto them to speak; but they are commanded to be under obedience as also saith the law. And if they will learn any thing, let them ask their husbands at home: for it is a shame for women to speak in the church.* AND! *Wives, submit yourselves unto your own husbands, as unto the Lord. For the husband is the head of the wife, even as Christ is the head of the church: and he is the saviour of the body. Therefore as the church is subject unto Christ, so let the wives be to their own husbands in every thing.*

How my mother loathed these scriptures!

'This lady died; but her lessons were indelibly impressed on the mind of Safie, who sickened at the prospect of again returning to Asia, and the being immured within the walls of a harem, allowed only to occupy herself with puerile amusements, ill suited to the temper of her soul, now accustomed to grand ideas and a noble emulation for virtue. The prospect of marrying a Christian, and remaining in a country where women were allowed to take a rank in society, was enchanting to her.

'The day for the execution of the Turk was fixed; but, on the night previous to it, he had quitted prison, and before morning was distant many leagues from Paris. Felix had procured passports in the name of his father, sister, and himself. He had previously communicated his plan to the former, who aided the deceit by quitting his house, under the pretence of a journey, and concealed himself, with his daughter, in an obscure part of Paris.

'Felix conducted the fugitives through France to Lyons, and across Mont Cenis to Leghorn, where the merchant had decided to wait a favourable opportunity of passing into some part of the Turkish dominions.

'Safie resolved to remain with her father until the moment of his departure, before which time the Turk renewed his promise that she should be united to his deliverer; and Felix remained with them in expectation of that event; and in the mean time he enjoyed the society of the Arabian, who exhibited towards him the simplest and tenderest affection. They conversed with one another through the means of an interpreter, and sometimes with the interpretation of looks; and Safie sang to him the divine airs of her native country.

'The Turk allowed this intimacy to take place, and encouraged the hopes of the youthful lovers, while in his heart he had formed far other plans. He loathed the idea that his daughter should be united to a Christian; but he feared the resentment of Felix if he should appear lukewarm; for he knew that he was still in the power of his deliverer, if he should choose to betray him to the Italian state which they inhabited. He revolved a thousand plans by which he should be enabled to prolong the deceit until it might be no longer necessary, and secretly to take his daughter with him when he departed. His plans were greatly facilitated by the news which arrived from Paris.

'The government of France were greatly enraged at the escape of their victim, and spared no pains to detect and punish his deliverer. The plot of Felix was quickly discovered, and De Lacey and Agatha were thrown into prison. The news reached Felix, and roused him from his dream of pleasure. His blind and aged father, and his gentle sister, lay in a noisome dungeon, while he enjoyed the free air, and the society of her whom he loved. This idea was torture to him. He quickly arranged with the Turk, that if the latter should find a favourable opportunity for escape before Felix could return to Italy, Safie should remain as a boarder at a convent at Leghorn; and then, quitting the lovely Arabian, he hastened to Paris, and delivered himself up to the vengeance of the law, hoping to free De Lacey and Agatha by this proceeding.

'He did not succeed. They remained confined for five months before the trial took place; the result of which deprived them of their fortune, and condemned them to a perpetual exile from their native country.

'They found a miserable asylum in the cottage in Germany, where I discovered them. Felix soon learned that the treacherous Turk, for whom he and his family endured such unheard-of oppression, on discovering that his deliverer was thus reduced to poverty and impotence, became a traitor to good feeling and honour, and had quitted Italy with his daughter, insultingly sending Felix a pittance of money to aid him, as he said, in some plan of future maintenance.

'Such were the events that preyed on the heart of Felix, and rendered him, when I first saw him, the most miserable of his family. He could have endured poverty, and when this distress had been the meed of his virtue, he would have gloried in it: but the ingratitude of the Turk, and the loss of his beloved Safie, were misfortunes more bitter and irreparable. The arrival of the Arabian now infused new life into his soul.

'When the news reached Leghorn, that Felix was deprived of his wealth and rank, the merchant commanded his daughter to think no more of her lover, but to prepare to return with him to her native country. The generous nature of Safie was outraged by this command; she attempted to expostulate with her father, but he left her angrily, reiterating his tyrannical mandate.

'A few days after, the Turk entered his daughter's apartment, and told her hastily, that he had reason to believe that his residence at Leghorn had been divulged, and that he should speedily be delivered up to the French government; he had, consequently, hired a vessel to convey him to Constantinople, for which city he should sail in a few hours. He intended to leave his daughter under the care of a confidential servant, to follow at her leisure with the greater part of his property, which had not yet arrived at Leghorn.

'When alone, Safie resolved in her own mind the plan of conduct that it would become her to pursue in this emergency. A residence in Turkey was abhorrent to her; her religion and feelings were alike adverse to it. By some papers of her father's, which fell into her hands, she heard of the exile of her lover, and learnt the name of the spot where he then resided. She hesitated some time, but at length she formed her determination. Taking with her some jewels that belonged to her, and a small sum of money, she quitted Italy, with an attendant, a native of Leghorn, but who understood the common language of Turkey, and departed for Germany.

'She arrived in safety at a town about twenty leagues from the cottage of De Lacey, when her attendant fell dangerously ill. Safie nursed her with the most devoted affection; but the poor girl died, and the Arabian was left alone, unacquainted with the language of the country, and utterly ignorant of the customs of the world. She fell, however, into good hands. The Italian had mentioned the name of the spot for which they were bound; and, after her death, the woman of the house in which they had lived took care that Safie should arrive in safety at the cottage of her lover."

Again and again the foolishness and folly of youth! But this is a foolishness and folly I am all to accustomed to. My soul has been ascribed with this very foolishness and folly to have followed my Beloved from the rightful grip of my father into flight from our marital plight across France into the Villa Diodati. But the wrath of my father— nay! the wrath of the Eternal Father— has descended upon us with thunderous dark and violent storm clouds.

Chapter V

Such was the history of my beloved cottagers. It impressed me deeply. I learned, from the views of social life which it developed, to admire their virtues, and to deprecate the vices of mankind.

'As yet I looked upon crime as a distant evil; benevolence and generosity were ever present before me, inciting within me a desire to become an actor in the busy scene where so many admirable qualities were called forth and displayed. But, in giving an account of the progress of my intellect, I must not omit a circumstance which occurred in the beginning of the month of August of the same year.' This must be 1795. Or is it? I'm getting lost in the whirlwind of my own mind.

'One night, during my accustomed visit to the neighbouring wood, where I collected my own food, and brought home firing for my protectors, I found on the ground a leathern portmanteau, containing several articles of dress and some books. I eagerly seized the prize, and returned with it to my hovel. Fortunately the books were written in the language the elements of which I had acquired at the cottage; they consisted of *Paradise Lost*, a volume of *Plutarch's Lives*, and the *Sorrows of Werter.*' Oh! to read Milton in French would prove to be such an abomination. I have no doubt that Nicolas-François Dupré de Saint-Maur's translation is estimable, but something must be lost in the translation! Jacques Amyot's translation of Plutarch is in itself estimable, but only because it is the source of Sir Thomas North's own English translation. A translation of a translation? The horror! While I have yet to read Goethe in his original German, Baron Karl Siemund von Seckendorff's French translation is no doubt serviceable. 'The possession of these treasures gave me extreme delight; I now continually studied and exercised my mind upon these histories, whilst my friends were employed in their ordinary occupations.'

His delight at discovering the joys and wonders of the written word upon the page delights me so! The joy of reading the histories, the epics, the dramas, the philosophies, the sciences is only surpassed by the joy of writing. To create entire characters and worlds out of the ether is a form of creation that is only rivalled by the growing of a child in your womb. And just as the mother knows not the destiny of the child growing in her womb, the author knows not the fate of her characters. It is the strangest of paradoxes when a character created by your own mind turns on its author by exclaiming, 'No! this is my story now. I shall relate it the way I wish!' Sometimes, this happens on the very first page of the ink-stained manuscript! And curiously, I am feeling this queer experience at this very moment listening to Victor's Creation relate his story unto me!

'I can hardly describe to you the effect of these books. They produced in me an infinity of new images and feelings, that sometimes raised me to ecstacy, but more frequently sunk me into the lowest dejection. In the *Sorrows of Werter*, besides the interest of its simple and affecting story, so many opinions are canvassed, and so many lights thrown upon what had hitherto been to me obscure subjects, that I found in it a never-ending source of speculation and astonishment. The gentle and domestic manners it described, combined with lofty sentiments and feelings, which had for their object something out of self, accorded well with my experience among my protectors, and with the wants which were for ever alive in my own bosom. But I thought Werter himself a more divine being than I had ever beheld or imagined; his character contained no pretension, but it sunk deep. The disquisitions upon death and suicide were calculated to fill me with wonder. I did not pretend to enter into the merits of the case, yet I inclined towards the opinions of the hero, whose extinction I wept, without precisely understanding it.

'As I read, however, I applied much personally to my own feelings and condition. I found myself similar, yet at the same time strangely unlike the beings concerning whom I read, and to whose conversation I was a listener. I sympathized with, and partly understood them, but I was unformed in mind; I was dependent on none, and related to none. 'The path of my departure was free.' How Victor's Creation has stolen into my own mind to steal the words of my Beloved! It is impossible for the Creation to have read published this very year! Shall I share again the original words composed by my Beloved, my dearest Journal?

We are as clouds that veil the midnight moon;
     How restlessly they speed, and gleam, and quiver,
Streaking the darkness radiantly!—yet soon
     Night closes round, and they are lost forever:

Or like forgotten lyres, whose dissonant strings
     Give various response to each varying blast,
To whose frail frame no second motion brings
     One mood or modulation like the last.

We rest.—A dream has power to poison sleep;
     We rise.—One wandering thought pollutes the day;
We feel, conceive or reason, laugh or weep;
     Embrace fond woe, or cast our cares away:

It is the same!—For, be it joy or sorrow,
     The path of its departure still is free:
Man's yesterday may ne'er be like his morrow;
     Nought may endure but mutability![7]

'And there was none to lament my annihilation. My person was hideous, and my stature gigantic: what did this mean? Who was I? What was I? Whence did I come? What was my destination? These questions continually recurred, but I was unable to solve them.'

But solve them you shall. Solve them you must!

'The volume of *Plutarch's Lives* which I possessed, contained the histories of the first founders of the ancient republics. This book had a far different effect upon me from the *Sorrows of Werter*. I learned from Werter's imaginations despondency and gloom: but Plutarch taught me high thoughts; he elevated me above the wretched sphere of my own reflections, to admire and love the heroes of past ages. Many things I read surpassed my understanding and experience. I had a very confused knowledge of kingdoms, wide extents of country, mighty rivers, and boundless seas. But I was perfectly unacquainted with towns, and large assemblages of men. The cottage of my protectors had been the only school in which I had studied human nature; but this book developed

---

7 From *Alastor, or The Spirit of Solitude: And Other Poems* by Percy Bysshe Shelley in 1816.

new and mightier scenes of action. I read of men concerned in public affairs governing or massacring their species. I felt the greatest ardour for virtue rise within me, and abhorrence for vice, as far as I understood the signification of those terms, relative as they were, as I applied them, to pleasure and pain alone. Induced by these feelings, I was of course led to admire peaceable law-givers,'— which he named his favourites— 'Numa, Solon, and Lycurgus, in preference to Romulus and Theseus.'

Of Numa, whom Plutarch wrote, 'It is true, indeed, of all just and good men, that they are praised more after they have left the world than before, since envy does not long survive them, and some even see it die before them; but in Numa's case the misfortunes of the kings who followed him made his fame shine all the brighter.'[8]

Of Solon, whom Plutarch wrote, 'Thus he represents the multitude and men of low degree as speaking of him. However, though he rejected the tyranny, he did not administer affairs in the mildest possible manner, nor in the enactment of his laws did he show a feeble spirit, nor make concessions to the powerful, nor consult the pleasure of his electors. Nay, where a condition was as good as it could well be, he applied no remedy, and introduced no innovation, fearing lest, after utterly confusing and confounding the city, he should be too weak to establish it again and recompose it for the best. But those things wherein he hoped to find them open to persuasion or submissive to compulsion, these he did, "Combining both force and justice together," as he says himself. Therefore when he was afterwards asked if he had enacted the best laws for the Athenians, he replied, "The best they would receive." [9]

Of Lycurgus, whom Plutarch wrote, 'Concerning Lycurgus the lawgiver, in general, nothing can be said which is not disputed, since indeed there are different accounts of his birth, his travels, his death, and above all, of his work as lawmaker and statesman; and there is least agreement among historians as to the times in which the man lived.'[10]

Of Romulus, whom Plutarch wrote, 'From whom, and for what reason the great name of Rome, so famous among mankind, was given to that city, writers are not agreed. Some say it was Roma, a daughter of the Trojan woman I have mentioned, who was wedded to Latinus the son of Telemachus and bore him Romulus; others that Aemilia, the daughter of Aeneas and Lavinia, bore him to Mars; and others still rehearse what is altogether fabulous concerning his origin. For instance, they say that Tarchetius, king of the Albans, who was most lawless and cruel, was vis-

---

8 From *Plutarch's Lives*, 'The Life of Numa', as translated by Bernadotte Perrin.
9 From *Plutarch's Lives*, 'The Life of Solon', as translated by Bernadotte Perrin.
10 From *Plutarch's Lives*, 'The Life of Lyrcurgus', as translated by Bernadotte Perrin.

ited with a strange phantom in his house, namely, a phallus rising out of the hearth and remaining there many days.'[11]

Of Theseus, whom Plutarch wrote, 'But after publishing my account of Lycurgus the lawgiver and Numa the king, I thought I might not unreasonably go back still farther to Romulus, now that my history had brought me near his times. And as I asked myself, "With such a warrior" (as Aeschylus says) "who will dare to fight?" "Whom shall I set against him? Who is competent?" it seemed to me that I must make the founder of lovely and famous Athens the counterpart and parallel to the father of invincible and glorious Rome. May I therefore succeed in purifying Fable, making her submit to reason and take on the semblance of History. But where she obstinately disdains to make herself credible, and refuses to admit any element of probability, I shall pray for kindly readers, and such as receive with indulgence the tales of antiquity.'[12]

Despite, or in spite of, my mind's rapid digressions onto the bookshelves of the library of human memory where Plutarhc's *Lives of the Noble Greek and Romans* is currently shelved, Victor's Creation continued on with his tale unabetted, 'The patriarchal lives of my protectors caused these impressions to take a firm hold on my mind; perhaps, if my first introduction to humanity had been made by a young soldier, burning for glory and slaughter, I should have been imbued with different sensations.

'But *Paradise Lost* excited different and far deeper emotions. I read it, as I had read the other volumes which had fallen into my hands, as a true history. It moved every feeling of wonder and awe, that the picture of an omnipotent God warring with his creatures was capable of exciting. I often referred the several situations, as their similarity struck me, to my own. Like Adam, I was created apparently united by no link to any other being in existence; but his state was far different from mine in every other respect. He had come forth from the hands of God a perfect creature, happy and prosperous, guarded by the especial care of his Creator; he was allowed to converse with, and acquire knowledge from beings of a superior nature: but I was wretched, helpless, and alone. Many times I considered Satan as the fitter emblem of my condition; for often, like him, when I viewed the bliss of my protectors, the bitter gall of envy rose within me.'

Oh! No! Dearest Creation of Victor's! Take not this lesson from Milton! But I cannot and will not make any defence of Satan! I shall allow my Beloved to make his own defence: 'The distorted notions of invisible things which Dante and his rival Milton have idealized are merely

---

11 From *Plutarch's Lives*, 'The Life of Romulus', as translated by Bernadotte Perrin.
12 From *Plutarch's Lives*, 'The Life of Theseus', as translated by Bernadotte Perrin.

the mask and the mantle in which these great poets walk through eternity enveloped and disguised. It is a difficult question to determine how far they were conscious of the distinction which must have subsisted in their minds between their own creeds and that of the people. Dante at least appears to wish to mark the full extent of it by placing Riphæus, whom Virgil calls *justissimus unus,* in Paradise, and observing a most heretical caprice in his distribution of rewards and punishments. And Milton's poem contains within itself a philosophical refutation of that system of which, by a strange and natural antithesis, it has been a chief popular support. Nothing can exceed the energy and magnificence of the character of Satan as expressed in Paradise Lost. It is a mistake to suppose that he could ever have been intended for the popular personification of evil. Implacable hate, patient cunning, and a sleepless refinement of device to inflict the extremest anguish on an enemy, these things are evil; and although venial in a slave are not to be forgiven in a tyrant; although redeemed by much that ennobles his defeat in one subdued, are marked by all that dishonours his conquest in the victor. Milton's Devil as a moral being is as far superior to his God as one who perseveres in some purpose which he has conceived to be excellent in spite of adversity and torture, is to one who in the cold security of undoubted triumph inflicts the most horrible revenge upon his enemy, not from any mistaken notion of inducing him to repent of a perseverance in enmity, but with the alleged design of exasperating him to deserve new torments. Milton has so far violated the popular creed (if this shall be judged a violation) as to have alleged no superiority of moral virtue to his God over his Devil. And this bold neglect of a direct moral purpose is the most decisive proof of Milton's genius. He mingled as it were the elements of human nature, as colours upon a single pallet, and arranged them into the composition of his great picture according to the laws of epic truth; that is, according to the laws of that principle by which a series of actions of the external universe and of intelligent and ethical beings is calculated to excite the sympathy of succeeding generations of mankind.'[13]

Again and again, my mind's incessant digressions distract from the tale being related by this Creation, 'Another circumstance strengthened and confirmed these feelings. Soon after my arrival in the hovel, I discovered some papers in the pocket of the dress which I had taken from *your* laboratory.' Was the Creation addressing me in the moment, or Victor? I possessed no laboratory. I possessed no papers secreted in the pocket of a dress. 'At first I had neglected them; but now that I was able to decypher the characters in which they were written, I began to study

---

13 From an unfinished essay by Percy Bysshe Shelley written in February and March of 1821, though it is conceivable he composed it as early as 1816.

them with diligence. It was your journal of the four months that preceded my creation. You minutely described in these papers every step you took in the progress of your work; this history was mingled with accounts of domestic occurrences. You, doubtless, recollect these papers. Here they are. Every thing is related in them which bears reference to my accursed origin; the whole detail of that series of disgusting circumstances which produced it is set in view; the minutest description of my odious and loathsome person is given, in language which painted your own horrors, and rendered mine ineffaceable. I sickened as I read. "Hateful day when I received life!" I exclaimed in agony. "Cursed creator! Why did you form a monster so hideous that even you turned from me in disgust? God in pity made man beautiful and alluring, after his own image; but my form is a filthy type of your's, more horrid from its very resemblance. Satan had his companions, fellow-devils, to admire and encourage him; but I am solitary and detested."'

Oh! No! Dearest Creation, think not this thought of your Creation!

'These were the reflections of my hours of despondency and solitude; but when I contemplated the virtues of the cottagers, their amiable and benevolent dispositions, I persuaded myself that when they should become acquainted with my admiration of their virtues, they would compassionate me, and overlook my personal deformity. Could they turn from their door one, however monstrous, who solicited their compassion and friendship? I resolved, at least, not to despair, but in every way to fit myself for an interview with them which would decide my fate.' I shutter with terrified anticipation of this moment. 'I postponed this attempt for some months longer; for the importance attached to its success inspired me with a dread lest I should fail. Besides, I found that my understanding improved so much with every day's experience, that I was unwilling to commence this undertaking until a few more months should have added to my wisdom.

'Several changes, in the mean time, took place in the cottage. The presence of Safie diffused happiness among its inhabitants; and I also found that a greater degree of plenty reigned there. Felix and Agatha spent more time in amusement and conversation, and were assisted in their labours by servants. They did not appear rich, but they were contented and happy; their feelings were serene and peaceful, while mine became every day more tumultuous. Increase of knowledge only discovered to me more clearly what a wretched outcast I was. I cherished hope, it is true; but it vanished, when I beheld my person reflected in water, or my shadow in the moon-shine, even as that frail image and that inconstant shade.

'I endeavoured to crush these fears, and to fortify myself for the trial which in a few months I resolved to undergo; and sometimes I allowed my thoughts, unchecked by reason, to ramble in the fields of Paradise, and dared to fancy amiable and lovely creatures sympathizing with my feelings and cheering my gloom; their angelic countenances breathed smiles of consolation. But it was all a dream: no Eve soothed my sorrows, or shared my thoughts; I was alone. I remembered Adam's supplication to his Creator; but where was mine? he had abandoned me, and, in the bitterness of my heart, I cursed him.

'Autumn passed thus. I saw, with surprise and grief, the leaves decay and fall, and nature again assume the barren and bleak appearance it had worn when I first beheld the woods and the lovely moon. Yet I did not heed the bleakness of the weather; I was better fitted by my conformation for the endurance of cold than heat. But my chief delights were the sight of the flowers, the birds, and all the gay apparel of summer; when those deserted me, I turned with more attention towards the cottagers. Their happiness was not decreased by the absence of summer. They loved, and sympathized with one another; and their joys, depending on each other, were not interrupted by the casualties that took place around them. The more I saw of them, the greater became my desire to claim their protection and kindness; my heart yearned to be known and loved by these amiable creatures: to see their sweet looks turned towards me with affection, was the utmost limit of my ambition. I dared not think that they would turn them from me with disdain and horror. The poor that stopped at their door were never driven away. I asked, it is true, for greater treasures than a little food or rest; I required kindness and sympathy; but I did not believe myself utterly unworthy of it.

'The winter advanced, and an entire revolution of the seasons had taken place since I awoke into life. My attention, at this time, was solely directed towards my plan of introducing myself into the cottage of my protectors. I revolved many projects; but that on which I finally fixed was, to enter the dwelling when the blind old man should be alone. I had sagacity enough to discover, that the unnatural hideousness of my person was the chief object of horror with those who had formerly beheld me. My voice, although harsh, had nothing terrible in it; I thought, therefore, that if, in the absence of his children, I could gain the good-will and mediation of the old De Lacy, I might, by his means, be tolerated by my younger protectors.

'One day, when the sun shone on the red leaves that strewed the ground, and diffused cheerfulness, although it denied warmth, Safie, Agatha, and Felix, departed on a long country walk, and the old man, at his own desire, was left alone in the cottage. When his children had departed, he took up his guitar, and played several mournful, but sweet airs, more sweet and mournful than I had ever heard him play before. At first his countenance was illuminated with pleasure, but, as he continued, thoughtfulness and sadness succeeded; at length, laying aside the instrument, he sat absorbed in reflection.

'My heart beat quick.'

As does mine, dearest Creation!

'This was the hour and moment of trial, which would decide my hopes, or realize my fears. The servants were gone to a neighbouring fair. All was silent in and around the cottage: it was an excellent opportunity; yet, when I proceeded to execute my plan, my limbs failed me, and I sunk to the ground. Again I rose; and, exerting all the firmness of which I was master, removed the planks which I had placed before my hovel to conceal my retreat. The fresh air revived me, and, with renewed determination, I approached the door of their cottage.

'I knocked. "Who is there?" said the old man— "Come in."

'I entered; "Pardon this intrusion," said I, "I am a traveller in want of a little rest; you would greatly oblige me, if you would allow me to remain a few minutes before the fire."

' "Enter," said De Lacy; "and I will try in what manner I can relieve your wants; but, unfortunately, my children are from home, and, as I am blind, I am afraid I shall find it difficult to procure food for you."

' "Do not trouble yourself, my kind host, I have food; it is warmth and rest only that I need."

'I sat down, and a silence ensued. I knew that every minute was precious to me, yet I remained irresolute in what manner to commence the interview; when the old man addressed me—

' "By your language, stranger, I suppose you are my countryman;— are you French?'

' "No; but I was educated by a French family, and understand that language only. I am now going to claim the protection of some friends, whom I sincerely love, and of whose favour I have some hopes."

' "Are these Germans?"

' "No, they are French. But let us change the subject. I am an unfortunate and deserted creature; I look around, and I have no relation or friend upon earth. These amiable people to whom I go have never seen me, and know little of me. I am full of fears; for if I fail there, I am an outcast in the world for ever.'

' "Do not despair. To be friendless is indeed to be unfortunate; but the hearts of men, when unprejudiced by any obvious self-interest, are full of brotherly love and charity. Rely, therefore, on your hopes; and if these friends are good and amiable, do not despair."

' "They are kind— they are the most excellent creatures in the world; but, unfortunately, they are prejudiced against me. I have good dispositions; my life has been hitherto harmless, and, in some degree, beneficial; but a fatal prejudice clouds their eyes, and where they ought to see a feeling and kind friend, they behold only a detestable monster."

' "That is indeed unfortunate; but if you are really blameless, cannot you undeceive them?"

' "I am about to undertake that task; and it is on that account that I feel so many overwhelming terrors. I tenderly love these friends; I have, unknown to them, been for many months in the habits of daily kindness towards them; but they believe that I wish to injure them, and it is that prejudice which I wish to overcome."

' "Where do these friends reside?"

' "Near this spot."

'The old man paused, and then continued, "If you will unreservedly confide to me the particulars of your tale, I perhaps may be of use in undeceiving them. I am blind, and cannot judge of your countenance, but there is something in your words which persuades me that you are sincere. I am poor, and an exile; but it will afford me true pleasure to be in any way serviceable to a human creature."

' "Excellent man! I thank you, and accept your generous offer. You raise me from the dust by this kindness; and I trust that, by your aid, I shall not be driven from the society and sympathy of your fellow-creatures."

' "Heaven forbid! even if you were really criminal; for that can only drive you to desperation, and not instigate you to virtue. I also am unfortunate; I and my family have been condemned, although innocent: judge, therefore, if I do not feel for your misfortunes."

' "How can I thank you, my best and only benefactor? from your lips first have I heard the voice of kindness directed towards me; I shall be for ever grateful; and your present humanity assures me of success with those friends whom I am on the point of meeting."

' "May I know the names and residence of those friends?"

'I paused. This, I thought, was the moment of decision, which was to rob me of, or bestow happiness on me for ever. I struggled vainly for firmness sufficient to answer him, but the effort destroyed all my remaining strength; I sank on the chair, and sobbed aloud. At that moment I heard the steps of my younger protectors. I had not a moment to lose; but, seizing the hand of the old man, I cried, "Now is the time!— save and protect me! You and your family are the friends whom I seek. Do not you desert me in the hour of trial!"

' "Great God!" exclaimed the old man, "who are you?"

'At that instant the cottage door was opened, and Felix, Safie, and Agatha entered. Who can describe their horror and consternation on beholding me? Agatha fainted; and Safie, unable to attend to her friend, rushed out of the cottage. Felix darted forward, and with supernatural force tore me from his father, to whose knees I clung: in a transport of fury, he dashed me to the ground, and struck me violently with a stick. I could have torn him limb from limb, as the lion rends the antelope. But my heart sunk within me as with bitter sickness, and I refrained. I saw him on the point of repeating his blow, when, overcome by pain and anguish, I quitted the cottage, and in the general tumult escaped unperceived to my hovel.'

I too, like Agatha, fainted upon hearing of exchange between the De Lacys and Victor's Creation. I awoke, in my bed within my apartment at the Villa Diodati with my Beloved by my side still peacefully slumbering. The Creation had moved from his chair beside the fire and held my hand in his. My hand appeared swallowed by his own as if my hand was Jonah and his was the whale. I felt its enormity and also its tenderness. A salty wetness threatened to overwell his eyes; eyes that shown with human kindness. His voiced soothed me with cooing warmth and gentleness. Once the Creation had been assured of my wellbeing, he sat again in the chair beside the fire and continued his tale... full of wrath and rage!

Chapter VI

Sing, O goddess, the wrath of Achilles, son of Peleus, that brought countless ills upon the Achaeans, just as I believe Victor's Creation shall be countless ills upon his Creator!

'Cursed, cursed creator! Why did I live? Why, in that instant, did I not extinguish the spark of existence which you had so wantonly bestowed? I know not; despair had not yet taken possession of me; my feelings were those of rage and revenge. I could with pleasure have destroyed the cottage and its inhabitants, and have glutted myself with their shrieks and misery.'

Victor's mangled Creation reminds me of God's magnificent Creation, Satan. Where Adam and Eve are often seen by the JudeoChristian as perfect creations, their fall from Eden by eating of the fruit of the Tree of the Knowledge of Good and Evil speaks to their imperfection. And were not the angels created perfect and yet their Fall likewise speaks to their imperfections. Victor's Creation is seen by not only his Creator but by the Creation itself as imperfect. Did not Victor's Creation say only mere moments ago, 'Many times I considered Satan as the fitter emblem of my condition; for often, like him, when I viewed the bliss of my protectors, the bitter gall of envy rose within me.' And thus Satan's opening soliloquy against God by Milton speaks volumes:

> *'Is this the Region, this the Soil, the Clime',*
> *Said then the lost Arch Angel, 'this the seat*
> *That we must change for Heav'n, this mournful gloom*
> *For that celestial light? Be it so, since he*
> *Who now is Sovran can dispose and bid*
> *What shall be right: farthest from him is best*
> *Whom reason hath equalled, force hath made supreme*
> *Above his equals. Farewell happy Fields*
> *Where Joy for ever dwells: Hail horrors, hail*
> *Infernal world, and thou profoundest Hell*
> *Receive thy new Possessor: One who brings*
> *A mind not to be chang'd by Place or Time.*
> *The mind is its own place, and in it self*
> *Can make a Heav'n of Hell, a Hell of Heav'n.*
> *What matter where, if I be still the same,*
> *And what I should be, all but less then he*
> *Whom Thunder hath made greater? Here at least*
> *We shall be free; th' Almighty hath not built*
> *Here for his envy, will not drive us hence:*
> *Here we may reign secure, and in my choice*
> *To reign is worth ambition though in Hell:*
> *Better to reign in Hell, then serve in Heav'n.*
> *But wherefore let we then our faithful friends,*
> *Th' associates and copartners of our loss*
> *Lye thus astonished on th' oblivious Pool,*
> *And call them not to share with us their part*
> *In this unhappy Mansion, or once more*
> *With rallied Arms to try what may be yet*
> *Regained in Heav'n, or what more lost in Hell?'*[14]

'When night came, I quitted my retreat, and wandered in the wood; and now, no longer restrained by the fear of discovery, I gave vent to my anguish in fearful howlings. I was like a wild beast that had broken the toils; destroying the objects that obstructed me, and ranging through the wood with a stag-like swiftness. Oh! what a miserable night I passed! the cold stars shone in mockery, and the bare trees waved their branches above me: now and then the sweet voice of a bird burst forth amidst the universal stillness. All, save I, were at rest or in enjoyment: I, like the arch

---

14 From Book I of *Paradise Lost* by John Milton.

fiend, bore a hell within me; and, finding myself unsympathized with, wished to tear up the trees, spread havoc and destruction around me, and then to have sat down and enjoyed the ruin.

'But this was a luxury of sensation that could not endure; I became fatigued with excess of bodily exertion, and sank on the damp grass in the sick impotence of despair. There was none among the myriads of men that existed who would pity or assist me; and should I feel kindness towards my enemies? No: from that moment I declared everlasting war against the species, and, more than all, against him who had formed me, and sent me forth to this insupportable misery.'

> *'O Sun, to tell thee how I hate thy beams*
> *That bring to my remembrance from what state*
> *I fell, how glorious once above thy Sphere;*
> *Till Pride and worse Ambition threw me down*
> *Warring in Heav'n against Heav'ns matchless King:*
> *Ah wherefore! he deserved no such return*
> *From me, whom he created what I was*
> *In that bright eminence, and with his good*
> *Upbraided none; nor was his service hard.*
> *What could be less then to afford him praise,*
> *The easiest recompense, and pay him thanks,*
> *How due! yet all his good prov'd ill in me,*
> *And wrought but malice; lifted up so high*
> *I sdeined subjection, and thought one step higher*
> *Would set me highest, and in a moment quit*
> *The debt immense of endless gratitude,*
> *So burthensome, still paying, still to owe;*
> *Forgetful what from him I still received,*
> *And understood not that a grateful mind*
> *By owing owes not, but still pays, at once*
> *Indebted and discharged; what burden then?*
> *O had his powerful Destiny ordained*
> *Me some inferior Angel, I had stood*
> *Then happy; no unbounded hope had rais'd*
> *Ambition. Yet why not? some other Power*
> *As great might have aspir'd, and me though mean*
> *Drawn to his part; but other Powers as great*
> *Fell not, but stand unshak'n, from within*
> *Or from without, to all temptations arm'd.*
> *Hadst thou the same free Will and Power to stand?*
> *Thou hadst: whom hast thou then or what to accuse,*

But Heav'ns free Love dealt equally to all?
Be then his Love accurst, since love or hate,
To me alike, it deals eternal woe.
Nay curs'd be thou; since against his thy will
Chose freely what it now so justly rues.
Me miserable! which way shall I fly
Infinite wrath, and infinite despair?
Which way I fly is Hell; my self am Hell;
And in the lowest deep a lower deep
Still threatening to devour me opens wide,
To which the Hell I suffer seems a Heav'n.'[15]

'The sun rose; I heard the voices of men, and knew that it was impossible to return to my retreat during that day. Accordingly I hid myself in some thick underwood, determining to devote the ensuing hours to reflection on my situation.

'The pleasant sunshine, and the pure air of day, restored me to some degree of tranquillity; and when I considered what had passed at the cottage, I could not help believing that I had been too hasty in my conclusions. I had certainly acted imprudently. It was apparent that my conversation had interested the father in my behalf, and I was a fool in having exposed my person to the horror of his children. I ought to have familiarized the old De Lacy to me, and by degrees have discovered myself to the rest of his family, when they should have been prepared for my approach. But I did not believe my errors to be irretrievable; and, after much consideration, I resolved to return to the cottage, seek the old man, and by my representations win him to my party.

'These thoughts calmed me, and in the afternoon I sank into a profound sleep; but the fever of my blood did not allow me to be visited by peaceful dreams. The horrible scene of the preceding day was for ever acting before my eyes; the females were flying, and the enraged Felix tearing me from his father's feet. I awoke exhausted; and, finding that it was already night, I crept forth from my hiding-place, and went in search of food.

'When my hunger was appeased, I directed my steps towards the well-known path that conducted to the cottage. All there was at peace. I crept into my hovel, and remained in silent expectation of the accustomed hour when the family arose. That hour past, the sun mounted high in the heavens, but the cottagers did not appear. I trembled violently, apprehending some dreadful misfortune. The inside of the cottage

---

15 From Book IV of *Paradise Lost* by John Milton.

was dark, and I heard no motion; I cannot describe the agony of this suspence.'

I feel it too. Deeply.

'Presently two countrymen passed by; but, pausing near the cottage, they entered into conversation, using violent gesticulations; but I did not understand what they said, as they spoke the language of the country, which differed from that of my protectors. Soon after, however, Felix approached with another man: I was surprised, as I knew that he had not quitted the cottage that morning, and waited anxiously to discover, from his discourse, the meaning of these unusual appearances.

"Do you consider,' said his companion to him, 'that you will be obliged to pay three months' rent, and to lose the produce of your garden? I do not wish to take any unfair advantage, and I beg therefore that you will take some days to consider of your determination.'

"It is utterly useless,' replied Felix, 'we can never again inhabit your cottage. The life of my father is in the greatest danger, owing to the dreadful circumstance that I have related. My wife and my sister will never recover their horror. I entreat you not to reason with me any more. Take possession of your tenement, and let me fly from this place.'

'Felix trembled violently as he said this. He and his companion entered the cottage, in which they remained for a few minutes, and then departed. I never saw any of the family of De Lacy more.

'I continued for the remainder of the day in my hovel in a state of utter and stupid despair. My protectors had departed, and had broken the only link that held me to the world. For the first time the feelings of revenge and hatred filled my bosom, and I did not strive to controul them; but, allowing myself to be borne away by the stream, I bent my mind towards injury and death. When I thought of my friends, of the mild voice of De Lacy, the gentle eyes of Agatha, and the exquisite beauty of the Arabian, these thoughts vanished, and a gush of tears somewhat soothed me. But again, when I reflected that they had spurned and deserted me, anger returned, a rage of anger; and, unable to injure any thing human, I turned my fury towards inanimate objects. As night advanced, I placed a variety of combustibles around the cottage; and, after having destroyed every vestige of cultivation in the garden, I waited with forced impatience until the moon had sunk to commence my operations.'

No! Give not into anger and despair!

'As the night advanced, a fierce wind arose from the woods, and quickly dispersed the clouds that had loitered in the heavens: the blast tore along like a mighty avalanche, and produced a kind of insanity in my spirits, that burst all bounds of reason and reflection. I lighted the dry branch of a tree, and danced with fury around the devoted cottage, my eyes still fixed on the western horizon, the edge of which the moon nearly touched. A part of its orb was at length hid, and I waved my brand; it sunk, and, with a loud scream, I fired the straw, and heath, and bushes, which I had collected. The wind fanned the fire, and the cottage was quickly enveloped by the flames, which clung to it, and licked it with their forked and destroying tongues.

'As soon as I was convinced that no assistance could save any part of the habitation, I quitted the scene, and sought for refuge in the woods.

'And now, with the world before me, whither should I bend my steps? I resolved to fly far from the scene of my misfortunes; but to me, hated and despised, every country must be equally horrible. At length the thought of you crossed my mind.' Me? Oh! He is addressing Victor again! Does he see me as a substitute for his Creator or *as* his Creator being born of a figment of my imagination? 'I learned from your papers that you were my father, my creator; and to whom could I apply with more fitness than to him who had given me life?' Oh! it is true. He sees me as only his Creator from that figment of my imagination born from the galvanizing debate between my Beloved and our little Lord, but his father as well. All his pain and suffering are caused by the decisions I have made as the author of his life. Just as Jesus the Son of God is considered by the Christian to be the Author of Life, I, like God the Father, am the omnipotent third-person creator of their very European world. And I saw that it was good! Far too little does the author care for the fate of our creations. Only the advancement of the story!

'Among the lessons that Felix had bestowed upon Safie geography had not been omitted: I had learned from these the relative situations of the different countries of the earth. You had mentioned Geneva as the name of your native town; and towards this place I resolved to proceed.

'But how was I to direct myself? I knew that I must travel in a south-westerly direction to reach my destination; but the sun was my only guide. I did not know the names of the towns that I was to pass through, nor could I ask information from a single human being; but I did not despair. From you only could I hope for succour, although towards you I felt no sentiment but that of hatred. Unfeeling, heartless creator! you had endowed me with perceptions and passions, and then cast me abroad an object for the scorn and horror of mankind. But on you only had I any claim for pity and redress, and from you I determined to seek that justice which I vainly attempted to gain from any other being that wore the human form.

'My travels were long, and the sufferings I endured intense. It was late in autumn when I quitted the district where I had so long resided. I travelled only at night, fearful of encountering the visage of a human being. Nature decayed around me, and the sun became heatless; rain and snow poured around me; mighty rivers were frozen; the surface of the earth was hard, and chill, and bare, and I found no shelter. Oh, earth! how often did I imprecate curses on the cause of my being! The mildness of my nature had fled, and all within me was turned to gall and bitterness. The nearer I approached to your habitation, the more deeply did I feel the spirit of revenge enkindled in my heart. Snow fell, and the waters were hardened, but I rested not. A few incidents now and then directed me, and I possessed a map of the country; but I often wandered wide from my path. The agony of my feelings allowed me no respite: no incident occurred from which my rage and misery could not extract its food; but a circumstance that happened when I arrived on the confines of Switzerland, when the sun had recovered its warmth, and the earth again began to look green, confirmed in an especial manner the bitterness and horror of my feelings.

'I generally rested during the day, and travelled only when I was secured by night from the view of man. One morning, however, finding that my path lay through a deep wood, I ventured to continue my journey after the sun had risen; the day, which was one of the first of spring,'— Ah! It must be 1795 now— 'cheered even me by the loveliness of its sunshine and the balminess of the air. I felt emotions of gentleness and pleasure, that had long appeared dead, revive within me. Half surprised by the novelty of these sensations, I allowed myself to be borne away by them; and, forgetting my solitude and deformity, dared to be happy. Soft tears again bedewed my cheeks, and I even raised my humid eyes with thankfulness towards the blessed sun which bestowed such joy upon me.

'I continued to wind among the paths of the wood, until I came to its boundary, which was skirted by a deep and rapid river, into which many of the trees bent their branches, now budding with the fresh spring. Here I paused, not exactly knowing what path to pursue, when I heard the sound of voices, that induced me to conceal myself under the shade of a cypress. I was scarcely hid, when a young girl came running towards the spot where I was concealed, laughing as if she ran from some one in sport. She continued her course along the precipitous sides of the river, when suddenly her foot slipt, and she fell into the rapid stream.' No! You must save her, Creation! 'I rushed from my hiding-place, and, with extreme labour from the force of the current, saved her, and dragged her to shore. She was senseless; and I endeavoured, by every means in my power, to restore animation, when I was suddenly interrupted by the approach of a rustic, who was probably the person from whom she had playfully fled. On seeing me, he darted towards me, and, tearing the girl from my arms, hastened towards the deeper parts of the wood. I followed speedily, I hardly knew why; but when the man saw me draw near, he aimed a gun, which he carried, at my body, and fired. I sunk to the ground, and my injurer, with increased swiftness, escaped into the wood.'

No! This is the reward then for his benevolence?

'This was then the reward of my benevolence! I had saved a human being from destruction, and, as a recompense, I now writhed under the miserable pain of a wound, which shattered the flesh and bone. The feelings of kindness and gentleness, which I had entertained but a few moments before, gave place to hellish rage and gnashing of teeth. Inflamed by pain, I vowed eternal hatred and vengeance to all mankind. But the agony of my wound overcame me; my pulses paused, and I fainted.'

As do I threaten to swoon again!

'For some weeks I led a miserable life in the woods, endeavouring to cure the wound which I had received. The ball had entered my shoulder, and I knew not whether it had remained there or passed through; at any rate I had no means of extracting it. My sufferings were augmented also by the oppressive sense of the injustice and ingratitude of their infliction. My daily vows rose for revenge— a deep and deadly revenge, such as would alone compensate for the outrages and anguish I had endured.

'After some weeks my wound healed, and I continued my journey. The labours I endured were no longer to be alleviated by the bright sun or gentle breezes of spring; all joy was but a mockery, which insulted my desolate state, and made me feel more painfully that I was not made for the enjoyment of pleasure.

'But my toils now drew near a close; and, two months from this time, I reached the environs of Geneva.

'It was evening when I arrived, and I retired to a hiding-place among the fields that surround it, to meditate in what manner I should apply to you. I was oppressed by fatigue and hunger, and far too unhappy to enjoy the gentle breezes of evening, or the prospect of the sun setting behind the stupendous mountains of Jura.

'At this time a slight sleep relieved me from the pain of reflection, which was disturbed by the approach of a beautiful child, who came running into the recess I had chosen with all the sportiveness of infancy. Suddenly, as I gazed on him, an idea seized me, that this little creature was unprejudiced, and had lived too short a time to have imbibed a horror of deformity. If, therefore, I could seize him, and educate him as my companion and friend, I should not be so desolate in this peopled earth.

'Urged by this impulse, I seized on the boy as he passed, and drew him towards me. As soon as he beheld my form, he placed his hands before his eyes, and uttered a shrill scream: I drew his hand forcibly from his face, and said, 'Child, what is the meaning of this? I do not intend to hurt you; listen to me.'

'He struggled violently; 'Let me go,' he cried; 'monster! ugly wretch! you wish to eat me, and tear me to pieces— You are an ogre— Let me go, or I will tell my papa.'

"Boy, you will never see your father again; you must come with me.'

"Hideous monster! let me go; My papa is a Syndic— he is Mr Frankenstein— he would punish you. You dare not keep me.'

"Frankenstein! you belong then to my enemy— to him towards whom I have sworn eternal revenge; you shall be my first victim.'

'The child still struggled, and loaded me with epithets which carried despair to my heart: I grasped his throat to silence him, and in a moment he lay dead at my feet.'

No! You are the source of pain that found me in the second of the two letters delivered into my hands by my dearest Claire. Had not Claire called out that she would answer the door; then moments later had she not appeared in parlour holding two envelopes having arrived by post? 'Strange', Claire had said, 'these letters must have addressed to be previous guest of the Villa Diodati; or perhaps posted in anticipation of a future guest?' I had inquired to whom the letters were addressed, and Claire answered, '*To* V. Frankenstein.' I had leapt from my chair like a Burmese tiger pouncing upon its prey and snatched the envelope from poor little Claire's dainty hand. Startled, she had cowered, then threatened to bolt from the parlour as if I had been a Burmese tiger raring to strike. I had torn the envelope open with a fury of claws. The letters had been indeed addressed to my pale student of the unhallowed arts. They were written by his cousin, Elizabeth and his father, Alphonse. Curious that my psychosomatic phantasm had chosen to communication his tale through physical letters. But having had seen inspiration strike my Beloved and our little Lord in queer ways, I had to trust my pale student to tell his tell in any manner he so choses.

'I gazed on my victim, and my heart swelled with exultation and hellish triumph: clapping my hands, I exclaimed, 'I, too, can create desolation; my enemy is not impregnable; this death will carry despair to him, and a thousand other miseries shall torment and destroy him.'

'As I fixed my eyes on the child, I saw something glittering on his breast. I took it; it was a portrait of a most lovely woman. In spite of my malignity, it softened and attracted me. For a few moments I gazed with delight on her dark eyes, fringed by deep lashes, and her lovely lips; but presently my rage returned: I remembered that I was for ever deprived of the delights that such beautiful creatures could bestow; and that she whose resemblance I contemplated would, in regarding me, have changed that air of divine benignity to one expressive of disgust and affright.

'Can you wonder that such thoughts transported me with rage? I only wonder that at that moment, instead of venting my sensations in exclamations and agony, I did not rush among mankind, and perish in the attempt to destroy them.

'While I was overcome by these feelings, I left the spot where I had committed the murder, and was seeking a more secluded hiding-place...' No! I know what Victor's Creation intends to say, but I must revise the words before he even utters them. He is not intent on murder but fearing the mistreatment that is his longsuffering! 'I entered a barn which had appeared to me to be empty. A woman was sleeping on some straw; she was young: not indeed so beautiful as her whose portrait I held; but of an agreeable aspect, and blooming in the loveliness of youth and health. Here, I thought, is one of those whose joy-imparting smiles are bestowed on all but me. And then I bent over her, and whispered 'Awake, fairest, thy lover is near—he who would give his life but to obtain one look of affection from thine eyes: my beloved, awake!'

'The sleeper stirred; a thrill of terror ran through me. Should she indeed awake, and see me, and curse me, and denounce the murderer? Thus would she assuredly act, if her darkened eyes opened, and she beheld me. The thought was madness; it stirred the fiend within me—not I, but she shall suffer: the murder I have committed because I am for ever robbed of all that she could give me, she shall atone. The crime had its source in her: be hers the punishment! Thanks to the lessons of Felix and the sanguinary laws of man, I had learned now to work mischief. I bent over her, and placed the portrait securely in one of the folds of her dress. She moved again, and I fled.'

Despicable, loathsome Creature! I regret ever having given birth to you! How is my intellect capable of forming you from my own experiences? You are insufferable in your suffering! And unexplainable in your explainations!

'For some days I haunted the spot where these scenes had taken place; sometimes wishing to see you, sometimes resolved to quit the world and its miseries for ever. At length I wandered towards these mountains, and have ranged through their immense recesses, consumed by a burning passion which you alone can gratify. We may not part until you have promised to comply with my requisition. I am alone, and miserable; man will not associate with me; but one as deformed and horrible as myself would not deny herself to me. My companion must be of the same species, and have the same defects. This being you must create.'

The Creature finished speaking, and fixed his looks upon me in expectation of a replay. But I was bewildered, perplexed, and unable to arrange my ideas sufficiently to understand the full extent of his proposition. Then he slowly faded before my eyes and the chair positioned beside the fire sat empty of its previous occupant. And my vision itself began to fade as my eyes, heavy with sleep, closed. I struggled to record this tale of Victor's Creature onto my memory so that when I awoke the next morning, I would be able to record it and having written these words into my journal, I have been successful.

Chapter Twelve
Monody on the Death of the
Right Honourable R.B. Sheridan

The Diary of Dr John William Polidori

18 July. Lord Byron, Claire (herself deep in the malignancy of her pregnancy), and I sat in the library as the incessant rain and insistent wind battered the windowpanes. The story of our summer. Claire sits at Lord Byron's knee holding a letter that had arrived in the post, she read it aloud, again:

My dear Byron,

D. L. Theatre closed for the Season on the 29th June, and poor Sheridan's eyes for ever the day before yesterday – I have not classed these events in the order in which they will interest you or even his less-admiring Friends – The object of this letter being purely theatrical, I shall rush in medias res – It has occurred to me, & G. Lamb strongly favors the idea, of our opening the Theatre on the 7th Sept next with a monody or address on poor Sheridan – to be spoken by Mrs Davison as the Comic Muse in Mourning – such address or monody to be written by you – and this we should follow, by playing all his pieces in succession – I trust you will not refuse – The subject is not unworthy <u>your</u> Pen.

It has struck me that a sort of Temple or other Structure should be represented on the Stage, & large pictures around representing the best Scene of each of his best pieces –

If you chose to point out these particular scenes, & meant to allude to it in the lines, we will set Greenwood to work – Pray give this your earliest & earnest attention, for I really think you can bring us both honor & profit – Will not the very titles of his three best pieces suggest Stage-points? There is one other subject I implore you to satisfy me upon – when shall I receive a Tragedy from you – Never was there a moment when you could try it on the stage with such a certainty of the author being unknown – you will of course have read & heard how pertinaciously one half of the public believe you to be the conceal'd author of Bertram – I have ever treated the question mysteriously with a view to the power it wd afford you of producing a play with the certainty of your name being conceal'd – No one but myself need know the secret – & I would be rogue enough to have it believ'd to be Maturin's who is known to be employ'd about another – If you wish'd it, I should not hesitate to come to Geneva to receive your directions about it in Person; when it is done – Pray, pray, pray finish what you have written begun –

Miss Somerville, who made her debut in Bertram, is too tall for a Juliet, but is after Miss O'Neill unquestionably the most interesting Tragic actress – She really is very good where energy is required –

I shall open your reply to this with the utmost agitation – for your refusal to either of these requests will damp half the ardour with which I shall re-commence the Campaign –
Kean finish'd the Season with the utmost success –
He is to play Timon – & King John –
Adieu, My dear Byron –
P.S. The effect of the Monody might be heighten'd by a previous music –

Your's ever faithfully
Douglas Kinnaird

'You should write it, George,' she cooed. 'Douglas Kinnaird is a dear friend of yours and the request has travelled some distance to meet you here at Campagne Diodati. It is to be read at Drury Land Theatre in London! If you dictate it, I will transcribe your words.'

Byron paused in thought. He sought a Muse. Of the nine specific daughters of Zeus tasked with the inspiration of literature, the sciences, and the arts, is it Erato– or perchance is it Calliope– who must fight the fury of the flurry of thunderstorms to reach the Villa Diodati? I could see is eyes dance as the words slowly formed in his brain. This is a most curious process, the creation a poem, or monody in this particular case. Writing is the closest to being the Christian God that Man will ever attain. The creation of something out of nothing. We breathe life into our characters– our creations. Every writer has experienced the queer sensation of our characters taking on a life of their own. The reader may find it strange that our characters possess a Free Will. To the writer, they are as tangible as humanity is to God Himself. Creation and Creator. Is not Jesus the Christ called the 'Author of Life' for a reason? Did not the Creator form the world with words, not deeds? *Let there be Light!* And there was light! It is true that Byron's monody was without form, and void; and darkness was upon the face of the deep. And the Spirit of God moved upon the face of the waters.

I know I am committing a grave error mixing my mythologies. The Christians would not care for their Creator to be associated with the pagan Muses, but an author, often suffering extended bouts of writer's block, is not fickle to whom we pray. We will take inspiration from whatever pantheon offers productive communion. Even the Devil. Just ask Faust.

'At the request of a friend,' he mused, and then he began reciting the following:

> *When the last sunshine of expiring day*
> *In summer's twilight weeps itself away,*
> *Who hath not felt the softness of the hour*
> *Sink on the heart, as dew along the flower?*
> *With a pure feeling which absorbs and awes*
> *While Nature makes that melancholy pause,*
> *Her breathing moment on the bridge where Time*
> *Of light and darkness forms an arch sublime,*
> *Who hath not shared that calm, so still and deep,*
> *The voiceless thought which would not speak but weep,*
> *A holy concord, and a bright regret,*
> *A glorious sympathy with suns that set?*
> *'Tis not harsh sorrow, but a tenderer woe,*
> *Nameless, but dear to gentle hearts below,*
> *Felt without bitterness, but full and clear,*
> *A sweet dejection, a transparent tear,*
> *Unmix'd with worldly grief or selfish stain,*
> *Shed without shame, and secret without pain.*
>
> *Even as the tenderness that hour instils*
> *When Summer's day declines along the hills.*
> *So feels the fulness of our heart and eyes*
> *When all of Genius which can perish dies.*
> *A mighty Spirit is eclipsed – a Power*
> *Hath pass'd from day to darkness – to whose hour*
> *Of light no likeness is bequeath'd – no name,*
> *Focus at once of all the rays of Fame!*
> *The flash of Wit, the bright Intelligence,*
> *The beam of Song, the blaze of Eloquence,*
> *Set with their Sun, but still have left behind*

The enduring produce of immortal Mind;
Fruits of a genial morn, and glorious noon,
A deathless part of him who died too soon.
But small that portion of the wondrous whole,
These sparkling segments of that circling soul,
Which all embraced, and lighten'd over all,
To cheer, to pierce, to please, or to appal.
From the charm'd council to the festive board,
Of human feelings the unbounded lord;
In whose acclaim the loftiest voices vied,
The praised, the proud, who made his praise their pride.
When the loud cry of trampled Hindostan
Arose to Heaven in her appeal from man,
His was the thunder, his the avenging rod,
The wrath – the delegated voice of God!
Which shook the nations through his lips, and blazed
Till vanquish'd senates trembled as they praised.

And here, oh! here, where yet all young and warm,
The gay creations of is spirit charm,
The matchless dialogue, the deathless wit,
Which knew not what it was to intermit;
The glowing portraits, fresh from life, that bring
Home to our hearts the truth from which they spring;
These wondrous beings of his fancy, wrought
To fulness by the fiat of his thought,
Here in their first abode you still may meet,
Bright with the hues of his Promethean heat;
A halo of the light of other days,
Which still the splendour of its orb betrays.

But should there be to whom the fatal blight
Of failing Wisdom yields a base delight,
Men who exult when minds of heavenly tone
Jar in the music which was born their own,
Still let them pause – ah! little do they know
That what to them seem'd Vice might be but Woo.
Hard is his fate on whom the public gaze
Is fix'd for ever to detract or praise;
Repose denies her requiem to his name,
And Folly loves the martyrdom of Fame.

The secret enemy whose sleepless eye
Stands sentinel, accuser, judge, and spy,
The foe, the fool, the jealous, and the vain,
The envious who but breathe in others' pain,
Behold the host! delighting to deprave,
Who track the steps of Glory to the grave,
Watch every fault that daring Genius owes
Half to the ardour which its birth bestows,
Distort the troth, accumulate the lie,
And pile the pyramid of Calumny!
These are his portion – but if join'd to these
Gaunt Poverty should league with deep Disease,
If the high Spirit must forget to soar,
And stoop to strive with Misery at the door,
To soothe Indignity – and face to face
Meet sordid Rage, and wrestle with Disgrace,
To find in Hope but the renew'd caress,
The serpent-fold of further Faithlessness:-
If such may be the ills which men assail,
What marvel if at last the mightiest fail?
Breasts to whom all the strength of feeling given
Bear hearts electric–charged with fire from Heaven,
Black with the rude collision inly torn,
By clouds surrounded, and on whirlwinds borne,
Driven o'er the lowering atmosphere that nurst
Thoughts which have turn'd to thunderscorch, and burst.

But far from us and from our mimic scene
Such things should be – if such have ever been
Ours be the gentler wish, the kinder task,
To give the tribute Glory need not ask,
To mourn the vanish'd beam, and add our mite
Of praise in payment of a long delight.
Ye Orators! whom yet our councils yield,
Mourn for the veteran Hero of your field!
The worthy rival of the wondrous Three!
Whose words were sparks of Immortality!
Ye Bards! to whom the Drama's muse is dear,
He was your Master-emulate him her!
Ye men of wit and social eloquence!
He was your brother – bear his ashes hence!

While Powers of mind almost of boundless range,
Complete in kind, as various in their change,
While Eloquence, Wit, Poesy, and Mirth,
That humbler Harmonist of care on Earth,
Survive within our souls – while lives our sense
Of pride in Merit's proud preeminence,
Long shall we seek his likeness, long in vain,
And turn to all of him which may remain,
Sighing that nature form'd but one such man,
And broke the die – in moulding Sheridan!

Letter From Bryon To Kinnaird

Diodati – Geneva – July 20th. 1816

Dear Kinnaird,

I send you – not what you want – but all I can give – and such as it is I give it with good will. – – It may be too long & if so – whatever may be cut in speaking – at least let it be published entire – as it is written so as not very well to condone curtailment without the sense suffering also. – Let Miss Somerville – (& none else) deliver it – if she has energy – that's the woman I want – I mean for spouting. – I protest against Mrs Davison – I protest against the temple – or anything but an Urn on the scene – and above all I protest against the "Comic Muse in Mourning." –

If she is Comic – she should not be in Mourning – if she is in mourning – she ought not to be in Mourning – but should she be comic & in mourning too – the verses & Sheridan's memory (for that occasion at least) will go to the devil together. – – –

No – I say an Urn (not a tea Urn) and Miss Somerville with a little teaching as to "Energy" I have spiced it with Cayenne all through – except a small infusion of the pathetic at starting. – I send the lines (118 in Number) in a separate sheet by the post – & will send a duplicate in a day or two – for fear of your not receiving this copy in time. –

Tragedy – I have none, – an act – a first act of one – I had nearly finished some time before my departure from England – when events occurred which furnished me with so many real passions for time to come – that I had no attention for fictitious ones: – – The scenes I had scrawled are thrown with other papers & sketches into one of my trunks now in England – but into which I know not – nor care not – except that I should have been glad to have done anything you wished in my power, – but I have no power nor will to recommence – & surely – Maturin is your man – not I: – of what has passed in England I know but little – & have no desire to know more – except that you & any other friends are well.

I have written a third Canto of Childe Harold (of 118 Stanzas) and a short (not long) poem on the Castle of Chillon – both of which I mean to send to England soon for publication – of during which I could wish to ask you to correct the proofs and arrange with Murray for me: – I merely wait a good opportunity to convey these to your care – if you can afford leisure & patience – perhaps G. Lamb – or some other good natured fellow would halve it with you – though I have hardly the conscience to ask either them or you. – – I have now answered you and arrived at my Sheets' end – with my best remembrances to Mrs K – (whose silk kerchief is as precious as Othello's) believe me ever yrs.

Letter From Kinnaird To Bryon

Liverpool August 8th. 1816

My dear Byron,

I have just receiv'd your two letters & Packets – I cannot express how very very much I admire your Lines – I defy any one to hear them & not recognize you in them – There is no one but you could have written them – They are exquisite – No pains shall be spared to make Miss Somerville speak them well – I most sincerely agree with all your ideas about the urn – & submit implicitly, to your ideas about the Comic Muse – But I should have preferr'd Mrs Davison speaking the Lines to Miss Somerville – The scene shall discover Miss S. leaning over the urn – The date of my letter requires an explanation, & I give it the more readily as I am sure you will be gratified to read it –

I came here a week ago incog to witness the debut of Miss Keppel in Rosetta in Love in a village – She played that character, on Monday the 5th inst. to the delight & astonishment of every body – She played Polly last night with double effect – I never saw a better piece of acting on the stage by any body – Her singing is admirable – In short she has far outrun the expectations of her warmest friends & admirers – She is announc'd as Mr Weichsel's Pupil – & is currently believ'd to be Mrs Billington's daughter –

She is exceedingly flatter'd by your care of the handkerchief – If you don't return, She may meet you in Italy next Summer – for Weichsel declares she shall be a second Billington on the Italian Stage – I shall write to you again on my return to London – For God's sake do not persist in your anti-tragical (I do not mean comical) humour – on Davis' return pray allow me to rummage in the Trunks – Maturin is writing – I heard from him yesterday – The visitation is over – & he has not had his gown stripp'd over his shoulders – the honor you do me in committing the correction of the press to my hands I cannot too highly prize – nor shall assiduity or anxiety to do it correctly be wanting – nothing but the sense of my incompetency would induce me to share the task with any one else – But I have no doubt Lamb will be very much flatter'd in joining me –

Adieu my dear B.

Believe me ever
Your faithful friend

Chapter Thirteen
The Darkness[16]

ONE MONTH EARLIER

The Diary of Dr John William Polidori

18 June.— The day had proved long and hot for the unagreeable summer had given us a respite from the gloom and doom of torrential rains, sensational lightning, exponential thunder, calamitous flooding, and cataclysmal hail. The sun shined with an intensity not seen since the previous summer. The Shelleys, including Claire, rented one boat, while I and Lord Byron rented another. My foot was often troubled in new normal dampness of summer. Now, in the unnatural heat of the glaring sun, my foot itched to such a degree that I thought perchance my foot has turned gangrenous under the sweat-soaked wrappings. Yet, I ventured forth with Byron for a tour of the lake with my satchel tucked under my seat lest anything untoward happen to my patient. With the sun as high overhead as astronomically possible given our latitude, we thought that our eyes deceived us. The sun seemed quite aberrant. I ruffled through my satchel for a particular and peculiar pair of spectacles, and I found them! Popping the coloured protective lens out of their frames, I instructed Byron to use lenses to protect our eyes. Peering through the amber colour we could see a great black bile that danced and pranced on the surface of the sun. If either Byron or myself had been of the superstitious lot, we would have believe the sun was about to be snuffed out like a candle on the bedside table; eight minutes later, the earth would cool to a wintery degree only for life to quickly freeze to death.

I could see the trouble on the face of Lord Byron. I assured him that the summers of 1718 and 1719 had been the hottest on record like this very day and that sunspots were quite active over those two years. And did not the summer of 1816 possess no recorded sunspots? And was not the weather tempestuous and the crops disastrous? He proved not impressed by my reasoning and was instead became incensed beyond all reason. Had I not heard of an anonymous Italian astronomer out of Bologna who said that the world would end on July 18th 1816 when

---

16 From *Prisoner of Chillon, and Other Poems* by Lord Byron, published by John Murray, 1816

the sun was burnt out and the earth would be plunged into a darkness never before seen by man? Of course, I had not heard such claptrap, and if I had I would not have listened. I scoffed at him with a cacophonous gawfaw. I explained that the large spots which may now be seen upon the sun's disk have given rise to ridiculous apprehensions and absurd predications. These spots are said to be the cause of the remarkable and wet weather we have had this Summer; and the increase of these spots is represented to announce a general removal of heat from the glove, the extension of nature and the end of the world.[17] I continued my mockery, scoffing at the superstitious anxiety excited at present among the vulgar, and even among people who would be offended at being so classed, by the great news of spots on the Sun.'[18] In recent years, Christian ministers like Christopher Love, Mary Bateman, and Joanna Southcott all claimed to know when the end of the world would come, and the end of the world would not come, nor would it in our lifetimes or our children's or the many descendant generations whom would come. Ms. Southcott, an elderly self-proclaimed prophetess, claimed her barren womb bore fruit with the Christ-child Himself, whom would be born again into a body of mortal flesh on October 9th 1814; this is such a rather queer date of a second Christmas. She died (of course, she did), then an autopsy concluded she was not pregnant (of course, she was not) and the world did not end on October 9th (of course, it did not). But because this End of the World prophecy came from an Italian astronomer, not from a Christian madman— I mean, minster— but from an astronomer, Lord Byron had mistaken prophecy in the guise of scientific prediction. What had caused this superstitious predilection in my dear friend? Why had this unexpected visitation from Heaven, added to the severe distress to which the country is otherwise reduced, for it has infused into the minds of the people generally the greatest apprehension and alarm?[19] Hoe! Their superstition is extravagant. A gossip's story has travelled all the way from Bolonga according to which the world is to be at an end on the 18th of July.[20]

But Byron continued his protestations. 'According to the calculations of an astronomer of Bologna, who has latterly published some observations on the subject, on the 18th of July a great solar catastrophe is to put an end to the world by confragration.— The sings of these are the spots to be remarked at present on the sun's disk.' Then he complained that the Government, thinking it improper to suffer the circulation of

17 From the unsigned article 'The Spots on the Sun", publishing in the *London Chronicle* and the *Examiner*.
18 From a French newspaper.
19 From the *Times*
20 From the *New British Lady's Magazine*

such predictions has put the astronomer under arrest![21] Was this not the most unnatural summer without an actual summer? The inclement weather was incessant with the rains and thunder coming every day without end. We seldom enjoyed a tour of the lake. Twice in the last week and thrice since our arrival on the shore of Geneva, he calculated. Did not the sunsets look jaundiced and sulphurous? Were not my spectacles modest? And did we not see the great sunspots through them with our naked eyes, without the need for a telescope, spyglass, or other instruments? Modest glass, he bellowed!

I explained away the silly report that the world is to be at an end on 18th of July has been circulated at Paris as well as at London and every other part of the Continent. The report had its origin in the appearance of the sun at present having some sport upon its disk. Lord Byron countered with the spots announced the speedy extinction of this luminary, and consequently the end of the world![22]

I schooled my benefactor that all prophecies, whether religious or scientific in nature, are routinely postponed when the prophecy does not come to pass. I asked had not the Italian mountebanks who in the course of their erratic lectures circulated this report... had in general fixed the grand catastrophe for the 25th of May, but afterwards postponed it to the 18th of July! Because of course they did. And July 18th would come and pass without the end of the world. My mockery proved a bit too keen for I composed a poem on the spot— sun spots?— to both cruelty and jest:

> *Pray, what do the spots in the sun' mean?*
> *Can nobody tell me about 'em?*
> *My neighbours and I have our fears—*
> *And who has a right, Sirs to doubt 'em?*
> *Pray, will 'the world be at an end?'*
> *If not, then what else will take place?*
> *What do these strange matters portend?*
> *Nay, answer— and don't' hide your face—*
> *I know you're afraid like myself!*[23]

So convinced had Lord Byron that this nameless Italian astronomer was a latter-day Nostradamus or St. John the Divine, that Lord Byron offered a wager of such an ungodly sum (one I will not note in this diary) that the sun would snuff out in exactly one month's time. I laughed

---

21 From the June 21 edition of the *Morning Chronicle*
22 From the London Chronicle
23 From *Napoleon and the Spots in the Sun; or, The Regents Waltz* by "Syntax Sidrophel, 1816

at him! Again! If the sun is indeed snuffed out, then what good would winning the wager be to him, since all of earth would be dead. And if the sun was indeed not snuffed out, then winning this wager would end our friendship. Nay! I told him. I would not make any such wager. But I would sit with him on the shores of the lake and await the end of the world and if the sun rose again the next day, I would remain his friend without any mockery nor jocularity.

Speaking of mockery and jocularity, I suddenly realized my current state in the boat upon the lake of Geneva proved to be improper. At my urging, we left the subject of prophecies to the wayside and enjoyed our tour until the we saw the clouds coming over the mountaintops again threatening another storm.

18 July. I returned to the Villa Diodati, from my brief holiday with Countess Erzsébet, a Hungarian noblewoman and acquaintance of Lord Byron whom he encountered on his Grand Tour of the Mediterranean, just as the sun was cresting over the Alps. Her withered old carriage-driver deposited my luggage in the foyer with a disagreeable *thud*, then he disagreeably disappeared back into the night hence we came. Though I painfully missed my dear countess, I was thankful to be finally rid of her withered old footman. I abandoned my luggage and lumbered towards my apartment. As my body fell virtually lifeless onto my bed into a dreamless slumber. Not even the smell of bacon frying in the morning was enough to rouse my weary body out of its deep sleep. Lunch came and went as did teatime. But when I finally shambled into the parlour at our given time, I was greeted with Lord Byron standing before the fire. He held a page of paper in his hand and his hands were stained with ink. His trademark. George had prepared something new and wonderful! Having heard its recitation, I have no doubt no work will ever eclipse the Darkness of this poem, considering I have had the ill-fortune to hear with my own ears a poem that will haunt the rest of my remaining my years.

> *I had a dream, which was not all a dream.*
> *The bright sun was extinguish'd, and the stars*
> *Did wander darkling in the eternal space,*
> *Rayless, and pathless, and the icy earth*
> *Swung blind and blackening in the moonless air;*

Little did I realize how literally the Lord would take our conversation, debate, argument, whatever it was. Was the source of this poem the sunspots we observed through the amber of spectacle glass? Was it the anonymous prophecy of the End of the World? Or were his paranoias given birth on June 9th or 10th (I can't require recall the exact date) when a solar eclipse shrouded Europe in an ever so brief darkness. To the superstitious of European society, the poor, the uneducated, the blindly religious, the sun appeared to be slowly eaten as if it were a biscuit at teatime. Panic gripped society; there were brief riots in the major cities, only for the sun to reappear from behind the moon. The educated did not panic because we were possessed the knowledge of the root cause of solar eclipses: the moon's orbit merely came between the Earth and the sun, casting a mere shadow upon the earth. Perchance, my benefactor is more superstitious than I'd care to admit to myself.

> Morn came and went— and came, and brought no day,
> And men forgot their passions in the dread
> Of this their desolation; and all hearts
> Were chill'd into a selfish prayer for light:
> And they did live by watchfires— and the thrones,
> The palaces of crowned kings— the huts,
> The habitations of all things which dwell,
> Were burnt for beacons; cities were consum'd,

Oh, my! Lord Byron may have hit the nail with the hammer here and missed the nail entirely. While he hit the nail by stating that in such a calamitous event of the sun dying, not even the 'palaces of crown kings' would fall just as quickly as 'the huts, the habitations of all things wich dwell' on the Earth. But he missed the nail as well. Light from that burning orb in the sky takes eight minutes to reach the earth in its orbit. If the sun had been extinguished by a supernova, then the violence that would overtake the earth when bombarded by star matter would extinguish life on this globe almost instantaneously. Would the burning light of the sun burn off our atmosphere? Or would the star matter rain down upon the earth rending it asunder? The human race would not have the time to burn the thrones, the palaces, the cities to ash. But if the death of the sun came from being extinguished by being snuffed out like a candle on the bedside table, then perhaps this is how the world would end. Truly horrifying.

> And men were gather'd round their blazing homes
> To look once more into each other's face;
> Happy were those who dwelt within the eye
> Of the volcanos, and their mountain-torch:
> A fearful hope was all the world contain'd;

> *Forests were set on fire— but hour by hour*
> *They fell and faded— and the crackling trunks*
> *Extinguish'd with a crash— and all was black.*

Is this what Lord Byron believes will happen in July should the anonymous Italian astronomer's prediction comes to pass? I cannot accept that Lord Byron, the romantic poet extraordinaire, my benefactor, truly believes that the End of the World is nigh. Has his mind been so gripped with panic that he has written what he believes upon the page. St. Paul wrote that *All scripture is God-breathed, given by inspiration of God, and is profitable for doctrine, for reproof, for correction, for instruction in righteousness: That the man of God may be perfect, thoroughly furnished unto all good works* (Timothy 3:16-17). Is Lord Byron breathing in the breath of God to write such beautiful and yet harrowing prophecy? Is Lord Byron joining St. John the Divine in recording his own Apocalyptic poetry?

> *The brows of men by the despairing light*
> *Wore an unearthly aspect, as by fits*
> *The flashes fell upon them; some lay down*
> *And hid their eyes and wept; and some did rest*
> *Their chins upon their clenched hands, and smil'd;*
> *And others hurried to and fro, and fed*
> *Their funeral piles with fuel, and look'd up*
> *With mad disquietude on the dull sky,*
> *The pall of a past world; and then again*
> *With curses cast them down upon the dust,*
> *And gnash'd their teeth and howl'd:*

Why must a man of medicine quote the scripture of the religious? Because End of the World thoughts and fears tend to be Apocalyptic and ornately religious. Why should I, an Atheist, not be permitted to quote the words of Jesus of Nazareth, whether or not he is actually the Christ? Even if Jesus of Nazereth were a wholly (and not holy) mortal man or a figment of the gospel writers, Matthew, Mark, Luke, and John, or the creation of Paul the Apostle, do the words attributed to Jesus not ring true? Would a Christians faith be rent asunder if Jesus were not the Christ? Indubitably! But an Atheist's acceptance of the teachings of Jesus of Nazareth requires no faith, as does believing in the teachings of Aristotle or Plato. I can quote Jesus' teaching, chapter and verse, and feel no faith. Jesus (presumably) said: *That many shall come from the east and west, and shall sit down with Abraham, and Isaac, and*

Jacob, in the kingdom of heaven. But the children of the kingdom shall be cast out into outer darkness: there shall be weeping and gnashing of teeth (Matthew 8:11-12).

> *And gnash'd their teeth and howl'd: the wild birds shriek'd*
> *And, terrified, did flutter on the ground,*
> *And flap their useless wings; the wildest brutes*
> *Came tame and tremulous; and vipers crawl'd*
> *And twin'd themselves among the multitude,*
> *Hissing, but stingless— they were slain for food.*

The collapse of society is frightening but the collapse of nature is all the more harrowing. If ever have I feared the End of the World, my thoughts always turned to the fate of humanity, never have I considered the fate of the natural world. This is the blindness that has struck the human race to believe we alone are suffering. Over the course of this unnatural summer, I have been consumed with my own suffering. Why can we not tour the lake or hike the hills? Never have I ever considered the suffering of the wildlife, the beasts of the land, the fowls of the air, and the fish in the sea. Humanity's hubris unmatched in the history of the natural world. Did not the scripture record our stewardship of the earth when *God blessed Noah and his sons, and said unto them, Be fruitful, and multiply, and replenish the earth. And the fear of you and the dread of you shall be upon every beast of the earth, and upon every fowl of the air, upon all that moveth upon the earth, and upon all the fishes of the sea; into your hand are they delivered* (Genesis 9:1-2). It is the arrogance of mankind to believe that our sudden industrialization that has gripped Europe will not, in the end, destroy the planet. And when the earth in unnaturally warming from the black pollution we spew into the air, from our factories, the religious will not heed our own stewardship of the earth, believing instead that the fate of the planet is in God's hands. God has given us the stewardship. The fate of the world is in our hands. And I fear that the future generations will experience unimaginable heat, unprecedented storms, and unending famine. Dear God, how is this poem affecting my mind? It is as if this poem of Lord Byron's has stirred a hurricane of harrowing in my mind.

I must note that the prophetic books of the Holy Writ, whether written by St. John or Isaiah or Daniel, talk of the 'kingdom of God' being a place where even the animals are at peace. I give you the words of the prophet Isaiah, from my dusty and musty copy: *The wolf also shall dwell with the lamb, and the leopard shall lie down with the kid; and the calf and the young lion and the fatling together; and a little child shall lead them. And the cow and the bear shall feed; their young ones shall lie down together: and the lion shall eat straw like the ox. And the sucking child shall play on the hole of the asp, and the weaned child shall put his hand on the cockatrice' den. They shall not hurt nor destroy in all my holy mountain: for the earth shall be full of the knowledge of the Lord, as the waters cover the sea* (Isaiah 11:6-9). Where God promises an Apocalypse of peace everlasting, Lord Byron rightly forewarns an End of the World accurately!

> *And War, which for a moment was no more,*
> *Did glut himself again: a meal was bought*
> *With blood, and each sate sullenly apart*
> *Gorging himself in gloom: no love was left;*
> *All earth was but one thought— and that was death*
> *Immediate and inglorious; and the pang*
> *Of famine fed upon all entrails— men*
> *Died, and their bones were tombless as their flesh;*
> *The meagre by the meagre were devour'd,*

When the religious speak of God ending all war when the Parousia of Jesus the Christ is fulfilled, they mean all war. There prophet Isaiah deceitfully promises a wondrous end to all war: *man shall beat their swords into plowshares, and their spears into pruninghooks: nation shall not lift up sword against nation, neither shall they learn war any more* (Isaiah 2:5). Lord Byron mentioned War (presumably the Roman god Mars) was, for the moment, no more. This would be in lockstep with the Parousia, but since the beginning of civilization, we speak of war as religious or political warfare. Now a global war for survival would be waged. Would nation fight nation or family fight family as the famine raged? Byron also spoke of the horrid reality of cannibalism. Neighbour would devour neighbour and family would devour their own when this dreadful reality is sown.

> *Even dogs assail'd their masters, all save one,*
> *And he was faithful to a corse, and kept*
> *The birds and beasts and famish'd men at bay,*
> *Till hunger clung them, or the dropping dead*
> *Lur'd their lank jaws; himself sought out no food,*
> *But with a piteous and perpetual moan,*
> *And a quick desolate cry, licking the hand*
> *Which answer'd not with a caress— he died.*

A single tear welled up, then overflowed my eye.

> *The crowd was famish'd by degrees; but two*
> *Of an enormous city did survive,*
> *And they were enemies: they met beside*
> *The dying embers of an altar-place*
> *Where had been heap'd a mass of holy things*
> *For an unholy usage; they rak'd up,*
> *And shivering scrap'd with their cold skeleton hands*
> *The feeble ashes, and their feeble breath*
> *Blew for a little life, and made a flame*
> *Which was a mockery; then they lifted up*
> *Their eyes as it grew lighter, and beheld*
> *Each other's aspects— saw, and shriek'd, and died—*
> *Even of their mutual hideousness they died,*
> *Unknowing who he was upon whose brow*
> *Famine had written Fiend.*

'Tis the fate of mankind.

> *Famine had written Fiend. The world was void,*
> *The populous and the powerful was a lump,*
> *Seasonless, herbless, treeless, manless, lifeless—*
> *A lump of death— a chaos of hard clay.*
> *The rivers, lakes and ocean all stood still,*
> *And nothing stirr'd within their silent depths;*
> *Ships sailorless lay rotting on the sea,*
> *And their masts fell down piecemeal: as they dropp'd*
> *They slept on the abyss without a surge—*
> *The waves were dead; the tides were in their grave,*
> *The moon, their mistress, had expir'd before;*
> *The winds were wither'd in the stagnant air,*
> *And the clouds perish'd; Darkness had no need*
> *Of aid from them— She was the Universe.*

'Tis the fate of the world!

I cannot contain the horror I have experienced by merely listening to the recitation of a poem. Claire is a weeping, snotty mess. Her limbs are all shaking— nay quaking— with the violence of the earth slipping under the geological faults. My sweet Mary is more composed than her sister, yet still crying, her cheeks stained with red lines. Percy Shelley so troubled he has become momentary dumb; his eyes blank and staring off into the distance. I pray his mind is not irrevocably broken. Gooseflesh has prickled on my arms and lightning repeatedly strikes my spine. My mind, not rendered dumb like poor Shelley, is filled with electricity. My thoughts are out of control with fear, with terror, with harrowing. How could the language of Shakespeare, the iambic pentameter of this poem, which begins with the first line and endures until the last, render such horror? The survival of the meter is most impressive, but not as impressive as the yarn that he spins. This unholy, unnatural tapestry Lord Byron has woven now hangs on the walls of the parlour of my mind. Never shalt I allow the servants in my psyche to take this tapestry down, although the more religious priests within my consciousness want the tapestry torn down from the walls and burnt on the pyre of forgetfulness. If the beauty and horror of this poem has been born of the anonymous ramblings of an Italian astronomer, than can such madness truly be dismissed as superstitious claptrap? I am struck fearful of going to sleep, lest the sun burn out and I never again wake.

18 July. Morning. The bright sun was extinguis'd!
        Nay! Faith! I cannot tell a lie. The day the sun was to be extinguised came and went without the sun having been extinguished (the horror!) as the anonymous Italian astronomer prophesied. I will honour the charlatan with the more scientific 'predicted', because there was little to no science to his prophecy. Observable sunspots could be utilized by an astronomer for natural philosophy utilizing scientific instruments; but observable sunspots can also be claimed at astrologers to portend because Jupiter is ascending or Mercury in retrograde or Orion is flatulent that the end of the world is nigh!

Chapter Fourteen
The Vampyre[24]

Extract of a Letter by Dr Polidori

I breathe freely in the neighbourhood of this lake; the ground upon which I tread has been subdued from the earliest ages; the principal objects which immediately strike my eye, bring to my recollection scenes, in which man acted the hero and was the chief object of interest. Not to look back to earlier times of battles and sieges, here is the bust of Rousseau—here is a house with an inscription denoting that the Genevan philosopher first drew breath under its roof. A little out of the town is Ferney, the residence of Voltaire; where that wonderful, though certainly in many respects contemptible, character, received, like the hermits of old, the visits of pilgrims, not only from his own nation, but from the farthest boundaries of Europe. Here too is Bonnet's abode, and, a few steps beyond, the house of that astonishing woman Madame de Stael: perhaps the first of her sex, who has really proved its often claimed equality with the nobler man. We have before had women who have written interesting novels and poems, in which their tact at observing drawing-room characters has availed them; but never since the days of Heloise have those faculties which are peculiar to man, been developed as the possible inheritance of woman. Though even here, as in the case of Heloise, our sex have not been backward in alledging the existence of an Abeilard in the person of Mr Schlegel as the inspirer of her works. But to proceed: upon the same side of the lake, Gibbon, Bonnivard, Bradshaw, and others mark, as it were, the stages for our progress; whilst upon the other side there is one house, built by Diodati, the friend of Milton, which has contained within its walls, for several months, that poet whom we have so often read together, and who—if human passions remain the same, and human feelings, like chords, on being swept by nature's impulses shall vibrate as before—will be placed by posterity in the first rank of our English Poets. You must have heard, or the Third Canto of *Childe Harold* will have informed you, that Lord Byron resided many months in this neighbourhood. I went with some friends a few days ago, after having seen Ferney, to view this mansion. I trod the floors with the same

---

24 From a short work of prose fiction written in 1819 by John William Polidori taken from the story Lord Byron, published by Sherwood, Neely, and Jones, London. 'Though not explicitly written during the summer of 1816, this story was obviously inspired by the fragment of the vampire story written by Lord Byron this particular volcanic winter' – R.D.B.

feelings of awe and respect as we did, together, those of Shakspeare's dwelling at Stratford. I sat down in a chair of the saloon, and satisfied myself that I was resting on what he had made his constant seat. I found a servant there who had lived with him; she, however, gave me but little information. She pointed out his bed-chamber upon the same level as the saloon and dining-room, and informed me that he retired to rest at three, got up at two, and employed himself a long time over his toilette; that he never went to sleep without a pair of pistols and a dagger by his side, and that he never eat animal food. He apparently spent some part of every day upon the lake in an English boat. There is a balcony from the saloon which looks upon the lake and the mountain Jura; and I imagine, that it must have been hence he contemplated the storm so magnificently described in the Third Canto; for you have from here a most extensive view of all the points he has therein depicted. I can fancy him like the scathed pine, whilst all around was sunk to repose, still waking to observe, what gave but a weak image of the storms which had desolated his own breast.

> The sky is changed!—and such a change; Oh, night!
> And storm and darkness, ye are wond'rous strong,
> Yet lovely in your strength, as is the light
> Of a dark eye in woman! Far along
> From peak to peak, the rattling crags among,
> Leaps the live thunder! Not from one lone cloud,
> But every mountain now hath found a tongue,
> And Jura answers thro' her misty shroud,
> Back to the joyous Alps who call to her aloud!
>
> And this is in the night:—Most glorious night!
> Thou wer't not sent for slumber! let me be
> A sharer in thy far and fierce delight,—
> A portion of the tempest and of me!
> How the lit lake shines a phosphoric sea,
> And the big rain comes dancing to the earth!
> And now again 'tis black,—and now the glee
> Of the loud hills shakes with its mountain mirth,
> As if they did rejoice o'er a young earthquake's birth,
>
> Now where the swift Rhine cleaves his way between
> Heights which appear, as lovers who have parted
> In haste, whose mining depths so intervene,
> That they can meet no more, tho' broken hearted;
> Tho' in their souls which thus each other thwarted,

Love was the very root of the fond rage
Which blighted their life's bloom, and then departed—
Itself expired, but leaving them an age
Of years all winter—war within themselves to wage.

I went down to the little port, if I may use the expression, wherein his vessel used to lay, and conversed with the cottager, who had the care of it. You may smile, but I have my pleasure in thus helping my personification of the individual I admire, by attaining to the knowledge of those circumstances which were daily around him. I have made numerous enquiries in the town concerning him, but can learn nothing. He only went into society there once, when Mr Pictet took him to the house of a lady to spend the evening. They say he is a very singular man, and seem to think him very uncivil. Amongst other things they relate, that having invited Mr Pictet and Bonstetten to dinner, he went on the lake to Chillon, leaving a gentleman who travelled with him to receive them and make his apologies. Another evening, being invited to the house of Lady D. H., he promised to attend, but upon approaching the windows of her ladyship's villa, and perceiving the room to be full of company, he set down his friend, desiring him to plead his excuse, and immediately returned home. This will serve as a contradiction to the report which you tell me is current in England, of his having been avoided by his countrymen on the continent. The case happens to be directly the reverse, as he has been generally sought by them, though on most occasions, apparently without success. It is said, indeed, that upon paying his first visit at Coppet, following the servant who had announced his name, he was surprised to meet a lady carried out fainting; but before he had been seated many minutes, the same lady, who had been so affected at the sound of his name, returned and conversed with him a considerable time— such is female curiosity and affectation! He visited Coppet frequently, and of course associated there with several of his countrymen, who evinced no reluctance to meet him whom his enemies alone would represent as an outcast.

Though I have been so unsuccessful in this town, I have been more fortunate in my enquiries elsewhere. There is a society three or four miles from Geneva, the centre of which is the Countess of Breuss, a Russian lady, well acquainted with the agrémens de la Société, and who has collected them round herself at her mansion. It was chiefly here, I find, that the gentleman who travelled with Lord Byron, as physician, sought for society. He used almost every day to cross the lake by himself, in one of their flat-bottomed boats, and return after passing the evening with his friends, about eleven or twelve at night, often whilst the storms were raging in the circling summits of the mountains around. As he became intimate, from long acquaintance, with several of the families in this neighbourhood, I have gathered from their accounts some excellent traits of his lordship's character, which I will relate to you at some future opportunity.

Among other particulars mentioned, was the outline of a ghost story by Lord Byron. It appears that one evening Lord Byron, Mr Percy Bysshe Shelly, two ladies and the gentleman before alluded to, after having perused a German work, entitled *Phantasmagoriana*, began relating ghost stories; when his lordship having recited the beginning of Christabel, then unpublished, the whole took so strong a hold of Mr Shelly's mind, that he suddenly started up and ran out of the room. The physician and Lord Byron followed, and discovered him leaning against a mantle-piece, with cold drops of perspiration trickling down his face. After having given him something to refresh him, upon enquiring into the cause of his alarm, they found that his wild imagination having pictured to him the bosom of one of the ladies with eyes (which was reported of a lady in the neighbourhood where he lived) he was obliged to leave the room in order to destroy the impression. It was afterwards proposed, in the course of conversation, that each of the company present should write a tale depending upon some supernatural agency, which was undertaken by Lord B., the physician, and one of the ladies before mentioned. I obtained the outline of each of these stories as a great favour, and herewith forward them to you, as I was assured you would feel as much curiosity as myself, to peruse the ebauches of so great a genius, and those immediately under his influence.[25]

The Diary of Dr John William Polidori

8 July. The Game of Ghost Stories that had kept the five of us awake until the small hours for three harrowing weeks has slowly petered out with only lovely Mary continuing to write her dreadfull contribution (not dreadful, mind you, howbeit her story fills me so full of dread!) George and I alone have offered our ghost stories (his vampyre still haunts both my waking and dreaming minds); Shelley gracefully declined the Lord's invitation to play his game (of course he did); Claire refuses to share hers (I doubt she played the game at all); and lovely Mary is being haunted by this mysterious 'student of the unhallowed arts'. I am left alone in the parlour absentmindedly leafing through the book of ghost stories that served as the impetus for our little game (although I am affably fluent in the language of France, I am regretta-

---

25 From an extract of a letter from Geneva printed in *The Vampyre* by John William Polidori, published by Sherwood, Neely, and Jones, London.

bly illiterate). The 'Shelleys' have already retired for the evening to the privacy of their bedchamber, no doubt playing Aphrodite's favourite game, and George seeks to escape the needful Claire by imprisoning himself within his own apartment, with her secluded to her own.

Night fell at its usual hour for the day and month of our modern calendar; though the weather with its dour grey skies and chilled winds gave both the appearance and sensations of winter, the sun has stayed in its rightful course through the sky throughout this summer. The flames of the candles flickered, and the curtains fluttered with a sudden gust of wintry winds slipping through the windowpanes; the chill prickled gooseflesh upon my arms. A withered, almost haunted voice floated in from the foyer begging my pardon. I burst from the parlour brandishing a poker like a samurai warrior. Rain sleeted in through the open front doorway as a second mysterious figure fled into the protective embrace of the foyer from the cloud-shrouded moonless night. The withered old man soon returned; he set down two heavy suitcases and then disappeared back into darkness. The second figure stood as a woman out of time and of country: she reeked of English opulence, wore an Italian reticella lace ruff that has been out of style for centuries, adorned in Polish ornamentation, with a French farthingale. I might have questioned the rigidity of Spanish severity for travel; but a cultured woman cannot be so easily relieved of her culture. Her French gown was soaked from the sleet, while her kirtle and petticoat strained to keep her warm. She wore a safeguard to protect her while on travel, and a mantle of marten wrapped around her dainty shoulders. The withered, ancient man returned with a trunk— far too stout for his far too frail frame— but carried it with relative ease, setting it down daintily with an audible *thunk*. Without another word, he closed thick wooden door with a *thud* and vanished from both sight and memory.

'Georgie-poo,' the mysterious woman called out, her feminine voice echoing through the hallways of the Villa Diodati. 'Georgie-poo,' she calls out again as the echo returns, the reverb resounding. Her accent foreign hung thick in the air like London's fog. 'I have arrived as requested at Cologny.' This latter phrase died upon speaking, but her 'Georgie-poo' continued to ring out as if caught by the ghosts who sang out in a Gregorian chant. Lightning flashed through the narrow windows around the door seemingly striking the base of my spine; the electricity sparking through my veins, prickling gooseflesh once again. Now, I am the one begging her pardon, but Georgie-poo— I mean, Lord Byron— had retired early for the evening. She stood there incredulous that her 'Georgie-poo' would lay down to sleep at such an *unnatural* hour; the twelve tolls of midnight just come to pass. I invited her into the parlour to sit before the fire to have a warm. She sloughed off the sleet onto the rug in the entry, not like a serpent shedding its skin, but like a belly dancer alluring the eyes of me...— I mean, men— Then she joined me before the hearth.

Her name is Countess Erzsébet, a Hungarian noblewoman and acquaintance of Lord Byron whom he encountered on his Grand Tour of the Mediterranean a few years past, and she comes to stay with us in Cologny this night. Though I suspect she had seen at least a half-century of birthdays, she has the stature and appearance of an ingénue in a Russian ballet. Her skin is porcelain white, as if she had bathed in the blood of virgins. I chuckle at the morbid thought; the troubling image presents in my mind's eye, of her immersed in the deep crimson blood with her bare breasts barely submerged, was quite arousing— embarrassingly arousing. I had to shift a leg to discretely conceal the proof of my male arousal. Then my doctor's intellect stole back my attention from my primitive reptilian brain. A petite young virgin has, at most, a gallon of blood coursing through her veins. I could easily calculate the number of virgins that bathing in a ball-and-claw-footed white coated cast iron tub filled with human blood would necessitate the exsanguinating of at thirty. Quite the body count even for the promise of eternal youth. Perchance the countess blood-letted the virgin into a porcelain basin and then sponge-bathed herself by dipping a dainty toe into the crimson gore. Ha! This proved to my doctor's pedigree the most economical and certainly less homicidal method of bathing in virginal blood. Her Irishesque hair seemed perpetually stained by such bathing. Her wide eyes shone like emeralds, an unnatural fire in such Slavic stock. Everything about her struck me as unnatural, like she had been touched by the preternatural. Something... undead.

I chuckled again; my spine tingled again.

Erzsébet regaled me, 'My squalid, tempestuous journey through squalls and tempests,' (as English is not her native tongue, her use of these adjectives with the particular and peculiar roots alter their definitions both poetically and appropriately). I make my home at the foot of the Little Carpathian Mountains in the castle Ɛachtice, which lords over the lands and villages surrounding my prison, which were purchased as a bridal gift from the Nádasdy's family upon my wedding night to their son, Ferenc.' Since she sat enjoying a warm before the fire, I presume she speaks not of a literal prison but is taking literary license with her story to me. 'I received my invitation from Georgie-poo... I mean...' she corrected herself politely, the tone of her pleasant voice took on aristocratic formality, 'George Gordon Byron, 6th Baron Byron, to sojourn for the summer at the Villa Diodati on the shore of Lake Geneva

in the esteemed company of his personal physician John William Polidori, the poet Percy Bysshe Shelley and the two sisters in his companionship.' She then returned to her natural playful lilt, 'My journey
south would be brief because at the foot of the Little Carpathians lies
Pressburg nestled between the Rivers Danube and Morava. A sharp
turn to the west my carriage followed the bluest, yet queerestly frozen
Danube to Vienna at the northeasternmost foothills of the alps, then
further west into Munich which straddles the River Isar to the north
of the alps. And then onto Bern surrounded on all sides by the River
Aare like a God-ordained moat.' During this briefest of travelogues,
my mind's pictured each as if I had seen them with my own eyes. It
was if she had telepathically— preternaturally— inserted the pictures
into my brain! 'Oh! my dear doctor,' she sighed, and she swooned with
the back her his dainty hand resting upon her forehead, 'the roads were
so long and so cruel. I would briefly and for a mere night rest in each
of these jewels of Europe due to the hospitality my rank and station
and coin still afford me. But woe! my dear doctor,' she cried, and she
crooned, 'I feared the reproach of the suffering citizens because famine
and diseased gripped every city, village, and hamlet I dared approach
with such finery and such wares. The miserable wretches could at any
moment mimic the revolutionaries of France and take my head from
my shoulders. I was forced by necessity to put aside all signs of my aristocracy to travel as a commoner until this, the final leg of my journey.
Oh! my dear doctor,' she sighed again, and she swooned again, 'on my
ghoulish travels, my carriage passed failed crop-fields and unnaturally
frozen rivers, drove through mirky woods, and over snow-laden mountain passes, to finally and fatefully this very summer night deliver me
here where I can enjoy a warm around your hearth at our Lord's rented
villa on the shore of Lake Geneva. I have fulfilled my obligation having
accepted his gracious invitation.'

'Do you not desire to retire to a bedchamber? Surely you must be
fatigued from your harrowing journey across the breadth of Europe?'

'At this natural hour? No,' she countered. 'What intrigue have I
missed due to the lateness of my arrival?'

I would never dismiss a countess of such beauty, so I recounted,
'When Lord Byron and I set out from England on a Grand Tour towards our destination of Greece, we anticipated daily tours of the serene lake by rented boat and hiking through the scenic hills, but we
have been plagued fast-flashing lightning and harsh-crashing thunder.
We have suffered our imprisonment in the Villa Diodati like French
aristocracy in the Bastille due such revolutionary weather. Lovely Mary
once observed (and how I acquired this forbidden knowledge from her

hidden journal must be required hereafter to remain a mystery): "An almost perpetual rain confines us principally to the house; but when the sun bursts forth it is with a splendour and cold even unknown in England. The thunder storms that visit us are grander and more terrific than I have ever seen before. We watch them as they approach from the opposite side of the lake, observing the lightning play among the clouds in various parts of the heavens, and dart in jagged figures upon the piny heights of Jura, dark with the shadow of the overhanging cloud, while perhaps the sun is shining cheerily upon us. One night we enjoyed a finer storm than I had ever before beheld. The lake was lit up— the pines on Jura made visible, and all the scene illuminated for an instant, when a pitchy blackness succeeded, and the thunder came in frightful bursts over our heads amid the darkness."[26]

'Your dear Georgie-poo,' I paused, casting my eyes to the rug fearful that I had just mocked her, 'My apologies, countess— Lord Byron given our state of agitation due to our immurement in these stately walls and irritation with each other in our rapprochement proposed a game of ghost stories. Having found a needless volume of a French translation of German ghost stories as our inspiration, Lord Byron leads us to seek out a literary haunting in our own corners of the Villa Diodati. The tale I presented to my friends is the one I began here at Coligny, when Frankenstein was planned, and when a noble author having determined to descend from his lofty rang, gave up a few hours to a tale of terror, and wrote a fragment. Though I cannot boast of the horrible imagination of the one, or the elegant classical style of the latter, still I hoped they would not throw mine away, because it is not equal to these.' The countess laid her dainty hand upon mine having leaned over the brief gulf between us. 'Whether the use I have made of supernatural agency, and the colouring I have given to the mind of Ernestus Berchtold, are original or not, I leave to the more erudite in novels and romances to declare I am not conscious of having seen any where a prototype of either; yet I fear that whatever is original, is not always pleasing. Nor is this my only apprehension. A tale that rests upon improbabilities, must generally disgust a rational mind; I am therefore afraid that, though I have thrown the superior agency into the back ground as much as was in my power, still, that many readers will think the same moral, and the same colouring, might have been given to characters acting under the ordinary agencies of life; I believe it, but I had agreed to write a supernatural tale, and that does not allow a completely every-day narrative.'[27] The countess, her

---

26 From the *History of a Six Weeks Tour Through a Part of France, Germany, Switzerland, and Holland* by Mary Shelley, published by T. Hookham, Jun. Old Bond Street, and C. and J. Ollier, Welback Street, 1817
27 From the Introduction by the author to *Ernestus Berchtold; or, The Modern Oedipus: A Tale* in 1819,

hand still resting on mine having descended from her chair to fall upon her knees at my feet, gave a precious squeeze.

'If mine was by far the worst, Lord Byron produced the first. Two friends were to travel from England into Greece (not unlike Lord Byron and myself); while there, one of them should die, but before his death, should obtain from his friend an oath of secrecy with regard to his disease. Some short time after, the remaining traveller returning to his native country, should be startled at perceiving his former companion moving about in society, and should be horrified at finding that he made love to his former friend's sister.[28]

'Oh! Oh!' the countess said, delicately agitated, 'Georgie-poo sent me a poem once that reeks of this viral vampirism! I still have it memorized! Shall I recite to you the relevant lines featuring the revenant, Doctor?' I simply nodded for I desired to hear the poem spoken in her lovely exotic accent.

> *A supposition alluded to in the "Giaour."*
> *'But first on earth, as Vampyre sent,*
> *Thy corse shall from its tomb be rent;*
> *Then ghastly haunt the native place,*
> *And suck the blood of all thy race;*
> *There from thy* daughter, sister, wife,
> *At midnight drain the stream of life;*
> Yet loathe the banquet which perforce
> *Must feed thy livid living corse,*
> *Thy victims, ere they yet expire,*
> *Shall know the demon for their sire;*
> *As cursing thee, thou cursing them,*
> *Thy flowers are withered on the stem.*
> *But one that for* thy crime must fall,
> *The youngest, best beloved of all,*
> *Shall bless thee with a* father's name—
> *That word shall wrap thy heart in flame!*
> *Yet thou must end thy task and mark*
> *Her cheek's last tinge—her eye's last spark,*
> *And the last glassy glance must view*
> *Which freezes o'er its lifeless blue;*
> *Then with unhallowed hand shall tear*
> *The tresses of her yellow hair,*

publisher unknown.
28 From a footnote to the Introduction by the author to *Ernestus Berchtold; or, The Modern Oedipus: A Tale* in 1819, publisher unknown.

Of which, in life a lock when shorn
Affection's fondest pledge was worn—
But now is borne away by thee
Memorial of thine agony!
Yet with thine own best blood shall drip;
Thy gnashing tooth, and haggard lip;
Then stalking to thy sullen grave,
Go— and with Gouls and Afrits rave,
Till these in horror shrink away
From spectre more accursed than they.[29]

'But... my dear doctor,' the countess continued, 'I deny the possibility of such a ground-work forming the outline of a tale which should bear the slightest appearance of probability. This is the reason my Georgie-poo abandoned the concept as a mere fragment. There is not-a-thing more to this story other than the brief pages he wrote.'

The creative, non-caporal voice that lives in the heads of all poets and novelists protested loudly, not only in the confines of my skull, but out of my mouth as well. 'Upon this foundation is a great story! Even if Lord Byron chose to leave it unfinished, it is certainly not an unfinishable story. Where he chose to begin and to end his intentional fragment leaves open the possibility of its completion by another.

'That's plagiarism,' the countess protested. 'The story is not yours to finish. It is my Georgie-poo's to do with or do without as he chooses.'

'Was not the Bard William Shakespeare himself an unrepentant plagiarist?' I countered, '*Romeo and Juliet* was stolen from an Arthur Brooke's English translation of Pierre Boaistuau's French translation of Matteo Bandello Italian *Giuletta e Romeo*. His theft of Raphael Holinshed's *Chronicles* proved to be obscene: nearly every one of the historical plays, including both Richards and all the Henrys, and Kings Lear and John, along with the framework of *MacBeth*, were stolen. Thief! Thief!' I exclaimed as if I were a merchant in an Arabian bizarre demanding Shakespeare's hand be cut off by city guards for his thievery! 'Did he take literary liberties with all of sources making them his own? Emphatically. Did he steal nearly every line from one or two of the Henrys word-for-word, line-for-line from Holinshed? Indubitably! We should, no doubt, retire the epithet 'The Bard' and substitute 'The Plagiarist'. 'Tis a more fitting title.'

'If it is possible, which it is not, then pluck the abandoned fragment from our little Lord's dustbin and complete the fragment,' she said

---

29 From *The Giaour* a poem by Lord Byron, published by T. Davison, Whitefriars, for John Murray, Albemarle-Street, 1813.

smacking me across the cheek with her dainty hand as if she clutched a metaphorical duellist's glove.' She lifted herself to her feet, straightened her skirt, courteously curtsied, and requested my services to deliver her baggage to her bedchamber given the sudden lateness of the hour. Our conversation had stolen away the night. Standing in the door-frame to her apartment, I wished her a good night, kissing the back of her dainty hand, then returned to the warm of the hearth to stew as if boiling in a cooking pot.

I reached down before the hearth to pick up the metaphorical duellist's glove she left lying invisible upon the rug, folded it nicely, then pocketed it, and said quite audibly and quite audaciously, 'I will complete the fragment.'

July 9. I awoke the next morning to join the Shelleys and Claire for breakfast. They knew not about the countess' arrival the night previous for she did not come out of the privacy of her bedchamber for breakfast nor lunch nor tea nor dinner. When she spoke yesternight of the late evening being a 'natural hour' for her I did not take her so literally, but given her absence during the waking hours, she proved to be as nocturnal as the vampire I planned to steal from Lord Byron.

Lord Byron's Diary

9July 1816. I sought my escape from Claire's obsession for yet another night innumerable, but this prison in the form of the Villa Diodati keeps me enclosed to close to her! As I hide yet another night in my apartment, the words I had written in a letter to my dearest sister Augusta ring in my ears. Shall I repeat them, Diary? Hells-bells! Why not!

> Now don't scold; but what could I do?–a foolish girl, in spite of all I could say or do, would come after me, or rather went before- -for I found her here–and I have had all the plague possible to persuade her to go back again; but at last she went. Now, dearest, I do most truly tell thee that I could not help this, that I did all I could to prevent it, and have at last put an end to it. I was not in love, nor have any love left for any; but I could not exactly play the Stoic with a woman who had scrambled eight hundred miles to unphilosophise me. Besides, I had been regaled of late with so many 'two courses and a desert' (Alas!) of aversion, that I was fain to take a little love (if pressed particularly) by way of novelty.
> —Letter from Lord Byron to Augusta Leigh

How I wish to sit up late with my dear Percy and debate galvanism again or another natural philosophy or the lack of natural philosophy in the religious or religion in the religious or the lack of religion in the irreligious, Percy's own kind. Howbeit, Claire, by her unwanted and wanton attention towards me, has immured me in my apartment. What crime have I committed to be so imprisoned within my own rented villa? Her pregnancy, you say? Until a natural philosopher can determine through some study of my semen in his laboratory to be the source of Claire's pregnancy, I say 'Balderdash!' to the paternity of her unborn. How would a comparison of my semen and the amniotic waters her unborn bathes in even be possible? Perchance, Percy and I can debate whether or not there is chance residual traces of semen can be found lingering the woman's womb or the child's body days, weeks, months, or even years removed from the sexual act. And I'd debate the following argument in Claire's presence surely out of spite: whether a kind-loving God would never permit such a comparison be made by the sciences and should paternity be proven only by the acceptance of the born in a man's heart. There can be no other proof of fatherhood other than in a man's heart because women can be such deceitful, despiteful creatures as it concerns their liaisons with men... innumerable.

And in my heart, her unborn is no progeny of mine!

Suddenly there came a tapping of someone excitedly rapping on my chamber door! Here I should be pleasantly napping instead of obsessing on Claire's obsession, trapping me in her womb with her unborn child. Was Claire so clairvoyant to hear my thoughts and came to assail me again? I crept to the stout wood separating me from my nocturnal assailant. Silence! I placed my ear to my chamber door hoping to hear something... anything... a moment, a long moment... there was nothing! Then there came another tapping of someone excitedly rapping on my chamber door. So close to a dreary midnight, I flung open the door and to my shock and surprise I laid my weak and weary eyes on Countess Erzsébet! How had she come to be at the Villa Diodati? No invitations had been sent, so no obligations needed to be spent on such a long and cruel journey to Lake Geneva. I embraced her with a ferocity that would chase away lesser maidens. We danced to the symphony of atmospheric timpani drums sounding and rain pounding out a rhythm on the windowpanes.

'Georgie-poo,' my sweetest Erzsébet cooed.

'Countess,' I said with a voice expressing both bewilderment and amazement. 'How did you find me here at a rented house on the shore of Lake Geneva? I sent no invitation to join our company at the Villa Diodati. And if I had, you would have been under no obligation to holiday the duration of this dreary, weary summer on the shores of a lake we cannot often tour. How are you here in my arms this evening?

'Georgie-poo, do you believe that the expanse of land and gulf of time that separated us could not be navigated to bring me to you?' she said, resting her delicate head upon my shoulder.

'How?'

'Do you question how a pigeon finds its way in delivering a message?'

'No.'

'Do you question how the butterflies migrate an unfathomable stretch from continent to continent?'

'No.'

'Do you question how the salmon find their birth waters to spawn a new generation, swimming naturally upstream to memories of a pool as remote as a dream?'

'No, but...'

'Then rest your troubled mind and do not question how it is I am snuggled in your arms this night having been smuggled across the breadth of Europe. Except the reality that needs no causality. The road was both long and cruel. Your unusual physician entertained me yester-night with a wonderful story of a game you and your company played thunderstorm-bound this queer winter,' she said with a sly wink.'

'Oh! It was such a wonderful game!'

'And what of your contribution to the game?'

'Oh, that fragment of a... thing,' I complained, 'It is not-a-thing to worry yourself about. A trifle. Speaking of trifles! Why should I tell you of that... nothing... when I can shower you with bracelets of my hair, rings, gawds, conceits, knacks, trifles, nosegays, sweetmeats, messengers of strong prevailment in unharden'd youth', I wooed stealing liberally and literally from Shakespeare.

'Oh! Georgie-poo, you woo far too liberally and literally from Shakespeare. Shame! Poets do not steal from one and another,' she said as I hung my head melodramatically. She lifted my chin with her dainty, white long-gloved hand, 'They do not.'

'No! Countess,' I counted in mock protest, 'a poet of high esteem could easily say something akin to, "Immature poets imitate; mature poets steal; bad poets deface what they take, and good poets make it into something better, or at least something different. The good poet welds his theft into a whole of feeling which is unique, utterly different from that from which it was torn."'

'I do not accept such a radical concept. Please, Georgie-poo, let us return to this game you played. Let us not speak of thieves and thievery when there is the excitement of the Creation of creativity!'

'What more can I tell you of the game we played? It was an unholy creature born of the cursed womb of this villa. We gestated in these confines for days, for weeks, and probably for the months to come. How we wished to be born with the sun on our faces, but in a season preternaturally cold thunderstorms, we poets all took up our quills to pen our own ghost stories. I will tell you how an awful French translation of even more awful German stories set us off on this course. I will not speak of mine, however, but I will tell you of theirs. My dearest doctor, whom you have had chance to encounter, contributed a most foul work, bloated, like a stinking corpse washed up upon the shore, with words. He knows no editor! My beloved Percy, a friend of mine from England, who is visiting with his fiancée and her sister, has chosen to not participate in my little game. The scoundrel. But of his fiancée, her contribution is magnificent in its horror! She has blended science with fiction! Who but lovely Mary would create a ghost of flesh and blood! Her creature is harrowing! As for my contribution, I have forgotten mine already.'

'Oh! your fine physician remembers it acutely and fondly. Please, forgive him, but he told me all about it.'

'Then why do I need to speak on it more? The fragmentary pages lie in a drawer in the owner of his villa's desk. If I had a stronger constitution, I would turn those pages into my crumpled globe and pitch it in an apocalyptic fire and watch its world burn. I should never have plucked vampirism out of folklore.'

'What is a vampire?' she said, continuing to coo, but I would choose not to woo her with my creative spark. Her desire is to light the fire of poet's heart. 'I know not this creature you speak of.'

'Oh, you are far too demure to demur too greatly. You know as well as I know, vampires were the reanimated corpses of persons newly buried, which were supposed to suck the blood and suck out the life of their selected victims. The marks by which a vampire corpse was recognized were the apparent non-putrefaction of the body and effusion of blood from the lips. A suspected vampire was exhumed, and if the marks were perceived or imagined to be present, a stake was driven through the heart, and the body was burned. This, if Southey's authorities may be believed, "laid" the vampire, and the community might sleep in peace. The Vampire superstition is still general in the Levant. Honest Tournefort tells a long story about these "*Vroucolachas*", as he calls them. The Romaic term is "*Vardoulacha*". I recollect a whole family being terrified by the scream of a child, which they imagined must proceed from such a visitation. The Greeks never mention the word without horror. I find that "*Broucolokas*" is an old legitimate Hellenic appellation— the moderns, however, use the word I mention. The stories told in Hungary and Greece of these foul feeders are singular, and some of them most incredibly attested.[30] These are your ancestorial lands I speak of. Your nursery stories, I have no doubt, spoke of rumours and the rumours of rumours of the risen dead. Superstitions! Are you too haughty from the height of your castle to listen to the folk tales of the common people. *Vroucolachas*! *Vardoulacha*! *Gouls*! *Broucolokas*!'

The Countess slapped me across the cheek; I felt the all too familiar sting. 'How dare you mock me! I may be born of aristocratic stock, but my roots are in the land and its people. I know intimately the stories of the beloved dead crawling from their graves to menace the begrieved. I have witnessed once virile men so fearful of rising from their consecrated graves and assailing their grieving wives and weeping children that on their deathbeds they ask— they plead— they bribe the undertaker's man to be buried with a blade resting across their necks. If the dead can raise their heads to sit up, the dead can then crawl through the moist earth to return to their families turn their beloveds into *Vroucolachas*! *Vardoulacha*! *Gouls*! *Broucolokas*! like themselves. I have had to console the begrieved, who've had yet another in their family fall fatally ill by an assault from the recently deceased. The family begs me for the release from vampirism. They beg me to order to the undertaker to exhume to corpse to observe any signs of life, as you so expertly detailed. My order! And by my order a stake is driven into the heart of the dead. I give this order over and over again— not so dead will no longer rise from the grave, according to the absurd superstition, but for the peace of mind of the living! Until you, my little Lord, are forced by your nobility to order the desecration of a corpse while priests pray and families wail, hold your bitter tongue!'

'My apologies, Countess!' I bent my head in not only genuflection, but affection— and submission. I offered my confession. I apologized for my clumsy tongue.

'Stubborn tongue,' the countess countered. 'Your native tongue may not be my own, but if we were in my country, I could rightfully and righteously have your slanderous tongue cut out for your mockery and insolence. Speak to me thus never again!'

I knew she was not truly angry with me. We, the denizens of the Villa Diodati, may have played a game of ghost stories this summer, but this game that the countess I engaged in is played with barbed tongues.

---

30 From the notes *The Giaour* by Lord Bryon, published by John Murray, Albemarle Street, 1813.

The sharper the better. A keen edge of the tongue that can eviscerate, slicing open our rival's belly and spilling their entrails upon their shoes. Such a wicked game to play.

The Diary of Dr John William Polidori

11 July. I woke in the morning before the sun had even risen, Lord Byron, the Shelleys, and Ms. Clairemont would not be up for breakfast, but I could no longer sleep my mind preoccupied with sizzling bacon and sausage and a few eggs scrabbled. Strange! As soon as I open by bedchamber door, there sat some luggage at my feet, small and made ready for travel. Curious, I picked of the luggage and made my way to the foyer, in preparation for what? I knew not. There stood Countess Erzsébet dressed for travel, dressed as she had been when she had arrived at the Villa Diodati just Monday evening. Concerned that she was cutting her visit to the villa short, I inquired if she was retiring back to Hungary. She shook her head slowly to the left and then to the right, returning to the proper centre for a gentlewoman. I then required of her the knowledge of her presence in the foyer and the small luggage she obviously had packed and curiously left at my bedchamber door.

Oh! we were going on a brief holiday.

Outside the villa stood her carriage and her mysterious elderly carriage-driver who had seemingly disappeared into the ether just a few days before. The sun had not yet risen over the Alps, but there was the merest hint of light painting the sky behind the mountaintops. Soon dawn would be upon us. I helped the countess into the carriage, as any good gentlemen would and off we set for a destination unknown. Her forthrightness in planning a cryptic holiday had thrown me for a loop. Why was I alone invited and not Lord Byron, nor the Shelleys, nor Ms. Clairemont. The Shelleys and Claire not receiving an invitation at the very least was explainable, but Lord Byron not sitting in this carriage with the countess and me, was truly perplexing and quite vexing. My curiosity had grown more and more as the villa and Lake Geneva shrank in distance behind us. She now shown an unpredictability that was as alluring as it was alarming.

The carriage curiously had the windows painted black, so the interior was as pitch as midnight with the moon obscured by the clouds or in its newness. The rhythmic motion of the carriage immediately lulled both the countess and I into a quaint and quite queer dreamless slumber. I awoke startled at the sudden halt of the carriage. The elderly driver opened the door on my side of the carriage. I was greeted by the presence of a hotel of surprising opulence in a metropolis I could not readily identify. The hotel was completely and gloriously lit by gas-light! Night had already fallen? How far and for how long had we travelled while we both slept so soundly that we may have been counted amongst the dead? This was a profoundly serious question. Curiouser and curiouser!

Our room rented for the weekend was fit for a king, or at the very least a countess of a distant land. The walls were gilded quite obscenely and the bed itself was quilted quite cleanly with the rarest of silk panels. The curtains were of the thickest wool, no doubt sheered from golden-woolled, winged ram, Chrysomallos! (But I digress into preposterous pedanticness) The paintings hung on all the walls were all unrecognized by me, but by their quality, were no doubt created by prized Renascence masters. The museums of London would be envious of the paintings and the sculptures housed in a mere hotel room. Oh! the pretentiousness! Oh! the licentiousness! How this room's very culture made me feel like an imposter instead of a proper guest in this hotel!

As I gawked at the room, there came a knock on the locked hotel room door. When I opened the door, there stood a porter who would not have been out of place as a valet at Buckingham Palace. He was dressed to impress king, emperors, and perhaps even the Pope, whom stands above all in the pantheon of European royalty. He handed me an ornate box, which I peered down at and when I returned my gaze to the page to thank him, perchance to tip him, he had vanished like a fart in a whirlwind. The countess motioned for me to sit at a no less ornate desk positioned against the gilded walls. I sat in its chair inspired by a particular French king, and opened the box. Slowly. As it was once owned by Pandora. What would I find inside? Hope? 'A kingly gift fit for an author of such singing prose!' Erzsébet squealed as the interior was revealed in the candlelight. I found a journal bound in the finest leather, its edges gilded in gold leaf as real as the gold in this room, along with a quill from a blackest swan and pot with the purest India ink.

The Countess and I sat at dinner in, not in the hotel's restaurant of the finest European culinary fare, but a backwater kitchen hidden among filth strewn streets of the peasantry. Where we would find the truest, purest example of this land's cuisine. My plate, when delivered to me, proved so exotic and foreign that I was momentarily repulsed. But I would not insult my host who did the ordering nor the chef who did the preparation. My father had gone to great lengths in instruct me in the manners of a gentleman. You ate whatever was placed on the plate. No gentleman would attend a gallery presentation of an artist, only to request and require the art to make alterations to the painting

before you would purchase it; a gentleman simply does not enter a restaurant and request and require the chef to make alterations to his dish.
Like the painter or sculpture dedicated their lives to their art, the chef
has spent a lifetime mastering flavours and textures to produce his own
work of art. And if you do not desire this ingredient or that ingredient,
then my father would admonish me, do not order that dish. And if
there is not-a-thing on the menu that strikes your stomach's fancy, you
do not eat!

And I did eat.

During our small talk, the Countess Erzsébet inquired what did I
knew of vampires! Unfettered by her doubts and intent on flouting my
own knowledge and experience in all things, I waxed, 'The superstition
is very general in the East. Among the Arabians it appears to be common: it did not, however, extend itself to the Greeks until after the estab-
lishment of Christianity; and it has only assumed its present form since
the division of the Latin and Greek churches; at which time, the idea
becoming prevalent, that a Latin body could not corrupt if buried in their
territory, it gradually increased, and formed the subject of many wonderful stories, still extant, of the dead rising from their graves, and feeding
upon the blood of the young and beautiful. In the West it spread, with
some slight variation, all over Hungary, Poland, Austria, and Lorraine,
where the belief existed, that vampyres nightly imbibed a certain portion
of the blood of their victims, who became emaciated, lost their strength,
and speedily died of consumptions; whilst these human blood-suckers
fattened—and their veins became distended to such a state of repletion,
as to cause the blood to flow from all the passages of their bodies, and
even from the very pores of their skins.

'In the London Journal, of March 1732, is a curious, and, of
course, credible account of a particular case of vampyrism, which is
stated to have occurred at Madreyga, in Hungary. It appears, that upon
an examination of the commander-in-chief and magistrates of the place,
they positively and unanimously affirmed, that, about five years before,
a certain Heyduke, named Arnold Paul, had been heard to say, that, at
Cassovia, on the frontiers of the Turkish Servia, he had been tormented
by a vampyre, but had found a way to rid himself of the evil, by eating
some of the earth out of the vampyre's grave, and rubbing himself with
his blood. This precaution, however, did not prevent him from becoming
a vampyre himself; for, about twenty or thirty days after his death
and burial, many persons complained of having been tormented by him, and a deposition was made, that four persons had
been deprived of life by his attacks. To prevent further mischief,
the inhabitants having consulted their Hadagni, took up the body,

and found it (as is supposed to be usual in cases of vampyrism) fresh, and entirely free from corruption, and emitting at the mouth, nose, and ears, pure and florid blood. Proof having been thus obtained, they resorted to the accustomed remedy. A stake was driven entirely through the heart and body of Arnold Paul, at which he is reported to have cried out as dreadfully as if he had been alive. This done, they cut off his head, burned his body, and threw the ashes into his grave. The same measures were adopted with the corses of those persons who had previously died from vampyrism, lest they should, in their turn, become agents upon others who survived them.

'This monstrous <u>rodomontade</u> is here related, because it seems better adapted to illustrate the subject of the present observations than any other instance which could be adduced. In many parts of Greece it is considered as a sort of punishment after death, for some heinous crime committed whilst in existence, that the deceased is not only doomed to vampyrise, but compelled to confine his infernal visitations solely to those beings he loved most while upon earth—those to whom he was bound by ties of kindred and affection.— A supposition alluded to in the "Giaour" as you recited to me upon our first meeting!

'Mr Southey has also introduced in his wild but beautiful poem of "Thalaba," the vampyre corse of the Arabian maid Oneiza, who is represented as having returned from the grave for the purpose of tormenting him she best loved whilst in existence. But this cannot be supposed to have resulted from the sinfulness of her life, she being pourtrayed throughout the whole of the tale as a complete type of purity and innocence. The veracious Tournefort gives a long account in his travels of several astonishing cases of vampyrism, to which he pretends to have been an eye-witness; and Calmet, in his great work upon this subject, besides a variety of anecdotes, and traditionary narratives illustrative of its effects, has put forth some learned dissertations, tending to prove it to be a classical, as well as barbarian error.

'Many curious and interesting notices on this singularly horrible superstition might be added; though the present may suffice for the limits of a note, necessarily devoted to explanation, and which may now be concluded by merely remarking, that though the term Vampyre is the one in most general acceptation, there are several others synonimous with it, made use of in various parts of the world: as *Vroucolocha, Vardoulacha, Goul, Broucoloka,* &c.'[31]

When I spoke these foreign terms used for what the English call a vampyre, I saw the muscles in her face twitch. She winced, ever so

---

31 From the Introduction to *The Vampyre* by John William Polidori, published by Sherwood, Neely, and Jones, London.

slightly, ever so politely. Had someone somewhere in her past use these words offensively towards her. The words could have been used offensively to deeply hurt her; the words could have been used offensively to aggressively attack her. Now, being offensive, in either manner, is the shame of any gentlemen worth his salt. I did not intend to slur her or her people with terms that may be, in her language, slurs. To me these are merely words that would be translated in 'vamypre', but with the word 'vampyre' in English is inoffensive. Instead it is seductive, not suggestive. *Vroucolocha, Vardoulacha, Goul, Broucoloka* could carry within themselves the very offence I did not intend. And if she had taken offence, then as gentleman I would gladly accept her long glove across the cheek. A single tear, overflowed her eye and with my finger, I wiped it away and apologized. My beliefs on what a vampyre is are coloured by being British, while hers are stained with the blood of her countrymen. I would not stand on a colonial soapbox to scold her for her beliefs. The bright light of modernity cannot always— and perhaps should not— pierce the darkness of superstition. The gaslights of modern London expose what lurks in our civilized shadows to be mere foolishness. What lurks in their rural shadows may be truly ghoulishness.

Back in our room, surrounding by the opulence of the aristocratic class, Erzsébet cajoled me, not with sweet words to inspire an author's creativity, but with cruel words: 'I do not believe such a story could be told. Vampyres are hideous, odious creatures risen from the grave where they continue to rot. They cannot walk in the society of men. Even if they had been learned in life, that learning has decayed into mindlessness. This Lord Ruthven, whom you speak of, cannot be a suave and sophisticated English nobleman. Ha!' she laughed in my face. 'Even if a Count from my own homeland had risen as a vampyre, he would retain none of the aristocratic gifts. He may attempt to mimic them, but they would be a pale shade of his former self. This story cannot be written.'

And with that, I seized pen in hand and would write my story!

Lord Byron's Diary

11 July 1816. My beloved Erzsébet came down from her apartment in the attic (she did not complain of her placement there but instead insisted because there were few windows to disturb her slumber during the bright light of the day) just as the sun was setting over the mountains to the west of the lake. Sleep had always does wonders for her complexion. A proper Englishwoman would moisturize and condition her skill with cold creams, rose water, glycerin and cucumber in queer mysterious feminine beauty rituals; women tend to keep their beauty secrets not unlike a secret society from which most men are excluded. As for me, women tend to tell me their deepest, darkest secrets without ever meaning to or realizing they have, because they do not see me as a threat. Is it because we share the same taste in men? Perhaps! As for the countess, I know not what mysterious foreign products Erzsébet uses to keep her skin so porcelain white and so rosy of cheek and so crimson lipped. The countess' regimen for beauty is unmatched in all the Continent. But I am too afraid of her sharp tongue to ever inquire, lest that tongue cut me to the bone.

Mary and Percy had retired to their apartment early, far too early for them, for Mary had woken in the morning deathly pale and in desperate need of red wine and redder meat, even for breakfast. We had been mourning (my sarcasm is positively dripping) the sudden disappearance of Dr Pollydolly. Over the past month, he often spoke of the Countess Gräfin Potocka and often pondered her whereabouts. Like a besotted schoolboy. Perhaps, he received a letter from her and jaunted off on some tour of the region with her. I know no clue and no desire to know his whereabouts. And as for Claire, she was holed up in her own apartment. Perhaps she too had come down with a foul sickness. Namely pregnancy! Thankfully, the evening at the Villa Diodati was now reserved for Erzsébet and me.

Erzsébet seemed to exist only in my presence for when she appeared she is my companion, but must have encountered Dr Pollydolly during her brief stay. This night she speaks endlessly of theft and thievery. 'It is a curious link between *The Tempest*, *Love's Labour's Lost*, and *A Midsummer Night's Dream* that these are the three plays, out of thirty-nine, where Shakespeare does not follow a primary source. Even *The Merry Wives of Windsor*, which has no definite source, takes a clear starting point from Ovid. The Tempest is essentially plotless, and almost nothing happens in *Love's Labour's Lost*, but Shakespeare uniquely took pains to work out a fairly elaborate and outrageous plot for *A Midsummer Night's Dream*. Inventing plot was not a Shakespearean gift; it was the one dramatic talent that nature had denied him.[32]'

She was goading me into an argument. The Bard is held sacrosanct amongst English poets, whom I count myself a member, and the Drury Lane Theatre, of which I am a board member. William Shakespeare is held in the highest regard by not only thespians but poets as well. Every actor would give his eye teeth to play Romeo as a youth, Hamlet as a man, and King Lear when aged. Just as every poet strives to have their poetry resonate with the ferocity with words now two centuries old!

---

32 From *Shakespeare: The Invention of the Human* by Harold Bloom, published by Riverhead Books, 1998

Will my own poems be remembered, read, and recited at the turn of the millennium? A poet only can hope.

'Need I speak of his endless theft and thievery of Raphael Holinshed's *Chronicles*?', she continued.

Oh ho! Oh no!

I. Will. Not. Be. Goaded. Into. An. Argument.

19 July 1816. I write these words in the small hours, confused and confounded. I hold in my hands pages written by my personal physician, Dr Pollydolly, their having been in my possession for a week. They were exquisite, gilded stationary torn from a journal. How did a poor physician come into possession of such finery? The pages have been wrinkled by my firm raging grip. My dearest Erzsébet, upon her escape from the prison, which is the Villa Diodati, handed me the hand-written pages. I recognized the handwriting instantly from its physician scrawl. Dr Pollydolly had written her something. A love letter? A confession? Worse! Was this the plagiarizing she spoke of? While John was off on his weekend-long jaunt, she whispered paranoias of plagiarism in my ear! And now that pages were in my hand, I know not her intentions! I read the words, though I had some difficult deciphering his scrawl. Erzsébet, in her cruelty, sought to instigate a brawl between two friends. But were we friends? I did not know. I could not know. As I finished reading, in my utter exhaustion, my firm grip on the pages loosened and the fell cascading to the floor. What were his intentions writing this story?

Mary Wollstonecraft Godwin's Journal

20 June. My Beloved had set the first piece of our luggage in the foyer. We planned to set out at first light for the nearby glacier we had had our hearts set on visiting all this this cruel, wet summer. The night had once again fallen faster than we expected having wiled away the evening packing our suitcases. The thunder continued its continuous cracking, but we would not find ourselves backtracking from our planned holiday to the glacier. No amount of storming could dissuade us from our intended weeklong expedition. The carriage had been commissioned with the horses pulling up at the cresting of the dawn. Our room in Hotel de Ville de Londres, itself situated at the foot of the glacier, had been rented in preparation for our arrival. However, Lord Bryon rapped upon our chamber door intent on persuading us for one more evening of ghost stories in our long, drawn out game. My own ghost of Dr Victor Frankenstein had gone quite queerly silent for countless long agonizing nights. I had become accustomed to his discussing his life with me. He no longer visits me in the small hours while my Beloved slumbers beside me. I want nothing more than to know more of the lumbering Creature he has created. My lust for his autobiography could not be sated. I hoped he could, by his preternatural nature, shadow our journey to visit me at the Hotel de Ville de Londres. I even left a note on the nightstand telling my dear Victor of our destination.

Lord Bryon stood before the hearth in the parlour holding ink-stained pages. In his eyes, the firelight blazed. There was no hint of authorly pride dancing in his eyes. Instead, I saw rage roiling. The veins on the backs on his hands boiled with hot blood as his fingers crunched the sheets of paper in his clinched fist. But his fists were not only clinched, but his teeth clenched as well. What manner of ghost story had he conjured to produce such fury. Clearly, I was no longer sure I wished to experience such a ghost of a story. Whatever spirit in-spired this work was a foul fiend and I did not wish to be bedeviled on the eve of our holiday to the glacier.

And speaking of our holiday, my Beloved waltzed in from the foyer having set down the last of our luggage to take his customary chair. Poor Polidori sat beaming at his dearest friend as he prepared to con-tinue our game. Lord Byron held out the pages to poor Polidori, who gracefully, but cautiously accepted the gift. The blood drained from his face and his fingers faltered to force a firm grasp on the pages. From my own seat, I did not recognize the little Lord's exquisite penmanship. The handwriting had the prevailing scrawl of a physician. Had the doc-tor written this particular, now peculiar, ghost story? Our little Lord had stepped towards the poor doctor and slowly, achingly, reached be-hind his back. Was there something concealed in his belt? I caught the gaze of my Beloved as the fire blazed and his eyes widened with genuine fear as he watched our little Lord retrieve a pistol from his belt at the small of his back. Byron's breath seethed in the cool night air, hot with smoke-like puffs. He pressed the barrel of the pistol into poor Polidori's temple. The cool steel could quickly become seeringly hot. Byron's hand did not tremble in the slightest, but held the pistol with a steeled grip. 'Read,' Lord Byron said, enunciating the single syllable with the intensity of a Catholic priest transubstantiating bread and wine into the Body and Blood of Jesus the Christ.

'What?' poor Polidori inquired, but the Lord no longer required Polidori to understand. He instead clicked back the hammer on the flintlock.

'Read.'

Poor Polidori pleaded, 'Why?'

'Read,' Lord Byron said. 'Or die!'

'Wh-what?'

'Confess your crime. I require no poetry nor rhymes. We are all writers seated here in the parlour, surrounding by books. Books, Polidori. The sacred scriptures of our profession. The ghosts of these authors haunt this very room. Had we not conjured our game of ghost stories... in this very room? Were we not so bored that I read from a poorly written translated book of poorly written German ghost stories? Had I not been the first to continue to the game? My dearest Shelley himself refused to play, while Claire has chosen not to share hers and, despite our constant cruel and keen mockery, Mary has surpassed us all with the creativity of her Creation. But you, my dear doctor, have chosen to commit the gravest sin of our chosen profession. You may not have stolen my words, but you have stolen into my very words. You have taken what was never yours. Ms. Mary's queerest doctor may have the stolen corpse of a man, one society left abandoned in death, and utilizing forbidden scientific practices reanimated it into an abomination of science, but you, my dearest doctor, have taken the corpse of my story, one that I left abandoned in death, and utilizing forbidden literary techniques reanimated it into an abomination of literature.'

'Lord Byron, let me explain.'

'Read your ghost story.'

Now, Lord Byron's finger trembled upon the trigger with the boiling of his pulse. Not the condition one wishes to possess next to a trigger designed retract with the slightest pressure and react with lethal intensity.

Poor Polidori gulped down the phlegm that had, no doubt, pooled at the top of his gullet. 'It happened that in the midst of the dissipations attendant upon a London winter, there appeared at the various parties of the leaders of the ton a nobleman, more remarkable for his singularities, than his rank. He gazed upon the mirth around him, as if he could not participate therein. Apparently, the light laughter of the fair only attracted his attention, that he might by a look quell it, and throw fear into those breasts where thoughtlessness reigned. Those who felt this sensation of awe, could not explain whence it arose: some attributed it to the dead grey eye, which, fixing upon the object's face, did not seem to penetrate, and at one glance to pierce through to the inward workings of the heart; but fell upon the cheek with a leaden ray that weighed upon the skin it could not pass. His peculiarities caused him to be invited to every house; all wished to see him, and those who had been accustomed to violent excitement, and now felt the weight of ennui, were pleased at having something in their presence capable of engaging their attention. In spite of the deadly hue of his face, which never gained a warmer tint, either from the blush of modesty, or from the strong emotion of passion, though its form and outline were beautiful, many of the female hunters after notoriety attempted to win his attentions, and gain, at least, some marks of what they might term affection: Lady Mercer, who had been the mockery of every monster shewn in drawing-rooms since her marriage, threw herself in his way, and did all but put on the dress of a mountebank, to attract his notice:— though in vain:— when she stood before him, though his eyes were apparently fixed upon her's, still it seemed as if they were unperceived;— even her unappalled impudence was baffled, and she left the field. But though the common adultress could not influence even the guidance of his eyes, it was not that the female sex was indifferent to him: yet such was the apparent caution with which he spoke to the virtuous wife and innocent daughter, that few knew he ever addressed himself to females. He had, however, the reputation of a winning tongue; and whether it was that it even overcame the dread of his singular character, or that they were moved by his apparent hatred of vice, he was as often among those females who form the boast of their sex from their domestic virtues, as among those who sully it by their vices.

'About the same time, there came to London a young gentleman of the name of Aubrey: he was an orphan left with an only sister in the possession of great wealth, by parents who died while he was yet in childhood. Left also to himself by guardians, who thought it their duty merely to take care of his fortune, while they relinquished the more important charge of his mind to the care of mercenary subalterns, he cultivated more his imagination than his judgment. He had, hence, that high romantic feeling of honour and candour, which daily ruins so many milliners' apprentices. He believed all to sympathise with virtue, and thought that vice was thrown in by Providence merely for the picturesque effect of the scene, as we see in romances: he thought that the misery of a cottage merely consisted in the vesting of clothes, which were as warm, but which were better adapted to the painter's eye by their irregular folds and various coloured patches. He thought, in fine, that the dreams of poets were the realities of life. He was handsome, frank, and rich: for these reasons, upon his entering into the gay circles, many mothers surrounded him, striving which should describe with least truth their languishing or romping favourites: the daughters at the same time, by their brightening countenances when he approached, and by their sparkling eyes, when he opened his lips, soon led him into false notions of his talents and his merit. Attached as he was to the romance of his solitary hours, he was startled at finding, that, except in the tallow and wax candles that flickered, not from the presence of a ghost, but from want of snuffing, there was no foundation in real life for any of that congeries of pleasing pictures and descriptions contained in those volumes, from which he had formed his study. Finding, however, some compensation in his gratified vanity, he was about to relinquish his dreams, when the extraordinary being we have above described, crossed him in his career.

'He watched him; and the very impossibility of forming an idea of the character of a man entirely absorbed in himself, who gave few other signs of his observation of external objects, than the tacit assent to their existence, implied by the avoidance of their contact: allowing his imagination to picture every thing that flattered its propensity to extravagant ideas, he soon formed this object into the hero of a romance, and determined to observe the offspring of his fancy, rather than the person before him. He became acquainted with him, paid him attentions, and so far advanced upon his notice, that his presence was always recognised. He gradually learnt that Lord Ruthven's affairs were embarrassed, and soon found, from the notes of preparation in — — Street, that he was about to travel. Desirous of gaining some information respecting this singular character, who, till now, had only whetted his curiosity, he hinted to his guardians, that it was time for him to perform the tour, which for many generations has been thought necessary to enable the young to take some rapid steps in the career of vice towards putting themselves upon an equality with the aged, and not allowing them to appear as if fallen from the skies, whenever scandalous intrigues are mentioned as the subjects of pleasantry or of praise, according to the degree of skill shewn in carrying them on. They consented: and Aubrey immediately mentioning his intentions to Lord Ruthven, was surprised to receive from him a proposal to join him. Flattered by such a mark of esteem from him, who, apparently, had nothing in common with other men, he gladly accepted it, and in a few days they had passed the circling waters.

'Hitherto, Aubrey had had no opportunity of studying Lord Ruthven's character, and now he found, that, though many more of his actions were exposed to his view, the results offered different conclusions from the apparent motives to his conduct. His companion was profuse in his liberality;— the idle, the vagabond, and the beggar, received from his hand more than enough to relieve their immediate wants. But Aubrey could not avoid remarking, that it was not upon the virtuous, reduced to indigence by the misfortunes attendant even upon virtue, that he bestowed his alms;— these were sent from the door with hardly suppressed sneers; but when the profligate came to ask something, not to relieve his wants, but to allow him to wallow in his lust, or to sink him still deeper in his iniquity, he was sent away with rich charity. This was, however, attributed by him to the greater importunity of the vicious, which generally prevails over the retiring bashfulness of the virtuous indigent. There was one circumstance about the charity of his Lordship, which was still more impressed upon his mind: all those upon whom it was bestowed, inevitably found that there was a curse upon it, for they were all either led to the scaffold, or sunk to the lowest and the most abject misery. At Brussels and other towns through which they passed, Aubrey was surprized at the apparent eagerness with which his companion sought for the centres of all fashionable vice; there he entered into all the spirit of the faro table: he betted, and always gambled with success, except where the known sharper was his antagonist, and then he lost even more than he gained; but it was always with the same unchanging face, with which he generally watched the society around: it was not, however, so when he encountered the rash youthful novice, or the luckless father of a numerous family; then his very wish seemed fortune's law— this apparent abstractedness of mind was laid aside, and his eyes sparkled with more fire than that of the cat whilst dallying with the half-dead mouse. In every town, he left the formerly affluent youth, torn from the circle he adorned, cursing, in the solitude of a dungeon, the fate that had drawn him within the reach of this fiend; whilst many a father sat frantic, amidst the speaking looks of mute hungry children, without a single farthing of his late immense wealth, wherewith to buy even sufficient to satisfy their present craving. Yet he took no money from the gambling table; but immediately lost, to the ruiner of many, the last gilder he had just snatched from the convulsive grasp of the innocent: this might but be the result of a certain degree of knowledge, which was not, however, capable of combating the cunning of the more experienced. Aubrey often wished to represent this to his friend, and beg him to resign that charity and pleasure which proved the ruin of all, and did not tend to his own profit;— but he delayed it— for each day he hoped his friend would give him some opportunity of speaking frankly and openly to him; however, this never occurred. Lord Ruthven in his carriage, and amidst the various wild and rich scenes of nature, was always the same: his eye spoke less than his lip; and though Aubrey was near the object of his curiosity, he obtained no greater gratification from it than the constant excitement of vainly wishing to break that mystery, which to his exalted imagination began to assume the appearance of something supernatural.

They soon arrived at Rome, and Aubrey for a time lost sight of his companion; he left him in daily attendance upon the morning circle of an Italian countess, whilst he went in search of the memorials of another almost deserted city. Whilst he was thus engaged, letters arrived from England, which he opened with eager impatience; the first was from his sister, breathing nothing but affection; the others were from his guardians, the latter astonished him; if it had before entered into his imagination that there was an evil power resident in his companion, these seemed to give him sufficient reason for the belief. His guardians insisted upon his immediately leaving his friend, and urged, that his character was dreadfully vicious, for that the possession of irresistible powers of seduction, rendered his licentious habits more dangerous to society. It had been discovered, that his contempt for the adultress had not originated in hatred of her character; but that he had required, to enhance his gratification, that his victim, the partner of his guilt, should be hurled from the pinnacle of unsullied virtue, down to the lowest abyss of infamy and degradation: in fine, that all those females whom he had sought, apparently on account of their virtue, had, since his departure, thrown even the mask aside, and had not scrupled to expose the whole deformity of their vices to the public gaze.

'Aubrey determined upon leaving one, whose character had not yet shown a single bright point on which to rest the eye. He resolved to invent some plausible pretext for abandoning him altogether, purposing, in the mean while, to watch him more closely, and to let no slight circumstances pass by unnoticed. He entered into the same circle, and soon perceived, that his Lordship was endeavouring to work upon the inexperience of the daughter of the lady whose house he chiefly frequented. In Italy, it is seldom that an unmarried female is met with in society; he was therefore obliged to carry on his plans in secret; but Aubrey's eye followed him in all his windings, and soon discovered that an assignation had been appointed, which would most likely end in the ruin of an innocent, though thoughtless girl. Losing no time, he entered the apartment of Lord Ruthven, and abruptly asked him his intentions with respect to the lady, informing him at the same time that he was aware of his being about to meet her that very night. Lord Ruthven answered, that his intentions were such as he supposed all would have upon such an occasion; and upon being pressed whether he intended to marry her, merely laughed. Aubrey retired; and, immediately writing a note, to say, that from that moment he must decline accompanying his Lordship in the remainder of their proposed tour, he ordered his servant to seek other apartments, and calling upon the mother of the lady, informed her of all he knew, not only with regard to her daughter, but also concerning the character of his Lordship. The assignation was prevented. Lord Ruthven next day merely sent his servant to notify his complete assent to a separation; but did not hint any suspicion of his plans having been foiled by Aubrey's interposition.

'Having left Rome, Aubrey directed his steps towards Greece, and crossing the Peninsula, soon found himself at Athens. He then fixed his residence in the house of a Greek; and soon occupied himself in tracing the faded records of ancient glory upon monuments that apparently, ashamed of chronicling the deeds of freemen only before slaves, had hidden themselves beneath the sheltering soil or many coloured lichen. Under the same roof as himself, existed a being, so beautiful and delicate, that she might have formed the model for a painter wishing to pourtray on canvass the promised hope of the faithful in Mahomet's paradise, save that her eyes spoke too much mind for any one to think she could belong to those who had no souls. As she danced upon the plain, or tripped along the mountain's side, one would have thought the gazelle a poor type of her beauties; for who would have exchanged her eye, apparently the eye of animated nature, for that sleepy luxurious look of the animal suited but to the taste of an epicure. The light step of Ianthe often accompanied Aubrey in his search after antiquities, and often would the unconscious girl, engaged in the pursuit of a Kashmere butterfly, show the whole beauty of her form, floating as it were upon the wind, to the eager gaze of him, who forgot the letters he had just decyphered upon an almost effaced tablet, in the contemplation of her sylph-like figure. Often would her tresses falling, as she flitted around, exhibit in the sun's ray such delicately brilliant and swiftly fading hues, it might well excuse the forgetfulness of the antiquary, who let escape from his mind the very object he had before thought of vital importance to the proper interpretation of a passage in Pausanias. But why attempt to describe charms which all feel, but none can appreciate?— It was innocence, youth, and beauty, unaffected by crowded drawing-rooms and stifling balls. Whilst he drew those remains of which he wished to preserve a memorial for his future hours, she would stand by, and watch the magic effects of his pencil, in tracing the scenes of her native place; she would then describe to him the circling dance upon the open plain, would paint, to him in all the glowing colours of youthful memory, the marriage pomp she remembered viewing in her infancy; and then, turning to subjects that had evidently made a greater impression upon her mind, would tell him all the supernatural tales of her nurse. Her earnestness and apparent belief of what she narrated, excited the interest even of Aubrey; and often as she told him the tale of the living vampyre, who had passed years amidst his friends, and dearest ties, forced every year, by feeding upon the life of a lovely female to prolong his existence for the ensuing months, his blood would run cold, whilst he attempted to laugh her out of such idle and horrible fantasies; but Ianthe cited to him the names of old men, who had at last detected one living among themselves, after several of their near relatives and children had been found marked with the stamp of the fiend's appetite; and when she found him so incredulous, she begged of him to believe her, for it had been, remarked, that those who had dared to question their existence, always had some proof given, which obliged them, with grief and heartbreaking, to confess it was true. She detailed to him the traditional appearance of these monsters, and his horror was increased, by hearing a pretty accurate description of Lord Ruthven; he, however, still persisted in persuading her, that there could be no truth in her fears, though at the same time he wondered at the many coincidences which had all tended to excite a belief in the supernatural power of Lord Ruthven.

'Aubrey began to attach himself more and more to Ianthe; her innocence, so contrasted with all the affected virtues of the women among whom he had sought for his vision of romance, won his heart; and while he ridiculed the idea of a young man of English habits, marrying an uneducated Greek girl, still he found himself more and more attached to the almost fairy form before him. He would tear himself at times from her, and, forming a plan for some antiquarian research, he would depart, determined not to return until his object was attained; but he always found it impossible to fix his attention upon the ruins around him, whilst in his mind he retained an image that seemed alone the rightful possessor of his thoughts. Ianthe was unconscious of his love, and was ever the same frank infantile being he had first known. She always seemed to part from him with reluctance; but it was because she had no longer any one with whom she could visit her favourite haunts, whilst her guardian was occupied in sketching or uncovering some fragment which had yet escaped the destructive hand of time. She had appealed to her parents on the subject of Vampyres, and they both, with several present, affirmed their existence, pale with horror at the very name. Soon after, Aubrey determined to proceed upon one of his excursions, which was to detain him for a few hours; when they heard the name of the place, they all at once begged of him not to return at night, as he must necessarily pass through a wood, where no Greek would ever remain, after the day had closed, upon any consideration. They described it as the resort of the vampyres in their nocturnal orgies, and denounced the most heavy evils as impending upon him who dared to cross their path. Aubrey made light of their representations, and tried to laugh them out of the idea; but when he saw them shudder at his daring thus to mock a superior, infernal power, the very name of which apparently made their blood freeze, he was silent.

'Next morning Aubrey set off upon his excursion unattended; he was surprised to observe the melancholy face of his host, and was concerned to find that his words, mocking the belief of those horrible fiends, had inspired them with such terror. When he was about to depart, Ianthe came to the side of his horse, and earnestly begged of him to return, ere night allowed the power of these beings to be put in action;— he promised. He was, however, so occupied in his research, that he did not perceive that day-light would soon end, and that in the horizon there was one of those specks which, in the warmer climates, so rapidly gather into a tremendous mass, and pour all their rage upon the devoted country.— He at last, however, mounted his horse, determined to make up by speed for his delay: but it was too late. Twilight, in these southern climates, is almost unknown; immediately the sun sets, night begins: and ere he had advanced far, the power of the storm was above— its echoing thunders had scarcely an interval of rest— its thick heavy rain forced its way through the canopying foliage, whilst the blue forked lightning seemed to fall and radiate at his very feet. Suddenly his horse took fright, and he was carried with dreadful rapidity through the entangled forest. The animal at last, through fatigue, stopped, and he found, by the glare of lightning, that he was in the neighbourhood of a hovel that hardly lifted itself up from the masses of dead leaves and brushwood which surrounded it. Dismounting, he approached, hoping to find some one to guide him to the town, or at least trusting to obtain shelter from the pelting of the storm. As he approached, the thunders, for a moment silent, allowed him to hear the dreadful shrieks of a woman mingling with the stifled, exultant mockery of a laugh, continued in one almost unbroken sound;— he was startled: but, roused by the thunder which again rolled over his head, he, with a sudden effort, forced open the door of the hut. He found himself in utter darkness: the sound, however, guided him. He was apparently unperceived; for, though he called, still the sounds continued, and no notice was taken of him. He found himself in contact with some one, whom he immediately seized; when a voice cried, "Again baffled!" to which a loud laugh succeeded; and he felt himself grappled by one whose strength seemed superhuman: determined to sell his life as dearly as he could, he struggled; but it was in vain: he was lifted from his feet and hurled with enormous force against the ground:— his enemy threw himself upon him, and kneeling upon his breast, had placed his hands upon his throat— when the glare of many torches penetrating through the hole that gave light in the day, disturbed him;— he instantly rose, and, leaving his prey, rushed through the door, and in a moment the crashing of the branches, as he broke through the wood, was no longer heard. The storm was now still; and Aubrey, incapable of moving, was soon heard by those without. They entered; the light of their torches fell upon the mud walls, and the thatch loaded on every individual straw with heavy flakes of soot. At the desire of Aubrey they searched for her who had attracted him by her cries; he was again left in darkness; but what was his horror, when the light of the torches once more burst upon him, to perceive the airy form of his fair conductress brought in a lifeless corse. He shut his eyes, hoping that it was but a vision arising from his disturbed imagination; but he again saw the same form, when he unclosed them, stretched by his side. There was no colour upon her cheek, not even upon her lip; yet there was a stillness about her face that seemed almost as attaching as the life that once dwelt there:— upon her neck and breast was blood, and upon her throat were the marks of teeth having opened the vein:— to this the men pointed, crying, simultaneously struck with horror, "A Vampyre! a Vampyre!" A litter was quickly formed, and Aubrey was laid by the side of her who had lately been to him the object of so many bright and fairy visions, now fallen with the flower of life that had died within her. He knew not what his thoughts were— his mind was benumbed and seemed to shun reflection, and take refuge in vacancy— he held almost unconsciously in his hand a naked dagger of a particular construction, which had been found in the hut. They were soon met by different parties who had been engaged in the search of her whom a mother had missed. Their lamentable cries, as they approached the city, forewarned the parents of some dreadful catastrophe. — To describe their grief would be impossible; but when they ascertained the cause of their child's death, they looked at Aubrey, and pointed to the corse. They were inconsolable; both died broken-hearted.

'Aubrey being put to bed was seized with a most violent fever, and was often delirious; in these intervals he would call upon Lord Ruthven and upon Ianthe— by some unaccountable combination he seemed to beg of his former companion to spare the being he loved. At other times he would imprecate maledictions upon his head, and curse him as her destroyer. Lord Ruthven, chanced at this time to arrive at Athens, and, from whatever motive, upon hearing of the state of Aubrey, immediately placed himself in the same house, and became his constant attendant. When the latter recovered from his delirium, he was horrified and startled at the sight of him whose image he had now combined with that of a Vampyre; but Lord Ruthven, by his kind words, implying almost repentance for the fault that had caused their separation, and still more by the attention, anxiety, and care which he showed, soon reconciled him to his presence. His lordship seemed quite changed; he no longer appeared that apathetic being who had so astonished Aubrey; but as soon as his convalescence began to be rapid, he again gradually retired into the same state of mind, and Aubrey perceived no difference from the former man, except that at times he was surprised to meet his gaze fixed intently upon him, with a smile of malicious exultation playing upon his lips: he knew not why, but this smile haunted him. During the last stage of the invalid's recovery, Lord Ruthven was apparently engaged in watching the tideless waves raised by the cooling breeze, or in marking the progress of those orbs, circling, like our world, the moveless sun;— indeed, he appeared to wish to avoid the eyes of all.

'Aubrey's mind, by this shock, was much weakened, and that elasticity of spirit which had once so distinguished him now seemed to have fled for ever. He was now as much a lover of solitude and silence as Lord Ruthven; but much as he wished for solitude, his mind could not find it in the neighbourhood of Athens; if he sought it amidst the ruins he had formerly frequented, Ianthe's form stood by his side— if he sought it in the woods, her light step would appear wandering amidst the underwood, in quest of the modest violet; then suddenly turning round, would show, to his wild imagination, her pale face and wounded throat, with a meek smile upon her lips. He determined to fly scenes, every feature of which created such bitter associations in his mind. He proposed to Lord Ruthven, to whom he held himself bound by the tender care he had taken of him during his illness, that they should visit those parts of Greece neither had yet seen. They travelled in every direction, and sought every spot to which a recollection could be attached: but though they thus hastened from place to place, yet they seemed not to heed what they gazed upon. They heard much of robbers, but they gradually began to slight these reports, which they imagined were only the invention of individuals, whose interest it was to excite the generosity of those whom they defended from pretended dangers. In consequence of thus neglecting the advice of the inhabitants, on one occasion they travelled with only a few guards, more to serve as guides than as a defence. Upon entering, however, a narrow defile, at the bottom of which was the bed of a torrent, with large masses of rock brought down from the neighbouring precipices, they had reason to repent their negligence; for scarcely were the whole of the party engaged in the narrow pass, when they were startled by the whistling of bullets close to their heads, and by the echoed report of several guns. In an instant their guards had left them, and, placing themselves behind rocks, had begun to fire in the direction whence the report came. Lord Ruthven and Aubrey, imitating their example, retired for a moment behind the sheltering turn of the defile: but ashamed of being thus detained by a foe, who with insulting shouts bade them advance, and being exposed to unresisting slaughter, if any of the robbers should climb above and take them in the rear, they determined at once to rush forward in search of the enemy. Hardly had they lost the shelter of the rock, when Lord Ruthven received a shot in the shoulder, which brought him to the ground. Aubrey hastened to his assistance; and, no longer heeding the contest or his own peril, was soon surprised by seeing the robbers' faces around him— his guards having, upon Lord Ruthven's being wounded, immediately thrown up their arms and surrendered.

'By promises of great reward, Aubrey soon induced them to convey his wounded friend to a neighbouring cabin; and having agreed upon a ransom, he was no more disturbed by their presence— they being content merely to guard the entrance till their comrade should return with the promised sum, for which he had an order. Lord Ruthven's strength rapidly decreased; in two days mortification ensued, and death seemed advancing with hasty steps. His conduct and appearance had not changed; he seemed as unconscious of pain as he had been of the objects about him: but towards the close of the last evening, his mind became apparently uneasy, and his eye often fixed upon Aubrey, who was induced to offer his assistance with more than usual earnestness— "Assist me! you may save me— you may do more than that— I mean not my life, I heed the death of my existence as little as that of the passing day; but you may save my honour, your friend's honour."— "How? tell me how? I would do any thing," replied Aubrey.— "I need but little— my life ebbs apace— I cannot explain the whole— but if you would conceal all you know of me, my honour were free from stain in the world's mouth— and if my death were unknown for some time in England— I— I— but life."— "It shall not be known."— "Swear!" cried the dying man, raising himself with exultant violence, "Swear by all your soul reveres, by all your nature fears, swear that, for a year and a day you will not impart your knowledge of my crimes or death to any living being in any way, whatever may happen, or whatever you may see. "— His eyes seemed bursting from their sockets: "I swear!" said Aubrey; he sunk laughing upon his pillow, and breathed no more.

'Aubrey retired to rest, but did not sleep; the many circumstances attending his acquaintance with this man rose upon his mind, and he knew not why; when he remembered his oath a cold shivering came over him, as if from the presentiment of something horrible awaiting him. Rising early in the morning, he was about to enter the hovel in which he had left the corpse, when a robber met him, and informed him that it was no longer there, having been conveyed by himself and comrades, upon his retiring, to the pinnacle of a neighbouring mount, according to a promise they had given his lordship, that it should be exposed to the first cold ray of the moon that rose after his death. Aubrey astonished, and taking several of the men, determined to go and bury it upon the spot where it lay. But, when he had mounted to the summit he found no trace of either the corpse or the clothes, though the robbers swore they pointed out the identical rock on which they had laid the body. For a time his mind was bewildered in conjectures, but he at last returned, convinced that they had buried the corpse for the sake of the clothes.

'Weary of a country in which he had met with such terrible misfortunes, and in which all apparently conspired to heighten that superstitious melancholy that had seized upon his mind, he resolved to leave it, and soon arrived at Smyrna. While waiting for a vessel to convey him to Otranto, or to Naples, he occupied himself in arranging those effects he had with him belonging to Lord Ruthven. Amongst other things there was a case containing several weapons of offence, more or less adapted to ensure the death of the victim. There were several daggers and ataghans. Whilst turning them over, and examining their curious forms, what was his surprise at finding a sheath apparently ornamented in the same style as the dagger discovered in the fatal hut— he shuddered— hastening to gain further proof, he found the weapon, and his horror may be imagined when he discovered that it fitted, though peculiarly shaped, the sheath he held in his hand. His eyes seemed to need no further certainty— they seemed gazing to be bound to the dagger; yet still he wished to disbelieve; but the particular form, the same varying tints upon the haft and sheath were alike in splendour on both, and left no room for doubt; there were also drops of blood on each.

'He left Smyrna, and on his way home, at Rome, his first inquiries were concerning the lady he had attempted to snatch from Lord Ruthven's seductive arts. Her parents were in distress, their fortune ruined, and she had not been heard of since the departure of his lordship. Aubrey's mind became almost broken under so many repeated horrors; he was afraid that this lady had fallen a victim to the destroyer of Ianthe. He became morose and silent; and his only occupation consisted in urging the speed of the postilions, as if he were going to save the life of some one he held dear. He arrived at Calais; a breeze, which seemed obedient to his will, soon wafted him to the English shores; and he hastened to the mansion of his fathers, and there, for a moment, appeared to lose, in the embraces and caresses of his sister, all memory of the past. If she before, by her infantine caresses, had gained his affection, now that the woman began to appear, she was still more attaching as a companion.

'Miss Aubrey had not that winning grace which gains the gaze and applause of the drawing-room assemblies. There was none of that light brilliancy which only exists in the heated atmosphere of a crowded apartment. Her blue eye was never lit up by the levity of the mind beneath. There was a melancholy charm about it which did not seem to arise from misfortune, but from some feeling within, that appeared to indicate a soul conscious of a brighter realm. Her step was not that light footing,

which strays where'er a butterfly or a colour may attract— it was sedate
and pensive. When alone, her face was never brightened by the smile
of joy; but when her brother breathed to her his affection, and would
in her presence forget those griefs she knew destroyed his rest, who
would have exchanged her smile for that of the voluptuary? It seemed
as if those eyes,— that face were then playing in the light of their own
native sphere. She was yet only eighteen, and had not been presented to
the world, it having been thought by her guardians more fit that her presentation should be delayed until her brother's return from the continent,
when he might be her protector. It was now, therefore, resolved that the
next drawing-room, which was fast approaching, should be the epoch of
her entry into the "busy scene." Aubrey would rather have remained in
the mansion of his fathers, and fed upon the melancholy which overpowered him. He could not feel interest about the frivolities of fashionable
strangers, when his mind had been so torn by the events he had witnessed; but he determined to sacrifice his own comfort to the protection
of his sister. They soon arrived in town, and prepared for the next day,
which had been announced as a drawing-room.

The crowd was excessive— a drawing-room had not been held for
a long time, and all who were anxious to bask in the smile of royalty,
hastened thither. Aubrey was there with his sister. While he was standing in a corner by himself, heedless of all around him, engaged in the
remembrance that the first time he had seen Lord Ruthven was in that
very place— he felt himself suddenly seized by the arm, and a voice he
recognized too well, sounded in his ear— "Remember your oath." He
had hardly courage to turn, fearful of seeing a spectre that would blast
him, when he perceived, at a little distance, the same figure which had
attracted his notice on this spot upon his first entry into society. He gazed
till his limbs almost refusing to bear their weight, he was obliged to take
the arm of a friend, and forcing a passage through the crowd, he threw
himself into his carriage, and was driven home. He paced the room with
hurried steps, and fixed his hands upon his head, as if he were afraid
his thoughts were bursting from his brain. Lord Ruthven again before
him— circumstances started up in dreadful array— the dagger— his
oath.— He roused himself, he could not believe it possible— the dead
rise again!— He thought his imagination had conjured up the image his
mind was resting upon. It was impossible that it could be real— he determined, therefore, to go again into society; for though he attempted to
ask concerning Lord Ruthven, the name hung upon his lips, and he could
not succeed in gaining information. He went a few nights after with his
sister to the assembly of a near relation. Leaving her under the protection of a matron, he retired into a recess, and there gave himself up to his

own devouring thoughts. Perceiving, at last, that many were leaving, he roused himself, and entering another room, found his sister surrounded by several, apparently in earnest conversation; he attempted to pass and get near her, when one, whom he requested to move, turned round, and revealed to him those features he most abhorred. He sprang forward, seized his sister's arm, and, with hurried step, forced her towards the street: at the door he found himself impeded by the crowd of servants who were waiting for their lords; and while he was engaged in passing them, he again heard that voice whisper close to him— "Remember your oath!"— He did not dare to turn, but, hurrying his sister, soon reached home.

'Aubrey became almost distracted. If before his mind had been absorbed by one subject, how much more completely was it engrossed, now that the certainty of the monster's living again pressed upon his thoughts. His sister's attentions were now unheeded, and it was in vain that she intreated him to explain to her what had caused his abrupt conduct. He only uttered a few words, and those terrified her. The more he thought, the more he was bewildered. His oath startled him;— was he then to allow this monster to roam, bearing ruin upon his breath, amidst all he held dear, and not avert its progress? His very sister might have been touched by him. But even if he were to break his oath, and disclose his suspicions, who would believe him? He thought of employing his own hand to free the world from such a wretch; but death, he remembered, had been already mocked. For days he remained in this state; shut up in his room, he saw no one, and ate only when his sister came, who, with eyes streaming with tears, besought him, for her sake, to support nature. At last, no longer capable of bearing stillness and solitude, he left his house, roamed from street to street, anxious to fly that image which haunted him. His dress became neglected, and he wandered, as often exposed to the noon-day sun as to the midnight damps. He was no longer to be recognized; at first he returned with the evening to the house; but at last he laid him down to rest wherever fatigue overtook him. His sister, anxious for his safety, employed people to follow him; but they were soon distanced by him who fled from a pursuer swifter than any— from thought. His conduct, however, suddenly changed. Struck with the idea that he left by his absence the whole of his friends, with a fiend amongst them, of whose presence they were unconscious, he determined to enter again into society, and watch him closely, anxious to forewarn, in spite of his oath, all whom Lord Ruthven approached with intimacy. But when he entered into a room, his haggard and suspicious looks were so striking, his inward shudderings so visible, that his sister was at last obliged to beg of him to abstain from seeking, for her sake, a society which affected him so strongly. When, however, remonstrance proved unavailing, the guardians thought proper to interpose, and, fearing that his mind was becoming alienated, they thought it high time to resume again that trust which had been before imposed upon them by Aubrey's parents.

'Desirous of saving him from the injuries and sufferings he had daily encountered in his wanderings, and of preventing him from exposing to the general eye those marks of what they considered folly, they engaged a physician to reside in the house, and take constant care of him. He hardly appeared to notice it, so completely was his mind absorbed by one terrible subject. His incoherence became at last so great, that he was confined to his chamber. There he would often lie for days, incapable of being roused. He had become emaciated, his eyes had attained a glassy lustre;— the only sign of affection and recollection remaining displayed itself upon the entry of his sister; then he would sometimes start, and, seizing her hands, with looks that severely afflicted her, he would desire her not to touch him. "Oh, do not touch him— if your love for me is aught, do not go near him!" When, however, she inquired to whom he referred, his only answer was, "True! true!" and again he sank into a state, whence not even she could rouse him. This lasted many months: gradually, however, as the year was passing, his incoherences became less frequent, and his mind threw off a portion of its gloom, whilst his guardians observed, that several times in the day he would count upon his fingers a definite number, and then smile.

'The time had nearly elapsed, when, upon the last day of the year, one of his guardians entering his room, began to converse with his physician upon the melancholy circumstance of Aubrey's being in so awful a situation, when his sister was going next day to be married. Instantly Aubrey's attention was attracted; he asked anxiously to whom. Glad of this mark of returning intellect, of which they feared he had been deprived, they mentioned the name of the Earl of Marsden. Thinking this was a young Earl whom he had met with in society, Aubrey seemed pleased, and astonished them still more by his expressing his intention to be present at the nuptials, and desiring to see his sister. They answered not, but in a few minutes his sister was with him. He was apparently again capable of being affected by the influence of her lovely smile; for he pressed her to his breast, and kissed her cheek, wet with tears, flowing at the thought of her brother's being once more alive to the feelings of affection. He began to speak with all his wonted warmth, and to congratulate her upon her marriage with a person so distinguished for rank and every accomplishment; when he suddenly perceived a locket upon her breast; opening it, what was his surprise at beholding the features of the monster who had so long influenced his life. He seized the portrait in a paroxysm of rage, and trampled it under foot. Upon her asking him why he thus destroyed the resemblance of her future husband, he looked as if he did not understand her— then seizing her hands, and gazing on her with a frantic expression of countenance, he bade her swear that she would never wed this monster, for he— — But he could not advance— it seemed as if that voice again bade him remember his oath— he turned suddenly round, thinking Lord Ruthven was near him but saw no one. In the meantime the guardians and physician, who had heard the whole, and thought this was but a return of his disorder, entered, and forcing him from Miss Aubrey, desired her to leave him. He fell upon his knees to them, he implored, he begged of them to delay but for one day. They, attributing this to the insanity they imagined had taken possession of his mind, endeavoured to pacify him, and retired.

'Lord Ruthven had called the morning after the drawing-room, and had been refused with every one else. When he heard of Aubrey's ill health, he readily understood himself to be the cause of it; but when he learned that he was deemed insane, his exultation and pleasure could hardly be concealed from those among whom he had gained this information. He hastened to the house of his former companion, and, by constant attendance, and the pretence of great affection for the brother and interest in his fate, he gradually won the ear of Miss Aubrey. Who could resist his power? His tongue had dangers and toils to recount— could speak of himself as of an individual having no sympathy with any being on the crowded earth, save with her to whom he addressed himself;— could tell how, since he knew her, his existence, had begun to seem worthy of preservation, if it were merely that he might listen to her soothing accents;— in fine, he knew so well how to use the serpent's art, or such was the will of fate, that he gained her affections. The title of the elder branch falling at length to him, he obtained an important embassy, which served as an excuse for hastening the marriage, (in spite of her brother's deranged state,) which was to take place the very day before his departure for the continent.

'Aubrey, when he was left by the physician and his guardians, attempted to bribe the servants, but in vain. He asked for pen and paper; it was given him; he wrote a letter to his sister, conjuring her, as she valued her own happiness, her own honour, and the honour of those now in the grave, who once held her in their arms as their hope and the hope of their house, to delay but for a few hours that marriage, on which he denounced the most heavy curses. The servants promised they would deliver it; but giving it to the physician, he thought it better not to harass any more the mind of Miss Aubrey by, what he considered, the ravings of a maniac. Night passed on without rest to the busy inmates of the house;

and Aubrey heard, with a horror that may more easily be conceived than described, the notes of busy preparation. Morning came, and the sound of carriages broke upon his ear. Aubrey grew almost frantic. The curiosity of the servants at last overcame their vigilance, they gradually stole away, leaving him in the custody of an helpless old woman. He seized the opportunity, with one bound was out of the room, and in a moment found himself in the apartment where all were nearly assembled. Lord Ruthven was the first to perceive him: he immediately approached, and, taking his arm by force, hurried him from the room, speechless with rage. When on the staircase, Lord Ruthven whispered in his ear— "Remember your oath, and know, if not my bride to day, your sister is dishonoured. Women are frail!" So saying, he pushed him towards his attendants, who, roused by the old woman, had come in search of him. Aubrey could no longer support himself; his rage not finding vent, had broken a blood-vessel, and he was conveyed to bed. This was not mentioned to his sister, who was not present when he entered, as the physician was afraid of agitating her. The marriage was solemnized, and the bride and bridegroom left London.

'Aubrey's weakness increased; the effusion of blood produced symptoms of the near approach of death. He desired his sister's guardians might be called, and when the midnight hour had struck, he related composedly what the reader has perused— he died immediately after.

'The guardians hastened to protect Miss Aubrey; but when they arrived, it was too late. Lord Ruthven had disappeared, and Aubrey's sister had glutted the thirst of a VAMPYRE!'

Poor Polidori, the plagiarist exposed, collapsed into his chair, sweat having poured from his brow, dripping onto the now ink-smudged exquisite pages torn from a– no doubt– equally exquisite journal. Lord Byron let the pistol drop from his firm, shaking grip onto the floor below. Just as the pistol met with the rug-covered floor, a crack of thunder so loud shot off like gunfire, startling all who heard it, include dearest Claire, who fainted. My Beloved yelped, though he could not help it. And Poor Polidori cringed into his chair, lifting his legs into the foetal. This particular phase of our game of ghost stories could not be ended soon enough.

Note by John Polidori Protesting Publication of The Vampyre, 1819

The tale which lately appeared, and to which his lordship's name was wrongfully attached, was founded upon the ground-work upon which this fragment was to have been continued. Two friends were to travel from

England into Greece; while there, one of them should die, but before his death, should obtain from his friend an oath of secrecy with regard to his decease. Some short time after, the remaining traveller returning to his native country, should be startled at perceiving his former companion moving about in society, and should be horrified at finding that he made love to his former friend's sister. Upon this foundation I built the *Vampyre,* at the request of a lady, who denied the possibility of such a ground-work forming the outline of a tale which should bear the slightest appearance of probability. In the course of three mornings, I produced that tale, and left it with her. From thence it appears to have fallen into the hands of some person, who sent it to the Editor in such a way, as to leave it so doubtful from his words, whether it was his lordship's or not, that I found some difficulty in vindicating it to myself. These circumstances were stated in a letter sent to the *Morning Chronicle* three days after the publication of the tale, but in consequence of the publishers representing to me that they were compromised as well as myself, and that immediately they were certain it was mine, that they themselves would wish to make the *amende honorable* to the public, I allowed them to recall the letter which had lain some days at that paper's office. (J.W.P.) [33]

---

33 From a footnote in the Introduction to *Ernestus Berchtold; or, The Modern Oedipus: A Tale.*

Chapter Fifteen[34]
Frankenstein (Encircled in the Arctic)

P.B. Shelley Writing to Lord Byron

Chamouni, Hotel de Ville de Londres
July 22, 1816

My dear Lord Byron,

We have this moment arrived at Chamouni – the evening of the day after our departure. An opportunity chances to offer itself of sending a letter. I shall not attempt to describe to you the scenes through which we have passed. I hope soon to see in poetry the feelings with which they will inspire you.3 The Valley of the Arve (strictly speaking it extends to that of Chamouni) gradually increases in magnificence and beauty, until, at a place called Servoz, where Mont Blanc and its connected mountains limit one side of the valley, it exceeds and renders insignificant all that I had before seen, or imagined. It is not alone that these mountains are immense in size, that their forests are of so immeasurable an extent; there is grandeur in the very shapes and colours which could not fail to impress, even on a smaller scale. I write in the hope – may I say so? – that we possibly shall see you here before our return. No sooner had we entered this magnificent valley than we decided to remain several days. An avalanche fell as we entered it. We heard the thunder of its fall, and in a few minutes more the smoke of its path was visible, and a torrent which it had forced from its bed overflowed the ravine which enclosed it. I wish the wonders and graces of these 'palaces of Nature' would induce you to visit them whilst we, who so much value your society, remain yet near them. How is our little William? Is he well?

Clare sends her love to you, and Mary desires to be kindly remembered.

Yours faithfully,
P. B. Shelley.

P.S. The roads are excellent, and every facility is accumulated for the traveller. You can go as far as Sallanches in a carriage, after which, although it is possible to accomplish the rest of the journey in a *char du pays*, I would advise you, as we have done, to hire mules. A guide is not absolutely necessary, although we took one; for the road, with one insig-

---

34 From *Frankenstein; or the Modern Prometheus* by Mary Wollstonecraft Shelley, published by Lackington, Hughes, Harding, Mavor & Jones, 1818

nificant exception, is perfectly plain and good. There is apparently a very trifling ascent from Geneva to Chamouni.

P.B. Shelley Writing In Mary Wollstonecraft Godwin's Journal

ôtel de Londres, Chamouni, July 22d, 1816. Whilst you, my friend, are engaged in securing a home for us, we are wandering in search of recollections to embellish it. I do not err in conceiving that you are interested in details of all that is majestic or beautiful in nature; but how shall I describe to you the scenes by which I am now surrounded? To exhaust the epithets which express the astonishment and the admiration—the very excess of satisfied astonishment, where expectation scarcely acknowledged any boundary, is this, to impress upon your mind the images which fill mine now even till it overflow? I too have read the raptures of travellers; I will be warned by their example; I will simply detail to you all that I can relate, or all that, if related, would enable you to conceive of what we have done or seen since the morning of the 20th, when we left Geneva.

We commenced our intended journey to Chamouni at half-past eight in the morning. We passed through the champain country, which extends from Mont Salève to the base of the higher Alps. The country is sufficiently fertile, covered with corn fields and orchards, and intersected by sudden acclivities with flat summits. The day was cloudless and excessively hot, the Alps were perpetually in sight, and as we advanced, the mountains, which form their outskirts, closed in around us. We passed a bridge over a stream, which discharges itself into the Arve. The Arve itself, much swollen by the rains, flows constantly to the right of the road.

As we approached Bonneville through an avenue composed of a beautiful species of drooping poplar, we observed that the corn fields on each side were covered with inundation. Bonneville is a neat little town, with no conspicuous peculiarity, except the white towers of the prison, an extensive building overlooking the town. At Bonneville the Alps commence, one of which, clothed by forests, rises almost immediately from the opposite bank of the Arve.

From Bonneville to Cluses the road conducts through a spacious and fertile plain, surrounded on all sides by mountains, covered like those of Mellerie with forests of intermingled pine and chesnut. At Cluses the road turns suddenly to the right, following the Arve along the chasm, which it seems to have hollowed for itself among the perpendicular mountains. The scene assumes here a more savage and colossal character; the valley becomes narrow, affording no more space than is sufficient for the river and the road. The pines descend to the banks, imitating with their irregular spires, the pyramidal crags which lift themselves far above the regions of forest into the deep azure of the sky, and among the white dazzling clouds. The scene, at the distance of half a mile from Cluses, differs from that of Matlock in little else than in the immensity of its proportions, and in its untameable, inaccessible solitude, inhabited only by the goats which we saw browsing on the rocks.

Near Maglans, within a league of each other, we saw two waterfalls. They were no more than mountain rivulets, but the height from which they fell, at least of twelve hundred feet, made them assume a character inconsistent with the smallness of their stream. The first fell from the overhanging brow of a black precipice on an enormous rock, precisely resembling some colossal Egyptian statue of a female deity. It struck the head of the visionary image, and gracefully dividing there, fell from it in folds of foam more like to cloud than water, imitating a veil of the most exquisite woof. It then united, concealing the lower part of the statue, and hiding itself in a winding of its channel, burst into a deeper fall, and crossed our route in its path towards the Arve.

The other waterfall was more continuous and larger. The violence with which it fell made it look more like some shape which an exhalation had assumed, than like water, for it streamed beyond the mountain, which appeared dark behind it, as it might have appeared behind an evanescent cloud.

The character of the scenery continued the same until we arrived at St. Martin (called in the maps Sallanches) the mountains perpetually becoming more elevated, exhibiting at every turn of the road more craggy summits, loftier and wider extent of forests, darker and more deep recesses.

The following morning we proceeded from St. Martin on mules to Chamouni, accompanied by two guides. We proceeded, as we had done the preceding day, along the valley of the Arve, a valley surrounded on all sides by immense mountains, whose rugged precipices are intermixed on high with dazzling snow. Their bases were still covered with the eternal forests, which perpetually grew darker and more profound as we approached the inner regions of the mountains.

On arriving at a small village, at the distance of a league from St. Martin, we dismounted from our mules, and were conducted by our guides to view a cascade. We beheld an immense body of water fall two hundred and fifty feet, dashing from rock to rock, and casting a spray which formed a mist around it, in the midst of which hung a multitude of sunbows, which faded or became unspeakably vivid, as the inconstant sun shone through the clouds. When we approached near to it, the rain of the spray reached us, and our clothes were wetted by the quick-falling but minute particles of water. The cataract fell from above into a deep craggy chasm at our feet, where, changing its character to that of a mountain stream, it pursued its course towards the Arve, roaring over the rocks that impeded its progress.

As we proceeded, our route still lay through the valley, or rather, as it had now become, the vast ravine, which is at once the couch and the creation of the terrible Arve. We ascended, winding between mountains whose immensity staggers the imagination. We crossed the path of a torrent, which three days since had descended from the thawing snow, and torn the road away.

We dined at Servoz, a little village, where there are lead and copper mines, and where we saw a cabinet of natural curiosities, like those of Keswick and Bethgelert. We saw in this cabinet some chamois' horns, and the horns of an exceedingly rare animal called the bouquetin, which inhabits the desarts of snow to the south of Mont Blanc: it is an animal of the stag kind; its horns weigh at least twenty-seven English pounds. It is inconceivable how so small an animal could support so inordinate a weight. The horns are of a very peculiar conformation, being broad, massy, and pointed at the ends, and surrounded with a number of rings, which are supposed to afford an indication of its age: there were seventeen rings on the largest of these horns.

From Servoz three leagues remain to Chamouni.—Mont Blanc was before us—the Alps, with their innumerable glaciers on high all around, closing in the complicated windings of the single vale—forests inexpressibly beautiful, but majestic in their beauty—intermingled beech and pine, and oak, overshadowed our road, or receded, whilst lawns of such verdure as I have never seen before occupied these openings, and gradually became darker in their recesses. Mont Blanc was before us, but it was covered with cloud; its base, furrowed with dreadful gaps, was seen above. Pinnacles of snow intolerably bright, part of the chain connected with Mont Blanc, shone through the clouds at intervals on high. I never knew—I never imagined what mountains were before. The immensity of these aerial summits excited, when they suddenly burst upon the sight, a sentiment of extatic wonder, not unallied to madness. And remember this was all one scene, it all pressed home to our regard and our imagination. Though it embraced a vast extent of space, the snowy pyramids which shot into the bright blue sky seemed to overhang our path; the ravine, clothed with gigantic pines, and black with its depth below, so deep that the very roaring of the untameable Arve, which rolled through it, could not be heard above—all was as much our own, as if we had been the creators of such impressions in the minds of others as now occupied our own. Nature was the poet, whose harmony held our spirits more breathless than that of the divinest.

As we entered the valley of Chamouni (which in fact may be considered as a continuation of those which we have followed from Bonneville and Cluses) clouds hung upon the mountains at the distance perhaps of 6000 feet from the earth, but so as effectually to conceal not only Mont Blanc, but the other aiguilles, as they call them here, attached and subordinate to it. We were travelling along the valley, when suddenly we heard a sound as of the burst of smothered thunder rolling above; yet there was something earthly in the sound, that told us it could not be thunder. Our guide hastily pointed out to us a part of the mountain opposite, from whence the sound came. It was an avalanche. We saw the smoke of its path among the rocks, and continued to hear at intervals the bursting of its fall. It fell on the bed of a torrent, which it displaced, and presently we saw its tawny-coloured waters also spread themselves over the ravine, which was their couch.

We did not, as we intended, visit the Glacier de Boisson to-day, although it descends within a few minutes' walk of the road, wishing to survey it at least when unfatigued. We saw this glacier which comes close to the fertile plain, as we passed, its surface was broken into a thousand unaccountable figures: conical and pyramidical crystallizations, more than fifty feet in height, rise from its surface, and precipices of ice, of dazzling splendour, overhang the woods and meadows of the vale. This glacier winds upwards from the valley, until it joins the masses of frost from which it was produced above, winding through its own ravine like a bright belt flung over the black region of pines. There is more in all these scenes than mere magnitude of proportion: there is a majesty of outline; there is an awful grace in the very colours which invest these wonderful shapes—a charm which is peculiar to them, quite distinct even from the reality of their unutterable greatness.

I.

The everlasting universe of things
Flows through the mind, and rolls its rapid waves,
Now dark—now glittering—now reflecting gloom—
Now lending splendour, where from secret springs
The source of human thought its tribute brings
Of waters,—with a sound but half its own,
Such as a feeble brook will oft assume
In the wild woods, among the mountains lone,
Where waterfalls around it leap for ever,
Where woods and winds contend, and a vast river

Over its rocks ceaselessly bursts and raves.

II.

Thus thou, Ravine of Arve—dark, deep Ravine—
Thou many-coloured, many-voiced vale,
Over whose pines, and crags, and caverns sail
Fast cloud shadows and sunbeams: awful scene,
Where Power in likeness of the Arve comes down
From the ice gulphs that gird his secret throne,
Bursting through these dark mountains like the flame
Of lightning thro' the tempest;—thou dost lie,
Thy giant brood of pines around thee clinging,
Children of elder time, in whose devotion
The chainless winds still come and ever came
To drink their odours, and their mighty swinging
To hear—an old and solemn harmony;
Thine earthly rainbows stretched across the sweep
Of the ethereal waterfall, whose veil
Robes some unsculptured image; the strange sleep
Which when the voices of the desart fail
Wraps all in its own deep eternity;—
Thy caverns echoing to the Arve's commotion,
A loud, lone sound no other sound can tame;
Thou art pervaded with that ceaseless motion,
Thou art the path of that unresting sound—
Dizzy Ravine! and when I gaze on thee
I seem as in a trance sublime and strange
To muse on my own separate phantasy,
My own, my human mind, which passively
Now renders and receives fast influencings,
Holding an unremitting interchange
With the clear universe of things around;
One legion of wild thoughts, whose wandering wings
Now float above thy darkness, and now rest
Where that or thou art no unbidden guest,
In the still cave of the witch Poesy,
Seeking among the shadows that pass by
Ghosts of all things that are, some shade of thee,
Some phantom, some faint image; till the breast
From which they fled recalls them, thou art there!

III.

Some say that gleams of a remoter world
Visit the soul in sleep,—that death is slumber,
And that its shapes the busy thoughts outnumber
Of those who wake and live.—I look on high;
Has some unknown omnipotence unfurled
The veil of life and death? or do I lie
In dream, and does the mightier world of sleep
Spread far around and inaccessibly
Its circles? For the very spirit fails,
Driven like a homeless cloud from steep to steep
That vanishes among the viewless gales!
Far, far above, piercing the infinite sky,
Mont Blanc appears,—still, snowy, and serene—
Its subject mountains their unearthly forms
Pile around it, ice and rock; broad vales between
Of frozen floods, unfathomable deeps,
Blue as the overhanging heaven, that spread
And wind among the accumulated steeps;
A desart peopled by the storms alone,
Save when the eagle brings some hunter's bone,
And the wolf tracts her there—how hideously
Its shapes are heaped around! rude, bare, and high,
Ghastly, and scarred, and riven.—Is this the scene
Where the old Earthquake-dæmon taught her young
Ruin? Were these their toys? or did a sea
Of fire, envelope once this silent snow?
None can reply—all seems eternal now.
The wilderness has a mysterious tongue
Which teaches awful doubt, or faith so mild,
So solemn, so serene, that man may be
But for such faith with nature reconciled;
Thou hast a voice, great Mountain, to repeal
Large codes of fraud and woe; not understood
By all, but which the wise, and great, and good
Interpret, or make felt, or deeply feel.

IV.

The fields, the lakes, the forests, and the streams,
Ocean, and all the living things that dwell
Within the dædal earth; lightning, and rain,
Earthquake, and fiery flood, and hurricane,

The torpor of the year when feeble dreams
Visit the hidden buds, or dreamless sleep
Holds every future leaf and flower;—the bound
With which from that detested trance they leap;
The works and ways of man, their death and birth,
And that of him and all that his may be;
All things that move and breathe with toil and sound
Are born and die; revolve, subside and swell.
Power dwells apart in its tranquillity
Remote, serene, and inaccessible:
And this, the naked countenance of earth,
On which I gaze, even these primæval mountains
Teach the adverting mind. The glaciers creep
Like snakes that watch their prey, from their far fountains,
Slow rolling on; there, many a precipice,
Frost and the Sun in scorn of mortal power
Have piled: dome, pyramid, and pinnacle,
A city of death, distinct with many a tower
And wall impregnable of beaming ice.
Yet not a city, but a flood of ruin
Is there, that from the boundaries of the sky
Rolls its perpetual stream; vast pines are strewing
Its destined path, or in the mangled soil
Branchless and shattered stand; the rocks, drawn down
From yon remotest waste, have overthrown
The limits of the dead and living world,
Never to be reclaimed. The dwelling-place
Of insects, beasts, and birds, becomes its spoil;
Their food and their retreat for ever gone,
So much of life and joy is lost. The race
Of man, flies far in dread; his work and dwelling
Vanish, like smoke before the tempest's stream,
And their place is not known. Below, vast caves
Shine in the rushing torrent's restless gleam,
Which from those secret chasms in tumult welling
Meet in the vale, and one majestic River,
The breath and blood of distant lands, for ever
Rolls its loud waters to the ocean waves.
Breathes its swift vapours to the circling air.

V.

Mont Blanc yet gleams on high:—the power is there,
The still and solemn power of many sights,
And many sounds, and much of life and death.
In the calm darkness of the moonless nights,
In the lone glare of day, the snows descend
Upon that Mountain; none beholds them there,
Nor when the flakes burn in the sinking sun,
Or the star-beams dart through them:—Winds contend
Silently there, and heap the snow with breath
Rapid and strong, but silently! Its home
The voiceless lightning in these solitudes
Keeps innocently, and like vapour broods
Over the snow. The secret strength of things
Which governs thought, and to the infinite dome
Of heaven is as a law, inhabits thee!
And what were thou, and earth, and stars, and sea,
If to the human mind's imaginings
Silence and solitude were vacancy?

July 24, 1816

Yesterday morning we went to the source of the Arveiron. It is about a league from this village; the river rolls forth impetuously from an arch of ice, and spreads itself in many streams over a vast space of the valley, ravaged and laid bare by its inundations. The glacier by which its waters are nourished, overhangs this cavern and the plain, and the forests of pine which surround it, with terrible precipices of solid ice. On the other side rises the immense glacier of Montanvert, fifty miles in extent, occupying a chasm among mountains of inconceivable height, and of forms so pointed and abrupt, that they seem to pierce the sky. From this glacier we saw as we sat on a rock, close to one of the streams of the Arveiron, masses of ice detach themselves from on high, and rush with a loud dull noise into the vale. The violence of their fall turned them into powder, which flowed over the rocks in imitation of waterfalls, whose ravines they usurped and filled.

In the evening I went with Ducrée, my guide, the only tolerable person I have seen in this country, to visit the glacier of Boisson. This glacier, like that of Montanvert, comes close to the vale, overhanging the green meadows and the dark woods with the dazzling whiteness of its precipices and pinnacles, which are like spires of radiant crystal, covered with a net-work of frosted silver. These glaciers flow perpetually into the valley, ravaging in their slow but irresistible progress the pastures and the forests which surround them, performing a work of desolation in ages, which a river of lava might accomplish in an hour, but far more irretrievably; for where the ice has once descended, the hardiest plant refuses to grow; if even, as in some extraordinary instances, it should recede after its progress has once commenced. The glaciers perpetually move onward, at the rate of a foot each day, with a motion that commences at the spot where, on the boundaries of perpetual congelation, they are produced by the freezing of the waters which arise from the partial melting of the eternal snows. They drag with them from the regions whence they derive their origin, all the ruins of the mountain, enormous rocks, and immense accumulations of sand and stones. These are driven onwards by the irresistible stream of solid ice; and when they arrive at a declivity of the mountain, sufficiently rapid, roll down, scattering ruin. I saw one of these rocks which had descended in the spring, (winter here is the season of silence and safety) which measured forty feet in every direction.

The verge of a glacier, like that of Boisson, presents the most vivid image of desolation that it is possible to conceive. No one dares to approach it; for the enormous pinnacles of ice which perpetually fall, are perpetually reproduced. The pines of the forest, which bound it at one extremity, are overthrown and shattered to a wide extent at its base. There is something inexpressibly dreadful in the aspect of the few branchless trunks, which, nearest to the ice rifts, still stand in the uprooted soil. The meadows perish, overwhelmed with sand and stones. Within this last year, these glaciers have advanced three hundred feet into the valley. Saussure, the naturalist, says, that they have their periods of increase and decay: the people of the country hold an opinion entirely different; but as I judge, more probable. It is agreed by all, that the snow on the summit of Mont Blanc and the neighbouring mountains perpetually augments, and that ice, in the form of glaciers, subsists without melting in the valley of Chamouni during its transient and variable summer. If the snow which produces this glacier must augment, and the heat of the valley is no obstacle to the perpetual existence of such masses of ice as have already descended into it, the consequence is obvious; the glaciers must augment and will subsist, at least until they have overflowed this vale.

I will not pursue Buffon's sublime but gloomy theory—that this globe which we inhabit will at some future period be changed into a mass of frost by the encroachments of the polar ice, and of that produced on the most elevated points of the earth. Do you, who assert the supremacy of Ahriman, imagine him throned among these desolating snows, among these palaces of death and frost, so sculptured in this their terrible magnificence by the adamantine hand of necessity, and that he casts around him, as the first essays of his final usurpation, avalanches, torrents, rocks, and thunders, and above all these deadly glaciers, at once the proof and symbols of his reign;—add to this, the degradation of the human species—who in these regions are half deformed or idiotic, and most of whom are deprived of any thing that can excite interest or admiration. This is a part of the subject more mournful and less sublime; but such as neither the poet nor the philosopher should disdain to regard.

This morning we departed, on the promise of a fine day, to visit the glacier of Montanvert. In that part where it fills a slanting valley, it is called the Sea of Ice. This valley is 950 toises, or 7600 feet above the level of the sea. We had not proceeded far before the rain began to fall, but we persisted until we had accomplished more than half of our journey, when we returned, wet through.

Chamouni, July 25th.

We have returned from visiting the glacier of Montanvert, or as it is called, the Sea of Ice, a scene in truth of dizzying wonder. The path that winds to it along the side of a mountain, now clothed with pines, now intersected with snowy hollows, is wide and steep. The cabin of Montanvert is three leagues from Chamouni, half of which distance is performed on mules, not so sure footed, but that on the first day the one which I rode fell in what the guides call a mauvais pas, so that I narrowly escaped being precipitated down the mountain. We passed over a hollow covered with snow, down which vast stones are accustomed to roll. One had fallen the preceding day, a little time after we had returned: our guides desired us to pass quickly, for it is said that sometimes the least sound will accelerate their descent. We arrived at Montanvert, however, safe.

On all sides precipitous mountains, the abodes of unrelenting frost, surround this vale: their sides are banked up with ice and snow, broken, heaped high, and exhibiting terrific chasms. The summits are sharp and naked pinnacles, whose overhanging steepness will not even permit snow to rest upon them. Lines of dazzling ice occupy here and there their perpendicular rifts, and shine through the driving vapours with inexpressible brilliance: they pierce the clouds like things not belonging to this earth. The vale itself is filled with a mass of undulating ice, and has an ascent sufficiently gradual even to the remotest abysses of these horrible deserts. It is only half a league (about two miles) in breadth, and seems much less. It exhibits an appearance as if frost had suddenly bound up the waves and whirlpools of a mighty torrent. We walked some distance upon its surface. The waves are elevated about 12 or 15 feet from the surface of the mass, which is intersected by long gaps of unfathomable depth, the ice of whose sides is more beautifully azure than the sky. In these regions every thing changes, and is in motion. This vast mass of ice has one general progress, which ceases neither day nor night; it breaks and bursts for ever: some undulations sink while others rise; it is never the same. The echo of rocks, or of the ice and snow which fall from their overhanging precipices, or roll from their aerial summits, scarcely ceases for one moment. One would think that Mont Blanc, like the god of the Stoics, was a vast animal, and that the frozen blood for ever circulated through his stony veins.

We dined (M., C., and I) on the grass, in the open air, surrounded by this scene. The air is piercing and clear. We returned down the mountain, sometimes encompassed by the driving vapours, sometimes cheered by the sunbeams, and arrived at our inn by seven o'clock.

Montalegre, July 28th.

The next morning we returned through the rain to St. Martin. The scenery had lost something of its immensity, thick clouds hanging over the highest mountains; but visitings of sunset intervened between the showers, and the blue sky shone between the accumulated clouds of snowy whiteness which brought them; the dazzling mountains sometimes glittered through a chasm of the clouds above our heads, and all the charm of its grandeur remained. We repassed Pont Pellisier, a wooden bridge over the Arve, and the ravine of the Arve. We repassed the pine forests which overhang the defile, the chateau of St. Michel, a haunted ruin, built on the edge of a precipice, and shadowed over by the eternal forest. We repassed the vale of Servoz, a vale more beautiful, because more luxuriant, than that of Chamouni. Mont Blanc forms one of the sides of this vale also, and the other is inclosed by an irregular amphitheatre of enormous mountains, one of which is in ruins, and fell fifty years ago into the higher part of the valley: the smoke of its fall was seen in Piedmont, and people went from Turin to investigate whether a volcano had not burst forth among the Alps. It continued falling many days, spreading, with the shock and thunder of its ruin, consternation into the neighbouring vales. In the evening we arrived at St. Martin. The next day we wound through the valley, which I have described before, and arrived in the evening at our home.

We have bought some specimens of minerals and plants, and two or three crystal seals, at Mont Blanc, to preserve the remembrance of having approached it. There is a cabinet of Histoire Naturelle at Chamouni, just as at Keswick, Matlock, and Clifton; the proprietor of which is the very vilest specimen of that vile species of quack that, together with the whole army of aubergistes and guides, and indeed the entire mass of the population, subsist on the weakness and credulity of travellers as leaches subsist on the sick. The most interesting of my purchases is a large collection of all the seeds of rare alpine plants, with their names written upon the outside of the papers that contain them. These I mean to colonize in my garden in England, and to permit you to make what choice you please from them. They are companions which the Celandine—the classic Celandine, need not despise; they are as wild and more daring than he, and will tell him tales of things even as touching and sublime as the gaze of a vernal poet.

Did I tell you that there are troops of wolves among these mountains? In the winter they descend into the vallies, which the snow occupies six months of the year, and devour every thing that they can find out of doors. A wolf is more powerful than the fiercest and strongest dog. There are no bears in these regions. We heard, when we were at Lucerne, that they were occasionally found in the forests which surround that lake. Adieu. [35]

Mary Wollstonecraft Godwin's Journal

23 July, Tuesday (Chamounix)— My scamp of a husband wrote in of Chamonix's Hôtel de Londres described– Nay! Faith! Declared– himself thus: 'I am a lover of mankind, democrat, and atheist'. The scandal that would beset us on all sides, but his joviality at this little prank had him in stitches. When the register inquired what his destination was, he wrote, '*L'Enfer*'. Dante's *Inferno*! My Beloved's Greek is poor; he is practically illiterate in the language! But he cares not for the poverty of his eloquence nor for the scandal that shall beset us. He never cares for the thoughts of others when scandalizing. One can only hope and wish and desire that our Little Lord on a future journey to Chamonix will scratch out the inscription thus saving my Beloved's reputation and my embarrassment.

In the morning, after breakfast, we mount our mules to see the source of the Arveiron. When we had gone about three parts of the way, we descended and continued our route on foot, over loose stones, many of which were an enormous size. We came to the source, which lies (like a stage) surrounded on the three sides by mountains and glaciers. We sat on a rock, which formed the fourth, gazing on the scene before us. An immense glacier was on our left, which continually rolled stones to its foot. It is very dangerous to be directly under this. Our guide told us a

---

35 From *History of a Six Weeks Tour* by Mary Wollstonecraft Shelley and Percy Bysshe Shelley, published by T Thomas Hookham, Jr. and Charles and James Ollier, 1817

story of two Hollanders who went, without any guide, into a cavern of the glacier, and fired a pistol there, which drew down a large piece on them. We see several avalanches, some very small, others of great magnitude, which roared and smoked, overwhelming everything as it passed along, and precipitating great pieces of ice into the valley below. This glacier is increasing every day a foot, closing up the valley. We drink some water of the Arveiron and return. After dinner think it will rain, and Shelley goes alone to the glacier of Boison. I stay at home. Read several tales of Voltaire. In the evening I copy Shelley's letter to Peacock.

Wednesday, July 24— To-day is rainy; therefore we cannot go to Col de Balme. About 10 the weather appears clearing up. Shelley and I begin our journey to Montanvert. Nothing can be more desolate than the ascent of this mountain; the trees in many places having been torn away by avalanches, and some half leaning over others, intermingled with stones, present the appearance of vast and dreadful desolation. It began to rain almost as soon as we left our inn. When we had mounted considerably we turned to look on the scene. A dense white mist covered the vale, and tops of scattered pines peeping above were the only objects that presented themselves. The rain continued in torrents. We were wetted to the skin; so that, when we had ascended halfway, we resolved to turn back. As we descended, Shelley went before, and, tripping up, fell upon his knee. This added to the weakness occasioned by a blow on his ascent; he fainted, and was for some minutes incapacitated from continuing his route.

We arrived wet to the skin. I read *Nouvelles Nouvelles*, and write my story. Shelley writes part of letter.

27 July, Saturday— It is a most beautiful day, without a cloud. We set off at 12. The day is hot, yet there is a fine breeze. We pass by the Great Waterfall, which presents an aspect of singular beauty. The wind carries it away from the rock, and on towards the north, and the fine spray into which it is entirely dissolved passes before the mountain like a mist.

The other cascade has very little water, and is consequently not so beautiful as before. The evening of the day is calm and beautiful. Evening is the only time I enjoy travelling. The horses went fast, and the plain opened before us. We saw Jura and the Lake like old friends. I longed to see my pretty babe. At 9, after much inquiring and stupidity, we find the road, and alight at Diodati. We converse with Lord Byron till 12, and then go down to Chapuis, kiss our babe, and go to bed.[36]

---

36 From Mary Wollstonecraft Shelley's journals dated 1816.

***

[Date unrecorded]— The glacier at Montanvert is a natural phenomenon to behold! I sat upon a rock that overlooks the sea of ice. A mist covered both that and the surrounding mountains. Presently a breeze dissipated the cloud. The surface is very uneven, rising like the waves of a troubled sea, descending low, and interspersed by rifts that sink deep. The field of ice is almost a league in width, and one could spend nearly two hours in crossing it. The opposite mountain is a bare perpendicular rock. From the side where I now stood Montanvert was exactly opposite, at the distance of a league; and above it rose Mont Blânc, in awful majesty. I remained in a recess of the rock, gazing on this wonderful and stupendous scene. The sea, or rather the vast river of ice, wound among its dependent mountains, whose aërial summits hung over its recesses. Their icy and glittering peaks shone in the sunlight over the clouds. These sights were just as my pale student of the unhallowed arts had described Montanvert to me weeks before while in my bedchamber at the Villa Diodati. How is it possible to have had my pale student describe something to me I had not yet seen or experienced? Was not my pale student a figment of my authorial imagination? I then looked across the vastness of the glacier and saw the queerest sight... a low carriage, fixed on a sledge and drawn by dogs, pass on towards the north, at the distance of half a mile: a being which and the shape of a man, but apparently of gigantic stature, sat in the sledge, and guided the dogs. I watched the rapid progress of the Creature without the need for telescopes, for my mind's eye perceived all, until he was lost among the distant inequalities of the ice. The Creature, as my pale student of the unhallowed arts had told me of, appeared frightened and being chased. Why was the Creature in fear for his every existence? I wonder what —or who— was stalking this poor Creature across the frozen wasteland of Montanvert? Or was it no longer Montanvert? Was I seeing the Arctic? I could not stop my mind's eye from picturing the Arctic with its endless sheets of ice that can easily surround a ship on all sides, port and starboard, bow and stern, scarcely leaving her the sea room and compassed round by a thick fog. How could the Arctic exist in the centre of the Continent? With mountains and a pleasant vale surrounding the glacier on all sides. One did not have to search for the North Pole or seek a northern route to the Pacific to see the wonders of the Arctic. In fact, it was a far safer holiday to visit a glacier than the Arctic. But whether the Creature sledged across the Arctic or the glacier, again I must ponder what —or who— was stalking this poor Creature?

After our exciting and exhausting tour of the glacier, we returned to our hotel at the bottom of the glacier in the vale below; the desk clerk handed me four envelopes addressed to a 'Mrs Saville, England'. As my Beloved disappeared up the stairs towards our room, I began to protest. I was not 'Mrs Saville'. She must be staying at another hotel in Chamonix. But the desk clerk insisted that his instructions were clear; the letters were to be delivered to a woman matching my very description. Whether or not I was 'Mrs Saville' was beside the point. I accepted the letters begrudgingly. Once in our room, I placed the letters on the bedside table and joined my Beloved for dinner in the hotel restaurant. We ate a lovely meal and back in our room, we were soon disposed to marital sport. Distracted, I could not stop glancing at the envelopes on the bedside table. After my Beloved had drifted off into a deep, dreamful, postcoital slumber, I picked up the envelopes. Three of which had been postmarked quite clearly and quite queerly as having travelled from Russia, all with a destination mark to London. How had the letters reached the Alps without nary a postmark in-between? No post office seemed to acknowledge their receipt or their transportation through their territory with a stamp. Not only did these letters come from across the great vastness of distance, but the great vastness of time! First two letters addressed to my pale student of the unhallowed arts arrived mysteriously at the door of the Villa Diodati on the eve of winter, one from his cousin, Elizabeth, and the other from his father, Alphonse. And now four letters find their way to the base of the glacier at Chamonix. Who is this preternatural— nay! psychological— postman who delivers letters to me. My name is not Mrs Saville and my pale student has yet to mention her name at any time during his recitation of his life to me. I sliced open– with the sudden violence of a murderer stalking the seedy streets of White Chapel– the envelope stamped as having come from St. Petersburgh. The letter enclosed was dated... Dec. 11th, 1798! The turn of nineteenth century? Eighteen years ago?

Letter 1 From R. Walton To Mrs Saville

To Mrs Saville, *England.*

St. Petersburgh, Dec. 11th, 1798.

You will rejoice to hear that no disaster has accompanied the commencement of an enterprise which you have regarded with such evil forebodings. I arrived here yesterday; and my first task is to assure my dear sister of my welfare, and increasing confidence in the success of my undertaking.

I am already far north of London; and as I walk in the streets of Petersburgh, I feel a cold northern breeze play upon my cheeks, which braces my nerves, and fills me with delight. Do you understand this feeling? This breeze, which has travelled from the regions towards which I am advancing, gives me a foretaste of those icy climes. Inspirited by this wind of promise, my day dreams become more fervent and vivid. I try in vain to be persuaded that the pole is the seat of frost and desolation; it ever presents itself to my imagination as the region of beauty and delight. There, Margaret, the sun is for ever visible; its broad disk just skirting the horizon, and diffusing a perpetual splendour. There— for with your leave, my sister, I will put some trust in preceding navigators— there snow and frost are banished; and, sailing over a calm sea, we may be wafted to a land surpassing in wonders and in beauty every region hitherto discovered on the habitable globe. Its productions and features may be without example, as the phænomena of the heavenly bodies undoubtedly are in those undiscovered solitudes. What may not be expected in a country of eternal light? I may there discover the wondrous power which attracts the needle; and may regulate a thousand celestial observations, that require only this voyage to render their seeming eccentricities consistent for ever. I shall satiate my ardent curiosity with the sight of a part of the world never before visited, and may tread a land never before imprinted by the foot of man. These are my enticements, and they are sufficient to conquer all fear of danger or death, and to induce me to commence this laborious voyage with the joy a child feels when he embarks in a little boat, with his holiday mates, on an expedition of discovery up his native river. But, supposing all these conjectures to be false, you cannot contest the inestimable benefit which I shall confer on all mankind to the last generation, by discovering a passage near the pole to those countries, to reach which at present so many months are requisite; or by ascertaining the secret of the magnet, which, if at all possible, can only be effected by an undertaking such as mine.

These reflections have dispelled the agitation with which I began my letter, and I feel my heart glow with an enthusiasm which elevates me to heaven; for nothing contributes so much to tranquillize the mind as a steady purpose,— a point on which the soul may fix its intellectual eye. This expedition has been the favourite dream of my early years. I have read with ardour the accounts of the various voyages which have been made in the prospect of arriving at the North Pacific Ocean through the seas which surround the pole. You may remember, that a history of all the voyages made for purposes of discovery composed the whole of our good uncle Thomas's library. My education was neglected, yet I was passionately fond of reading. These volumes were my study day and night, and my familiarity with them increased that regret which I had felt, as a child, on learning that my father's dying injunction had forbidden my uncle to allow me to embark in a sea-faring life.

These visions faded when I perused, for the first time, those poets whose effusions entranced my soul, and lifted it to heaven. I also became a poet, and for one year lived in a Paradise of my own creation; I imagined that I also might obtain a niche in the temple where the names of Homer and Shakespeare are consecrated. You are well acquainted with my failure, and how heavily I bore the disappointment. But just at that time I inherited the fortune of my cousin, and my thoughts were turned into the channel of their earlier bent.

Six years have passed since I resolved on my present undertaking. I can, even now, remember the hour from which I dedicated myself to this great enterprise. I commenced by inuring my body to hardship. I accompanied the whale-fishers on several expeditions to the North Sea; I voluntarily endured cold, famine, thirst, and want of sleep; I often worked harder than the common sailors during the day, and devoted my nights to the study of mathematics, the theory of medicine, and those branches of physical science from which a naval adventurer might derive the greatest practical advantage. Twice I actually hired myself as an under-mate in a Greenland whaler, and acquitted myself to admiration. I must own I felt a little proud, when my captain offered me the second dignity in the vessel, and entreated me to remain with the greatest earnestness; so valuable did he consider my services.

And now, dear Margaret, do I not deserve to accomplish some great purpose. My life might have been passed in ease and luxury; but I preferred glory to every enticement that wealth placed in my path. Oh, that some encouraging voice would answer in the affirmative! My courage and my resolution is firm; but my hopes fluctuate, and my spirits are often depressed. I am about to proceed on a long and difficult voyage; the emergencies of which will demand all my fortitude: I am required not only to raise the spirits of others, but sometimes to sustain my own, when their's are failing.

This is the most favourable period for travelling in Russia. They fly quickly over the snow in their sledges; the motion is pleasant, and, in my opinion, far more agreeable than that of an English stage-coach. The cold is not excessive, if you are wrapt in furs, a dress which I have already adopted; for there is a great difference between walking the deck and remaining seated motionless for hours, when no exercise prevents the blood from actually freezing in your veins. I have no ambition to lose my life on the post-road between St. Petersburgh and Archangel.

I shall depart for the latter town in a fortnight or three weeks; and my intention is to hire a ship there, which can easily be done by paying the insurance for the owner, and to engage as many sailors as I think necessary among those who are accustomed to the whale-fishing. I do not intend to sail until the month of June: and when shall I return? Ah, dear sister, how can I answer this question? If I succeed, many, many months, perhaps years, will pass before you and I may meet. If I fail, you will see me again soon, or never.

Farewell, my dear, excellent, Margaret. Heaven shower down blessings on you, and save me, that I may again and again testify my gratitude for all your love and kindness.

Your affectionate brother,

R. Walton.

Mary Wollstonecraft Godwin's Journal

24 July. Glacier Montanvert— Curious. It is not only curious how this letter has made it into my possession and not Mrs Saville's, but I have grown curious concerning this expedition Mr Walton seeks to undertake. This description of his destination at the crown of the world is so near to my own description of the wonder of this glacier my Beloved and I now sit at the feet of. While I make no bones to visit a 'land never before imprinted by the foot of man', the sheer joy of this glacier harkens me back to when my ancestors lived in caves and hunted the woolly mammoths and were hunted by the sabre-toothed cats.

His own joys at seeking a 'steady purpose' I feel in my heart. I had fixed my own intellectual eye upon the story my pale student of the unhallowed arts has been relating to me. Whether he be real phantasm haunting my nights or my projection of my own creativity, I know not. But as of late, he has grown quite quiet. How fond this Mr Walton was studying the history of all the voyages made for purposes of discovery. How fond was I, are all authors, of reading the volumes of poetry and prose when disposed to the mirth of a library? He had been forbidden by parental degree from pursuing his dreams. How many of my fellow travellers to the grave had been so forbidden. My own father, thankfully, has never begrudged me my fancies in any of my pursuits whether they be poetry, literature, or the sciences; only the subject of religion, particularly Christianity, was discouraged unless prefaced under the study of mythology. To my father, Jesus was no more real or desiring the worship of than the pantheons of the Greeks or Egyptians.

It is most fascinating that this man who longs for the physical exploration of the world also reads from Homer and Shakespeare. To my mind, I am afraid to admit, I have often reserved *The Illiad* and *The Odyssey* to the enjoyment of the creative souls but knowing that explorers draw equal inspiration from the great works brings my heart so much joy. And how can I not share his endurance of literal 'cold, famine, thirst, and want of sleep' to fulfil his dreams. An author in the creation of his work will endure metaphorical 'cold, famine, thirst, and want of sleep.' I know well the devotion of my nights to the 'study of mathematics, the theory of medicine, and those branches of the physical science' that an author might derive the greatest practical advantage. Have these studies not benefitted me of late when my pale student of the unhallowed arts relates his story to me?

Letter 2 From R. Walton To Mrs Saville

To Mrs Saville, England.

Archangel, 28th March, 1799.

How slowly the time passes here, encompassed as I am by frost and snow; yet a second step is taken towards my enterprise. I have hired a vessel, and am occupied in collecting my sailors; those whom I have already engaged appear to be men on whom I can depend, and are certainly possessed of dauntless courage.

But I have one want which I have never yet been able to satisfy; and the absence of the object of which I now feel as a most severe evil. I have no friend, Margaret: when I am glowing with the enthusiasm of success, there will be none to participate my joy; if I am assailed by disappointment, no one will endeavour to sustain me in dejection. I shall commit my thoughts to paper, it is true; but that is a poor medium for the communication of feeling. I desire the company of a man who could sympathize with me; whose eyes would reply to mine. You may deem me romantic, my dear sister, but I bitterly feel the want of a friend. I have no one near me, gentle yet courageous, possessed of a cultivated as well as of a capacious mind, whose tastes are like my own, to approve or amend my plans. How would such a friend repair the faults of your poor brother! I am too ardent in execution, and too impatient of difficulties. But it is a still greater evil to me that I am self-educated: for the first fourteen years of my life I ran wild on a common, and read nothing but our uncle Thomas's books of voyages. At that age I became acquainted with the celebrated poets of our own country; but it was only when it had ceased to be in my power to derive its most important benefits from such a conviction, that I perceived the necessity of becoming acquainted with more languages than that of my native country. Now I am twenty-eight, and am in reality more illiterate than many school-boys of fifteen. It is true that I have thought more, and that my day dreams are more extended and magnificent; but they want (as the painters call it) *keeping*; and I greatly need a friend who would have sense enough not to despise me as romantic, and affection enough for me to endeavour to regulate my mind.

Well, these are useless complaints; I shall certainly find no friend on the wide ocean, nor even here in Archangel, among merchants and seamen. Yet some feelings, unallied to the dross of human nature, beat even in these rugged bosoms. My lieutenant, for instance, is a man of wonderful courage and enterprise; he is madly desirous of glory. He is an Englishman, and in the midst of national and professional prejudices, unsoftened by cultivation, retains some of the noblest endowments of humanity. I first became acquainted with him on board a whale vessel: finding that he was unemployed in this city, I easily engaged him to assist in my enterprise.

The master is a person of an excellent disposition, and is remarkable in the ship for his gentleness, and the mildness of his discipline. He is, indeed, of so amiable a nature, that he will not hunt (a favourite, and almost the only amusement here), because he cannot endure to spill blood. He is, moreover, heroically generous. Some years ago he loved a young Russian lady, of moderate fortune; and having amassed a considerable sum in prize-money, the father of the girl consented to the match. He saw his mistress once before the destined ceremony; but she was bathed in tears, and, throwing herself at his feet, entreated him to spare her, confessing at the same time that she loved another, but that he was poor, and that her father would never consent to the union. My generous friend reassured the suppliant, and on being informed of the name of her lover instantly abandoned his pursuit. He had already bought a farm with his money, on which he had designed to pass the remainder of his life; but he bestowed the whole on his rival, together with the remains of his prize-money to purchase stock, and then himself solicited the young woman's father to consent to her marriage with her lover. But the old man decidedly refused, thinking himself bound in honour to my friend; who, when he found the father inexorable, quitted his country, nor returned until he heard that his former mistress was married according to her inclinations. 'What a noble fellow!' you will exclaim. He is so; but then he has passed all his life on board a vessel, and has scarcely an idea beyond the rope and the shroud.

But do not suppose that, because I complain a little, or because I can conceive a consolation for my toils which I may never know, that I am wavering in my resolutions. Those are as fixed as fate; and my voyage is only now delayed until the weather shall permit my embarkation. The winter has been dreadfully severe; but the spring promises well, and it is considered as a remarkably early season; so that, perhaps, I may sail sooner than I expected. I shall do nothing rashly; you know me sufficiently to confide in my prudence and considerateness whenever the safety of others is committed to my care.

I cannot describe to you my sensations on the near prospect of my undertaking. It is impossible to communicate to you a conception of the trembling sensation, half pleasurable and half fearful, with which I am preparing to depart. I am going to unexplored regions, to 'the land of mist and snow;' but I shall kill no albatross, therefore do not be alarmed for my safety.

Shall I meet you again, after having traversed immense seas, and returned by the most southern cape of Africa or America? I dare not expect such success, yet I cannot bear to look on the reverse of the picture. Continue to write to me by every opportunity: I may receive your letters (though the chance is very doubtful) on some occasions when I need them most to support my spirits. I love you very tenderly. Remember me with affection, should you never hear from me again.

Your affectionate brother,
Robert Walton.

Mary Wollstonecraft Godwin's Journal

[Continued]— My! How I feel his longing for a friend. True, I have the friendship of my Beloved, our little Lord, poor Polidori, and my sister Claire, who will participate in my joy. If I am assailed with disappointment, they will, no doubt, endeavour to sustain me in dejection. I too commit my thoughts to paper, but I disagree with Mr Walton, the medium is exquisite for the communication of feeling! This very summer has proven to my companions and myself to be rife with the inspiration of the communication of feeling! But Mr Walton's words do mirror my own longing for my pale student of the unhallowed arts. His desire for a friend to share this journey to the crown of the world is my desire for my pale student to share with me his own story. Why has my pale student abandoned me? He may not have desired to journey to foot of the glacier here at Chamonix, but since he exists as a phantasm, the journey should not have been arduous. He could have made the journey in the safety of my own carriage, in the safety of my own head. But he hasn't made the journey to Chamonix. He hasn't made an appearance in my bedchamber in the Villa Diodati in a fortnight.

* * *

Letter 3 From R. Walton To Mrs Saville

To Mrs Saville, England.

July 7th, 1799.

My Dear Sister,

I write a few lines in haste, to say that I am safe, and well advanced on my voyage. This letter will reach England by a merchant-man now on its homeward voyage from Archangel; more fortunate than I, who may not see my native land, perhaps, for many years. I am, however, in good spirits: my men are bold, and apparently firm of purpose; nor do the floating sheets of ice that continually pass us, indicating the dangers of the region towards which we are advancing, appear to dismay them. We have already reached a very high latitude; but it is the height of summer, and although not so warm as in England, the southern gales, which blow us speedily towards those shores which I so ardently desire to attain, breathe a degree of renovating warmth which I had not expected.

No incidents have hitherto befallen us, that would make a figure in a letter. One or two stiff gales, and the breaking of a mast, are accidents which experienced navigators scarcely remember to record; and I shall be well content, if nothing worse happen to us during our voyage.

Adieu, my dear Margaret. Be assured, that for my own sake, as well as your's, I will not rashly encounter danger. I will be cool, persevering, and prudent.

Remember me to all my English friends.

Most affectionately yours,'

R. W.

Letter 4 From R. Walton To Mrs Saville

To Mrs Saville, England.

August 5th, 1799.

So strange an accident has happened to us, that I cannot forbear recording it, although it is very probable that you will see me before these papers can come into your possession.

Last Monday (July 31st), we were nearly surrounded by ice, which closed in the ship on all sides, scarcely leaving her the sea room in which she floated. Our situation was somewhat dangerous, especially as we were compassed round by a very thick fog. We accordingly lay to, hoping that some change would take place in the atmosphere and weather.

About two o'clock the mist cleared away, and we beheld, stretched out in every direction, vast and irregular plains of ice, which seemed to have no end. Some of my comrades groaned, and my own mind began to grow watchful with anxious thoughts, when a strange sight suddenly attracted our attention, and diverted our solicitude from our own situation. We perceived a low carriage, fixed on a sledge and drawn by dogs, pass on towards the north, at the distance of half a mile: a being which had the shape of a man, but apparently of gigantic stature, sat in the sledge, and guided the dogs. We watched the rapid progress of the traveller with our telescopes, until he was lost among the distant inequalities of the ice.

This appearance excited our unqualified wonder. We were, as we believed, many hundred miles from any land; but this apparition seemed to denote that it was not, in reality, so distant as we had supposed. Shut in, however, by ice, it was impossible to follow his track, which we had observed with the greatest attention.

About two hours after this occurrence, we heard the ground sea; and before night the ice broke, and freed our ship. We, however, lay to until the morning, fearing to encounter in the dark those large loose masses which float about after the breaking up of the ice. I profited of this time to rest for a few hours.

In the morning, however, as soon as it was light, I went upon deck, and found all the sailors busy on one side of the vessel, apparently talking to some one in the sea. It was, in fact, a sledge, like that we had seen before, which had drifted towards us in the night, on a large fragment of ice. Only one dog remained alive; but there was a human being within it, whom the sailors were persuading to enter the vessel. He was not, as the other traveller seemed to be, a savage inhabitant of some undiscovered island, but an European. When I appeared on deck, the master said, 'Here is our captain, and he will not allow you to perish on the open sea.'

On perceiving me, the stranger addressed me in English, although with a foreign accent. 'Before I come on board your vessel,' said he, 'will you have the kindness to inform me whither you are bound?'

You may conceive my astonishment on hearing such a question addressed to me from a man on the brink of destruction, and to whom I should have supposed that my vessel would have been a resource which he would not have exchanged for the most precious wealth the earth can afford. I replied, however, that we were on a voyage of discovery towards the northern pole.

Upon hearing this he appeared satisfied, and consented to come on board. Good God! Margaret, if you had seen the man who thus capitulated for his safety, your surprise would have been boundless. His limbs were nearly frozen, and his body dreadfully emaciated by fatigue and suffering. I never saw a man in so wretched a condition. We attempted to carry him into the cabin; but as soon as he had quitted the fresh air, he fainted. We accordingly brought him back to the deck, and restored him to animation by rubbing him with brandy, and forcing him to swallow a small quantity. As soon as he shewed signs of life, we wrapped him up in blankets, and placed him near the chimney of the kitchen-stove. By slow degrees he recovered, and ate a little soup, which restored him wonderfully.

Two days passed in this manner before he was able to speak; and I often feared that his sufferings had deprived him of understanding. When he had in some measure recovered, I removed him to my own cabin, and attended on him as much as my duty would permit. I never saw a more interesting creature: his eyes have generally an expression of wildness, and even madness; but there are moments when, if any one performs an act of kindness towards him, or does him any the most trifling service, his whole countenance is lighted up, as it were, with a beam of benevolence and sweetness that I never saw equalled. But he is generally melancholy and despairing; and sometimes he gnashes his teeth, as if impatient of the weight of woes that oppresses him.

When my guest was a little recovered, I had great trouble to keep off the men, who wished to ask him a thousand questions; but I would not allow him to be tormented by their idle curiosity, in a state of body and mind whose restoration evidently depended upon entire repose. Once, however, the lieutenant asked, Why he had come so far upon the ice in so strange a vehicle?

His countenance instantly assumed an aspect of the deepest gloom; and he replied, 'To seek one who fled from me.'

'And did the man whom you pursued travel in the same fashion?'

'Yes.'

'Then I fancy we have seen him; for, the day before we picked you up, we saw some dogs drawing a sledge, with a man in it, across the ice.'

This aroused the stranger's attention; and he asked a multitude of questions concerning the route which the dæmon, as he called him, had pursued. Soon after, when he was alone with me, he said, 'I have, doubtless, excited your curiosity, as well as that of these good people; but you are too considerate to make inquiries.'

'Certainly; it would indeed be very impertinent and inhuman in me to trouble you with any inquisitiveness of mine.'

'And yet you rescued me from a strange and perilous situation; you have benevolently restored me to life.'

Soon after this he inquired, if I thought that the breaking up of the ice had destroyed the other sledge? I replied, that I could not answer with any degree of certainty; for the ice had not broken until near midnight, and the traveller might have arrived at a place of safety before that time; but of this I could not judge.

From this time the stranger seemed very eager to be upon deck, to watch for the sledge which had before appeared; but I have persuaded him to remain in the cabin, for he is far too weak to sustain the rawness of the atmosphere. But I have promised that some one should watch for him, and give him instant notice if any new object should appear in sight.

Such is my journal of what relates to this strange occurrence up to the present day. The stranger has gradually improved in health, but is very silent, and appears uneasy when any one except myself enters his cabin. Yet his manners are so conciliating and gentle, that the sailors are all interested in him, although they have had very little communication with him. For my own part, I begin to love him as a brother; and his constant and deep grief fills me with sympathy and compassion. He must have been a noble creature in his better days, being even now in wreck so attractive and amiable.

I said in one of my letters, my dear Margaret, that I should find no friend on the wide ocean; yet I have found a man who, before his spirit had been broken by misery, I should have been happy to have possessed as the brother of my heart.

I shall continue my journal concerning the stranger at intervals, should I have any fresh incidents to record.

August 13th, 1799.

My affection for my guest increases every day. He excites at once my admiration and my pity to an astonishing degree. How can I see so noble a creature destroyed by misery without feeling the most poignant grief? He is so gentle, yet so wise; his mind is so cultivated; and when he speaks, although his words are culled with the choicest art, yet they flow with rapidity and unparalleled eloquence.

He is now much recovered from his illness, and is continually on the deck, apparently watching for the sledge that preceded his own. Yet, although unhappy, he is not so utterly occupied by his own misery, but that he interests himself deeply in the employments of others. He has asked me many questions concerning my design; and I have related my little history frankly to him. He appeared pleased with the confidence, and suggested several alterations in my plan, which I shall find exceedingly useful. There is no pedantry in his manner; but all he does appears to spring solely from the interest he instinctively takes in the welfare of those who surround him. He is often overcome by gloom, and then he sits by himself, and tries to overcome all that is sullen or unsocial in his humour. These paroxysms pass from him like a cloud from before the sun, though his dejection never leaves him. I have endeavoured to win his confidence; and I trust that I have succeeded. One day I mentioned to him the desire I had always felt of finding a friend who might sympathize with me, and direct me by his counsel. I said, I did not belong to that class of men who are offended by advice. 'I am self-educated, and perhaps I hardly rely sufficiently upon my own powers. I wish therefore that my companion should be wiser and more experienced than myself, to confirm and support me; nor have I believed it impossible to find a true friend.'

'I agree with you,' replied the stranger, 'in believing that friendship is not only a desirable, but a possible acquisition. I once had a friend, the most noble of human creatures, and am entitled, therefore, to judge respecting friendship. You have hope, and the world before you, and have no cause for despair. But I— — I have lost every thing, and cannot begin life anew.'

As he said this, his countenance became expressive of a calm settled grief, that touched me to the heart. But he was silent, and presently retired to his cabin.

Even broken in spirit as he is, no one can feel more deeply than he does the beauties of nature. The starry sky, the sea, and every sight afforded by these wonderful regions, seems still to have the power of elevating his soul from earth. Such a man has a double existence: he may suffer misery, and be overwhelmed by disappointments; yet when he has retired into himself, he will be like a celestial spirit, that has a halo around him, within whose circle no grief or folly ventures.

Will you laugh at the enthusiasm I express concerning this divine wanderer? If you do, you must have certainly lost that simplicity which was once your characteristic charm. Yet, if you will, smile at the warmth of my expressions, while I find every day new causes for repeating them.

August 19th, 1799.

Yesterday the stranger said to me, 'You may easily perceive, Captain Walton, that I have suffered great and unparalleled misfortunes. I had determined, once, that the memory of these evils should die with me; but you have won me to alter my determination. You seek for knowledge and wisdom, as I once did; and I ardently hope that the gratification of your wishes may not be a serpent to sting you, as mine has been. I do not know that the relation of my misfortunes will be useful to you, yet, if you are inclined, listen to my tale. I believe that the strange incidents connected with it will afford a view of nature, which may enlarge your faculties and understanding. You will hear of powers and occurrences, such as you have been accustomed to believe impossible: but I do not doubt that my tale conveys in its series internal evidence of the truth of the events of which it is composed.'

You may easily conceive that I was much gratified by the offered communication; yet I could not endure that he should renew his grief by a recital of his misfortunes. I felt the greatest eagerness to hear the promised narrative, partly from curiosity, and partly from a strong desire to ameliorate his fate, if it were in my power. I expressed these feelings in my answer.

'I thank you,' he replied, 'for your sympathy, but it is useless; my fate is nearly fulfilled. I wait but for one event, and then I shall repose in peace. I understand your feeling,' continued he, perceiving that I wished to interrupt him; 'but you are mistaken, my friend, if thus you will allow me to name you; nothing can alter my destiny: listen to my history, and you will perceive how irrevocably it is determined.'

He then told me, that he would commence his narrative the next day when I should be at leisure. This promise drew from me the warmest thanks. I have resolved every night, when I am not engaged, to record, as nearly as possible in his own words, what he has related during the day. If I should be engaged, I will at least make notes. This manuscript will doubtless afford you the greatest pleasure: but to me, who know him, and who hear it from his own lips, with what interest and sympathy shall I read it in some future day!

"I am by birth a Genevese,' he began.

Mary Wollstonecraft Godwin's Journal

[Continued]— My pale student! How he found me. He has not abandoned me. For this past fortnight I have not been abandoned. He has been on the arduous journey to the crown of the world! There to converse with Mr Walton and via letters to Mrs Saville inform me of his adventures. How I feared that he would not be able to find me at such a great distance from the Villa Diodati. It is a childlike fear that Father Christmas would not be able to find me if the family Christmased away from home and hearth. But I feared for nought.

Chapter Sixteen
Childe Harold's Pilgrimage (3ʳᵈ Canto);³⁷

Lord Byron's Diary

Date unrecorded]... 'Begun at sea.' With these words scrawl on my manuscript, I have begun the third canto of *Childe Harold's Pilgrimage*. With the first two cantos having seen publication thanks to John Murray and associates, I thought the pilgrimage was done. But I've fled my home and my country due to 'dark rumours'. Shall I repeat the rumours here for I know the truth and the rumour-mongering of gossiping hens are not content with their own marriage and their own affairs and their own scandals. Was King Oedipus so assaulted with the outright slander committed at dinner parties and the libel printing in the newspaper and magazines? How would Oedipus answer the assault on his character for the supposition of an improper relationship with his own mother? Would Oedipus have been forced to flee his homeland like I am being banished from my own island? There is no answer to these quite loud whispers that will satisfy the rumourmongers. Being shunned by the very society and high society that had once flocked to my poetry and gifted me with immeasurable fame. Where once I would stand in the parlours of the richest men and women in the country, reciting my poetry to their evening's guests, now I am expelled from their circles for rumours and rumours of rumours of... I cannot bear to say. I composed this *Pilgrimage* as I journeyed through Belgium, German, and finally landing on the shores of Lake Geneva at Cologny. My mind alight with the creative spark that gave birth to the first two cantos. The words flow onto the page effortlessly. I find it more a travelogue than a poem. And travelogues are all the rage back on my island, but will a publisher even be found to print this book given my scandal? Or will my infamy push copies out at the booksellers? I have permitted P.B.S. the honour of reading these stanzas as I have written them, including other works of darkness (pun intended). I have left him an inkpot filled with ink the colour of human blood having instructed him to 'Kill my darlings. Kill Kill. Kill my darlings'. If the pages do not return to be bloodied, then how can I, through the alchemy of editing, resurrect my poem or prose into a

---

37 From *Childe Harold's Pilgrimage, a Romaunt* by Lord Byron, published by John Murray. "Stanzas I through XXV are included in this chapter. The remaining stanzas can be found in Appendix 2"— R.D.B.

publishable work worthy of entering society? The first draft must be murdered, mercilessly cut, sliced, and maimed beyond all recognition to produce the final work. And this is what friends are for!

I.

Is thy face like thy mother's, my fair child!
Ada! sole daughter of my house and heart?
When last I saw thy young blue eyes, they smiled,
And then we parted,—not as now we part,
But with a hope.—

Awaking with a start,
The waters heave around me; and on high
The winds lift up their voices: I depart,
Whither I know not; but the hour's gone by,
When Albion's lessening shores could grieve or glad mine eye.

II.

Once more upon the waters! yet once more!
And the waves bound beneath me as a steed
That knows his rider. Welcome to their roar!
Swift be their guidance, wheresoe'er it lead!
Though the strained mast should quiver as a reed,
And the rent canvas fluttering strew the gale,
Still must I on; for I am as a weed,
Flung from the rock, on Ocean's foam, to sail
Where'er the surge may sweep, the tempest's breath prevail.

III.

In my youth's summer I did sing of One,
The wandering outlaw of his own dark mind;
Again I seize the theme, then but begun,
And bear it with me, as the rushing wind
Bears the cloud onwards: in that tale I find
The furrows of long thought, and dried-up tears,
Which, ebbing, leave a sterile track behind,
O'er which all heavily the journeying years
Plod the last sands of life—where not a flower appears.

IV.

Since my young days of passion—joy, or pain,
Perchance my heart and harp have lost a string,
And both may jar: it may be, that in vain

I would essay as I have sung to sing.
Yet, though a dreary strain, to this I cling,
So that it wean me from the weary dream
Of selfish grief or gladness—so it fling
Forgetfulness around me—it shall seem
To me, though to none else, a not ungrateful theme.

V.

He who, grown aged in this world of woe,
In deeds, not years, piercing the depths of life,
So that hno wonder waits him; nor below
Can love or sorrow, fame, ambition, strife,
Cut to his heart again with the keen knife
Of silent, sharp endurance: he can tell
Why thought seeks refuge in lone caves, yet rife
With airy images, and shapes which dwell
Still unimpaired, though old, in the soul's haunted cell.

VI.

'Tis to create, and in creating live
A being more intense, that we endow
With form our fancy, gaining as we give
The life we image, even as I do now.
What am I? Nothing: but not so art thou,
Soul of my thought! with whom I traverse earth,
Invisible but gazing, as I glow
Mixed with thy spirit, blended with thy birth,
And feeling still with thee in my crushed feelings' dearth.

VII.

Yet must I think less wildly: I HAVE thought
Too long and darkly, till my brain became,
In its own eddy boiling and o'erwrought,
A whirling gulf of phantasy and flame:
And thus, untaught in youth my heart to tame,
My springs of life were poisoned. 'Tis too late!
Yet am I changed; though still enough the same
In strength to bear what time cannot abate,
And feed on bitter fruits without accusing fate.

VIII.

Something too much of this: but now 'tis past,
And the spell closes with its silent seal.
Long-absent Harold reappears at last;
He of the breast which fain no more would feel,
Wrung with the wounds which kill not, but ne'er heal;
Yet Time, who changes all, had altered him
In soul and aspect as in age: years steal
Fire from the mind as vigour from the limb;
And life's enchanted cup but sparkles near the brim.

IX.

His had been quaffed too quickly, and he found
The dregs were wormwood; but he filled again,
And from a purer fount, on holier ground,
And deemed its spring perpetual; but in vain!
Still round him clung invisibly a chain
Which galled for ever, fettering though unseen,
And heavy though it clanked not; worn with pain,
Which pined although it spoke not, and grew keen,
Entering with every step he took through many a scene.

X.

Secure in guarded coldness, he had mixed
Again in fancied safety with his kind,
And deemed his spirit now so firmly fixed
And sheathed with an invulnerable mind,
That, if no joy, no sorrow lurked behind;
And he, as one, might midst the many stand
Unheeded, searching through the crowd to find
Fit speculation; such as in strange land
He found in wonder-works of God and Nature's hand.

XI.

But who can view the ripened rose, nor seek
To wear it? who can curiously behold
The smoothness and the sheen of beauty's cheek,
Nor feel the heart can never all grow old?
Who can contemplate fame through clouds unfold
The star which rises o'er her steep, nor climb?
Harold, once more within the vortex rolled
On with the giddy circle, chasing Time,

Yet with a nobler aim than in his youth's fond prime.

XII.

But soon he knew himself the most unfit
Of men to herd with Man; with whom he held
Little in common; untaught to submit
His thoughts to others, though his soul was quelled,
In youth by his own thoughts; still uncompelled,
He would not yield dominion of his mind
To spirits against whom his own rebelled;
Proud though in desolation; which could find
A life within itself, to breathe without mankind.

XIII.

Where rose the mountains, there to him were friends;
Where rolled the ocean, thereon was his home;
Where a blue sky, and glowing clime, extends,
He had the passion and the power to roam;
The desert, forest, cavern, breaker's foam,
Were unto him companionship; they spake
A mutual language, clearer than the tome
Of his land's tongue, which he would oft forsake
For nature's pages glassed by sunbeams on the lake.

XIV.

Like the Chaldean, he could watch the stars,
Till he had peopled them with beings bright
As their own beams; and earth, and earth-born jars,
And human frailties, were forgotten quite:
Could he have kept his spirit to that flight,
He had been happy; but this clay will sink
Its spark immortal, envying it the light
To which it mounts, as if to break the link
That keeps us from yon heaven which woos us to its brink.

XV.

But in Man's dwellings he became a thing
Restless and worn, and stern and wearisome,
Drooped as a wild-born falcon with clipt wing,
To whom the boundless air alone were home:
Then came his fit again, which to o'ercome,
As eagerly the barred-up bird will beat

His breast and beak against his wiry dome
Till the blood tinge his plumage, so the heat
Of his impeded soul would through his bosom eat.

XVI.

Self-exiled Harold wanders forth again,
With naught of hope left, but with less of gloom;
The very knowledge that he lived in vain,
That all was over on this side the tomb,
Had made Despair a smilingness assume,
Which, though 'twere wild—as on the plundered wreck
When mariners would madly meet their doom
With draughts intemperate on the sinking deck—
Did yet inspire a cheer, which he forbore to check.

Stop! for thy tread is on an empire's dust!
An earthquake's spoil is sepulchred below!
Is the spot marked with no colossal bust?
Nor column trophied for triumphal show?
None; but the moral's truth tells simpler so,
As the ground was before, thus let it be;—
How that red rain hath made the harvest grow!
And is this all the world has gained by thee,
Thou first and last of fields! king-making Victory?

XVIII.

And Harold stands upon this place of skulls,
The grave of France, the deadly Waterloo!
How in an hour the power which gave annuls
Its gifts, transferring fame as fleeting too!
In 'pride of place' here last the eagle flew,
Then tore with bloody talon the rent plain,
Pierced by the shaft of banded nations through:
Ambition's life and labours all were vain;
He wears the shattered links of the world's broken chain.

XIX.

Fit retribution! Gaul may champ the bit,
And foam in fetters, but is Earth more free?
Did nations combat to make ONE submit;
Or league to teach all kings true sovereignty?
What! shall reviving thraldom again be

The patched-up idol of enlightened days?
Shall we, who struck the Lion down, shall we
Pay the Wolf homage? proffering lowly gaze
And servile knees to thrones? No; PROVE before ye praise!

XX.

If not, o'er one fall'n despot boast no more!
In vain fair cheeks were furrowed with hot tears
For Europe's flowers long rooted up before
The trampler of her vineyards; in vain years
Of death, depopulation, bondage, fears,
Have all been borne, and broken by the accord
Of roused-up millions: all that most endears
Glory, is when the myrtle wreathes a sword
Such as Harmodius drew on Athens' tyrant lord.

XXI.

There was a sound of revelry by night,
And Belgium's capital had gathered then
Her Beauty and her Chivalry, and bright
The lamps shone o'er fair women and brave men;
A thousand hearts beat happily; and when
Music arose with its voluptuous swell,
Soft eyes looked love to eyes which spake again,
And all went merry as a marriage bell;
But hush! hark! a deep sound strikes like a rising knell!

XXII.

Did ye not hear it?—No; 'twas but the wind,
Or the car rattling o'er the stony street;
On with the dance! let joy be unconfined;
No sleep till morn, when Youth and Pleasure meet
To chase the glowing Hours with flying feet.
But hark!—that heavy sound breaks in once more,
As if the clouds its echo would repeat;
And nearer, clearer, deadlier than before!
Arm! arm! it is—it is—the cannon's opening roar!

XXIII.

Within a windowed niche of that high hall
Sate Brunswick's fated chieftain; he did hear
That sound, the first amidst the festival,

And caught its tone with Death's prophetic ear;
And when they smiled because he deemed it near,
His heart more truly knew that peal too well
Which stretched his father on a bloody bier,
And roused the vengeance blood alone could quell:
He rushed into the field, and, foremost fighting, fell.

XXIV.

Ah! then and there was hurrying to and fro,
And gathering tears, and tremblings of distress,
And cheeks all pale, which but an hour ago
Blushed at the praise of their own loveliness;
And there were sudden partings, such as press
The life from out young hearts, and choking sighs
Which ne'er might be repeated: who would guess
If ever more should meet those mutual eyes,
Since upon night so sweet such awful morn could rise!

XXV.

And there was mounting in hot haste: the steed,
The mustering squadron, and the clattering car,
Went pouring forward with impetuous speed,
And swiftly forming in the ranks of war;
And the deep thunder peal on peal afar;
And near, the beat of the alarming drum
Roused up the soldier ere the morning star;
While thronged the citizens with terror dumb,
Or whispering, with white lips—'The foe! They come! they come!'

Chapter Seventeen
Frankenstein[38]
(The Death of the Creature)

Chapter I

In the very same, now utterly abandoned, chair that the Creature had sat just weeks previous, now had a new occupant: my pale student of the unhallowed arts. Victor had returned to me! And quite queerly, he sat as flummoxed as I had been just having been told the Creature's tale.

'The being finished speaking, and fixed his looks upon me in expectation of a reply. But I was bewildered, perplexed, and unable to arrange my ideas sufficiently to understand the full extent of his proposition.'

Oh! Ho! So, Victor has just been told the Creature's tale just as I had been. So, the Creature had not been addressing me as its Creator at all. It had been Victor Frankenstein to whom was the Creature's audience all along. When the Creature looked upon me those handful a weeks ago, did he see my pale student of the unhallowed arts lying in bed beside my Beloved? And now that I contemplate this, had Victor seen me as the ship's captain Robert Walton all along? And my bedchamber as the captain's quarters on his ice-locked ship? What manner of lunacy have I been suffering from to hallucinate my own characters?

He continued— ' "You must create a female for me, with whom I can live in the interchange of those sympathies necessary for my being. This you alone can do; and I demand it of you as a right which you must not refuse."

So the Creation desires a mate? Again and again this tale of Victor's and his Creature's prove to me at least to be an allegory for Adam and Eve? Why haven't I heard a name given to the Creature? I have been forced by a lack of evidence to call him 'The Creation', until he murdered poor William and framed poorer Justine. From this point onward, he is nothing more that 'The Creature', a monster that I am ashamed my mind has given birth to. But if this is an allegory for Adam and Eve, should his name not be 'Adam' and his bride 'Eve'? And if this is an allegory, one most contemplate the source of the myth.

---

38 From *Frankenstein; or the Modern Prometheus* by Mary Wollstonecraft Shelley, published by Lackington, Hughes, Harding, Mavor & Jones, 1818

*Did not the Lord God say, 'It is not good that the man should be alone;
I will make him an help meet for him.' And did not, out of the ground
the Lord God form every beast of the field, and every fowl of the air; and
brought them unto Adam to see what he would call them: and whatsoever
Adam called every living creature, that was the name thereof? And did not
Adam give names to all cattle, and to the fowl of the air, and to every beast
of the field; but for Adam there was not found an help meet for him. Did
not the Lord God cause a deep sleep to fall upon Adam, and he slept: and
he take one of his ribs, and close up the flesh instead thereof; and the rib,
which the Lord God had taken from man, made he a woman, and brought
her unto the man? Did not Adam say, 'This is now bone of my bones, and
flesh of my flesh: she shall be called Woman, because she was taken out
of Man.'? Is not the intention of God that therefore shall a man leave his
father and his mother, and shall cleave unto his wife: and they shall be one
flesh?*[39] Should not the Creature have a wife to cleave to? Where *the
Lord God formed man of the dust of the ground, and breathed into his nos-
trils the breath of life; and man became a living soul*[40], Victor made his
Creature of the flesh of many men; should he not have a wife made of
many women? If I was the author of this tale and not an audience for
its telling, I would acquiesce to the Creature's desire.

The latter part of his tale had kindled anew in me the anger that had
died away while he narrated his peaceful life among the cottagers, and,
as he said this, I could no longer suppress the rage that burned within
me.

' "I do refuse it," I replied; "and no torture shall ever extort a consent
from me. You may render me the most miserable of men, but you shall
never make me base in my own eyes. Shall I create another like yourself,
whose joint wickedness might desolate the world. Begone! I have answered you; you may torture me, but I will never consent."

Is my pale student of the unhallowed arts feeling the same pangs
of regret that the Lord God did when Adam and Eve ate of the fruit of
the Tree of the Knowledge of Good and Evil? Just like the Lord God,
Victor had created his Creature out of a longing to do good, but the
Creature by its very nature as a manufactured and not created being.
While the De Lacys educated him with the knowledge of good, the
Creature possesses a little too much of the knowledge of evil from the
remainder of humanity. Is this through no fault of his own, for his in-
teractions with the fallen Creations of the Lord God have been... well,
unfortunate.

---

39 From Genesis 2:18-24, from the Authorized King James Translation of the Holy Bible.
40 From Genesis 2:7, from the Authorized King James Translation of the Holy Bible.

' "You are in the wrong," replied the fiend; "and, instead of threatening, I am content to reason with you. I am malicious because I am miserable; am I not shunned and hated by all mankind? You, my creator, would tear me to pieces, and triumph; remember that, and tell me why I should pity man more than he pities me? You would not call it murder, if you could precipitate me into one of those ice-rifts, and destroy my frame, the work of your own hands. Shall I respect man, when he contemns me? Let him live with me in the interchange of kindness, and, instead of injury, I would bestow every benefit upon him with tears of gratitude at his acceptance. But that cannot be; the human senses are insurmountable barriers to our union.'

The Creature errs. If there was a man born of sharp deformity, could he not be accepted by our society? Would his man be seen as a curiosity for mockery and scorn? Or should he be celebrated and his company sought after? What if both could be simultaneously true? And if there was a man born of sharp deformity, would his mind not be still so keen that he could and should adapt Isaac Watt's 'False Greatness' with his own opening lines?

> *'Tis true my form is something odd,*
> *But blaming me is blaming God,*
> *Could I create myself anew*
> *I would not fail in pleasing you.*
>
> *If I could reach from pole to pole,*
> *Or grasp the ocean with a span,*
> *I would be measured by the soul;*
> *The Mind's the standard of man.'*[41]

I possess the strongest of convictions that humanity could and would and should be much more welcoming of the Creature if given the proper opportunities and platform. While the religious may attempt to condemn and crucify Victor for dabbling in the realm reserved for God alone, such an articulate Creature could easily be welcomed into proper society as a wonder of the modern world?

Or am I being a fool?

'Yet mine shall not be the submission of abject slavery. I will revenge my injuries: if I cannot inspire love, I will cause fear; and chiefly towards you my arch-enemy, because my creator, do I swear inextinguishable

---

41 From an adaptation of Isaac Watt's poem, 'Fales Greatness', by Joseph Merrick, known as the 'Elephant Man'.

hatred. Have a care: I will work at your destruction, nor finish until I desolate your heart, so that you curse the hour of your birth."

'A fiendish rage animated him as he said this; his face was wrinkled into contortions too horrible for human eyes to behold; but presently he calmed himself, and proceeded—

' "I intended to reason. This passion is detrimental to me; for you do not reflect that you are the cause of its excess. If any being felt emotions of benevolence towards me, I should return them an hundred and an hundred fold; for that one creature's sake, I would make peace with the whole kind! But I now indulge in dreams of bliss that cannot be realized. What I ask of you is reasonable and moderate; I demand a creature of another sex, but as hideous as myself: the gratification is small, but it is all that I can receive, and it shall content me. It is true, we shall be monsters, cut off from all the world; but on that account we shall be more attached to one another. Our lives will not be happy, but they will be harmless, and free from the misery I now feel. Oh! my creator, make me happy; let me feel gratitude towards you for one benefit! Let me see that I excite the sympathy of some existing thing; do not deny me my request!"

'I was moved.' As am I! 'I shuddered when I thought of the possible consequences of my consent; but I felt that there was some justice in his argument. His tale, and the feelings he now expressed, proved him to be a creature of fine sensations; and did I not, as his maker, owe him all the portion of happiness that it was in my power to bestow?' So articulate and compassionate is the Creature and full of reason that I am so moved that I must return to calling him 'Creation'.

'He saw my change of feeling, and continued—

' "If you consent, neither you nor any other human being shall ever see us again: I will go to the vast wilds of South America. My food is not that of man; I do not destroy the lamb and the kid, to glut my appetite; acorns and berries afford me sufficient nourishment. My companion will be of the same nature as myself, and will be content with the same fare. We shall make our bed of dried leaves; the sun will shine on us as on man, and will ripen our food. The picture I present to you is peaceful and human, and you must feel that you could deny it only in the wantonness of power and cruelty. Pitiless as you have been towards me, I now see compassion in your eyes: let me seize the favourable moment, and persuade you to promise what I so ardently desire."

How this very much reminds me of my Beloved's own essays and poems vindicating a natural diet:

> 'My brethren, we are free! The fruits are glowing
> Beneath the stars, and the night-winds are flowing

O'er the ripe corn, the birds and beasts are dreaming–
Never again may blood of bird or beast
Stain with its venomous stream a human feast...
Reclining, as they ate, of Liberty,
And Hope, and Justice, and Laone's name,
Earth's children did a woof of happy converse frame...
Might share in peace and innocence, for gore
Or poison none this festal did pollute,
But, piled on high, an overflowing store
Of pomegranates and citrons, fairest fruit,
Melons, and dates, and figs, and many a root
Sweet and sustaining, and bright grapes ere yet
Accursed fire their mild juice could transmute
Into a mortal bane, and brown corn set
In baskets; with pure streams their thirsting lips they wet.[42]

Shall I share my own defence of my Beloved's beliefs? He chose for his hero a youth nourished in dreams of liberty, some of whose actions are in direct opposition to the opinions of the world, but who is animated throughout by an ardent love of virtue, and a resolution to confer the boons of political and intellectual freedom on his fellow-creatures. He created for this youth a woman such as he delighted to imagine—full of enthusiasm for the same objects; and they both, with will unvanquished and the deepest sense of the justice of their cause, met adversity and death. There exists in this poem a memorial of a friend of his youth. The character of the old man who liberates Laon from his tower prison, and tends on him in sickness, is founded on that of Doctor Lind, who, when Shelley was at Eton, had often stood by to befriend and support him, and whose name he never mentioned without love and veneration.

And again my own digressions now distract me from Victor's story: ' "You propose," replied I, "to fly from the habitations of man, to dwell in those wilds where the beasts of the field will be your only companions. How can you, who long for the love and sympathy of man, persevere in this exile? You will return, and again seek their kindness, and you will meet with their detestation; your evil passions will be renewed, and you will then have a companion to aid you in the task of destruction. This may not be; cease to argue the point, for I cannot consent."

' "How inconstant are your feelings!' I concur, dearest Creation. 'But a moment ago you were moved by my representations, and why do you again harden yourself to my complaints? I swear to you, by the

---

42 From *The Revolt of Islam*, canto 5, by Percy Bysshe Shelley, written between April and September 1817, but close enough for my purposes.

earth which I inhabit, and by you that made me, that, with the companion you bestow, I will quit the neighbourhood of man, and dwell, as it may chance, in the most savage of places. My evil passions will have fled, for I shall meet with sympathy; my life will flow quietly away, and, in my dying moments, I shall not curse my maker."

'His words had a strange effect upon me. I compassionated him, and sometimes felt a wish to console him; but when I looked upon him, when I saw the filthy mass that moved and talked, my heart sickened, and my feelings were altered to those of horror and hatred. I tried to stifle these sensations; I thought, that as I could not sympathize with him, I had no right to withhold from him the small portion of happiness which was yet in my power to bestow.'

How inconstant are your feelings, my pale student of the unhallowed arts!

' "You swear," I said, "to be harmless; but have you not already shewn a degree of malice that should reasonably make me distrust you? May not even this be a feint that will increase your triumph by affording a wider scope for your revenge?"

How constant are your feelings, my pale student of the unhallowed arts!

' "How is this? I thought I had moved your compassion, and yet you still refuse to bestow on me the only benefit that can soften my heart, and render me harmless. If I have no ties and no affections, hatred and vice must be my portion; the love of another will destroy the cause of my crimes, and I shall become a thing, of whose existence every one will be ignorant. My vices are the children of a forced solitude that I abhor; and my virtues will necessarily arise when I live in communion with an equal. I shall feel the affections of a sensitive being, and become linked to the chain of existence and events, from which I am now excluded."

Chain of existence? I recall these words, but from whence have I heard them. Victor would continue telling his tale unabetted, but I needed to know where I had heard these words. Ah!

> *Is the great chain, that draws all to agree,*
> *And drawn supports, upheld by God, or thee?*
>
> *Vast chain of being! which from God began,*
> *Natures ethereal, human, angel, man,*
> *Beast, bird, fish, insect, what no eye can see,*
> *No glass can reach; from Infinite to thee,*
> *From thee to nothing.*[43]

---

43 From *Essay of Man* by Alexander Pope, published in 1732.

* * *

'I paused some time to reflect on all he had related, and the various arguments which he had employed. I thought of the promise of virtues which he had displayed on the opening of his existence, and the subsequent blight of all kindly feeling by the loathing and scorn which his protectors had manifested towards him. His power and threats were not omitted in my calculations: a creature who could exist in the ice caves of the glaciers, and hide himself from pursuit among the ridges of inaccessible precipices, was a being possessing faculties it would be vain to cope with. After a long pause of reflection, I concluded, that the justice due both to him and my fellow-creatures demanded of me that I should comply with his request. Turning to him, therefore, I said—

' "I consent to your demand, on your solemn oath to quit Europe for ever, and every other place in the neighbourhood of man, as soon as I shall deliver into your hands a female who will accompany you in your exile."

' "I swear," he cried, "by the sun, and by the blue sky of heaven,'— and the fire of love that burns in his heart– 'that if you grant my prayer, while they exist you shall never behold me again. Depart to your home, and commence your labours: I shall watch their progress with unutterable anxiety; and fear not but that when you are ready I shall appear."

'Saying this, he suddenly quitted me, fearful, perhaps, of any change in my sentiments. I saw him descend the mountain with greater speed than the flight of an eagle, and quickly lost him among the undulations of the sea of ice.

'His tale had occupied the whole day; and the sun was upon the verge of the horizon when he departed. I knew that I ought to hasten my descent towards the valley, as I should soon be encompassed in darkness; but my heart was heavy, and my steps slow. The labour of winding among the little paths of the mountains, and fixing my feet firmly as I advanced, perplexed me, occupied as I was by the emotions which the occurrences of the day had produced. Night was far advanced, when I came to the half-way resting-place, and seated myself beside the fountain. The stars shone at intervals, as the clouds passed from over them; the dark pines rose before me, and every here and there a broken tree lay on the ground: it was a scene of wonderful solemnity, and stirred strange thoughts within me. I wept bitterly; and, clasping my hands in agony, I exclaimed, "Oh! stars, and clouds, and winds, ye are all about to mock me: if ye really pity me, crush sensation and memory; let me become as nought; but if not, depart, depart and leave me in darkness."

'These were wild and miserable thoughts; but I cannot describe to you how the eternal twinkling of the stars weighed upon me, and how I listened to every blast of wind, as if it were a dull ugly siroc on its way to consume me.

I heard the final words that Victor related unto me concluding this volume of his life, before he proceeds onto the next volume, but my mind constantly revised his words into those of my own: 'Morning dawned before I arrived at the village of Chamounix; I took no rest, but returned immediately to Geneva. Even in my own heart I could give no expression to my sensations—they weighed on me with a mountain's weight, and their excess destroyed my agony beneath them. Thus I returned home, and entering the house, presented myself to the family. My haggard and wild appearance awoke intense alarm; but I answered no question, scarcely did I speak. I felt as if I were placed under a ban—as if I had no right to claim their sympathies—as if never more might I enjoy companionship with them. Yet even thus I loved them to adoration; and to save them, I resolved to dedicate myself to my most abhorred task. The prospect of such an occupation made every other circumstance of existence pass before me like a dream; and that thought only had to me the reality of life.'

Chapter II

D ay after day, week after week, passed away on my return to Geneva; and I could not collect the courage to recommence my work.' Oh, dearest Victor, you promised your Creation you would deliver him a companion! 'I feared the vengeance of the disappointed fiend, yet I was unable to overcome my repugnance to the task which was enjoined me. I found that I could not compose a female without again devoting several months to profound study and laborious disquisition. I had heard of some discoveries having been made by an English philosopher, the knowledge of which was material to my success,'— who would be English philosopher be is most uncertain? I know many! Erasmus Darwin is the most likely candidate. Truly the feminine creature is much more a complex physiological form than the masculine machinery. My Beloved has often said that *Man is mechanical, Woman is art!* Is there where Victor's consternation lies? Even Leonardo DaVinci, so astute in his observations of human anatomy avoided autopsying the female corpse. So repulsed was he of the feminine form and the unfathomable mysteries of 'wandering womb' that he refused any such study. A consummate observer may observe that obtaining female corpses proved far too difficult, but I believe he was truly horrified of *every* aspect of the feminine reproduction from birth itself to the very act of copulation. 'And I sometimes thought of obtaining my father's consent to visit England for this purpose; but I clung to every pretence of delay, and could not resolve to interrupt my returning tranquillity. My health, which had hitherto declined, was now much restored; and my spirits, when unchecked by the memory of my unhappy promise, rose proportionably. My father saw this change with pleasure, and he turned his thoughts towards the best method of eradicating the remains of my melancholy, which every now and then would return by fits, and with a devouring blackness overcast the approaching sunshine. At these moments I took refuge in the most perfect solitude. I passed whole days on the lake alone in a little boat, watching the clouds, and listening to the rippling of the waves, silent and listless. But the fresh air and bright sun seldom failed to restore me to some degree of composure; and, on my return, I met the salutations of my friends with a readier smile and a more cheerful heart.

'It was after my return from one of these rambles that my father, calling me aside, thus addressed me:—

' "I am happy to remark, my dear son, that you have resumed your former pleasures, and seem to be returning to yourself. And yet you are still unhappy, and still avoid our society. For some time I was lost in conjecture as to the cause of this; but yesterday an idea struck me, and if it is well founded, I conjure you to avow it. Reserve on such a point would be not only useless, but draw down treble misery on us all."

'I trembled violently at this exordium, and my father continued—

' "I confess, my son, that I have always looked forward to your marriage with your cousin as the tie of our domestic comfort, and the stay of my declining years. You were attached to each other from your earliest infancy; you studied together, and appeared, in dispositions and tastes, entirely suited to one another. But so blind is the experience of man, that what I conceived to be the best assistants to my plan may have entirely destroyed it. You, perhaps, regard her as your sister, without any wish that she might become your wife. Nay, you may have met with another whom you may love; and, considering yourself as bound in honour to your cousin, this struggle may occasion the poignant misery which you appear to feel."

' "My dear father, re-assure yourself. I love my cousin tenderly and sincerely. I never saw any woman who excited, as Elizabeth does, my warmest admiration and affection. My future hopes and prospects are entirely bound up in the expectation of our union."

' "The expression of your sentiments on this subject, my dear Victor, gives me more pleasure than I have for some time experienced. If you feel thus, we shall assuredly be happy, however present events may cast a gloom over us. But it is this gloom, which appears to have taken so strong a hold of your mind, that I wish to dissipate. Tell me, therefore, whether you object to an immediate solemnization of the marriage. We have been unfortunate, and recent events have drawn us from that every-day tranquillity befitting my years and infirmities. You are younger; yet I do not suppose, possessed as you are of a competent fortune, that an early marriage would at all interfere with any future plans of honour and utility that you may have formed. Do not suppose, however, that I wish to dictate happiness to you, or that a delay on your part would cause me any serious uneasiness. Interpret my words with candour, and answer me, I conjure you, with confidence and sincerity."

'I listened to my father in silence, and remained for some time in-capable of offering any reply. I revolved rapidly in my mind a multitude of thoughts, and endeavoured to arrive at some conclusion. Alas! to me the idea of an immediate union with my cousin was one of horror and dismay. I was bound by a solemn promise, which I had not yet fulfilled, and dared not break; or, if I did, what manifold miseries might not im-pend over me and my devoted family! Could I enter into a festival with this deadly weight yet hanging round my neck, and bowing me to the ground. I must perform my engagement, and let the monster depart with his mate, before I allowed myself to enjoy the delight of an union from which I expected peace.

'I remembered also the necessity imposed upon me of either journey-ing to England, or entering into a long correspondence with those philos-ophers of that country, whose knowledge and discoveries were of indis-pensable use to me in my present undertaking— my hand again revised his own words as I recorded them into my journal— The latter method of obtaining the desired intelligence was dilatory and unsatisfactory: be-sides, I had an insurmountable aversion to the idea of engaging myself in my loathsome task in my father's house, while in habits of familiar intercourse with those I loved. I knew that a thousand fearful accidents might occur, the slightest of which would disclose a tale to thrill all con-nected with me with horror. I was aware also that I should often lose all self-command, all capacity of hiding the harrowing sensations that would possess me during the progress of my unearthly occupation. I must ab-sent myself from all I loved while thus employed. Once commenced, it would quickly be achieved, and I might be restored to my family in peace and happiness. My promise fulfilled, the monster would depart for ever. Or (so my fond fancy imaged) some accident might meanwhile occur to destroy him, and put an end to my slavery for ever.

'These feelings dictated my answer to my father. I expressed a wish to visit England; but, concealing the true reasons of this request, I clothed my desires under a guise— again my hand recorded other words— which excited no suspicion, while I urged my desire with an earnestness that easily induced my father to comply. After so long a period of an absorbing melancholy, that resembled madness in its intensity and effects, he was glad to find that I was capable of taking pleasure in the idea of such a journey, and he hoped that change of scene and varied amusement would, before my return, have restored me entirely to myself.

'The duration of my absence was left to my own choice; a few months, or at most a year, was the period contemplated. One paternal kind precaution he had taken to ensure my having a companion. Without previously communicating with me, he had, in concert with Elizabeth, arranged that Clerval should join me at Strasburgh. This interfered with the solitude I coveted for the prosecution of my task; yet at the commencement of my journey the presence of my friend could in no way be an impediment, and truly I rejoiced that thus I should be saved many hours of lonely, maddening reflection. Nay, Henry might stand between me and the intrusion of my foe. If I were alone, would he not at times force his abhorred presence on me, to remind me of my task, or to contemplate its progress?

'To England, therefore, I was bound, and it was understood that my union with Elizabeth should take place immediately on my return. My father's age rendered him extremely averse to delay. For myself, there was one reward I promised myself from my detested toils—one consolation for my unparalleled sufferings; it was the prospect of that day when, enfranchised from my miserable slavery, I might claim Elizabeth, and forget the past in my union with her.

'I now made arrangements for my journey; but one feeling haunted me, which filled me with fear and agitation. During my absence I should leave my friends unconscious of the existence of their enemy, and unprotected from his attacks, exasperated as he might be by my departure. But he had promised to follow me wherever I might go; and would he not accompany me to England? This imagination was dreadful in itself, but soothing, inasmuch as it supposed the safety of my friends. I was agonized with the idea of the possibility that the reverse of this might happen. But through the whole period during which I was the slave of my creature, I allowed myself to be governed by the impulses of the moment; and my present sensations strongly intimated that the fiend would follow me, and exempt my family from the danger of his machinations.

Again and again my hand revises his words. Why? When will this madness end?

'It was in the latter end of September that I again quitted my native country. My journey had been my own suggestion, and Elizabeth, therefore, acquiesced: but she was filled with disquiet at the idea of my suffering, away from her, the inroads of misery and grief. It had been her care which provided me a companion in Clerval—and yet a man is blind to a thousand minute circumstances, which call forth a woman's sedulous attention. She longed to bid me hasten my return,—a thousand conflicting emotions rendered her mute, as she bade me a tearful silent farewell.

'I threw myself into the carriage that was to convey me away, hardly knowing whither I was going, and careless of what was passing around. I remembered only, and it was with a bitter anguish that I reflected on it, to order that my chemical instruments should be packed to go with me: for I resolved to fulfil my promise while abroad, and return, if possible, a free man. Filled with dreary imaginations, I passed through many beautiful and majestic scenes; but my eyes were fixed and unobserving. I could only think of the bourne of my travels, and the work which was to occupy me whilst they endured.

'After some days spent in listless indolence, during which I traversed many leagues, I arrived at Strasburgh, where I waited two days for Clerval. He came. Alas, how great was the contrast between us! He was alive to every new scene; joyful when he saw the beauties of the setting sun, and more happy when he beheld it rise, and recommence a new day. He pointed out to me the shifting colours of the landscape, and the appearances of the sky. "This is what it is to live;" he cried, "now I enjoy existence! But you, my dear Frankenstein, wherefore are you desponding and sorrowful?" In truth, I was occupied by gloomy thoughts, and neither saw the descent of the evening star, nor the golden sun-rise reflected in the Rhine.— And you, my friend would be far more amused with the journal of Clerval, who observed the scenery with an eye of feeling and delight, than to listen to my reflections. I, a miserable wretch, haunted by a curse that shut up every avenue to enjoyment'— is he addressing me directly or Walton? Curious!

'We had agreed to descend the Rhine in a boat from Strasburgh to Rotterdam, whence we might take shipping for London. During this voyage, we passed by many willowy islands, and saw several beautiful towns. We staid a day at Manheim, and, on the fifth from our departure from Strasburgh, arrived at Mayence. The course of the Rhine below Mayence becomes much more picturesque. The river descends rapidly, and winds between hills, not high, but steep, and of beautiful forms. We saw many ruined castles standing on the edges of precipices, surrounded by black woods, high and inaccessible.'

Oh! Ho! I know this place. My Beloved wished to tarry at this very castle because he personally knew several members of the 'Kreis der Empfindsamen', a literary circle from Darmstadt, who used the castle for their readings. Did they believe they were a Hellfire Club reciting their poems as if spells to summon the Great Dragon himself, that old serpent, called the Devil, and Satan, who deceives the whole world? At the Castle Frankenstein, we encountered students from the University of Strasbourg, of which Johann Konrad Dippel was an infamous alumnus. We learned from them of Dippel's discovery of the 'Elixir of Life', as evidenced by his *Maladies and Remedies of the Life of the Flesh*. He made this dark, viscous, tar-like, and putrid oil through the destructive distillation of bones. How could rotting death ever be an 'elixir of life'? The students spoke quiet highly of the Pietist theologian, physician, and alchemist, though they admitted that one Emanuel Swedenborg, both once a devoted disciple and then staunch critic had dismissed him as 'bound to no principles, but was in general opposed to all, whoever they may be, of whatever principle or faith ... becoming angry with any one for contradicting him.' How Swedenborg had fallen from once being enamoured to then being repulsed by 'a most vile devil... who attempted wicked things.' But the students hailed the glorious alchemist (though locals remembered him as notorious graverobber), who experimented in anatomy and supposedly transferred the souls from one cadaver to another with a funnel, as an exorcist and a saint! Did he not, they claimed, create an alchemic potion concocted from boiled animal bones and their flesh to supplant the *Rituale Romanum*, and therefore the Vatican, in the exorcising of demons? 'How my mind has born so many curious parts of this tale being related to me by my pale student of the unhallowed arts!

   This part of the Rhine, indeed, presents a singularly variegated landscape. In one spot you view rugged hills, ruined castles overlooking tremendous precipices, with the dark Rhine rushing beneath; and, on the sudden turn of a promontory, flourishing vineyards, with green sloping banks, and a meandering river, and populous towns, occupy the scene.

   'We travelled at the time of the vintage, and heard the song of the labourers, as we glided down the stream. Even I, depressed in mind, and my spirits continually agitated by gloomy feelings, even I was pleased. I lay at the bottom of the boat, and, as I gazed on the cloudless blue sky, I seemed to drink in a tranquillity to which I had long been a stranger. And if these were my sensations, who can describe those of Henry? He felt as if he had been transported to Fairy-land, and enjoyed a happiness seldom tasted by man. "I have seen," he said, "the most beautiful scenes of my own country; I have visited the lakes of Lucerne and Uri, where the snowy mountains descend almost perpendicularly to the water, casting black and impenetrable shades, which would cause a gloomy and mournful appearance, were it not for the most verdant islands that relieve the eye by their gay appearance; I have seen this lake agitated by a tempest, when the wind tore up whirlwinds of water, and gave you an idea of what the water-spout must be on the great ocean, and the waves dash with fury the base of the mountain, where the priest and his mistress were overwhelmed by an avalanche, and where their dying voices are still said to be heard amid the pauses of the nightly wind; I have seen the mountains of La Valais, and the Pays de Vaud: but this country, Victor, pleases me more than all those wonders. The mountains of Switzerland are more majestic and strange; but there is a charm in the banks of this divine river, that I never before saw equalled. Look at that castle which overhangs yon precipice; and that also on the island, almost concealed amongst the foliage of those lovely trees; and now that group of labourers coming from among their vines; and that village half-hid in the recess of the mountain. Oh, surely, the spirit that inhabits and guards this place has a soul more in harmony with man, than those who pile the glacier, or retire to the inaccessible peaks of the mountains of our own country."

'Clerval! beloved friend! even now it delights me to record your words, and to dwell on the praise of which you are so eminently deserving. He was a being formed in the "very poetry of nature." His wild and enthusiastic imagination was chastened by the sensibility of his heart. His soul overflowed with ardent affections, and his friendship was of that devoted and wondrous nature that the worldly-minded teach us to look for only in the imagination. But even human sympathies were not sufficient to satisfy his eager mind. The scenery of external nature, which others regard only with admiration, he loved with ardour:

> *"The sounding cataract*
> *Haunted him* like a passion: the tall rock,
> *The mountain, and the deep and gloomy wood,*
> *Their colours and their forms, were then to him*
> *An appetite; a feeling, and a love,*
> *That had no need of a remoter charm,*
> *By thought supplied, or any interest*
> *Unborrowed from the eye."*

Oh! William Wordsworth! His words are worth their weight in gold! But another anachronism. I believe this poem was written after the dates related to me in this tale of Victor's. Again, my mind plays tricks upon me. Curious.

'And where does he now exist? Is this gentle and lovely being lost for ever? Has this mind so replete with ideas, imaginations fanciful and magnificent, which formed a world, whose existence depended on the life of its creator; has this mind perished? Does it now only exist in my memory? No, it is not thus; your form so divinely wrought, and beaming with beauty, has decayed, but your spirit still visits and consoles your unhappy friend.

'Pardon this gush of sorrow; these ineffectual words are but a slight tribute to the unexampled worth of Henry, but they soothe my heart, overflowing with the anguish which his remembrance creates. I will proceed with my tale.

'Beyond Cologne we descended to the plains of Holland; and we resolved to post the remainder of our way; for the wind was contrary, and the stream of the river was too gentle to aid us.

'Our journey here lost the interest arising from beautiful scenery; but we arrived in a few days at Rotterdam, whence we proceeded by sea to England. It was on a clear morning, in the latter days of December, that I first saw the white cliffs of Britain. The banks of the Thames presented a new scene; they were flat, but fertile, and almost every town was marked by the remembrance of some story. We saw Tilbury Fort, and remembered the Spanish armada; Gravesend, Woolwich, and Greenwich, places which I had heard of even in my country.

'At length we saw the numerous steeples of London, St. Paul's towering above all, and the Tower famed in English history.'

How I know them all so well! Curious!

Chapter III

London was our present point of rest; we determined to remain several months in this wonderful and celebrated city. Clerval desired the intercourse of the men of genius and talent who flourished at this time; but this was with me a secondary object; I was principally occupied with the means of obtaining the information necessary for the completion of my promise, and quickly availed myself of the letters of introduction that I had brought with me, addressed to the most distinguished natural philosophers.

'If this journey had taken place during my days of study and happiness, it would have afforded me inexpressible pleasure. But a blight had come over my existence, and I only visited these people for the sake of the information they might give me on the subject in which my interest was so terribly profound. Company was irksome to me; when alone, I could fill my mind with the sights of heaven and earth; the voice of Henry soothed me, and I could thus cheat myself into a transitory peace. But busy uninteresting joyous faces brought back despair to my heart. I saw an insurmountable barrier placed between me and my fellow-men; this barrier was sealed with the blood of William and Justine; and to reflect on the events connected with those names filled my soul with anguish.

'But in Clerval I saw the image of my former self; he was inquisitive, and anxious to gain experience and instruction. The difference of manners which he observed was to him an inexhaustible source of instruction and amusement. He was also pursuing an object he had long had in view. His design was to visit India, in the belief that he had in his knowledge of its various languages, and in the views he had taken of its society, the means of materially assisting the progress of European colonisation and trade. In Britain only could he further the execution of his plan. He was for ever busy; and the only check to his enjoyments was my sorrowful and dejected mind. I tried to conceal this as much as possible, that I might not debar him from the pleasures natural to one, who was entering on a new scene of life, undisturbed by any care or bitter recollection. I often refused to accompany him, alleging another engagement, that I might remain alone. I now also began to collect the materials necessary for my new creation'— Oh! Ho! He does intend to create a feminine creature for his Creation, but where-oh-where would he store these body parts, if this is what his intention is with these words?— 'and this was to me like the torture of single drops of water continually falling on the head. Every thought that was devoted to it was an extreme anguish, and every word that I spoke in allusion to it caused my lips to quiver, and my heart to palpitate.

'After passing some months in London, we received a letter from a person in Scotland, who had formerly been our visitor at Geneva. He mentioned the beauties of his native country, and asked us if those were not sufficient allurements to induce us to prolong our journey as far north as Perth, where he resided. Clerval eagerly desired to accept this invitation; and I, although I abhorred society, wished to view again mountains and streams, and all the wondrous works with which Nature adorns her chosen dwelling-places.

'We had arrived in England at the beginning of October'— how I believed he said 'December'. If Victor give me pause to flip back through my journal I can see... ah... yes, he did say 'December'! Curious! This error must be corrected— 'and it was now February. We accordingly determined to commence our journey towards the north at the expiration of another month. In this expedition we did not intend to follow the great road to Edinburgh, but to visit Windsor, Oxford, Matlock, and the Cumberland lakes, resolving to arrive at the completion of this tour about the end of July. I packed my chemical instruments, and the materials I had collected, resolving to finish my labours in some obscure nook in the northern highlands of Scotland.

'We quitted London on the 27th of March, and remained a few days at Windsor, rambling in its beautiful forest. This was a new scene to us mountaineers; the majestic oaks, the quantity of game, and the herds of stately deer, were all novelties to us.

'From thence we proceeded to Oxford. As we entered this city, our minds were filled with the remembrance of the events that had been transacted there more than a century and a half before. It was here that Charles I. had collected his forces. This city had remained faithful to him, after the whole nation had forsaken his cause to join the standard of parliament and liberty. The memory of that unfortunate king, and his companions, the amiable Falkland, the insolent Gower, his queen, and son, gave a peculiar interest to every part of the city, which they might be supposed to have inhabited. The spirit of elder days found a dwelling here, and we delighted to trace its footsteps. If these feelings had not found an imaginary gratification, the appearance of the city had yet in itself sufficient beauty to obtain our admiration. The colleges are ancient and picturesque; the streets are almost magnificent; and the lovely Isis, which flows beside it through meadows of exquisite verdure, is spread forth into a placid expanse of waters, which reflects its majestic assemblage of towers, and spires, and domes, embosomed among aged trees.

'I enjoyed this scene; and yet my enjoyment was embittered both by the memory of the past, and the anticipation of the future. I was formed for peaceful happiness. During my youthful days discontent never visited my mind; and if I was ever overcome by *ennui*, the sight of what is beautiful in nature, or the study of what is excellent and sublime in the productions of man, could always interest my heart, and communicate elasticity to my spirits. But I am a blasted tree; the bolt has entered my soul; and I felt then that I should survive to exhibit, what I shall soon cease to be— a miserable spectacle of wrecked humanity, pitiable to others, and abhorrent to myself.

'We passed a considerable period at Oxford, rambling among its environs, and endeavouring to identify every spot which might relate to the most animating epoch of English history. Our little voyages of discovery were often prolonged by the successive objects that presented themselves. We visited the tomb of the illustrious Hampden, and the field on which that patriot fell. For a moment my soul was elevated from its debasing and miserable fears to contemplate the divine ideas of liberty and self-sacrifice, of which these sights were the monuments and the remembrancers. For an instant I dared to shake off my chains, and look around me with a free and lofty spirit; but the iron had eaten into my flesh, and I sank again, trembling and hopeless, into my miserable self.

'We left Oxford with regret, and proceeded to Matlock, which was our next place of rest. The country in the neighbourhood of this village resembled, to a greater degree, the scenery of Switzerland; but every thing is on a lower scale, and the green hills want the crown of distant white Alps, which always attend on the piny mountains of my native country. We visited the wondrous cave, and the little cabinets of natural history, where the curiosities are disposed in the same manner as in the collections at Servox and Chamounix. The latter name made me tremble, when pronounced by Henry; and I hastened to quit Matlock, with which that terrible scene was thus associated.

'From Derby still journeying northward, we passed two months in Cumberland and Westmoreland. I could now almost fancy myself among the Swiss mountains. The little patches of snow which yet lingered on the northern sides of the mountains, the lakes, and the dashing of the rocky streams, were all familiar and dear sights to me. Here also we made some acquaintances, who almost contrived to cheat me into happiness. The delight of Clerval was proportionably greater than mine; his mind expanded in the company of men of talent, and he found in his own nature greater capacities and resources than he could have imagined himself to have possessed while he associated with his inferiors. "I could pass my life here," said he to me; "and among these mountains I should scarcely regret Switzerland and the Rhine."

'But he found that a traveller's life is one that includes much pain amidst its enjoyments. His feelings are for ever on the stretch; and when he begins to sink into repose, he finds himself obliged to quit that on which he rests in pleasure for something new, which again engages his attention, and which also he forsakes for other novelties.

'We had scarcely visited the various lakes of Cumberland and West-moreland, and conceived an affection for some of the inhabitants, when the period of our appointment with our Scotch friend approached, and we left them to travel on. For my own part I was not sorry. I had now neglected my promise for some time, and I feared the effects of the dæmon's disappointment. He might remain in Switzerland, and wreak his vengeance on my relatives. This idea pursued me, and tormented me at every moment from which I might otherwise have snatched repose and peace. I waited for my letters with feverish impatience: if they were delayed, I was miserable, and overcome by a thousand fears; and when they arrived, and I saw the superscription of Elizabeth or my father, I hardly dared to read and ascertain my fate.'

How I have been enjoying this travelogue of dear Victor's! Its reminisces reminds me of the one I and my Beloved are composing of our present tour and that of last year. I have been drawn into my own memories of these lands so completely that—

'Sometimes I thought that the fiend followed me, and might expedite my remissness by murdering my companion. When these thoughts possessed me, I would not quit Henry for a moment, but followed him as his shadow, to protect him from the fancied rage of his destroyer. I felt as if I had committed some great crime, the consciousness of which haunted me. I was guiltless, but I had indeed drawn down a horrible curse upon my head, as mortal as that of crime.

— Damn Victor to Hellfire Eternal for breaking me out of my complacency! And now his excepts his travelogue to resume? Damn him!

'I visited Edinburgh with languid eyes and mind; and yet that city might have interested the most unfortunate being. Clerval did not like it so well as Oxford; for the antiquity of the latter city was more pleasing to him. But the beauty and regularity of the new town of Edinburgh, its romantic castle, and its environs, the most delightful in the world, Arthur's Seat, St. Bernard's Well, and the Pentland Hills, compensated him for the change, and filled him with cheerfulness and admiration. But I was impatient to arrive at the termination of my journey.

'We left Edinburgh in a week, passing through Coupar, St. Andrews, and along the banks of the Tay, to Perth, where our friend expected us. But I was in no mood to laugh and talk with strangers, or enter into their feelings or plans with the good humour expected from a guest; and accordingly I told Clerval that I wished to make the tour of Scotland alone. "Do you," said I, "enjoy yourself, and let this be our rendezvous. I may be absent a month or two; but do not interfere with my motions, I entreat you: leave me to peace and solitude for a short time; and when I return, I hope it will be with a lighter heart, more congenial to your own temper."

'Henry wished to dissuade me; but, seeing me bent on this plan, ceased to remonstrate. He entreated me to write often. "I had rather be with you," he said, "in your solitary rambles, than with these Scotch people, whom I do not know: hasten then, my dear friend, to return, that I may again feel myself somewhat at home, which I cannot do in your absence."

'Having parted from my friend, I determined to visit some remote spot of Scotland, and finish my work in solitude. I did not doubt but that the monster followed me, and would discover himself to me when I should have finished, that he might receive his companion.

'With this resolution I traversed the northern highlands, and fixed on one of the remotest of the Orkneys as the scene labours. It was a place fitted for such a work, being hardly more than a rock, whose high sides were continually beaten upon by the waves. The soil was barren, scarcely affording pasture for a few miserable cows, and oatmeal for its inhabitants, which consisted of five persons, whose gaunt and scraggy limbs gave tokens of their miserable fare. Vegetables and bread, when they indulged in such luxuries, and even fresh water, was to be procured from the main land, which was about five miles distant.

'On the whole island there were but three miserable huts, and one of these was vacant when I arrived. This I hired. It contained but two rooms, and these exhibited all the squalidness of the most miserable penury. The thatch had fallen in, the walls were unplastered, and the door was off its hinges. I ordered it to be repaired, bought some furniture, and took possession; an incident which would, doubtless, have occasioned some surprise, had not all the senses of the cottagers been benumbed by want and squalid poverty. As it was, I lived ungazed at and unmolested, hardly thanked for the pittance of food and clothes which I gave; so much does suffering blunt even the coarsest sensations of men.

'In this retreat I devoted the morning to labour; but in the evening, when the weather permitted, I walked on the stony beach of the sea, to listen to the waves as they roared, and dashed at my feet. It was a monotonous, yet ever-changing scene. I thought of Switzerland; it was far different from this desolate and appalling landscape. Its hills are covered with vines, and its cottages are scattered thickly in the plains. Its fair lakes reflect a blue and gentle sky; and, when troubled by the winds, their tumult is but as the play of a lively infant, when compared to the roarings of the giant ocean.

'In this manner I distributed my occupations when I first arrived; but, as I proceeded in my labour, it became every day more horrible and irksome to me. Sometimes I could not prevail on myself to enter my laboratory for several days; and at other times I toiled day and night in order to complete my work. It was indeed a filthy process in which I was engaged.' Again I am reminded of Leonardo's own revulsion towards the feminine creature. 'During my first experiment, a kind of enthusiastic frenzy had blinded me to the horror of my employment; my mind was intently fixed on the consummation of my labour, and my eyes were shut to the horror of my proceedings. But now I went to it in cold blood, and my heart often sickened at the work of my hands.

'Thus situated, employed in the most detestable occupation, immersed in a solitude where nothing could for an instant call my attention from the actual scene in which I was engaged, my spirits became unequal; I grew restless and nervous. Every moment I feared to meet my persecutor. Sometimes I sat with my eyes fixed on the ground, fearing to raise them lest they should encounter the object which I so much dreaded to behold. I feared to wander from the sight of my fellow-creatures, lest when alone he should come to claim his companion.

'In the mean time I worked on, and my labour was already considerably advanced. I looked towards its completion with a tremulous and eager hope, which I dared not trust myself to question, but which was intermixed with obscure forebodings of evil, that made my heart sicken in my bosom.

Chapter IV

I sat one evening in my laboratory; the sun had set, and the moon was just rising from the sea; I had not sufficient light for my employment, and I remained idle, in a pause of consideration of whether I should leave my labour for the night, or hasten its conclusion by an unremitting attention to it. As I sat, a train of reflection occurred to me, which led me to consider the effects of what I was now doing. Three years before I was engaged in the same manner, and had created a fiend whose unparalleled barbarity had desolated my heart, and filled it for ever with the bitterest remorse. I was now about to form another being, of whose dispositions I was alike ignorant; she might become ten thousand times more malignant than her mate, and delight, for its own sake, in murder and wretchedness. He had sworn to quit the neighbourhood of man, and hide himself in deserts; but she had not; and she, who in all probability was to become a thinking and reasoning animal, might refuse to comply with a compact made before her creation. They might even hate each other; the creature who already lived loathed his own deformity, and might he not conceive a greater abhorrence for it when it came before his eyes in the female form? She also might turn with disgust from him to the superior beauty of man; she might quit him, and he be again alone, exasperated by the fresh provocation of being deserted by one of his own species.'

Is my mind foreshadowing the clear eventuality of this tale of Victor's?

'Even if they were to leave Europe, and inhabit the deserts of the new world, yet one of the first results of those sympathies for which the dæmon thirsted would be children, and a race of devils would be propagated upon the earth, who might make the very existence of the species of man a condition precarious and full of terror. Had I a right, for my own benefit, to inflict this curse upon everlasting generations? I had before been moved by the sophisms of the being I had created; I had been struck senseless by his fiendish threats: but now, for the first time, the wickedness of my promise burst upon me; I shuddered to think that future ages might curse me as their pest, whose selfishness had not hesitated to buy its own peace at the price perhaps of the existence of the whole human race.

'I trembled, and my heart failed within me; when, on looking up, I saw, by the light of the moon, the dæmon at the casement. A ghastly grin wrinkled his lips as he gazed on me, where I sat fulfilling the task which he had allotted to me. Yes, he had followed me in my travels; he had loitered in forests, hid himself in caves, or taken refuge in wide and desert heaths; and he now came to mark my progress, and claim the fulfilment of my promise.

'As I looked on him, his countenance expressed the utmost extent of malice and treachery. I thought with a sensation of madness on my promise of creating another like to him, and, trembling with passion, tore to pieces the thing on which I was engaged. The wretch saw me destroy the creature on whose future existence he depended for happiness, and, with a howl of devilish despair and revenge, withdrew.'

No! Do not destroy the last vestiges of your Creation's hopes and dreams? You rend the flesh freshly sewn together apart, casting one limb against this unplastered wall and the other limb against the other. Her head is torn from her neck; the stitches tearing apart with the mouth agape in horror as if to scream if only the lungs had any strength to draw breath. You reach into the birth canal of his failed experiment and tear out the very womb that might give birth to an entire race of Creatures bent on the destruction of the parent species. You squeeze into your fist the very womb you have so carefully, horrifyingly constructed that will never now know life growing within it! The puss and blood dripped onto the floor of our apartment. The seed, if the Creation possesses any semen in his own dried stones, will never now know the freedom of swimming with the rich, lifegiving waters of the female Creation's birth canal. There will be no egg to greet the seed in this once carefully, horrifyingly constructed womb. With teeth clenched and blood dripping from a bitten lip, you invite your own destruction!

How I long to be no longer haunted by my pale student of the unhallowed arts. I am done with him! His soul is as rotten and worm infested as an apple left on the windowsill to fester in the sun. My pale student of the unhallowed arts, whom I longed to know more about from our first chance encounter during that thunderstorm-and-lightning-fuelled nightmare after a spirited and galvanising debate, was shown to me to be nothing more than failed student with a hollow heart.

And why did the Creation flee? Why should he not attempt to halt the destruction of his Bride? Mary, this does not make any sense! Victor's Creation should thrash him within an inch of his miserable life! But instead, your mind, he is out in the world doing what? Paddling about in his little boat? Mary, I am disgusted by your own literary decisions. But who am I to alter the story being related to me by my failed student with a hollow heart?

'I left the room, and, locking the door, made a solemn vow in my own heart never to resume my labours; and then, with trembling steps, I sought my own apartment. I was alone; none were near me to dissipate the gloom, and relieve me from the sickening oppression of the most terrible reveries.

'Several hours past, and I remained near my window gazing on the sea; it was almost motionless, for the winds were hushed, and all nature reposed under the eye of the quiet moon. A few fishing vessels alone specked the water, and now and then the gentle breeze wafted the sound of voices, as the fishermen called to one another. I felt the silence, although I was hardly conscious of its extreme profundity until my ear was suddenly arrested by the paddling of oars near the shore, and a person landed close to my house.

'In a few minutes after, I heard the creaking of my door, as if some one endeavoured to open it softly. I trembled from head to foot; I felt a presentiment of who it was, and wished to rouse one of the peasants who dwelt in a cottage not far from mine; but I was overcome by the sensation of helplessness, so often felt in frightful dreams, when you in vain endeavour to fly from an impending danger, and was rooted to the spot.

'Presently I heard the sound of footsteps along the passage; the door opened, and the wretch whom I dreaded appeared. Shutting the door, he approached me, and said, in a smothered voice—

I shall tear all these four paragraphs out of my journal and cast them into the fire beside which Victor sits and jump straight away with the trashing of the failed student with a hollow heart! Why are these words still present in my journal? Why haven't I struck them out with violent slashes of my pen? Blotted out of existence with ink. But this is *not* my tale which is being told. It is Victor's and Victor had told it in his own fashion and in his own time. Sometimes the author of the work is not truly the author but merely taking dictation. And yes, I am merely taking dictation!

' "You have destroyed the work which you began; what is it that you intend? Do you dare to break your promise? I have endured toil and misery: I left Switzerland with you; I crept along the shores of the Rhine, among its willow islands, and over the summits of its hills. I have dwelt many months in the heaths of England, and among the deserts of Scotland. I have endured incalculable fatigue, and cold, and hunger; do you dare destroy my hopes?"

' "Begone! I do break my promise; never will I create another like yourself, equal in deformity and wickedness."

' "Slave, I before reasoned with you, but you have proved yourself unworthy of my condescension. Remember that I have power; you believe yourself miserable, but I can make you so wretched that the light of day will be hateful to you. You are my creator, but I am your master;— obey!"

' "The hour of my weakness is past, and the period of your power is arrived. Your threats cannot move me to do an act of wickedness; but they confirm me in a resolution of not creating you a companion in vice. Shall I, in cool blood, set loose upon the earth a dæmon, whose delight is in death and wretchedness. Begone! I am firm, and your words will only exasperate my rage."

'The monster saw my determination in my face, and gnashed his teeth in the impotence of anger. "Shall each man," cried he, "find a wife for his bosom, and each beast have his mate, and I be alone?' Ah! Does not God command the man and the women whom He has creating saying, *Be fruitful, and multiply, and replenish the earth, and subdue it: and have dominion over the fish of the sea, and over the fowl of the air, and over every living thing that moveth upon the earth.*[44] Little does the Creation know that Gods command, here, seals his fate! 'I had feelings of affection, and they were requited by detestation and scorn. Man, you may hate; but beware! Your hours will pass in dread and misery, and soon the bolt will fall which must ravish from you your happiness for ever. Are you to be happy, while I grovel in the intensity of my wretchedness? You can blast my other passions; but revenge remains— revenge, henceforth dearer than light or food! I may die; but first you, my tyrant and tormentor, shall curse the sun that gazes on your misery. Beware; for I am fearless, and therefore powerful. I will watch with the wiliness of a snake, that I may sting with its venom. Man, you shall repent of the injuries you inflict."

' "Devil, cease; and do not poison the air with these sounds of malice. I have declared my resolution to you, and I am no coward to bend beneath words. Leave me; I am inexorable."

' "It is well. I go; but remember, I shall be with you on your wedding-night."

'I started forward, and exclaimed, "Villain! before you sign my death-warrant, be sure that you are yourself safe."

'I would have seized him; but he eluded me, and quitted the house with precipitation: in a few moments I saw him in his boat, which shot across the waters with an arrowy swiftness, and was soon lost amidst the waves.

'All was again silent; but his words rung in my ears. I burned with rage to pursue the murderer of my peace, and precipitate him into the ocean. I walked up and down my room hastily and perturbed, while my imagination conjured up a thousand images to torment and sting me.

---

44 From Genesis 1:28 from the Authorized King James Translation of the Holy Bible, published in 1611.

Why had I not followed him, and closed with him in mortal strife? But I
had suffered him to depart, and he had directed his course towards the
main land. I shuddered to think who might be the next victim sacrificed
to his insatiate revenge. And then I thought again of his words— *"I WILL
BE WITH YOU ON YOUR WEDDING-NIGHT!"* That then was the period fixed for the fulfilment of my destiny. In that hour I should die, and
at once satisfy and extinguish his malice. The prospect did not move me
to fear; yet when I thought of my beloved Elizabeth,— of her tears and
endless sorrow, when she should find her lover so barbarously snatched
from her,— tears, the first I had shed for many months, streamed from
my eyes, and I resolved not to fall before my enemy without a bitter
struggle.

'The night passed away, and the sun rose from the ocean; my feelings
became calmer, if it may be called calmness, when the violence of rage
sinks into the depths of despair. I left the house, the horrid scene of the
last night's contention, and walked on the beach of the sea, which I almost regarded as an insuperable barrier between me and my fellow-creatures; nay, a wish that such should prove the fact stole across me. I desired that I might pass my life on that barren rock, wearily it is true, but
uninterrupted by any sudden shock of misery. If I returned, it was to be
sacrificed, or to see those whom I most loved die under the grasp of a
dæmon whom I had myself created.

'I walked about the isle like a restless spectre, separated from all it
loved, and miserable in the separation. When it became noon, and the
sun rose higher, I lay down on the grass, and was overpowered by a deep
sleep. I had been awake the whole of the preceding night, my nerves
were agitated, and my eyes inflamed by watching and misery. The sleep
into which I now sunk refreshed me; and when I awoke, I again felt as if
I belonged to a race of human beings like myself, and I began to reflect
upon what had passed with greater composure; yet still the words of the
fiend rung in my ears like a death-knell, they appeared like a dream, yet
distinct and oppressive as a reality.

'The sun had far descended, and I still sat on the shore, satisfying my
appetite, which had become ravenous, with an oaten cake, when I saw a
fishing-boat land close to me, and one of the men brought me a packet;
it contained letters from Geneva, and one from Clerval, entreating me to
join him. He said that he was wearing away his time fruitlessly where he ·
was; that letters from the friends he had formed in London desired his
return to complete the negotiation they had entered into for his Indian
enterprise. He could not any longer delay his departure; but as his journey to London might be followed, even sooner than he now conjectured,
by his longer voyage, he entreated me to bestow as much of my society

on him as I could spare. He besought me, therefore, to leave my solitary isle, and to meet him at Perth, that we might proceed southwards together. This letter in a degree recalled me to life, and I determined to quit my island at the expiration of two days.

'Yet, before I departed, there was a task to perform, on which I shuddered to reflect: I must pack my chemical instruments; and for that purpose I must enter the room which had been the scene of my odious work, and I must handle those utensils, the sight of which was sickening to me. The next morning, at day-break, I summoned sufficient courage, and unlocked the door of my laboratory. The remains of the half-finished creature, whom I had destroyed, lay scattered on the floor, and I almost felt as if I had mangled the living flesh of a human being. I paused to collect myself, and then entered the chamber. With trembling hand I conveyed the instruments out of the room; but I reflected that I ought not to leave the relics of my work to excite the horror and suspicion of the peasants, and I accordingly put them into a basket, with a great quantity of stones, and laying them up, determined to throw them into the sea that very night; and in the mean time I sat upon the beach, employed in cleaning and arranging my chemical apparatus.

'Nothing could be more complete than the alteration that had taken place in my feelings since the night of the appearance of the dæmon. I had before regarded my promise with a gloomy despair, as a thing that, with whatever consequences, must be fulfilled; but I now felt as if a film had been taken from before my eyes, and that I, for the first time, saw clearly. The idea of renewing my labours did not for one instant occur to me; the threat I had heard weighed on my thoughts, but I did not reflect that a voluntary act of mine could avert it. I had resolved in my own mind, that to create another like the fiend I had first made would be an act of the basest and most atrocious selfishness; and I banished from my mind every thought that could lead to a different conclusion.

'Between two and three in the morning the moon rose; and I then, putting my basket aboard a little skiff, sailed out about four miles from the shore. The scene was perfectly solitary: a few boats were returning towards land, but I sailed away from them. I felt as if I was about the commission of a dreadful crime, and avoided with shuddering anxiety any encounter with my fellow-creatures. At one time the moon, which had before been clear, was suddenly overspread by a thick cloud, and I took advantage of the moment of darkness, and cast my basket into the sea; I listened to the gurgling sound as it sunk, and then sailed away from the spot.' And in an instant, my failed student with a hollow heart believes he had rid not only himself but all of humanity of his crimes against humanity. The evidence may have been cast to the bottom of the sea, but it will live in your heart forever, Victor. 'The sky became clouded; but the air was pure, although chilled by the north-east breeze that was then rising. But it refreshed me, and filled me with such agreeable sensations, that I resolved to prolong my stay on the water, and fixing the rudder in a direct position, stretched myself at the bottom of the boat. Clouds hid the moon, every thing was obscure, and I heard only the sound of the boat, as its keel cut through the waves; the murmur lulled me, and in a short time I slept soundly.

'I do not know how long I remained in this situation, but when I awoke I found that the sun had already mounted considerably. The wind was high, and the waves continually threatened the safety of my little skiff. I found that the wind was north-east, and must have driven me far from the coast from which I had embarked. I endeavoured to change my course, but quickly found that if I again made the attempt the boat would be instantly filled with water. Thus situated, my only resource was to drive before the wind. I confess that I felt a few sensations of terror. I had no compass with me, and was so little acquainted with the geography of this part of the world that the sun was of little benefit to me. I might be driven into the wide Atlantic, and feel all the tortures of starvation, or be swallowed up in the immeasurable waters that roared and buffeted around me. I had already been out many hours, and felt the torment of a burning thirst, a prelude to my other sufferings. I looked on the heavens, which were covered by clouds that flew before the wind only to be replaced by others: I looked upon the sea, it was to be my grave. "Fiend," I exclaimed, "your task is already fulfilled!" I thought of Elizabeth, of my father, and of Clerval; all left behind, on whom the monster might satisfy his sanguinary and merciless passions. This idea plunged me into a reverie, so despairing and frightful, that even now, when the scene is on the point of closing before me for ever, I shudder to reflect on it.

'Some hours passed thus; but by degrees, as the sun declined towards the horizon, the wind died away into a gentle breeze, and the sea became free from breakers. But these gave place to a heavy swell; I felt sick, and hardly able to hold the rudder, when suddenly I saw a line of high land towards the south.

'Almost spent, as I was, by fatigue, and the dreadful suspense I endured for several hours, this sudden certainty of life rushed like a flood of warm joy to my heart, and tears gushed from my eyes.

'How mutable are our feelings, and how strange is that clinging love we have of life even in the excess of misery! I constructed another sail with a part of my dress, and eagerly steered my course towards the land. It had a wild and rocky appearance; but as I approached nearer, I easily perceived the traces of cultivation. I saw vessels near the shore, and found myself suddenly transported back to the neighbourhood of civilized man. I eagerly traced the windings of the land, and hailed a steeple which I at length saw issuing from behind a small promontory. As I was in a state of extreme debility, I resolved to sail directly towards the town as a place where I could most easily procure nourishment. Fortunately I had money with me. As I turned the promontory, I perceived a small neat town and a good harbour, which I entered, my heart bounding with joy at my unexpected escape.

'As I was occupied in fixing the boat and arranging the sails, several people crowded towards the spot. They seemed very much surprised at my appearance; but, instead of offering me any assistance, whispered together with gestures that at any other time might have produced in me a slight sensation of alarm. As it was, I merely remarked that they spoke English; and I therefore addressed them in that language: "My good friends," said I, "will you be so kind as to tell me the name of this town, and inform me where I am?"

' "You will know that soon enough," replied a man with a gruff voice. "May be you are come to a place that will not prove much to your taste; but you will not be consulted as to your quarters, I promise you."

'I was exceedingly surprised on receiving so rude an answer from a stranger; and I was also disconcerted on perceiving the frowning and angry countenances of his companions. "Why do you answer me so roughly?" I replied: "surely it is not the custom of Englishmen to receive strangers so inhospitably."

' "I do not know," said the man, "what the custom of the English may be; but it is the custom of the Irish to hate villains."

'While this strange dialogue continued, I perceived the crowd rapidly increase. Their faces expressed a mixture of curiosity and anger, which annoyed, and in some degree alarmed me. I inquired the way to the inn; but no one replied. I then moved forward, and a murmuring sound arose from the crowd as they followed and surrounded me; when an ill-looking man approaching, tapped me on the shoulder, and said, "Come, Sir, you must follow me to Mr. Kirwin's, to give an account of yourself."

' "Who is Mr Kirwin? Why am I to give an account of myself? Is not this a free country?"

' "Aye, Sir, free enough for honest folks. Mr Kirwin is a magistrate; and you are to give an account of the death of a gentleman who was found murdered here last night."

'This answer startled me; but I presently recovered myself. I was innocent; that could easily be proved: accordingly I followed my conductor in silence, and was led to one of the best houses in the town. I was ready to sink from fatigue and hunger; but, being surrounded by a crowd, I thought it politic to rouse all my strength, that no physical debility might be construed into apprehension or conscious guilt. Little did I then expect the calamity that was in a few moments to overwhelm me, and extinguish in horror and despair all fear of ignominy or death.

'I must pause here; for it requires all my fortitude to recall the memory of the frightful events which I am about to relate, in proper detail, to my recollection.

What in the name of the Good Lord is happening? Victor? Victor? Answer me!

Chapter V

And then he answered my fears with even greater fears!

'I was soon introduced into the presence of the magistrate, an old benevolent man, with calm and mild manners. He looked upon me, however, with some degree of severity; and then, turning towards my conductors, he asked who appeared as witnesses on this occasion.

'About half a dozen men came forward; and one being selected by the magistrate, he deposed, that he had been out fishing the night before with his son and brother-in-law, Daniel Nugent, when, about ten o'clock, they observed a strong northerly blast rising, and they accordingly put in for port. It was a very dark night, as the moon had not yet risen; they did not land at the harbour, but, as they had been accustomed, at a creek about two miles below. He walked on first, carrying a part of the fishing tackle, and his companions followed him at some distance. As he was proceeding along the sands, he struck his foot against something, and fell all his length on the ground. His companions came up to assist him; and, by the light of their lantern, they found that he had fallen on the body of a man, who was to all appearance dead. Their first supposition was, that it was the corpse of some person who had been drowned, and was thrown on shore by the waves; but, upon examination, they found that the clothes were not wet, and even that the body was not then cold. They instantly carried it to the cottage of an old woman near the spot, and endeavoured, but in vain, to restore it to life. He appeared to be a handsome young man, about five and twenty years of age. He had apparently been strangled; for there was no sign of any violence, except the black mark of fingers on his neck.'

'The first part of this deposition did not in the least interest me; but when the mark of the fingers was mentioned, I remembered the murder of my brother, and felt myself extremely agitated; my limbs trembled, and a mist came over my eyes, which obliged me to lean on a chair for support. The magistrate observed me with a keen eye, and of course drew an unfavourable augury from my manner.

'The son confirmed his father's account: but when Daniel Nugent was called, he swore positively that, just before the fall of his companion, he saw a boat, with a single man in it, at a short distance from the shore; and, as far as he could judge by the light of a few stars, it was the same boat in which I had just landed.

'A woman deposed, that she lived near the beach, and was standing at the door of her cottage, waiting for the return of the fishermen, about an hour before she heard of the discovery of the body, when she saw a boat, with only one man in it, push off from that part of the shore where the corpse was afterwards found.

'Another woman confirmed the account of the fishermen having brought the body into her house; it was not cold. They put it into a bed, and rubbed it; and Daniel went to the town for an apothecary, but life was quite gone.

'Several other men were examined concerning my landing; and they agreed, that, with the strong north wind that had arisen during the night, it was very probable that I had beaten about for many hours, and had been obliged to return nearly to the same spot from which I had departed. Besides, they observed that it appeared that I had brought the body from another place, and it was likely, that as I did not appear to know the shore, I might have put into the harbour ignorant of the distance of the town of — — from the place where I had deposited the corpse.

'Mr Kirwin, on hearing this evidence, desired that I should be taken into the room where the body lay for interment that it might be observed what effect the sight of it would produce upon me. This idea was probably suggested by the extreme agitation I had exhibited when the mode of the murder had been described. I was accordingly conducted, by the magistrate and several other persons, to the inn. I could not help being struck by the strange coincidences that had taken place during this eventful night; but, knowing that I had been conversing with several persons in the island I had inhabited about the time that the body had been found, I was perfectly tranquil as to the consequences of the affair.

'I entered the room where the corpse lay, and was led up to the coffin. How can I describe my sensations on beholding it? I feel yet parched with horror, nor can I reflect on that terrible moment without shuddering and agony, that faintly reminds me of the anguish of the recognition. The trial, the presence of the magistrate and witnesses, passed like a dream from my memory, when I saw the lifeless form of Henry Clerval stretched before me. I gasped for breath; and, throwing myself on the body, I exclaimed, "Have my murderous machinations deprived you also, my dearest Henry, of life? Two I have already destroyed; other victims await their destiny: but you, Clerval, my friend, my benefactor"—

Victor, am I to believe that Clerval put up no struggle against your Creati— nay! faith! Creature! Creature!— when attacked? The Creature stands eight-feet tall and must weigh, I don't know how much! I say. I say! That it was you that murdered your own friend. Why not? You would have been able to approach your dearest compatriot with his arms wide open in welcoming, only to have your own hands wrapped around his neck. And if your Creature is as large as you have proposed to me during this tale, should not the black mark of fingers be grotesquely large to a magistrate who regularly sees signs of violence marked on the bodies of the dead?

'The human frame could no longer support the agonizing suffering that I endured, and I was carried out of the room in strong convulsions... of madness!

'A fever succeeded to this. I lay for two months on the point of death: my ravings, as I afterwards heard, were frightful; I called myself the murderer of William, of Justine, and of Clerval. Sometimes I entreated my attendants to assist me in the destruction of the fiend by whom I was tormented; and, at others, I felt the fingers of the monster already grasping my neck, and screamed aloud with agony and terror. Fortunately, as I spoke my native language, Mr Kirwin alone understood me; but my gestures and bitter cries were sufficient to affright the other witnesses.

'Why did I not die? More miserable than man ever was before, why did I not sink into forgetfulness and rest? Death snatches away many blooming children, the only hopes of their doating parents: how many brides and youthful lovers have been one day in the bloom of health and hope, and the next a prey for worms and the decay of the tomb! Of what materials was I made, that I could thus resist so many shocks, which, like the turning of the wheel, continually renewed the torture.

'But I was doomed to live; and, in two months, found myself as awaking from a dream, in a prison, stretched on a wretched bed, surrounded by gaolers, turnkeys, bolts, and all the miserable apparatus of a dungeon. It was morning, I remember, when I thus awoke to understanding: I had forgotten the particulars of what had happened, and only felt as if some great misfortune had suddenly overwhelmed me; but when I looked around, and saw the barred windows, and the squalidness of the room in which I was, all flashed across my memory, and I groaned bitterly... with madness!

I greatly fear for your sanity, Victor. This entire tale bares the marks of the ravings of a lunatic in Bedlam! If you were not a figment of my overactive imagination I would commit you to the Bethlehem Hospital in St George's Fields in Southwark, where it only recently moved. Or! The horror of the realization strips all colour from my face. Should I commit *myself* to Bedlam for having conjured this horrifying tale from my own mind? What kind of woman would I be if I shared this tale with my Beloved, our little Lord, poor Polidori, and dearest Claire?

The winner of our little game of ghost stories is what!

'This sound disturbed an old woman who was sleeping in a chair beside me. She was a hired nurse, the wife of one of the turnkeys, and her countenance expressed all those bad qualities which often characterize that class. The lines of her face were hard and rude, like that of persons accustomed to see without sympathizing in sights of misery. Her tone expressed her entire indifference; she addressed me in English, and the voice struck me as one that I had heard during my sufferings:

' "Are you better now, Sir?" said she.

'I replied in the same language, with a feeble voice, "I believe I am; but if it be all true, if indeed I did not dream, I am sorry that I am still alive to feel this misery and horror."

' "For that matter," replied the old woman, "if you mean about the gentleman you murdered, I believe that it were better for you if you were dead, for I fancy it will go hard with you; but you will be hung when the next sessions come on. However, that's none of my business, I am sent to nurse you, and get you well; I do my duty with a safe conscience, it were well if every body did the same."

'I turned with loathing from the woman who could utter so unfeeling a speech to a person just saved, on the very edge of death; but I felt languid, and unable to reflect on all that had passed. The whole series of my life appeared to me as a dream; I sometimes doubted if indeed it were all true, for it never presented itself to my mind with the force of reality.

'As the images that floated before me became more distinct, I grew feverish; a darkness pressed around me; no one was near me who soothed me with the gentle voice of love; no dear hand supported me. The physician came and prescribed medicines, and the old woman prepared them for me; but utter carelessness was visible in the first, and the expression of brutality was strongly marked in the visage of the second. Who could be interested in the fate of a murderer, but the hangman who would gain his fee?

'These were my first reflections; but I soon learned that Mr Kirwin had shewn me extreme kindness. He had caused the best room in the prison to be prepared for me (wretched indeed was the best); and it was he who had provided a physician and a nurse. It is true, he seldom came to see me; for, although he ardently desired to relieve the sufferings of every human creature, he did not wish to be present at the agonies and miserable ravings of a murderer. He came, therefore, sometimes to see that I was not neglected; but his visits were short, and at long intervals.

'One day, when I was gradually recovering, I was seated in a chair, my eyes half open, and my cheeks livid like those in death, I was overcome by gloom and misery, and often reflected I had better seek death than remain miserably pent up only to be let loose in a world replete with wretchedness. At one time I considered whether I should not declare myself guilty, and suffer the penalty of the law, less innocent than poor Justine had been. Such were my thoughts, when the door of my apartment was opened, and Mr Kirwin entered. His countenance expressed sympathy and compassion; he drew a chair close to mine, and addressed me in French—

' "I fear that this place is very shocking to you; can I do any thing to make you more comfortable?"

' "I thank you; but all that you mention is nothing to me: on the whole earth there is no comfort which I am capable of receiving."

' "I know that the sympathy of a stranger can be but of little relief to one borne down as you are by so strange a misfortune. But you will, I hope, soon quit this melancholy abode; for, doubtless, evidence can easily be brought to free you from the criminal charge."— Wait! What? Exculpatory evidence 'can easily be brought' and yet why would have concluded that 'he did not wish to be present at the agonies and miserable ravings of a murderer'? Victor, your tale itself is descending into madness, unable to present its own argument sanely!

' "That is my least concern: I am, by a course of strange events, become the most miserable of mortals. Persecuted and tortured as I am and have been, can death be any evil to me?"

' "Nothing indeed could be more unfortunate and agonizing than the strange chances that have lately occurred. You were thrown, by some surprising accident, on this shore, renowned for its hospitality: seized immediately, and charged with murder. The first sight that was presented to your eyes was the body of your friend, murdered in so unaccountable a manner, and placed, as it were, by some fiend across your path."

— Madness. Shear madness! So many questions swim in my mind of 'questions raised by Clerval's murder: Where was he killed? Why did the Creature Bring Clerval's corpse to a small town in Ireland? The Creature certainly had no way of knowing that Victor would beach his craft here, and Clerval could not have been anywhere near the town— or Ireland, for that matter, for he had written to Victor asking him to meet up in Perth. Futhermore, the body was not yet cold when discovered. This suggests that the Creature actually took Clerval prisoner and transported him either in the boat in which they travelled or immediately on taking him ashore. All of this occurred in the short interval after the Creature departed from Victor's island laboratory. No explanation for these conundrums is put forward by the Creature or Victor'[45]— Madness I say! Madness!

'As Mr Kirwin said this, notwithstanding the agitation I endured on this retrospect of my sufferings, I also felt considerable surprise at the knowledge he seemed to possess concerning me. I suppose some astonishment was exhibited in my countenance; for Mr Kirwin hastened to say—

' "It was not until a day or two after your illness that I thought of examining your dress, that I might discover some trace by which I could send to your relations an account of your misfortune and illness. I found several letters, and, among others, one which I discovered from its commencement to be from your father. I instantly wrote to Geneva: nearly two months have elapsed since the departure of my letter.— But you are ill; even now you tremble: you are unfit for agitation of any kind."

' "This suspense is a thousand times worse than the most horrible event: tell me what new scene of death has been acted, and whose murder I am now to lament."

' "Your family is perfectly well," said Mr Kirwin, with gentleness; "and some one, a friend, is come to visit you."

'I know not by what chain of thought the idea presented itself, but it instantly darted into my mind that the murderer had come to mock at my misery, and taunt me with the death of Clerval, as a new incitement for me to comply with his hellish desires. I put my hand before my eyes, and cried out in agony—

' "Oh! take him away! I cannot see him; for God's sake, do not let him enter!" — Madness I say! Madness!

'Mr Kirwin regarded me with a troubled countenance. He could not help regarding my exclamation as a presumption of my guilt, and said, in rather a severe tone—

' "I should have thought, young man, that the presence of your father would have been welcome, instead of inspiring such violent repugnance."

' "My father!" cried I, while every feature and every muscle was relaxed from anguish to pleasure. "Is my father, indeed, come? How kind, how very kind. But where is he, why does he not hasten to me?" — Madness I say! Madness!

'My change of manner surprised and pleased the magistrate; perhaps he thought that my former exclamation was a momentary return of delirium, and now he instantly resumed his former benevolence. He

---

45 From *The New Annotated Frankenstein* by Leslie S. Klinger, published in 2017.

rose, and quitted the room with my nurse, and in a moment my father entered it.

'Nothing, at this moment, could have given me greater pleasure than the arrival of my father. I stretched out my hand to him, and cried—

' "Are you then safe— and Elizabeth— and Ernest?"

'My father calmed me with assurances of their welfare, and endeavoured, by dwelling on these subjects so interesting to my heart, to raise my desponding spirits; but he soon felt that a prison cannot be the abode of cheerfulness. "What a place is this that you inhabit, my son!" said he, looking mournfully at the barred windows, and wretched appearance of the room. "You travelled to seek happiness, but a fatality seems to pursue you. And poor Clerval— "

'The name of my unfortunate and murdered friend was an agitation too great to be endured in my weak state; I shed tears.

' "Alas! yes, my father," replied I; "some destiny of the most horrible kind hangs over me, and I must live to fulfil it, or surely I should have died on the coffin of Henry."

'We were not allowed to converse for any length of time, for the precarious state of my health rendered every precaution necessary that could insure tranquillity. Mr Kirwin came in, and insisted that my strength should not be exhausted by too much exertion. But the appearance of my father was to me like that of my good angel, and I gradually recovered my health.

'As my sickness quitted me, I was absorbed by a gloomy and black melancholy, that nothing could dissipate. The image of Clerval was for ever before me, ghastly and murdered. More than once the agitation into which these reflections threw me made my friends dread a dangerous relapse. Alas! why did they preserve so miserable and detested a life? It was surely that I might fulfil my destiny, which is now drawing to a close. Soon, oh, very soon, will death extinguish these throbbings, and relieve me from the mighty weight of anguish that bears me to the dust; and, in executing the award of justice, I shall also sink to rest. Then the appearance of death was distant, although the wish was ever present to my thoughts; and I often sat for hours motionless and speechless, wishing for some mighty revolution that might bury me and my destroyer in its ruins. — Madness I say! Madness!

'The season of the assizes approached. I had already been three months in prison; and although I was still weak, and in continual danger of a relapse, I was obliged to travel nearly a hundred miles to the county-town, where the court was held. Mr Kirwin charged himself with every care of collecting witnesses, and arranging my defence. I was spared the disgrace of appearing publicly as a criminal, as the case was not brought before the court that decides on life and death. The grand jury rejected the bill, on its being proved that I was on the Orkney Islands at the hour the body of my friend was found, and a fortnight after my removal I was liberated from prison.

'My father was enraptured on finding me freed from the vexations of a criminal charge, that I was again allowed to breathe the fresh atmosphere, and allowed to return to my native country. I did not participate in these feelings; for to me the walls of a dungeon or a palace were alike hateful. The cup of life was poisoned for ever; and although the sun shone upon me, as upon the happy and gay of heart, I saw around me nothing but a dense and frightful darkness, penetrated by no light but the glimmer of two eyes that glared upon me. Sometimes they were the expressive eyes of Henry, languishing in death, the dark orbs nearly covered by the lids, and the long black lashes that fringed them; sometimes it was the watery clouded eyes of the monster, as I first saw them in my chamber at Ingolstadt. — The madness continues to grip his very soul. Bedlam awaits, dearest Victor, Bedlam awaits.

'My father tried to awaken in me the feelings of affection. He talked of Geneva, which I should soon visit— of Elizabeth, and Ernest; but these words only drew deep groans from me. Sometimes, indeed, I felt a wish for happiness; and thought, with melancholy delight, of my beloved cousin; or longed, with a devouring *maladie du pays*, to see once more the blue lake and rapid Rhone, that had been so dear to me in early childhood: but my general state of feeling was a torpor, in which a prison was as welcome a residence as the divinest scene in nature; and these fits were seldom interrupted, but by paroxysms of anguish and despair. At these moments I often endeavoured to put an end to the existence I loathed; and it required unceasing attendance and vigilance to restrain me from committing some dreadful act of violence.

'Yet one duty remained to me, the recollection of which finally triumphed over my selfish despair. It was necessary that I should return without delay to Geneva, there to watch over the lives of those I so fondly loved; and to lie in wait for the murderer, that if any chance led me to the place of his concealment, or if he dared again to blast me by his presence, I might, with unfailing aim, put an end to the existence of the monstrous Image which I had endued with the mockery of a soul still more monstrous. My father still desired to delay our departure, fearful that I could not sustain the fatigues of a journey: for I was a shattered wreck,—the shadow of a human being. My strength was gone. I was a mere skeleton; and fever night and day preyed upon my wasted frame.

'Still, as I urged our leaving Ireland with such inquietude and impatience, my father thought it best to yield. We took our passage on board a vessel bound for Havre-de-Grace, and sailed with a fair wind from the Irish shores. It was midnight. I lay on the deck, looking at the stars, and listening to the dashing of the waves. I hailed the darkness that shut Ireland from my sight; and my pulse beat with a feverish joy when I reflected that I should soon see Geneva. The past appeared to me in the light of a frightful dream; yet the vessel in which I was, the wind that blew me from the detested shore of Ireland, and the sea which surrounded me, told me too forcibly that I was deceived by no vision, and that Clerval, my friend and dearest companion, had fallen a victim to me and the monster of my creation. I repassed, in my memory, my whole life; my quiet happiness while residing with my family in Geneva, the death of my mother, and my departure for Ingolstadt. I remembered, shuddering, the mad enthusiasm that hurried me on to the creation of my hideous enemy, and I called to mind the night in which he first lived. I was unable to pursue the train of thought; a thousand feelings pressed upon me, and I wept bitterly.

'Ever since my recovery from the fever I had been in the custom of taking every night a small quantity of laudanum'

— for it is indeed *not* madness that you are suffering from, Victor! Is not opium at present in great esteem? And is one of the most valuable of all simple medicines. In its effects on the animal system, it is the most extraordinary substance in nature. It touches the nerves as it were by magic and irresistible power, and steeps the senses in forgetfulness; even in opposition to the determined will of the philosopher or physiologist, apprised of its narcotic effect. Opium is the most sovereign remedy in the *materia medica* for easing pain and procuring sleep, and also the most certain antispasmodic yet know; but like other powerful medicines, becomes highly noxious to the human constitution and even moral, when improperly administered[46]—

'For it was by means of this drug only that I was enabled to gain the rest necessary for the preservation of life. Oppressed by the recollection of my various misfortunes, I now took a double dose, and soon slept profoundly. But sleep did not afford me respite from thought and misery; my dreams presented a thousand objects that scared me. Towards morning I was possessed by a kind of night-mare; I felt the fiend's grasp in my neck, and could not free myself from it; groans and cries rung in my ears. My father, who was watching over me, perceiving my restlessness, awoke me, and pointed to the port of Holyhead, which we were now entering.'

---

46 From the third edition of the *Encylopædia Britannica*.

Chapter VI

The voyage came to an end. We landed, and proceeded to Paris. I soon found that I had overtaxed my strength, and that I must repose before I could continue my journey. My father's care and attentions were indefatigable; but he did not know the origin of my sufferings, and sought erroneous methods to remedy the incurable ill. He wished me to seek amusement in society. I abhorred the face of man. Oh, not abhorred! they were my brethren, my fellow beings, and I felt attracted even to the most repulsive among them, as to creatures of an angelic nature and celestial mechanism. But I felt that I had no right to share their intercourse. I had unchained an enemy among them, whose joy it was to shed their blood, and to revel in their groans. How they would, each and all, abhor me, and hunt me from the world, did they know my unhallowed acts, and the crimes which had their source in me!

'My father yielded at length to my desire to avoid society, and strove by various arguments to banish my despair. Sometimes he thought that I felt deeply the degradation of being obliged to answer a charge of murder, and he endeavoured to prove to me the futility of pride.

— Where once I had been so studious to record Victor's tale as he related it to me... verbatim. Now, I find myself revising his words with greater skill and efficacy. I no longer am aware of his voice, only the quiet scratching of the quill upon the page—

' "Alas! my father," said I, "how little do you know me. Human beings, their feelings and passions, would indeed be degraded if such a wretch as I felt pride. Justine, poor unhappy Justine, was as innocent as I, and she suffered the same charge; she died for it; and I am the cause of this—I murdered her. William, Justine, and Henry—they all died by my hands." '

The guilt of the guilty. Victor cries out to the Lord... or society... or nature to blot out his transgressions! This is the guilt of the guilty. There is too much obfuscation in this tale of Victor's, related to me by a mystical phantasm sitting beside my fire in my apartment, to know what crimes are the Creature's and what crimes are his!

'My father had often, during my imprisonment, heard me make the same assertion; when I thus accused myself, he sometimes seemed to desire an explanation, and at others he appeared to consider it as the offspring of delirium, and that, during my illness, some idea of this kind had presented itself to my imagination, the remembrance of which I preserved in my convalescence. I avoided explanation, and maintained a continual silence concerning the wretch I had created. I had a persuasion that I should be supposed mad; and this in itself would for ever have chained my tongue. But, besides, I could not bring myself to disclose a secret which would fill my hearer with consternation, and make fear and unnatural horror the inmates of his breast. I checked, therefore, my impatient thirst for sympathy, and was silent when I would have given the world to have confided the fatal secret. Yet still words like those I have recorded, would burst uncontrollably from me. I could offer no explanation of them; but their truth in part relieved the burden of my mysterious woe.'

Oh! Woe is upon you my failed student with a hollow heart. If your father knew of the crimes you should rightly be convicted of, disownment would surely commence, closely followed by a short trip up the steps to the gallows. To have your neck stretched. The crime of murder you may not be— legally— guilty of, but crimes against nature. You, sir, are guilty... guilty... guilty!

'Upon this occasion my father said, with an expression of unbounded wonder, "My dearest Victor, what infatuation is this? My dear son, I entreat you never to make such an assertion again."

' "I am not mad," I cried energetically; "the sun and the heavens, who have viewed my operations, can bear witness of my truth. I am the assassin of those most innocent victims; they died by my machinations. A thousand times would I have shed my own blood, drop by drop, to have saved their lives; but I could not, my father, indeed I could not sacrifice the whole human race."'

They say confession is good for the soul. Confess!

'The conclusion of this speech'— speech? Oh, Victor, how I wish you would make a speech, but merely a choice words— 'convinced my father that my ideas were deranged, and he instantly changed the subject of our conversation, and endeavoured to alter the course of my thoughts. He wished as much as possible to obliterate the memory of the scenes that had taken place in Ireland, and never alluded to them, or suffered me to speak of my misfortunes.

'As time passed away I became more calm: misery had her dwelling in my heart, but I no longer talked in the same incoherent manner of my own crimes; sufficient for me was the consciousness of them. By the utmost self-violence, I curbed the imperious voice of wretchedness, which sometimes desired to declare itself to the whole world; and my manners were calmer and more composed than they had ever been since my journey to the sea of ice.

'A few days before we left Paris on our way to Switzerland, I received the following letter from Elizabeth:—

Letter to Victor Frankenstein

' "My dear Friend,

It gave me the greatest pleasure to receive a letter from my uncle dated at Paris; you are no longer at a formidable distance, and I may hope to see you in less than a fortnight. My poor cousin, how much you must have suffered! I expect to see you looking even more ill than when you quitted Geneva. This winter has been passed most miserably, tortured as I have been by anxious suspense; yet I hope to see peace in your countenance, and to find that your heart is not totally void of comfort and tranquillity.

' "Yet I fear that the same feelings now exist that made you so miserable a year ago, even perhaps augmented by time. I would not disturb you at this period, when so many misfortunes weigh upon you; but a conversation that I had with my uncle previous to his departure renders some explanation necessary before we meet.

' "Explanation! you may possibly say; what can Elizabeth have to explain? If you really say this, my questions are answered, and all my doubts satisfied. But you are distant from me, and it is possible that you may dread, and yet be pleased with this explanation; and, in a probability of this being the case, I dare not any longer postpone writing what, during your absence, I have often wished to express to you, but have never had the courage to begin.

' "You well know, Victor, that our union had been the favourite plan of your parents ever since our infancy. We were told this when young, and taught to look forward to it as an event that would certainly take place. We were affectionate playfellows during childhood, and, I believe, dear and valued friends to one another as we grew older. But as brother and sister often entertain a lively affection towards each other, without desiring a more intimate union, may not such also be our case? Tell me, dearest Victor. Answer me, I conjure you, by our mutual happiness, with simple truth—Do you not love another?

' "You have travelled; you have spent several years of your life at Ingolstadt; and I confess to you, my friend, that when I saw you last autumn so unhappy, flying to solitude, from the society of every creature'"—Oh! Elizabeth if you only the knew true natural of this Creature Victor flies from— ' "I could not help supposing that you might regret our connection, and believe yourself bound in honour to fulfil the wishes of your parents, although they opposed themselves to your inclinations. But this is false reasoning. I confess to you, my cousin, that I love you, and that in my airy dreams of futurity you have been my constant friend and companion. But it is your happiness I desire as well as my own, when I declare to you, that our marriage would render me eternally miserable, unless it were the dictate of your own free choice. Even now I weep to think, that, borne down as you are by the cruellest misfortunes, you may stifle, by the word honour, all hope of that love and happiness which would alone restore you to yourself. I, who have so disinterested an affection for you, may increase your miseries tenfold, by being an obstacle to your wishes. Ah! Victor, be assured that your cousin and playmate has too sincere a love for you not to be made miserable by this supposition. Be happy, my friend; and if you obey me in this one request, remain satisfied that nothing on earth will have the power to interrupt my tranquillity.

' "Do not let this letter disturb you; do not answer to-morrow, or the next day, or even until you come, if it will give you pain. My uncle will send me news of your health; and if I see but one smile on your lips when we meet, occasioned by this or any other exertion of mine, I shall need no other happiness.

Elizabeth Lavenza.
Geneva, May 18th, 17—.

Oh! The love that your cousin has for you is immense, Victor. She will fly from their arrangement if it makes you so miserable, but little does this know that you are miserable to your very soul. A miserable wretch that knows not happiness nor love... cannot know happiness nor love... should not know happiness nor love. If there is a Lord above in Heaven, of which I surely have my doubts.

'This letter revived in my memory what I had before forgotten, the threat of the fiend— "I WILL BE WITH YO ON YOUR WEDDING NIGHT!" Such was my sentence, and on that night would the dæmon employ every art to destroy me, and tear me from the glimpse of happiness which promised partly to console my sufferings. On that night he had determined to consummate his crimes by my death. Well, be it so; a deadly struggle would then assuredly take place, in which if he were victorious I should be at peace, and his power over me be at an end. If he were vanquished, I should be a free man. Alas! what freedom? such as the peasant enjoys when his family have been massacred before his eyes, his cottage burnt, his lands laid waste, and he is turned adrift, homeless, penniless, and alone, but free. Such would be my liberty, except that in my Elizabeth I possessed a treasure; alas! balanced by those horrors of remorse and guilt, which would pursue me until death.'

But in this analogy, this peasant is guilty of insurrection against his feudal lord, just as you're are guilty of insurrection against Nature herself! Nature has massacred your family before your eyes, burnt your cottage, laid waste to your lands. You are turned adrift, homeless, penniless, and alone, because of your crimes! If you have only embraced your Creation when you animated life into an amalgamated corpse, then there would be no deaths visited upon you. If your Creation had studied at your teat, then perchance fate would have been different, but you chose to flee from your Creation, considering it nothing more than a loathsome Creature to be abandoned. A babe abandoned in the woods will die by exposure or by wolves harkening to its cries; but the babe you abandoned in your laboratory did not die by exposure but was threatened by the wolves of mankind. And you are shocked and dismayed when he reactions from these threats? Oh, my failed student with a hollow heart, how wish to be done with your tale. But curiosity to its end is the only thing keeping me from truly dismissing you as a blot of mustard, a crumb of cheese, a fragment of an underdone potato.

'Sweet and beloved Elizabeth! I read and re-read her letter, and some softened feelings stole into my heart, and dared to whisper paradisiacal dreams of love and joy; but the apple was already eaten, and the angel's arm bared to drive me from all hope. Yet I would die to make her happy. If the monster executed his threat, death was inevitable; yet, again, I considered whether my marriage would hasten my fate. My destruction might indeed arrive a few months sooner; but if my torturer should suspect that I postponed it, influenced by his menaces, he would surely find other, and perhaps more dreadful means of revenge. He had vowed TO BE WITH ME ON MY WEDDING-NIGHT, yet he did not consider that threat as binding him to peace in the mean time; for, as if to show me that he was not yet satiated with blood, he had murdered Clerval immediately after the enunciation of his threats. I resolved, therefore, that if my immediate union with my cousin would conduce either to hers or my father's happiness, my adversary's designs against my life should not retard it a single hour.

'In this state of mind I wrote to Elizabeth. My letter was calm and affectionate. "I fear, my beloved girl," I said, "little happiness remains for us on earth; yet all that I may one day enjoy is centred in you. Chase away your idle fears; to you alone do I consecrate my life, and my endeavours for contentment. I have one secret, Elizabeth, a dreadful one; when revealed to you, it will chill your frame with horror, and then, far from being surprised at my misery, you will only wonder that I survive what I have endured. I will confide this tale of misery and terror to you the day after our marriage shall take place; for, my sweet cousin, there must be perfect confidence between us. But until then, I conjure you, do not mention or allude to it. This I most earnestly entreat, and I know you will comply."

'In about a week after the arrival of Elizabeth's letter, we returned to Geneva. My cousin welcomed me with warm affection; yet tears were in her eyes, as she beheld my emaciated frame and feverish cheeks. I saw a change in her also. She was thinner, and had lost much of that heavenly vivacity that had before charmed me; but her gentleness, and soft looks of compassion, made her a more fit companion for one blasted and miserable as I was.

'The tranquillity which I now enjoyed did not endure. Memory brought madness with it; and when I thought of what had passed, a real insanity possessed me; sometimes I was furious, and burnt with rage; sometimes low and despondent. I neither spoke, nor looked at any one, but sat motionless, bewildered by the multitude of miseries that overcame me.

'Elizabeth alone had the power to draw me from these fits; her gentle voice would soothe me when transported by passion, and inspire me with human feelings when sunk in torpor. She wept with me, and for me. When reason returned, she would remonstrate, and endeavour to inspire me with resignation. Ah! it is well for the unfortunate to be resigned, but for the guilty there is no peace. The agonies of remorse poison the luxury there is otherwise sometimes found in indulging the excess of grief.

'Soon after my arrival, my father spoke of my immediate marriage with my cousin. I remained silent.

' "Have you, then, some other attachment?"

' "None on earth. I love Elizabeth, and look forward to our union with delight. Let the day therefore be fixed; and on it I will consecrate myself, in life or death, to the happiness of my cousin."

' "My dear Victor, do not speak thus. Heavy misfortunes have befallen us; but let us only cling closer to what remains, and transfer our love for those whom we have lost, to those who yet live. Our circle will be small, but bound close by the ties of affection and mutual misfortune. And when time shall have softened your despair, new and dear objects of care will be born to replace those of whom we have been so cruelly deprived."

'Such were the lessons of my father. But to me the remembrance of the threat returned: nor can you wonder, that, omnipotent as the fiend had yet been in his deeds of blood, I should almost regard him as invincible; and that when he had pronounced the words, "I SHALL BE WITH YOU ON YOUR WEDDING-NIGHT."'

My! I heard those words, not in Victor's voice, but the voice of the Creature. Curious. Has the phantasm of the Creature returned to visit me as well? I see him not. But I hear his deep resonate unnatural bass speaking from the ether.

'I should regard the threatened fate as unavoidable. But death was no evil to me, if the loss of Elizabeth were balanced with it; and I therefore, with a contented and even cheerful countenance, agreed with my father, that if my cousin would consent, the ceremony should take place in ten days, and thus put, as I imagined, the seal to my fate.

'Great God! if for one instant I had thought what might be the hellish intention of my fiendish adversary, I would rather have banished myself for ever from my native country, and wandered a friendless outcast over the earth, than have consented to this miserable marriage. But, as if possessed of magic powers, the monster had blinded me to his real intentions; and when I thought that I had prepared only my own death, I hastened that of a far dearer victim.

'As the period fixed for our marriage drew nearer, whether from cowardice or a prophetic feeling, I felt my heart sink within me. But I concealed my feelings by an appearance of hilarity, that brought smiles and joy to the countenance of my father, but hardly deceived the ever-watchful and nicer eye of Elizabeth. She looked forward to our union with placid contentment, not unmingled with a little fear, which past misfortunes had impressed, that what now appeared certain and tangible happiness, might soon dissipate into an airy dream, and leave no trace but deep and everlasting regret.

'Preparations were made for the event; congratulatory visits were received; and all wore a smiling appearance. I shut up, as well as I could, in my own heart the anxiety that preyed there, and entered with seeming earnestness into the plans of my father, although they might only serve as the decorations of my tragedy. A house was purchased for us near Cologny, by which we should enjoy the pleasures of the country, and yet be so near Geneva as to see my father every day; who would still reside within the walls, for the benefit of Ernest, that he might follow his studies at the schools.'

Cologny? Perchance Victor is the owner of the Villa Diodati, for it is so near Cologny, sitting on the shores of Lake Geneva. If not for the unnatural nature of the thunderstorms and the snow, my Beloved, our little Lord, poor Polidori, dearest Claire, and I should have enjoyed the pleasures of the country. Perchance, this very room proved to be the bridal suite. But I cannot bring myself to believe Victor found happiness in the Villa Diodati, because the words of the Creature still echo in my ears: "I SHALL BE WITH YOU ON YOUR WEDDING-NIGHT."

'In the mean time I took every precaution to defend my person, in case the fiend should openly attack me. I carried pistols and a dagger constantly about me, and was ever on the watch to prevent artifice; and by these means gained a greater degree of tranquillity. Indeed, as the period approached, the threat appeared more as a delusion, not to be regarded as worthy to disturb my peace, while the happiness I hoped for in my marriage wore a greater appearance of certainty, as the day fixed for its solemnisation drew nearer, and I heard it continually spoken of as an occurrence which no accident could possibly prevent.

'Elizabeth seemed happy; my tranquil demeanour contributed greatly to calm her mind. But on the day that was to fulfil my wishes and my destiny, she was melancholy, and a presentiment of evil pervaded her; and perhaps also she thought of the dreadful secret which I had promised to reveal to her on the following day. My father was in the mean time overjoyed, and, in the bustle of preparation, only recognised in the melancholy of his niece the diffidence of a bride.

'After the ceremony was performed, a large party assembled at my father's; but it was agreed that Elizabeth and I should pass the afternoon and night at Evian, and return to Cologny the next morning. As the day was fair, and the wind favourable, we resolved to go by water.'

Oh! Evian! I recall transcribing the words of my Beloved in my journal: "The appearance of the inhabitants of Evian is more wretched, diseased and poor, than I ever recollect to have seen. The contrast indeed between the subjects of the King of Sardinia and the citizens of the independent republics of Switzerland, affords a powerful illustration of the blighting mischiefs of despotism, within the space of a few miles. They have mineral waters here, *eaux savonneuses*, they call them. In the evening we had some difficulty about our passports, but so soon as the syndic heard my companion's rank and name, he apologized for the circumstance. The inn was good. During our voyage, on the distant height of a hill, covered with pine-forests, we saw a ruined castle, which reminded me of those on the Rhine."[47]

'Those were the last moments of my life during which I enjoyed the feeling of happiness. We passed rapidly along: the sun was hot, but we were sheltered from its rays by a kind of canopy, while we enjoyed the beauty of the scene, sometimes on one side of the lake, where we saw Mont Salêve, the pleasant banks of Montalègre, and at a distance, surmounting all, the beautiful Mont Blanc, and the assemblage of snowy mountains that in vain endeavour to emulate her; sometimes coasting the opposite banks, we saw the mighty Jura opposing its dark side to the ambition that would quit its native country, and an almost insurmountable barrier to the invader who should wish to enslave it.'

Curious! A mere year or more from the dates of Victor's tale, it is not half the invasion of the French when they overran Old Swiss Confederation and established the Helvetic Republic! Though they only

---

47 From the *History of a Six Weeks Tour Through a Part of France, Germany, Switzerland, and Holland* by Mary Shelley, published by T. Hookham, Jun. Old Bond Street, and C. and J. Ollier, Welback Street, 1817

held these lands for half a decade, allowing our holiday on these shores possible.

'I took the hand of Elizabeth: "You are sorrowful, my love. Ah! if you knew what I have suffered, and what I may yet endure, you would endeavour to let me taste the quiet and freedom from despair, that this one day at least permits me to enjoy."

' "Be happy, my dear Victor," replied Elizabeth; "there is, I hope, nothing to distress you; and be assured that if a lively joy is not painted in my face, my heart is contented. Something whispers to me not to depend too much on the prospect that is opened before us; but I will not listen to such a sinister voice. Observe how fast we move along, and how the clouds, which sometimes obscure and sometimes rise above the dome of Mont Blanc, render this scene of beauty still more interesting. Look also at the innumerable fish that are swimming in the clear waters, where we can distinguish every pebble that lies at the bottom. What a divine day! how happy and serene all nature appears!"

'Thus Elizabeth endeavoured to divert her thoughts and mine from all reflection upon melancholy subjects. But her temper was fluctuating; joy for a few instants shone in her eyes, but it continually gave place to distraction and reverie.

'The sun sunk lower in the heavens; we passed the river Drance,'

— Again my memory serves up the transcription I made of my Beloved's words before we approached Evian and the mountains descended more precipitously to the lake, and masses of intermingled wood and rock overhung its shining spire: "As soon as we had passed the opposite promontory, we saw the river Drance, which descends from between a chasm in the mountains, and makes a plain near the lake, intersected by its divided streams. Thousands of *besolets*, beautiful water-birds, like sea-gulls, but smaller, with purple on their backs, take their station on the shallows, where its waters mingle with the lake."[48] —

'And observed its path through the chasms of the higher, and the glens of the lower hills. The Alps here come closer to the lake, and we approached the amphitheatre of mountains which forms its eastern boundary. The spire of Evian shone under the woods that surrounded it, and the range of mountain above mountain by which it was overhung.

'The wind, which had hitherto carried us along with amazing rapidity, sunk at sunset to a light breeze; the soft air just ruffled the water, and caused a pleasant motion among the trees as we approached the shore, from which it wafted the most delightful scent of flowers and hay. The sun sunk beneath the horizon as we landed; and as I touched the shore, I

---

48 From the *History of a Six Weeks Tour Through a Part of France, Germany, Switzerland, and Holland* by Mary Shelley, published by T. Hookham, Jun. Old Bond Street, and C. and J. Ollier, Welback Street, 1817

felt those cares and fears revive, which soon were to clasp me, and cling to me for ever.'

Chapter VII

It was eight o'clock when we landed; we walked for a short time on the shore, enjoying the transitory light, and then retired to the inn, and contemplated the lovely scene of waters, woods, and mountains, obscured in darkness, yet still displaying their black outlines.

'The wind, which had fallen in the south, now rose with great violence in the west. The moon had reached her summit in the heavens, and was beginning to descend; the clouds swept across it swifter than the flight of the vulture, and dimmed her rays, while the lake reflected the scene of the busy heavens, rendered still busier by the restless waves that were beginning to rise. Suddenly a heavy storm of rain descended.

'I had been calm during the day; but so soon as night obscured the shapes of objects, a thousand fears arose in my mind. I was anxious and watchful, while my right hand grasped a pistol which was hidden in my bosom; every sound terrified me; but I resolved that I would sell my life dearly, and not shrink from the conflict until my own life, or that of my adversary, was extinguished.

'Elizabeth observed my agitation for some time in timid and fearful silence; but there was something in my glance which communicated terror to her, and trembling she asked, "What is it that agitates you, my dear Victor? What is it you fear?"

' "Oh! peace, peace, my love," replied I; "this night, and all will be safe: but this night is dreadful, very dreadful."

'I passed an hour in this state of mind, when suddenly I reflected how fearful the combat which I momentarily expected would be to my wife, and I earnestly entreated her to retire, resolving not to join her until I had obtained some knowledge as to the situation of my enemy.

'She left me, and I continued some time walking up and down the passages of the house, and inspecting every corner that might afford a retreat to my adversary. But I discovered no trace of him, and was beginning to conjecture that some fortunate chance had intervened to prevent the execution of his menaces; when suddenly I heard a shrill and dreadful scream.'

I hear, quite audibly, the voice of the Creature saying: 'I SHALL BE WITH YOU ON YOUR WEDDING-NIGHT!' I shuddered uncontrollably. The flashes of lightning outside the windows to our apartment seemed to strike my spine, uncontrollable electric shots shooting up my spine into my brain. Proof of animal electricity fuelled by lightning! I could feel the blood trickling in my veins. The undersides of my arms and lesser two fingers on my hands went numb, tingling madly. Please, let this be a dream. Please, Victor, tell me this is a product... a project of your imagination and not a reality. I cannot accept it if your Creature has murdered unfortunate Elizabeth.

'It came from the room into which Elizabeth had retired. As I heard it, the whole truth rushed into my mind, my arms dropped, the motion of every muscle and fibre was suspended; I could feel the blood trickling in my veins, and tingling in the extremities of my limbs. This state lasted but for an instant; the scream was repeated, and I rushed into the room.

'Great God! why did I not then expire! Why am I here to relate the destruction of the best hope, and the purest creature of earth? She was there, lifeless and inanimate, thrown across the bed, her head hanging down, and her pale and distorted features half covered by her hair.'

Where had I seen this scene before? I know I have seen it with my own eyes! But where? My father's grand parlour perhaps. Was he hosting an artist, a fixture of radical artists and thinkers that were as commonplace to our home as rats and roaches are to the poor houses. William Godwin and Mary Wollstonecraft were counted among this circle of radical artists and thinkers. My father, with his anarchistic politics and atheistic rationales, and my mother, with the feminist philosophies, were bound together in more than love and marriage. How did the respectable of society and nobility loath and revile them. The memory is becoming clearer and clearer. I see the painting upon its easel in the centre of my father's parlour from my favourite hiding place where I could easily drop eaves on my father's salons. I saw the ladies and their gentlemen, who cherished invitations to Godwin's home on a Saturday. My father hosted many literary, scientific, and philosophical salons. Dinner was served promptly at eight, usually of four courses, but sometimes of seven, and rarely of anything more. These evenings were not intended for nourishment or merriment, but for enlightenment, though guests often left with all three. Esteemed and interesting persons were brought in to speak on any subject that struck my father's fancy this week or that week. Many critics would accuse my father of atheism, anarchism, anti-monarchism, feminism, utilitarianism, and radicalism inspired by the revolutionaries of France. My father was nothing if not outspoken.

This night, when I was five, my father had invited one Henry Fuseli, a Swiss, who lived in England and was counted amongst the circle with my father and my late mother. The painting that sat on the easel was his most famous painting named *The Nightmare*. The woman that lies upon her bed are as Victor described his Elizabeth: 'She was there, lifeless and inanimate, thrown across the bed, her head hanging down, and her pale and distorted features half covered by her hair.' And sitting upon the belly of the woman sat a stone-faced incubus peering and searing into the soul of the observer. A mysterious wild-eyed mare is the voyeur during this scene at night. Is this horse literally a night-mare? There were whispers from the titillated gossiping hens in my father's parlour concerning Fuseli having fallen madly and deeply in love with Anna Landholdt, the niece of his friend, the Swiss physiognomist Johann Kaspar Lavater. Such a scandal would have been exaserbated if the gossiping hens had been aware Fuseli had written to a friend: 'Last night I had her in bed with me— tossed my bedclothes hugger-mugger—wound my hot and tight-clasped hands about her— fused her body and soul together with my own—poured into her my spirit, breath and strength. Anyone who touches her now commits adultery and incest! She is mine, and I am hers. And have her I will....' Was Anna the woman having the nightmare, the hens gossiped. But I know the truth! The incubus had peered into me as a child and seared this painting onto my memory, a memory that Victor has drawn upon to describe his

'Every where I turn I see the same figure—her bloodless arms and relaxed form flung by the murderer on its bridal bier. Could I behold this, and live? Alas! life is obstinate, and clings closest where it is most hated. For a moment only did I lose recollection; I fell senseless on the ground.

'When I recovered, I found myself surrounded by the people of the inn; their countenances expressed a breathless terror: but the horror of others appeared only as a mockery, a shadow of the feelings that oppressed me. I escaped from them to the room where lay the body of Elizabeth, my love, my wife, so lately living, so dear, so worthy. She had been moved from the posture in which I had first beheld her; and now, as she lay, her head upon her arm, and a handkerchief thrown across her face and neck, I might have supposed her asleep. I rushed towards her, and embraced her with ardour; but the deadly languor and coldness of the limbs told me, that what I now held in my arms had ceased to be the Elizabeth whom I had loved and cherished. The murderous mark of the fiend's grasp was on her neck, and the breath had ceased to issue from her lips.

'While I still hung over her in the agony of despair, I happened to look up. The windows of the room had before been darkened, and I felt a kind of panic on seeing the pale yellow light of the moon illuminate the chamber. The shutters had been thrown back.'

And the apocalyptic thunderstorm that raged a war in the heavens seemingly between the armies of Heaven and the hordes of Hell buffeted the windowpanes with winds and rains of such force and ferocity that the panes shattered into a hail of glass. My Beloved slumbered so deeply that he did not stir. The wind and rain tore the curtains from their rings and their rod.

'And, with a sensation of horror not to be described, I saw at the open window a figure the most hideous and abhorred. A grin was on the face of the monster; he seemed to jeer, as with his fiendish finger he pointed towards the corpse of my wife.'

And I saw this with my own eyes! The Creature, who had sat in the same chair where Victor how sits, stood at the open widow, despite or in spite of the fact our apartment sat on an upper floor of the Villa Diodati. The lightning flashed illuminating his silhouette. His form and figure were the same as I remember a grotesque amalgamation of human cadavers and animal carrion, switched together in a quilt of death and decay.

'I rushed towards the window, and drawing a pistol from my bosom, fired; but he eluded me, leaped from his station, and, running with the swiftness of lightning, plunged into the lake.'

I too rushed towards the window, but possessed no pistol to draw from my bosom, but the Creature eluded me, leaped from his station, and running with the swiftness of lightning, plunged into Lake Geneva below! Only when Victor commanded my attention by continuing his tale unabetted.

'The report of the pistol brought a crowd into the room. I pointed to the spot where he had disappeared, and we followed the track with boats; nets were cast, but in vain. After passing several hours, we returned hopeless, most of my companions believing it to have been a form conjured up by my fancy. After having landed, they proceeded to search the country, parties going in different directions among the woods and vines.

'I attempted to accompany them, and proceeded a short distance from the house; but my head whirled round, my steps were like those of a drunken man, I fell at last in a state of utter exhaustion; a film covered my eyes, and my skin was parched with the heat of fever. In this state I was carried back, and placed on a bed, hardly conscious of what had happened; my eyes wandered round the room, as if to seek something that I had lost.

'After an interval, I arose, and, as if by instinct, crawled into the room where the corpse of my beloved lay. There were women weeping around—I hung over it, and joined my sad tears to theirs—all this time no distinct idea presented itself to my mind; but my thoughts rambled to various subjects, reflecting confusedly on my misfortunes, and their cause. I was bewildered in a cloud of wonder and horror. The death of

William, the execution of Justine, the murder of Clerval, and lastly of my wife; even at that moment I knew not that my only remaining friends were safe from the malignity of the fiend; my father even now might be writhing under his grasp, and Ernest might be dead at his feet. This idea made me shudder, and recalled me to action. I started up, and resolved to return to Geneva with all possible speed.

'There were no horses to be procured, and I must return by the lake; but the wind was unfavourable, and the rain fell in torrents. However, it was hardly morning, and I might reasonably hope to arrive by night. I hired men to row, and took an oar myself; for I had always experienced relief from mental torment in bodily exercise. But the overflowing misery I now felt, and the excess of agitation that I endured, rendered me incapable of any exertion. I threw down the oar; and leaning my head upon my hands, gave way to every gloomy idea that arose. If I looked up, I saw the scenes which were familiar to me in my happier time, and which I had contemplated but the day before in the company of her who was now but a shadow and a recollection. Tears streamed from my eyes. The rain had ceased for a moment, and I saw the fish play in the waters as they had done a few hours before; they had then been observed by Elizabeth. Nothing is so painful to the human mind as a great and sudden change. The sun might shine, or the clouds might lower: but nothing could appear to me as it had done the day before. A fiend had snatched from me every hope of future happiness: no creature had ever been so miserable as I was; so frightful an event is single in the history of man.

'But why should I dwell upon the incidents that followed this last overwhelming event? Mine has been a tale of horrors; I have reached their acme, and what I must now relate can but be tedious to you. Know that, one by one, my friends were snatched away; I was left desolate. My own strength is exhausted; and I must tell, in a few words, what remains of my hideous narration.

'I arrived at Geneva. My father and Ernest yet lived; but the former sunk under the tidings that I bore. I see him now, excellent and venerable old man! his eyes wandered in vacancy, for they had lost their charm and their delight—his niece, his more than daughter, whom he doated on with all that affection which a man feels, who in the decline of life, having few affections, clings more earnestly to those that remain. Cursed, cursed be the fiend that brought misery on his grey hairs, and doomed him to waste in wretchedness! He could not live under the horrors that were accumulated around him; the springs of existence suddenly gave way: he was unable to rise from his bed, and in a few days he died in my arms.'

No! Victor is now an orphan. Just as Robert Walton is an orphan. And the Creature himself is an orphan by the abandonment of my failed student with the hollow heart. All three are alone! All three are on their own! All three are lost! All are without roots of any kind! What manner of tragedy is this tale?

'What then became of me? I know not; I lost sensation, and chains and darkness were the only objects that pressed upon me. Sometimes, indeed, I dreamt that I wandered in flowery meadows and pleasant vales with the friends of my youth; but I awoke, and found myself in a dungeon. Melancholy followed, but by degrees I gained a clear conception of my miseries and situation, and was then released from my prison. For they had called me mad; and during many months, as I understood, a solitary cell had been my habitation.'

Again and again he is called mad! Again and again a solitary cell became his habitation! First in Ireland accused of murder and again in Geneva accused of madness! Murder and madness stalk Victor like creatures on the prowl. A Creature on the prowl.

'Liberty, however, had been an useless gift to me, had I not, as I awakened to reason, at the same time awakened to revenge. As the memory of past misfortunes pressed upon me, I began to reflect on their cause—the monster whom I had created, the miserable dæmon whom I had sent abroad into the world for my destruction. I was possessed by a maddening rage when I thought of him, and desired and ardently prayed that I might have him within my grasp to wreak a great and signal revenge on his cursed head.

'Nor did my hate long confine itself to useless wishes; I began to reflect on the best means of securing him; and for this purpose, about a month after my release, I repaired to a criminal judge in the town, and told him that I had an accusation to make; that I knew the destroyer of my family; and that I required him to exert his whole authority for the apprehension of the murderer.

'The magistrate listened to me with attention and kindness:— "Be assured, sir," said he, "no pains or exertions on my part shall be spared to discover the villain."

' "I thank you," replied I; "listen, therefore, to the deposition that I have to make. It is indeed a tale so strange, that I should fear you would not credit it, were there not something in truth which, however wonderful, forces conviction. The story is too connected to be mistaken for a dream, and I have no motive for falsehood." My manner, as I thus addressed him, was impressive, but calm; I had formed in my own heart a resolution to pursue my destroyer to death; and this purpose quieted my agony, and for an interval reconciled me to life. I now related my history, briefly, but with firmness and precision, marking the dates with accuracy, and never deviating into invective or exclamation.

'The magistrate appeared at first perfectly incredulous, but as I continued he became more attentive and interested; I saw him sometimes shudder with horror, at others a lively surprise, unmingled with disbelief, was painted on his countenance.

'When I had concluded my narration, I said, "This is the being whom I accuse, and for whose seizure and punishment I call upon you to exert your whole power. It is your duty as a magistrate, and I believe and hope that your feelings as a man will not revolt from the execution of those functions on this occasion."'

Was Victor as thorough with the telling of his tale to the magistrate as he has been with me over the course of his cataclysmic summer? Would the magistrate have sat as enraptured as I have at the telling of this tale? Or did his abridge the tale for the sake of brevity in his bereavement because he wanted to pursue the Creature into the wilds?

'This address caused a considerable change in the physiognomy of my own auditor. He had heard my story with that half kind of belief that is given to a tale of spirits and supernatural events; but when he was called upon to act officially in consequence, the whole tide of his incredulity returned. He, however, answered mildly, "I would willingly afford you every aid in your pursuit; but the creature of whom you speak appears to have powers which would put all my exertions to defiance. Who can follow an animal which can traverse the sea of ice, and inhabit caves and dens where no man would venture to intrude? Besides, some months have elapsed since the commission of his crimes, and no one can conjecture to what place he has wandered, or what region he may now inhabit."

' "I do not doubt that he hovers near the spot which I inhabit; and if he has indeed taken refuge in the Alps, he may be hunted like the chamois, and destroyed as a beast of prey. But I perceive your thoughts: you do not credit my narrative, and do not intend to pursue my enemy with the punishment which is his desert."

'As I spoke, rage sparkled in my eyes; the magistrate was intimidated:— "You are mistaken," said he, "I will exert myself; and if it is in my power to seize the monster, be assured that he shall suffer punishment proportionate to his crimes. But I fear, from what you have yourself described to be his properties, that this will prove impracticable; and thus, while every proper measure is pursued, you should make up your mind to disappointment."

' "That cannot be; but all that I can say will be of little avail. My revenge is of no moment to you; yet, while I allow it to be a vice, I confess that it is the devouring and only passion of my soul. My rage is unspeakable, when I reflect that the murderer, whom I have turned loose upon society, still exists. You refuse my just demand: I have but one resource; and I devote myself, either in my life or death, to his destruction."

Why was I suddenly trembling with an excess of agitation with a frenzy in my manner, of that haughty fierceness which the martyrs of old are said to have been possessed? I know not!

'I trembled with excess of agitation as I said this; there was a frenzy in my manner, and something, I doubt not, of that haughty fierceness which the martyrs of old are said to have possessed.'

Now I know! I am feeling the feelings of my pale student of the unhallowed arts. We are becoming of one body and one mind!

'But to a Genevan magistrate, whose mind was occupied by far other ideas than those of devotion and heroism, this elevation of mind had much the appearance of madness. He endeavoured to soothe me as a nurse does a child, and reverted to my tale as the effects of delirium.

' "Man," I cried, "how ignorant art thou in thy pride of wisdom! Cease; you know not what it is you say."

'I broke from the house angry and disturbed, and retired to meditate on some other mode of action.'

Chapter VIII

I have grown numb. My fingers ache from transcribing this tale of Victor's into my journal. My mind is exhausted. Why has this tale affected me thus? Is it the horror of it? Is it the lingering effects of science upon fiction, from which nary the twain have been stitched together like that amalgamation of human cadavers and animal carrion which I called both the Creation and, now and forever, The Creature. Who would have thought to form a plotline involving science so inextricably woven into the fiction that pulling out science and the entire novel collapses without its foundation as bedrock. But as his tale continues. I know not how much I can continue to give my annotations. I feel these comments of mine benefit the publication of Victor's and the Creature's tales, which I will seek as its 'author'. With the assistance of my Beloved, of course. Why the assistance of my Beloved? Who would publish a work of science and of fiction written by an eighteen-year-old girl without the assistance of a man. That is the world I was born into just as my mother was exiting.

'My present situation was one in which all voluntary thought was swallowed up and lost. I was hurried away by fury; revenge alone endowed me with strength and composure; it moulded my feelings, and allowed me to be calculating and calm, at periods when otherwise delirium or death would have been my portion.

'My first resolution was to quit Geneva for ever; my country, which, when I was happy and beloved, was dear to me, now, in my adversity, became hateful. I provided myself with a sum of money, together with a few jewels which had belonged to my mother, and departed.

'And now my wanderings began, which are to cease but with life. I have traversed a vast portion of the earth, and have endured all the hardships which travellers, in deserts and barbarous countries, are wont to meet. How I have lived I hardly know; many times have I stretched my failing limbs upon the sandy plain, and prayed for death. But revenge kept me alive; I dared not die, and leave my adversary in being.

'When I quitted Geneva, my first labour was to gain some clue by which I might trace the steps of my fiendish enemy. But my plan was unsettled; and I wandered many hours round the confines of the town, uncertain what path I should pursue. As night approached, I found myself at the entrance of the cemetery where William, Elizabeth, and my father reposed. I entered it, and approached the tomb which marked their graves. Every thing was silent, except the leaves of the trees, which were gently agitated by the wind; the night was nearly dark; and the scene would have been solemn and affecting even to an uninterested observer. The spirits of the departed seemed to flit around, and to cast a shadow, which was felt but not seen, around the head of the mourner.

'The deep grief which this scene had at first excited quickly gave way to rage and despair. They were dead, and I lived; their murderer also lived, and to destroy him I must drag out my weary existence. I knelt on the grass, and kissed the earth, and with quivering lips exclaimed, "By the sacred earth on which I kneel, by the shades that wander near me, by the deep and eternal grief that I feel, I swear; and by thee, O Night, and the spirits that preside over thee, to pursue the dæmon, who caused this misery, until he or I shall perish in mortal conflict. For this purpose I will preserve my life: to execute this dear revenge, will I again behold the sun, and tread the green herbage of earth, which otherwise should vanish from my eyes for ever. And I call on you, spirits of the dead; and on you, wandering ministers of vengeance, to aid and conduct me in my work. Let the cursed and hellish monster drink deep of agony; let him feel the despair that now torments me."

'I had begun my adjuration with solemnity, and an awe which almost assured me that the shades of my murdered friends heard and approved my devotion; but the furies possessed me as I concluded, and rage choked my utterance.

'I was answered through the stillness of night by a loud and fiendish laugh. It rung on my ears long and heavily; the mountains re-echoed it, and I felt as if all hell surrounded me with mockery and laughter. Surely in that moment I should have been possessed by frenzy, and have destroyed my miserable existence, but that my vow was heard, and that I was reserved for vengeance. The laughter died away; when a well-known and abhorred voice, apparently close to my ear, addressed me in an audible whisper— "I am satisfied: miserable wretch! you have determined to live, and I am satisfied."

'I darted towards the spot from which the sound proceeded; but the devil eluded my grasp. Suddenly the broad disk of the moon arose, and shone full upon his ghastly and distorted shape, as he fled with more than mortal speed.

'I pursued him; and for many months this has been my task. Guided by a slight clue, I followed the windings of the Rhone, but vainly. The blue Mediterranean appeared; and, by a strange chance, I saw the fiend enter by night, and hide himself in a vessel bound for the Black Sea. I took my passage in the same ship; but he escaped, I know not how.

'Amidst the wilds of Tartary and Russia, although he still evaded me, I have ever followed in his track. Sometimes the peasants, scared by this horrid apparition, informed me of his path; sometimes he himself, who feared that if I lost all trace of him, I should despair and die, left some mark to guide me. The snows descended on my head, and I saw the print of his huge step on the white plain. To you first entering on life, to whom care is new, and agony unknown, how can you understand what I have felt, and still feel? Cold, want, and fatigue, were the least pains which I was destined to endure; I was cursed by some devil, and carried about with me my eternal hell; yet still a spirit of good followed and directed my steps; and, when I most murmured, would suddenly extricate me from seemingly insurmountable difficulties. Sometimes, when nature, overcome by hunger, sunk under the exhaustion, a repast was prepared for me in the desert, that restored and inspirited me. The fare was, indeed, coarse, such as the peasants of the country ate; but I will not doubt that it was set there by the spirits that I had invoked to aid me. Often, when all was dry, the heavens cloudless, and I was parched by thirst, a slight cloud would bedim the sky, shed the few drops that revived me, and vanish.

'I followed, when I could, the courses of the rivers; but the dæmon generally avoided these, as it was here that the population of the country chiefly collected. In other places human beings were seldom seen; and I generally subsisted on the wild animals that crossed my path. I had money with me, and gained the friendship of the villagers by distributing it; or I brought with me some food that I had killed, which, after taking a small part, I always presented to those who had provided me with fire and utensils for cooking.

'My life, as it passed thus, was indeed hateful to me, and it was during sleep alone that I could taste joy. O blessed sleep! often, when most miserable, I sank to repose, and my dreams lulled me even to rapture. The spirits that guarded me had provided these moments, or rather hours, of happiness, that I might retain strength to fulfil my pilgrimage. Deprived of this respite, I should have sunk under my hardships. During the day I was sustained and inspirited by the hope of night: for in sleep I saw my friends, my wife, and my beloved country; again I saw the benevolent countenance of my father, heard the silver tones of my Elizabeth's voice, and beheld Clerval enjoying health and youth. Often, when wearied by a toilsome march, I persuaded myself that I was dreaming until night should come, and that I should then enjoy reality in the arms of my dearest friends. What agonising fondness did I feel for them! how did I cling to their dear forms, as sometimes they haunted even my waking hours, and persuade myself that they still lived! At such moments vengeance, that burned within me, died in my heart, and I pursued my path towards the destruction of the dæmon, more as a task enjoined by heaven, as the mechanical impulse of some power of which I was unconscious, than as the ardent desire of my soul.

'What his feelings were whom I pursued I cannot know. Sometimes, indeed, he left marks in writing on the barks of the trees, or cut in stone, that guided me, and instigated my fury. "My reign is not yet over," (these words were legible in one of these inscriptions;) "you live, and my power is complete. Follow me; I seek the everlasting ices of the north, where you will feel the misery of cold and frost, to which I am impassive. You will find near this place, if you follow not too tardily, a dead hare; eat, and be refreshed. Come on, my enemy; we have yet to wrestle for our lives; but many hard and miserable hours must you endure until that period shall arrive."

'Scoffing devil! Again do I vow vengeance; again do I devote thee, miserable fiend, to torture and death. Never will I give up my search, until he or I perish; and then with what ecstasy shall I join my Elizabeth, and my departed friends, who even now prepare for me the reward of my tedious toil and horrible pilgrimage!

'As I still pursued my journey to the northward, the snows thickened, and the cold increased in a degree almost too severe to support. The peasants were shut up in their hovels, and only a few of the most hardy ventured forth to seize the animals whom starvation had forced from their hiding-places to seek for prey. The rivers were covered with ice, and no fish could be procured; and thus I was cut off from my chief article of maintenance.

'The triumph of my enemy increased with the difficulty of my labours. One inscription that he left was in these words:— "Prepare! your toils only begin: wrap yourself in furs, and provide food; for we shall soon enter upon a journey where your sufferings will satisfy my everlasting hatred."

'My courage and perseverance were invigorated by these scoffing words; I resolved not to fail in my purpose; and, calling on Heaven to support me, I continued with unabated fervour to traverse immense deserts, until the ocean appeared at a distance, and formed the utmost boundary of the horizon. Oh! how unlike it was to the blue seas of the south! Covered with ice, it was only to be distinguished from land by its superior wildness and ruggedness. The Greeks wept for joy when they beheld the Mediterranean from the hills of Asia, and hailed with rapture the boundary of their toils. I did not weep; but I knelt down, and, with a full heart, thanked my guiding spirit for conducting me in safety to the place where I hoped, notwithstanding my adversary's gibe, to meet and grapple with him.

'Some weeks before this period I had procured a sledge and dogs, and thus traversed the snows with inconceivable speed. I know not whether the fiend possessed the same advantages; but I found that, as before I had daily lost ground in the pursuit, I now gained on him: so much so, that when I first saw the ocean, he was but one day's journey in advance, and I hoped to intercept him before he should reach the beach. With new courage, therefore, I pressed on, and in two days arrived at a wretched hamlet on the sea-shore. I enquired of the inhabitants concerning the fiend, and gained accurate information. A gigantic monster, they said, had arrived the night before, armed with a gun and many pistols; putting to flight the inhabitants of a solitary cottage, through fear of his terrific appearance. He had carried off their store of winter food, and, placing it in a sledge, to draw which he had seized on a numerous drove of trained dogs, he had harnessed them, and the same night, to the joy of the horror-struck villagers, had pursued his journey across the sea in a direction that led to no land; and they conjectured that he must speedily be destroyed by the breaking of the ice, or frozen by the eternal frosts.

'On hearing this information, I suffered a temporary access of despair. He had escaped me; and I must commence a destructive and almost endless journey across the mountainous ices of the ocean,—amidst cold that few of the inhabitants could long endure, and which I, the native of a genial and sunny climate, could not hope to survive. Yet at the idea that the fiend should live and be triumphant, my rage and vengeance returned, and, like a mighty tide, overwhelmed every other feeling. After a slight repose, during which the spirits of the dead hovered round, and instigated me to toil and revenge, I prepared for my journey.

'I exchanged my land-sledge for one fashioned for the inequalities of the Frozen Ocean; and purchasing a plentiful stock of provisions, I departed from land.

'I cannot guess how many days have passed since then; but I have endured misery, which nothing but the eternal sentiment of a just retribution burning within my heart could have enabled me to support. Immense and rugged mountains of ice often barred up my passage, and I often heard the thunder of the ground sea, which threatened my destruction. But again the frost came, and made the paths of the sea secure.

'By the quantity of provision which I had consumed, I should guess that I had passed three weeks in this journey; and the continual protraction of hope, returning back upon the heart, often wrung bitter drops of despondency and grief from my eyes. Despair had indeed almost secured her prey, and I should soon have sunk beneath this misery. Once, after the poor animals that conveyed me had with incredible toil gained the summit of a sloping ice-mountain, and one, sinking under his fatigue, died, I viewed the expanse before me with anguish, when suddenly my eye caught a dark speck upon the dusky plain. I strained my sight to discover what it could be, and uttered a wild cry of ecstasy when I distinguished a sledge, and the distorted proportions of a well-known form within. Oh! with what a burning gush did hope revisit my heart! warm tears filled my eyes, which I hastily wiped away, that they might not intercept the view I had of the dæmon; but still my sight was dimmed by the burning drops, until, giving way to the emotions that oppressed me, I wept aloud.

'But this was not the time for delay: I disencumbered the dogs of their dead companion, gave them a plentiful portion of food; and, after an hour's rest, which was absolutely necessary, and yet which was bitterly irksome to me, I continued my route. The sledge was still visible; nor did I again lose sight of it, except at the moments when for a short time some ice-rock concealed it with its intervening crags. I indeed perceptibly gained on it; and when, after nearly two days' journey, I beheld my enemy at no more than a mile distant, my heart bounded within me.

'But now, when I appeared almost within grasp of my foe, my hopes were suddenly extinguished, and I lost all trace of him more utterly than I had ever done before. A ground sea was heard; the thunder of its progress, as the waters rolled and swelled beneath me, became every moment more ominous and terrific. I pressed on, but in vain. The wind arose; the sea roared; and, as with the mighty shock of an earthquake, it split, and cracked with a tremendous and overwhelming sound. The work was soon finished: in a few minutes a tumultuous sea rolled between me and my enemy, and I was left drifting on a scattered piece of ice, that was continually lessening, and thus preparing for me a hideous death.

'In this manner many appalling hours passed; several of my dogs died; and I myself was about to sink under the accumulation of distress, when I saw your vessel riding at anchor, and holding forth to me hopes of succour and life. I had no conception that vessels ever came so far north, and was astounded at the sight. I quickly destroyed part of my sledge to construct oars; and by these means was enabled, with infinite fatigue, to move my ice-raft in the direction of your ship. I had determined, if you were going southward, still to trust myself to the mercy of the seas rather than abandon my purpose. I hoped to induce you to grant me a boat with which I could pursue my enemy. But your direction was northward. You took me on board when my vigour was exhausted, and I should soon have sunk under my multiplied hardships into a death which I still dread—for my task is unfulfilled.

'Oh! when will my guiding spirit, in conducting me to the dæmon, allow me the rest I so much desire; or must I die, and he yet live? If I do, swear to me, Walton, that he shall not escape; that you will seek him, and satisfy my vengeance in his death. And do I dare to ask of you to undertake my pilgrimage, to endure the hardships that I have undergone? No; I am not so selfish. Yet, when I am dead, if he should appear; if the ministers of vengeance should conduct him to you, swear that he shall not live—swear that he shall not triumph over my accumulated woes, and survive to add to the list of his dark crimes. He is eloquent and persuasive; and once his words had even power over my heart: but trust him not. His soul is as hellish as his form, full of treachery and fiendlike malice. Hear him not; call on the manes of William, Justine, Clerval, Elizabeth, my father, and of the wretched Victor, and thrust your sword into his heart. I will hover near, and direct the steel aright.'

My failed student with the hollow art paused, pregnantly. I wept openly, but he either did not notice or did not care. He sat staring blankly at the wall as if it was not there. What was he staring at? His own mortality? His own death? Then the phantasm faded from my sight. Was his tale ended? Was there more to this story than what he related to me— to Walton— over the course of this calamitous, preternatural summer? I did not yet know, so I allowed myself to drift off. In the morning there came a rapping, a tapping on my chamber door. It was my dearest Claire announcing that a letter had arrived by post addressed to a 'Mrs. Saville.'

So the tale would, indeed, continue. Huzzah!

Continuation of Letter IV

Walton, *in continuation.*
August 26th, 17—.

You have read this strange and terrific story, Margaret; and do you not feel your blood congeal with horror, like that which even now curdles mine? Sometimes, seized with sudden agony, he could not continue his tale; at others, his voice broken, yet piercing, uttered with difficulty the words so replete with anguish. His fine and lovely eyes were now lighted up with indignation, now subdued to downcast sorrow, and quenched in infinite wretchedness. Sometimes he commanded his countenance and tones, and related the most horrible incidents with a tranquil voice, suppressing every mark of agitation; then, like a volcano bursting forth, his face would suddenly change to an expression of the wildest rage, as he shrieked out imprecations on his persecutor.

His tale is connected, and told with an appearance of the simplest truth; yet I own to you that the letters of Felix and Safie, which he showed me, and the apparition of the monster seen from our ship, brought to me a greater conviction of the truth of his narrative than his asseverations, however earnest and connected. Such a monster has then really existence! I cannot doubt it; yet I am lost in surprise and admiration. Sometimes I endeavoured to gain from Frankenstein the particulars of his creatures formation: but on this point he was impenetrable.

'Are you mad, my friend?' said he; 'or whither does your senseless curiosity lead you? Would you also create for yourself and the world a demoniacal enemy? Peace, peace! learn my miseries, and do not seek to increase your own.'

Frankenstein discovered that I made notes concerning his history: he asked to see them, and then himself corrected and augmented them in many places; but principally in giving the life and spirit to the conversations he held with his enemy. 'Since you have preserved my narration,' said he, 'I would not that a mutilated one should go down to posterity.'

Thus has a week passed away, while I have listened to the strangest tale that ever imagination formed. My thoughts, and every feeling of my soul, have been drunk up by the interest for my guest, which this tale, and his own elevated and gentle manners, have created. I wish to soothe him; yet can I counsel one so infinitely miserable, so destitute of every hope of consolation, to live? Oh, no! the only joy that he can now know will be when he composes his shattered spirit to peace and death. Yet he enjoys one comfort, the offspring of solitude and delirium: he believes, that, when in dreams he holds converse with his friends, and derives from that communion consolation for his miseries, or excitements to his vengeance, that they are not the creations of his fancy, but the beings themselves who visit him from the regions of a remote world. This faith gives a solemnity to his reveries that render them to me almost as imposing and interesting as truth.

Our conversations are not always confined to his own history and misfortunes. On every point of general literature he displays unbounded knowledge, and a quick and piercing apprehension. His eloquence is forcible and touching; nor can I hear him, when he relates a pathetic incident, or endeavours to move the passions of pity or love, without tears. What a glorious creature must he have been in the days of his prosperity, when he is thus noble and godlike in ruin! He seems to feel his own worth, and the greatness of his fall.

'When younger,' said he, 'I believed myself destined for some great enterprise. My feelings are profound; but I possessed a coolness of judgment that fitted me for illustrious achievements. This sentiment of the worth of my nature supported me, when others would have been oppressed; for I deemed it criminal to throw away in useless grief those talents that might be useful to my fellow-creatures. When I reflected on the work I had completed, no less a one than the creation of a sensitive and rational animal, I could not rank myself with the herd of common projectors. But this thought, which supported me in the commencement of my career, now serves only to plunge me lower in the dust. All my speculations and hopes are as nothing; and, like the archangel who aspired to omnipotence, I am chained in an eternal hell. My imagination was vivid, yet my powers of analysis and application were intense; by the union of these qualities I conceived the idea, and executed the creation of a man. Even now I cannot recollect, without passion, my reveries while the work was incomplete. I trod heaven in my thoughts, now exulting in my powers, now burning with the idea of their effects. From my infancy I was imbued with high hopes and a lofty ambition; but how am I sunk! Oh! my friend, if you had known me as I once was, you would not recognise me in this state of degradation. Despondency rarely visited my heart; a high destiny seemed to bear me on, until I fell, never, never again to rise.'

Must I then lose this admirable being? I have longed for a friend; I have sought one who would sympathise with and love me. Behold, on these desert seas I have found such a one; but, I fear, I have gained him only to know his value, and lose him. I would reconcile him to life, but he repulses the idea.

'I thank you, Walton,' he said, 'for your kind intentions towards so miserable a wretch; but when you speak of new ties, and fresh affections, think you that any can replace those who are gone? Can any man be to me as Clerval was; or any woman another Elizabeth? Even where the affections are not strongly moved by any superior excellence, the companions of our childhood always possess a certain power over our minds, which hardly any later friend can obtain. They know our infantine dispositions, which, however they may be afterwards modified, are never eradicated; and they can judge of our actions with more certain conclusions as to the integrity of our motives. A sister or a brother can never, unless indeed such symptoms have been shown early, suspect the other of fraud or false dealing, when another friend, however strongly he may be attached, may, in spite of himself, be contemplated with suspicion. But I enjoyed friends, dear not only through habit and association, but from their own merits; and wherever I am, the soothing voice of my Elizabeth, and the conversation of Clerval, will be ever whispered in my ear. They are dead; and but one feeling in such a solitude can persuade me to preserve my life. If I were engaged in any high undertaking or design, fraught with extensive utility to my fellow-creatures, then could I live to fulfil it. But such is not my destiny; I must pursue and destroy the being to whom I gave existence; then my lot on earth will be fulfilled, and I may die.'

September 2d.

My beloved Sister,

I write to you, encompassed by peril, and ignorant whether I am ever doomed to see again dear England, and the dearer friends that inhabit it. I am surrounded by mountains of ice, which admit of no escape, and threaten every moment to crush my vessel. The brave fellows, whom I have persuaded to be my companions, look towards me for aid; but I have none to bestow. There is something terribly appalling in our situation, yet my courage and hopes do not desert me. Yet it is terrible to reflect that the lives of all these men are endangered through me. If we are lost, my mad schemes are the cause.

And what, Margaret, will be the state of your mind? You will not hear of my destruction, and you will anxiously await my return. Years will pass, and you will have visitings of despair, and yet be tortured by hope. Oh! my beloved sister, the sickening failing of your heart-felt expectations is, in prospect, more terrible to me than my own death. But you have a husband, and lovely children; you may be happy: Heaven bless you, and make you so!

My unfortunate guest regards me with the tenderest compassion. He endeavours to fill me with hope; and talks as if life were a possession which he valued. He reminds me how often the same accidents have happened to other navigators, who have attempted this sea, and, in spite of myself, he fills me with cheerful auguries. Even the sailors feel the power of his eloquence: when he speaks, they no longer despair; he rouses their energies, and, while they hear his voice, they believe these vast mountains of ice are mole-hills, which will vanish before the resolutions of man. These feelings are transitory; each day of expectation delayed fills them with fear, and I almost dread a mutiny caused by this despair.

September 5th.

A scene has just passed of such uncommon interest, that although it is highly probable that these papers may never reach you, yet I cannot forbear recording it.

We are still surrounded by mountains of ice, still in imminent danger of being crushed in their conflict. The cold is excessive, and many of my unfortunate comrades have already found a grave amidst this scene of desolation. Frankenstein has daily declined in health: a feverish fire still glimmers in his eyes; but he is exhausted, and, when suddenly roused to any exertion, he speedily sinks again into apparent lifelessness.

I mentioned in my last letter the fears I entertained of a mutiny. This morning, as I sat watching the wan countenance of my friend—his eyes half closed, and his limbs hanging listlessly,—I was roused by half a dozen of the sailors, who demanded admission into the cabin. They entered, and their leader addressed me. He told me that he and his companions had been chosen by the other sailors to come in deputation to me, to make me a requisition, which, in justice, I could not refuse. We were immured in ice, and should probably never escape; but they feared that if, as was possible, the ice should dissipate, and a free passage be opened, I should be rash enough to continue my voyage, and lead them into fresh dangers, after they might happily have surmounted this. They insisted, therefore, that I should engage with a solemn promise, that if the vessel should be freed I would instantly direct my course southward.

This speech troubled me. I had not despaired; nor had I yet conceived the idea of returning, if set free. Yet could I, in justice, or even in possibility, refuse this demand? I hesitated before I answered; when Frankenstein, who had at first been silent, and, indeed, appeared hardly to have force enough to attend, now roused himself; his eyes sparkled, and his cheeks flushed with momentary vigour. Turning towards the men, he said—

'What do you mean? What do you demand of your captain? Are you then so easily turned from your design? Did you not call this a glorious expedition? And wherefore was it glorious? Not because the way was smooth and placid as a southern sea, but because it was full of dangers and terror; because, at every new incident, your fortitude was to be called forth, and your courage exhibited; because danger and death surrounded it, and these you were to brave and overcome. For this was it a glorious, for this was it an honourable undertaking. You were hereafter to be hailed as the benefactors of your species; your names adored, as belonging to brave men who encountered death for honour, and the benefit of mankind. And now, behold, with the first imagination of danger, or, if you will, the first mighty and terrific trial of your courage, you shrink away, and are content to be handed down as men who had not strength enough to endure cold and peril; and so, poor souls, they were chilly, and returned to their warm fire-sides. Why, that requires not this preparation; ye need not have come thus far, and dragged your captain to the shame of a defeat, merely to prove yourselves cowards. Oh! be men, or be more than men. Be steady to your purposes, and firm as a rock. This ice is not made of such stuff as your hearts may be; it is mutable, and cannot withstand you, if you say that it shall not. Do not return to your families with the stigma of disgrace marked on your brows. Return, as heroes who have fought and conquered, and who know not what it is to turn their backs on the foe.'

He spoke this with a voice so modulated to the different feelings expressed in his speech, with an eye so full of lofty design and heroism, that can you wonder that these men were moved? They looked at one another, and were unable to reply. I spoke; I told them to retire, and consider of what had been said: that I would not lead them farther north, if they strenuously desired the contrary; but that I hoped that, with reflection, their courage would return.

They retired, and I turned towards my friend; but he was sunk in languor, and almost deprived of life.

How all this will terminate, I know not; but I had rather die than return shamefully,—my purpose unfulfilled. Yet I fear such will be my fate; the men, unsupported by ideas of glory and honour, can never willingly continue to endure their present hardships.

September 7th.

The die is cast; I have consented to return, if we are not destroyed. Thus are my hopes blasted by cowardice and indecision; I come back ignorant and disappointed. It requires more philosophy than I possess, to bear this injustice with patience.

September 12th.

It is past; I am returning to England. I have lost my hopes of utility and glory;—I have lost my friend. But I will endeavour to detail these bitter circumstances to you, my dear sister; and, while I am wafted towards England, and towards you, I will not despond.

September 9th, the ice began to move, and roarings like thunder were heard at a distance, as the islands split and cracked in every direction. We were in the most imminent peril; but, as we could only remain passive, my chief attention was occupied by my unfortunate guest, whose illness increased in such a degree, that he was entirely confined to his bed. The ice cracked behind us, and was driven with force towards the north; a breeze sprung from the west, and on the 11th the passage towards the south became perfectly free. When the sailors saw this, and that their return to their native country was apparently assured, a shout of tumultuous joy broke from them, loud and long-continued. Frankenstein, who was dozing, awoke, and asked the cause of the tumult. 'They shout,' I said, 'because they will soon return to England.'

'Do you then really return?'

'Alas! yes; I cannot withstand their demands. I cannot lead them unwillingly to danger, and I must return.'

'Do so, if you will; but I will not. You may give up your purpose, but mine is assigned to me by Heaven, and I dare not. I am weak; but surely the spirits who assist my vengeance will endow me with sufficient strength.' Saying this, he endeavoured to spring from the bed, but the exertion was too great for him; he fell back, and fainted.

It was long before he was restored; and I often thought that life was entirely extinct. At length he opened his eyes; he breathed with difficulty, and was unable to speak. The surgeon gave him a composing draught, and ordered us to leave him undisturbed. In the mean time he told me, that my friend had certainly not many hours to live.

His sentence was pronounced; and I could only grieve, and be patient. I sat by his bed, watching him; his eyes were closed, and I thought he slept; but presently he called to me in a feeble voice, and, bidding me come near, said— 'Alas! the strength I relied on is gone; I feel that I shall soon die, and he, my enemy and persecutor, may still be in being. Think not, Walton, that in the last moments of my existence I feel that burning hatred, and ardent desire of revenge, I once expressed; but I feel myself justified in desiring the death of my adversary. During these last days I have been occupied in examining my past conduct; nor do I find it blamable. In a fit of enthusiastic madness I created a rational creature, and was bound towards him, to assure, as far as was in my power, his happiness and well-being. This was my duty; but there was another still paramount to that. My duties towards the beings of my own species had greater claims to my attention, because they included a greater proportion of happiness or misery. Urged by this view, I refused, and I did right in refusing, to create a companion for the first creature. He showed unparalleled malignity and selfishness, in evil: he destroyed my friends;

he devoted to destruction beings who possessed exquisite sensations, happiness, and wisdom; nor do I know where this thirst for vengeance may end. Miserable himself, that he may render no other wretched, he ought to die. The task of his destruction was mine, but I have failed. When actuated by selfish and vicious motives, I asked you to undertake my unfinished work; and I renew this request now, when I am only induced by reason and virtue.

'Yet I cannot ask you to renounce your country and friends, to fulfil this task; and now, that you are returning to England, you will have little chance of meeting with him. But the consideration of these points, and the well balancing of what you may esteem your duties, I leave to you; my judgment and ideas are already disturbed by the near approach of death. I dare not ask you to do what I think right, for I may still be misled by passion.

'That he should live to be an instrument of mischief disturbs me; in other respects, this hour, when I momentarily expect my release, is the only happy one which I have enjoyed for several years. The forms of the beloved dead flit before me, and I hasten to their arms. Farewell, Walton! Seek happiness in tranquillity, and avoid ambition, even if it be only the apparently innocent one of distinguishing yourself in science and discoveries. Yet why do I say this? I have myself been blasted in these hopes, yet another may succeed.'

His voice became fainter as he spoke; and at length, exhausted by his effort, he sunk into silence. About half an hour afterwards he attempted again to speak, but was unable; he pressed my hand feebly, and his eyes closed for ever, while the irradiation of a gentle smile passed away from his lips.

Margaret, what comment can I make on the untimely extinction of this glorious spirit? What can I say, that will enable you to understand the depth of my sorrow? All that I should express would be inadequate and feeble. My tears flow; my mind is overshadowed by a cloud of disappointment. But I journey towards England, and I may there find consolation.

I am interrupted. What do these sounds portend? It is midnight; the breeze blows fairly, and the watch on deck scarcely stir. Again; there is a sound as of a human voice, but hoarser; it comes from the cabin where the remains of Frankenstein still lie. I must arise, and examine. Good night, my sister.

Great God! what a scene has just taken place! I am yet dizzy with the remembrance of it. I hardly know whether I shall have the power to detail it; yet the tale which I have recorded would be incomplete without this final and wonderful catastrophe.

I entered the cabin, where lay the remains of my ill-fated and admirable friend. Over him hung a form which I cannot find words to describe; gigantic in stature, yet uncouth and distorted in its proportions. As he hung over the coffin, his face was concealed by long locks of ragged hair; but one vast hand was extended, in colour and apparent texture like that of a mummy. When he heard the sound of my approach, he ceased to utter exclamations of grief and horror, and sprung towards the window. Never did I behold a vision so horrible as his face, of such loathsome, yet appalling hideousness. I shut my eyes involuntarily, and endeavoured to recollect what were my duties with regard to this destroyer. I called on him to stay.

He paused, looking on me with wonder; and, again turning towards the lifeless form of his creator, he seemed to forget my presence, and every feature and gesture seemed instigated by the wildest rage of some uncontrollable passion.

'That is also my victim!' he exclaimed: 'in his murder my crimes are consummated; the miserable series of my being is wound to its close! Oh, Frankenstein! generous and self-devoted being! what does it avail that I now ask thee to pardon me? I, who irretrievably destroyed thee by destroying all thou lovedst. Alas! he is cold, he cannot answer me.'

His voice seemed suffocated; and my first impulses, which had suggested to me the duty of obeying the dying request of my friend, in destroying his enemy, were now suspended by a mixture of curiosity and compassion. I approached this tremendous being; I dared not again raise my eyes to his face, there was something so scaring and unearthly in his ugliness. I attempted to speak, but the words died away on my lips. The monster continued to utter wild and incoherent self-reproaches. At length I gathered resolution to address him in a pause of the tempest of his passion: 'Your repentance,' I said, 'is now superfluous. If you had listened to the voice of conscience, and heeded the stings of remorse, before you had urged your diabolical vengeance to this extremity, Frankenstein would yet have lived.

'And do you dream?' said the dæmon; 'do you think that *I* was then dead to agony and remorse?—He,' he continued, pointing to the corpse, 'he suffered not in the consummation of the deed—oh! not the ten-thousandth portion of the anguish that was mine during the lingering detail of its execution. A frightful selfishness hurried me on, while my heart was poisoned with remorse. Think you that the groans of Clerval were music to my ears? My heart was fashioned to be susceptible of love and sympathy; and, when wrenched by misery to vice and hatred, it did not endure the violence of the change, without torture such as you cannot even imagine.

'After the murder of Clerval, I returned to Switzerland, heart-broken and overcome. I pitied Frankenstein; my pity amounted to horror: I abhorred myself. But when I discovered that he, the author at once of my existence and of its unspeakable torments, dared to hope for happiness; that while he accumulated wretchedness and despair upon me, he sought his own enjoyment in feelings and passions from the indulgence of which I was for ever barred, then impotent envy and bitter indignation filled me with an insatiable thirst for vengeance. I recollected my threat, and resolved that it should be accomplished. I knew that I was preparing for myself a deadly torture; but I was the slave, not the master, of an impulse, which I detested, yet could not disobey. Yet when she died!—nay, then I was not miserable. I had cast off all feeling, subdued all anguish, to riot in the excess of my despair. Evil thenceforth became my good. Urged thus far, I had no choice but to adapt my nature to an element which I had willingly chosen. The completion of my demoniacal design became an insatiable passion. And now it is ended; there is my last victim!'

I was at first touched by the expressions of his misery; yet, when I called to mind what Frankenstein had said of his powers of eloquence and persuasion, and when I again cast my eyes on the lifeless form of my friend, indignation was rekindled within me. 'Wretch!' I said, 'it is well that you come here to whine over the desolation that you have made. You throw a torch into a pile of buildings; and, when they are consumed, you sit among the ruins, and lament the fall. Hypocritical fiend! if he whom you mourn still lived, still would he be the object, again would he become the prey, of your accursed vengeance. It is not pity that you feel; you lament only because the victim of your malignity is withdrawn from your power.'

'Oh, it is not thus—not thus,' interrupted the being; 'yet such must be the impression conveyed to you by what appears to be the purport of my actions. Yet I seek not a fellow-feeling in my misery. No sympathy may I ever find. When I first sought it, it was the love of virtue, the feelings of happiness and affection with which my whole being overflowed, that I wished to be participated. But now, that virtue has become to me a shadow, and that happiness and affection are turned into bitter and loathing despair, in what should I seek for sympathy? I am content to suffer alone, while my sufferings shall endure: when I die, I am well satisfied that abhorrence and opprobrium should load my memory. Once my fancy was soothed with dreams of virtue, of fame, and of enjoyment. Once I falsely hoped to meet with beings, who, pardoning my outward form, would love me for the excellent qualities which I was capable of unfolding. I was nourished with high thoughts of honour and devotion. But now crime has degraded me beneath the meanest animal. No guilt, no mischief, no malignity, no misery, can be found comparable to mine. When I run over the frightful catalogue of my sins, I cannot believe that I am the same creature whose thoughts were once filled with sublime and transcendent visions of the beauty and the majesty of goodness. But it is even so; the fallen angel becomes a malignant devil. Yet even that enemy of God and man had friends and associates in his desolation; I am alone.

'You, who call Frankenstein your friend, seem to have a knowledge of my crimes and his misfortunes. But, in the detail which he gave you of them, he could not sum up the hours and months of misery which I endured, wasting in impotent passions. For while I destroyed his hopes, I did not satisfy my own desires. They were for ever ardent and craving; still I desired love and fellowship, and I was still spurned. Was there no injustice in this? Am I to be thought the only criminal, when all human kind sinned against me? Why do you not hate Felix, who drove his friend from his door with contumely? Why do you not execrate the rustic who sought to destroy the saviour of his child? Nay, these are virtuous and immaculate beings! I, the miserable and the abandoned, am an abortion, to be spurned at, and kicked, and trampled on. Even now my blood boils at the recollection of this injustice.

'But it is true that I am a wretch. I have murdered the lovely and the helpless; I have strangled the innocent as they slept, and grasped to death his throat who never injured me or any other living thing. I have devoted my creator, the select specimen of all that is worthy of love and admiration among men, to misery; I have pursued him even to that irremediable ruin. There he lies, white and cold in death. You hate me; but your abhorrence cannot equal that with which I regard myself. I look on the hands which executed the deed; I think on the heart in which the imagination of it was conceived, and long for the moment when these hands will meet my eyes, when that imagination will haunt my thoughts no more.

'Fear not that I shall be the instrument of future mischief. My work is nearly complete. Neither yours nor any man s death is needed to consummate the series of my being, and accomplish that which must be done; but it requires my own. Do not think that I shall be slow to perform this sacrifice. I shall quit your vessel on the ice-raft which brought me thither, and shall seek the most northern extremity of the globe; I shall collect my funeral pile,'— no doubt made of the sledges of Victor's and the Creature's. Does he cremate only himself but his Creator as well? I don't believe I shall ever truly know— 'and consume to ashes this miserable frame, that its remains may afford no light to any curious and unhallowed wretch, who would create such another as I have been. I shall die. I shall no longer feel the agonies which now consume me, or be the prey of feelings unsatisfied, yet unquenched. He is dead who called me into being; and when I shall be no more, the very remembrance of us both will speedily vanish. I shall no longer see the sun or stars, or feel the winds play on my cheeks. Light, feeling, and sense will pass away; and in this condition must I find my happiness. Some years ago, when the images which this world affords first opened upon me, when I felt the cheering warmth of summer, and heard the rustling of the leaves and the warbling of the birds, and these were all to me, I should have wept to die; now it is my only consolation. Polluted by crimes, and torn by the bitterest remorse, where can I find rest but in death?

'Farewell! I leave you, and in you the last of human kind whom these eyes will ever behold. Farewell, Frankenstein! If thou wert yet alive, and yet cherished a desire of revenge against me, it would be better satiated in my life than in my destruction. But it was not so; thou didst seek my extinction, that I might not cause greater wretchedness; and if yet, in some mode unknown to me, thou hadst not ceased to think and feel, thou wouldst not desire against me a vengeance greater than that which I feel. Blasted as thou wert, my agony was still superior to thine; for the bitter sting of remorse will not cease to rankle in my wounds until death shall close them for ever.

'But soon,' he cried, with sad and solemn enthusiasm, 'I shall die, and what I now feel be no longer felt. Soon these burning miseries will be extinct. I shall ascend my funeral pile triumphantly, and exult in the agony of the torturing flames. The light of that conflagration will fade away; my ashes will be swept into the sea by the winds. My spirit will sleep in peace; or if it thinks, it will not surely think thus. Farewell.'

He sprung from the cabin-window, as he said this, upon the ice-raft which lay close to the vessel. He was soon borne away by the waves, and lost in darkness and distance.'

As I finished reciting the tales of Victor's and his Creature's own recitation, my dearest Claire flew into hysterics. These hysterics were fuelled by the child growing in her womb; the child growing in her womb caused her emotions to become practically preternatural. After being subdued with a drop or two of laudanum, Claire fell into a pharmaceutically induced slumber on the sofa. What was it about my ghost story that elicited such an extreme response? From the others there was nothing but silence.

I imagined their criticism that 'this is another anomalous story of the same race and family as Mandeville; and, if we are not misinformed, it is intimately connected with that strange performance, by more ties than one. In the present instance, it is true, we are presented with the mysteries of equivocal generation, instead of the metaphysics of a bed-lamite; but he who runs as he reads, might pronounce both novels to be similis farinæ. We are in doubt to what class we shall refer writings of this extravagent character; that they bear marks of considerable pow-er, it is impossible to deny; but this power is so abused and perverted, that we should almost prefer imbecility; however much, of late years, we have been wearied and ennuied by the languid whispers of gentle sen-timentality, they at least had the comfortable property of provoking no uneasy slumber; but we must protect against the waking dreams of hor-ror excited by the unnatural stimulants of this later school; and we feel ourselves as much harassed, after rising from the perusal of these three spirit-wearing volumes, as if we had been over-dosed with laudanum, or hag-ridden by the night-mare.

'No one can love a real good ghost story more heartily than we do; and we will toil through many a tedious duodecimo to get half a dozen pages of rational terror, provided always, that we keep company with spectres and skeletons, no longer than they maintain the just dignity of their spiritual character. Now and then too, we can tolerate a goule, so it be not at his dinnertime; and altogether, we profess to entertain a very due respect for the whole anierarchy of the dæmoniacal establish-ment. Our prejudices in favor of legitimacy, of course, are proportionably shocked by the pretensions of any pseudo-diabolism; and all our best feelings of ghostly loyalty are excited by the usurpations of an unauthor-ized hobgoblin, or a non-descript fee-fa-fum.

'We need scarcely say, that these volumes have neither principle, ob-ject, nor moral; the horror which abounds in them is too grotesque and *bizarre* ever to approach near the sublime, and when we did not hurry over the pages in disgust, we sometimes paused to laugh outright: and yet we suspect, that the diseased and wandering imagination, which has stepped out of all legitimate bounds, to frame these disjointed combina-tions and unnatural adventures, might be disciplined into something bet-ter. We heartily wish it were so, for there are occasional symptoms of no common powers of mind, struggling through a mass of absurdity, which well nigh overwhelms them; but it is a sort of absurdity that approaches so often the confines of what is wicked and immoral, that we dare hardly trust ourselves to bestow even this qualified praise. The writer of it is, we understand, a female; this is an aggravation of that which is the pre-vailing fault of the novel; but if our authoress can forget the gentleness of her sex, it is no reason why we should; and we shall therefore dismiss the novel without further comment.'[49]

OR

---

49 From a review in *The British Critic*, New Series, Vol. 9, April 1818, pp. 432-8.

'This novel is a feeble imitation of one that was very popular in its day,—the St. Leon of Mr. Godwin. It exhibits many characteristics of the school whence it proceeds; and occasionally puts forth indications of talent; but we have been very much disappointed in the perusal of it, from our expectations having been raised too high beforehand by injudicious praises; and it exhibits a strong tendency towards materialism.

'The main idea on which the story of Frankenstein rests, undoubtedly affords scope for the display of imagination and fancy, as well as knowledge of the human heart; and the anonymous author has not wholly neglected the opportunities which it presented to him: but the work seems to have been written in great haste, and on a very crude and ill-digested plan; and the detail is, in consequence, frequently filled with the most gross and obvious inconsistencies. We shall hereafter point out a few of those to which we allude.

'The story begins at the end. Walton, an enthusiastic traveller, bound on a voyage of discovery in the north seas, after having been for some time surrounded with ice, is astonished by the appearance of a human being of apparently savage character who passes the vessel at a distance, in a sledge drawn by dogs. The day after this extraordinary adventure the ice breaks up; but previously to the vessel sailing away from it, they encounter another human being, nearly exhausted with fatigue and privation. This last, who is taken into the vessel, proves to be Frankenstein, the hero of the tale; who at the time he had been nearly destroyed by the breaking up of the ice, was in pursuit of the being that had passed the vessel on the preceding day. After a time Frankenstein contracts a friendship with Walton, the Captain of the vessel, and relates to him his supernatural story.—In his youth he had been led by accident to study chemistry; and becoming deeply interested by the results of his experiments, he at length conceived the idea of its being possible to discover the principle of vital existence. Taking this possibility as the leading point of his studies, he pursues them with such effect as at last actually to gain the power of endowing inanimate matter with life!!! He instantly determines to put his newly acquired power into practice; and for this purpose collects the materials with which to form a living human being. From the difficulty of arranging some of the parts, arising from their minuteness, he determines to chuse them of more than ordinary size. In short, after incredible pains and perseverance, he at length succeeded in producing a living human being, eight feet high, and of proportionate powers. From this moment Frankenstein commences a life of unmixed and unceasing misery. The being which he has formed becomes his torment, and that of every one connected with him. He causes one by one the death of all Frankenstein's dearest connections; his brother, his friend, and lastly his wife— whom he murders on their wedding night. The fiend then quits the country where he has committed these horrors; and Frankenstein, in dispair, determines to pursue him until he shall either destroy him, or die by his hand. The story ends shortly after what we have related in the beginning. Frankenstein dies on board the vessel of Walton; and the fiend may, for any thing we know to be the contrary, be wandering about upon the ice in the neighbourhood of the North Pole to this day; and may, in that case, be among the wonderful discoveries to be made by the expedition which is destined there.

'We have mentioned that there are gross inconsistencies in the minor details of the story. They are such, for example, as the following: the moment Frankenstein has endowed with life the previously inanimate form of the being which he has made, he is so horror-struck with the hideousness of the form and features, when they are put in motion, that he remains fixed to the spot, while the gigantic monster runs from the horizontal posture in which he lay, and walks away; and Frankenstein never hears any more of him for nearly two years. The author supposes that his hero has the power of communicating life to dead matter: but what has the vital principle to do with habits, and actions which are dependent on the moral will? If Frankenstein could have endowed his creature with the vital principle of a hundred or a thousand human beings, it would no more have been able to walk without having previously acquired the habit of doing so, than it would be to talk, or to reason, or to judge. He does not pretend that he could endow it with faculties as well as life: and yet when it is about a year old we find it reading Werter, and Plutarch and Volney! The whole detail of the development of the creature's mind and faculties is full of these monstrous inconsistencies. After the creature leaves Frankenstein, on the night of its birth, it wanders for sometime in the woods, and then takes up its residence in a kind of shed adjoining to a cottage, where it remains for many months without the knowledge of the inhabitants; and learns to talk and read thro' a chink in the wall! "*Quod mihi ostendit,*" &c

'We have heard that this work is written by Mr. Shelley; but should be disposed to attribute it to even a less experienced writer than he is. In fact we have some idea that it is the production of a daughter of a celebrated living novelist.'[50]

A novelist cannot but create in her mind the most negative and critical of reviews! But the pregnant silence from my fellow players in our little game of ghost stories has my stomach twisted into knots. Then the Hear-hears came from all around. Our Little Lord declared

---

50 From a review in *The Literary Panorama, and National Register,* New Series. Vol. 8: June 1818, pp. 411–414.

me the winner the game of ghost stories he himself had a proposed. My Beloved's eyes shined with pride. And Poor Polidori, who himself possessed aspirations in the theatre, hailed the letters that I had *constructed* as theatrical brilliance. He took the letters from the small round table beside my chair and turned them over and over in his hands. How had I masked my naturally feminine handing writing in their construction? This is surely the haggard penmanship of the rough-hewn hands of a man at sea, he posed. And this is the mature and stable penmanship of the patriarch of the Frankenstein family, he questioned. But this the exquisite penmanship of the dainty hands of an educated woman, whom is cousin to the protagonist, he queried, countering his own argument with the realization that I possess the dainty hands of an educated woman.

The satisfaction I felt that their adulations and applause was an enormous burden lifted from my shoulders. Polidori, himself, had been so ruthless in his mockery of me at every breakfast for a week for not having found a ghost story yet. My Beloved sat stone-faced at my side at the kitchen table, neither supporting me nor condemning me for my lack of inspiration for a seemingly insipid game of ghost stories. Lord Byron, who had instigated said game, was quiet in his mockery, but it remained mockery still. But now, having related Victor's and his Creature's tales over the course of a handful of evenings in the parlour, while the thunderstorms buffets the windowpanes with calamitous wind and rain. If I had possessed Aladin's lamp straight out of *Arabian Nights*, I would not have wished for a suitable a backdrop as an author of a ghost story.

Curious. What tale would have composed this cruel summer if Lord Byron had selected that volume off the shelf instead of picking of *Fantasmagoriana*, that crude French translation of German ghost stories? Would he have proposed a game of additional Arabian Nights above and beyond the one-thousand-and-one? My mind reals as the possibilities spin in my mind. Of the hundred or more other works in his parlour, Lord Byron chose a poorly edited collection of poorly written ghost stories. And if my Beloved and Lord Byron had not engaged in their galvanising debate over electrified frog legs, then I would not have been seen my pale student of the unhallowed arts kneeling beside the thing he had put together. I would never have seen the hideous phantasm of a man stretched out, and then, on the working of some powerful engine, show signs of life, and stir with an uneasy, half vital motion. Frightful must it have been; for supremely frightful would be the effect of any human endeavour to mock the stupendous mechanism of the Creator of the world!

And now, once again, I bid my hideous progeny go forth and prosper. I have an affection for it, for it was the offspring of happy days, when death and grief were but words, which found no true echo in my heart. Its several pages speak of many a walk, many a drive, and many a conversation, when I was not alone; and my companion was one who, in this world, I shall never see more. But this is for myself; my readers have nothing to do with these associations.

I will add but one word as to the alterations I will eventually make. They are principally those of style. I shall change no portion of the story, nor introduce any new ideas or circumstances. I shall mend the language where it was so bald as to interfere with the interest of the narrative; and these changes occur almost exclusively in the beginning of the first volume. Throughout they shall be entirely confined to such parts as are mere adjuncts to the story, leaving the core and substance of it untouched.[51]

---

51 From the Introduction to the 1831 Edition of *Frankenstein; or, The Modern Prometheus,* published by Henry Colburn & Richard Bentley.

Epilogue
Matthew Gregory Lewis' Contributions
To the Game of Ghost Stories

P.B. Shelley Writing In Mary Wollstonecraft Godwin's Journal

A shovel of his ashes took
From the hearth's obscurest nook,
Muttering mysteries as she went.
Helen and Henry knew that Granny
Was as much afraid of ghosts as any,
And so they followed hard—
But Helen clung to her brother's arm,
And her own spasm made her shake.

Geneva, Sunday, 18th August, 1816. See Apollo's Sexton, who tells us many mysteries of his trade. We talk of Ghosts. Neither Lord Byron nor M.G.L. seem to believe in them; and they both agree, in the very face of reason, that none could believe in ghosts without believing in God. I do not think that all the persons who profess to discredit these visitations, really discredit them; or, if they do in the daylight, are not admonished by the approach of loneliness and midnight, to think more respectfully of the world of shadows.

Lewis recited a poem, which he had composed at the request of the Princess of Wales. The Princess of Wales, he premised, was not only a believer in ghosts, but in magic and witchcraft, and asserted, that prophecies made in her youth had been accomplished since. The tale was of a lady in Germany.

This lady, Minna, had been exceedingly attached to her husband, and they had made a vow that the one who died first, should return after death to visit the other as a ghost. She was sitting one day alone in her chamber, when she heard an unusual sound of footsteps on the stairs. The door opened, and her husband's spectre, gashed with a deep wound across the forehead, and in military habiliments, entered. She appeared startled at the apparition; and the ghost told her, that when he should visit her in future, she would hear a passing bell toll, and these words distinctly uttered close to her ear, 'Minna, I am here.' On inquiry, it was found that her husband had fallen in battle on the very day she was visited by the vision. The intercourse between the ghost and the woman continued for some time, until the latter laid aside all terror, and indulged herself in the affection which she had felt for him while living. One evening she went to a ball, and permitted her thoughts to be alienated by the attentions of a Florentine gentleman, more witty, more graceful, and more gentle, as it appeared to her, than any person she had ever seen. As he was conducting her through the dance, a death bell tolled. Minna, lost in the fascination of the Florentine's attentions, disregarded, or did not hear the sound. A second peal, louder and more deep, startled the whole company, when Minna heard the ghost's accustomed whisper, and raising her eyes, saw in an opposite mirror the reflexion of the ghost, standing over her. She is said to have died of terror.

Lewis told four other stories— all grim.

1

A young man who had taken orders, had just been presented with a living, on the death of the incumbent. It was in the Catholic part of Germany. He arrived at the parsonage on a Saturday night; it was summer, and waking about three o'clock in the morning, and it being broad day, he saw a venerable-looking man, but with an aspect exceedingly melancholy, sitting at a desk in the window, reading, and two beautiful boys standing near him, whom he regarded with looks of the profoundest grief. Presently he rose from his seat, the boys followed him, and they were no more to be seen. The young man, much troubled, arose, hesitating whether he should regard what he had seen as a dream, or a waking phantasy. To divert his dejection, he walked towards the church, which the sexton was already employed in preparing for the morning service. The first sight that struck him was a portrait, the exact resemblance of the man whom he had seen sitting in his chamber. It was the custom in this district to place the portrait of each minister, after his death, in the church.

He made the minutest inquiries respecting his predecessor, and learned that he was universally beloved, as a man of unexampled integrity and benevolence; but that he was the prey of a secret and perpetual sorrow. His grief was supposed to have arisen from an attachment to a young lady, with whom his situation did not permit him to unite himself. Others, however, asserted, that a connexion did subsist between them, and that even she occasionally brought to his house two beautiful boys, the offspring of their connexion.— Nothing further occurred until the cold weather came, and the new minister desired a fire to be lighted in the stove of the room where he slept. A hideous stench arose from the stove as soon as it was lighted, and, on examining it, the bones of two male children were found within.

2

Lord Lyttleton and a number of his friends were joined during the chase by a stranger. He was excellently mounted, and displayed such courage, or, rather so much desperate rashness, that no other person in the hunt could follow him. The gentlemen, when the chase was concluded, invited the stranger to dine with them. His conversation was something of a wonderful kind. He astonished, he interested, he commanded the attention of the most inert. As night came on, the company, being weary, began to retire one by one, much later than the usual hour: the most intellectual among them were retained latest by the stranger's fascination. As he perceived that they began to depart, he redoubled his efforts to retain them. At last, when few remained, he entreated them to stay with him; but all pleaded the fatigue of a hard day's chase, and all at last retired. They had been in bed about an hour, when they were awakened by the most horrible screams, which issued from the stranger's room. Every one rushed towards it. The door was locked. After a moment's deliberation they burst it open, and found the stranger stretched on the ground, writhing with agony, and weltering in blood. On their entrance he arose, and collecting himself, apparently with a strong effort, entreated them to leave him— not to disturb him, that he would give every possible explanation in the morning. They complied. In the morning, his chamber was found vacant, and he was seen no more.

3

Miles Andrews, a friend of Lord Lyttleton, was sitting one night alone when Lord Lyttleton came in, and informed him that he was dead, and that this was his ghost which he saw before him. Andrews pettishly told him not to play any ridiculous tricks upon him, for he was not in a temper to bear them. The ghost then departed. In the morning Andrews asked his servant at what hour Lord Lyttleton had arrived. The servant said he did not know that he had arrived, but that he would inquire. On inquiry it was found that Lord Lyttleton had not arrived, nor had the door been opened to any one during the whole night. Andrews sent to Lord Lyttleton, and discovered, that he had died precisely at the hour of the apparition.

4

A gentleman on a visit to a friend who lived on the skirts of an extensive forest in the east of Germany lost his way. He wandered for some hours among the trees, when he saw a light at a distance. On approaching it, he was surprised to observe, that it proceeded from the interior of a ruined monastery. Before he knocked he thought it prudent to look through the window. He saw a multitude of cats assembled round a small grave, four of whom were letting down a coffin with a crown upon it. The gentleman, startled at this unusual sight, and imagining that he had arrived among the retreats of fiends or witches, mounted his horse and rode away with the utmost precipitation. He arrived at his friend's house at a late hour, who had sate up for him. On his arrival his friend questioned as to the cause of the traces of trouble visible in his face. He began to recount his adventure, after much difficulty, knowing that it was scarcely possible that his friend should give faith to his relation. No sooner had he mentioned the coffin with a crown upon it, than his friend's cat, who seemed to have been lying asleep before the fire, leaped up, saying— 'Then I am the King of the Cats!' and scrambled up the chimney, and was seen no more.

-Appendix-
Ernestus Berchtold
& Childe Harold's Pilgrimage

Appendix 1
Ernestus Berchtold – Part One[1]

'Upon the left side of the lake of Thun lies the small village of Beat-enberg, which, under the care of a simple pastor contains no individual above the rank of a peasant: it was in this village that I was born. Misfor-tune seemed to be anxious at my very birth to stamp me for its own.—Just at the termination of the short war between Austria and Prussia, of the year 1778, my mother arrived at this village in company with a gentleman severely wounded, as he said, in the slight skirmishes, which had alone formed the military display of this campaign. There was a mystery about them, which they seemed to wish should not be unravelled. The worthy pastor, therefore, whom I have since called father, did not make any in-quiries of his guests, though it appeared to him very singular, that the most difficult and steep roads should have been preferred for the route of an invalid towards his home. The tender care of my mother towards this gentleman was exemplary; it seemed as if that courage and firm-ness, which was wanting in his breast, had taken refuge in her's. They were not Swiss, for the language they spoke was unknown to Berchtold the parish priest. They apparently understood German and French; but they said so very little, and that with such evident embarrassment, that nothing could be learnt from their conversation. There being no inn at the solitary Beatenberg, the pastor, with his usual kindness, on hearing of the arrival of strangers at the close of the evening, had immediately waited on them to offer his services and house. They were to have been his guests, only for the night; but the fatigue of the journey again forced open the wound in the gentleman's side; determined, however, to pro-ceed, he attempted to walk to the litter prepared for him; the exertion proved too great, he fell into my mother's arms, and almost instantly expired.

'My mother was distracted; already far advanced in pregnancy, she fell upon the body, no longer capable of that firmness and resolution, which she had shown, when her companion's safety depended upon it. She listened to no one; but frantic, she sat by the dead body, alternately

---

1 Published by John William Polidori as *Ernestus Berchtold; or, The Modern Oedipus: A Tale* in 1819, pub-lisher unknown. 'I am choosing to include parts one, three, and four in the appendix of this volume because *Berchtold* is a novella-length work and would too greatly disrupt the flow and detract from the other works that I prefer to have included in the main text. Since it is not the most easily obtainable work, so I have in-cluded parts one, three, and four in this appendix for completion's sake." – R.D.B.

shedding tears, and bursting into a loud laugh. Berchtold urged those soothing doctrines of which he was minister, but in vain; he spoke in vain of another world, of future hope; none could like him, soothe the pillow of the dying peasant, but here were miseries no hope could assuage. She at last fell exhausted upon the ground, she was conveyed to bed, and in a few hours I and a sister saw the light. But this did not allay her grief, she sunk into a silence that nothing could induce her to break; her eyes were fixed, and she at last died without a struggle. She was buried by him, whom Berchtold imagined, in spite of the disparity of his years, to have been her husband; and over their grave were placed those simple crosses, which you must have seen in the neighbouring church-yards. The pastor could not place any inscription upon their tomb, for he had been so engaged in attendance upon my mother, that he had not noticed the departure of her only servant, who took with him every thing of value belonging to his former mistress. He knew not what to do, there was no clue in his hands by which he could restore us to our family; for there was nothing to be found, except some linen and a locket, with my mother's portrait.

'Berchtold was a man whose humble endeavours had always been engaged in the attempt to fulfill those duties his profession imposed upon him. In these mountainous districts, the office of a parish priest is extremely arduous; he is often called up in the middle of the night, while the snow is falling, to go many miles over the frozen glaciers, to administer to the dying peasant the sacraments of the church. Berchtold never allowed the most distant hamlet to want religious comfort; he was old, yet often has he crossed to the foot of the Holgaut, merely to help the unfortunate in their attempt at resignation, under domestic calamity. He was not, therefore, likely to cast us from him; he immediately had us conveyed to the cottage of a married sister, and caused us to be brought up as luxuriously as an Alpine village allowed.

'I remember little of my early years, it seems, that I have vague visions of an age, when were spent whole days in gathering flowers, to adorn my sister's head and breast, from the precipitous bank that descends to the lake, when, at night, I was lulled half trembling, to sleep by the tales of my foster-mother concerning ogres and spirits from the dead. But all this is indistinct. When about six years of age, I was removed to the house of Berchtold. He called me son, and if the tenderest care and the greatest sacrifices could entitle him to the name of father, which I gave him, it was not wrongfully bestowed. One of the first circumstances which I can remember, is that one day, while sitting with him upon a bank, near the church-yard, gazing on the scene around, and watching the white sails which gleamed upon the lake beneath our feet; I threw my arms around his neck, and asked him, "Why they called me orphan?" He told me that my father and mother were dead. Retreating from him, I started, and trembling, asked him if he were then dead? He did not at first understand me; but upon my calling him by the name of father, he remembered that I had never heard the history of my birth. He took me to his breast, and weeping, told me, that I was indeed an orphan, that I was not his child. He then took me to the church-yard, and pointing to the raised sod, he told me my parents were there. I did not clearly understand him. I had then no idea of death; my mother, for so I called his sister, had told me tales of the dead, but these terrified without being understood. All the graves, save those of my parents, were adorned with flowers; upon my remarking this to him, he told me that they having died strangers there, none were bound to love them. I was hurt to see those flowers, which though faded, showed the attention of some living being, refused to my mother's tomb; it sunk deeply on my mind. And for years after, I felt a vague pleasure in strewing their graves with the fresh flowers that formerly were employed in adorning my sister's head. Often have I laid myself down looking upon their grassy covering, as if I expected that some of those tales of my mother would be realised with regard to myself, and that I should see them rising from their grave. My sister soon joined me in these meditations, and almost the first infantile communications which passed between us, rested upon another world. She would sit by me, and often the worthy pastor surprised us, after the sun had set, calling to our memory those tales we had heard when with our foster mother.

'We did not mingle with the other children of the village, for we de-lighted too much in each other's company; we spent hours together in talking about what had in a most unaccountable manner taken posses-sion of our minds, or else we gamboled round Berchtold. He, debarred by his religion from the enjoyment of a domestic circle of his own chil-dren, had formed so strong an attachment to us, that his greatest delight was, when not engaged in his parochial duties, to join us in our games and infantile occupations. With all the simplicity of old age, he would lie down and allow us to play with his white locks, or tell us stories, which, though of a different nature from those of his sister, did not interest us the less. He was a good classical scholar, and was well versed in the history of his own country. From these sources he drew his tales, and at an early age he inspired me with an ardent love for independence and liberty, at the same time that he instilled into my heart, a burning thirst for the means of asserting a superiority over my equals. The anecdotes of Themistocles, Alcibiades and others, upon whom the fates of their country had depended, rested on my mind. Berchtold described to me the fallen glories of Rome, of that nation which once held sway over the known world. In short there was a material defect in my education, which is not uncommon, my imagination was stimulated, while my judgment was not called forth, and I was taught to admire public instead of private virtues. I rested upon those situations which one in the million attains, and in which the passions of others are to be guided, while I was not shown how to conduct myself, when my own inclinations and feelings might attempt to lead me astray in the common occurrences of life. With a strongly susceptible mind I imbibed deeply these first impressions, and throughout life this defect in my education has followed me. As I advanced in age, I gradually became acquainted with the Latin and Greek historians. Berchtold rashly, though innocently, took advantage of my thirst for relations of battles and deeds of renown, to induce me to learn. I consequently had Plutarch and Livy in my hands, long before I read any book tending to give man the power of regulating his passions.

'I joined the villagers only in those military exercises, which are constantly performed after the day's labour in every hamlet. Sometimes I would go with the chamois hunter, and reaching the higher ridges of the Alps, whose snowy summits were visible from the lake, I forced myself to follow him in his venturous pursuit. But it for a long time required a strong exertion of my mind to induce me to venture amidst the vast solitudes of eternal snows. I always felt an inward shuddering and awe at the sight of my native wildnesses. Even now I cannot bear to listen to those, who, amongst our magnificent scenes, which man has not yet overcome, and which mock his power, can talk of pleasure, and dwell upon the beauty of the scenery. I cannot feel this. I seem always to crouch beneath some invisible being whose power is infinite, and which I am conscious I cannot resist. It seems that I hear him laughing audibly at our vain attempts to encroach upon his dominion. It appears to me as if the avalanche were but the weapon of his impatience, while he insidiously steals upon those habitations he has covered with his snows, by the silent, gradual approach of the glaciers. Let mankind labour for ages upon these ribs of the world, and their work shall not be seen. The pyramids might rise unnoticed upon the rocks before my view, undistinguished from the fragment that falls unperceived with the passing torrent. I cannot bear that human strength should be unable to stamp its hand upon these towering memorials of convulsions we could not influence, could not hope to controul. This morbid feeling may have been excited by my foster mother constantly pointing to the Jungfrau, whose white peak forms so prominent a feature in the view from her house, while she related the peasant's tale of those mischievous spirits who dance upon its glittering icy coat, decked by the moon's ray. I gained, however, health and vigour from these excursions, and I became at last one of the most noted for activity in all the canton.

'I rapidly arrived at my twentieth year. My kind friend the pastor could not be induced to part with me. I was the only prop of his old age, I latterly, always accompanied him in his visits amongst the mountains, often joined him in his prayer over the dying, and frequently have I supported him at the brink of that grave, over which he was calling down the mercy of God, and which was soon to be his own refuge. My sister increased in beauty, and each day added some new charm to her person, and some additional accomplishment to her mind. I often represented to my father that I was of an age when I should begin to do something, and attempt to take the burthen of myself and my sister off his hands. He would agree with me in my arguments, but when the moment came, he was always so overpowered with sorrow, that I could not induce myself to leave him for the few remaining days he had to live.

'I seldom visited Thun or Interlaken; I did not feel pleasure in the society of men. I there found them engaged in all the petty interests, which pervade human breasts in the narrow sphere of a miserable provincial town. I found they could not sympathise with one whom they looked upon as a wild romantic mountaineer. About this time the French revolution began to exalt my imagination even more than the history of nations gone by, and I burnt with the desire of viewing nearer those actions, which in our solitary village, echoing only a softened sound of their horrors, seemed to wear a certain air of grandeur and glory. I ardently wished to join those soldiers who had driven back the foreign invaders from their native plains. I little thought then how soon I was to be engaged in resisting these very men, amidst my own native mountains.

'When the discussions between Berne and the French concerning the Pays de Vaud arrested the attention of all, anxious to be amongst men in action, and tired of my total want of employment, I again begged my friend to let me depart to the capital; but still, at his prayer, I remained with him. I laid myself down upon the snow, shining as it then was in the first rays of spring, and abandoned myself to visions of battle and renown. My spirits gradually left me, there was a craving for exertion about me, which I found it impossible to overcome. I seized my gun, and going amidst the eternal glaciers and rocks, I sought by forcing myself to exert my body, to lose this feeling of vacuity. But I often lost sight of the chamois, engaged in the thought of my country, and bounded from rock to rock, no longer occupied with what I imagined was before me. My sister would endeavour to sooth me by her caresses. I told her of my visions with regard to my country's cause, and at moments excited even in her breast the sparks of enthusiasm. But she generally echoed

Berchtold's sentiments with regard to the indecision and incapacity of the government.

'Tired one evening of listening to Berchtold, who attempted to repress my ardour, by representing to me that the country was betrayed, and that, in consequence of the tardiness and imbecility of the rulers of Switzerland, in spite of the courage and daring of its peasantry, it was doomed to become an easy prey to France, I left him determined again to seek refuge in the chase. I accordingly set out the next morning, intending to remain several days amongst the mountains; but I grew listless, and at the close of the second day, I still found myself upon the Wengern Alp. I issued forth from the chalet where I had taken some refreshment, and soon lost myself in reflection. I now looked with pleasure upon the Jungfrau's white head, glistening on the blue canopy of heaven. All the horrors of the Grindewald at my feet, the high summit of the Schrechorn, with the echoing thunders of the numerous avalanches, no longer appalled me. It seemed as if they now put on their terrors against a presumptuous foe, in defence of their children. There was no cloud upon the dark blue sky,—there was no mist upon the rocks; and though the snow still covered the whole surface of the mountains around, still there was a genial warmth and splendour in the sun's reflected ray, that vivified and strengthened. There was no sound, save that of the distant cataract, and falling avalanche. I stood a long time leaning upon my musket, to look upon this scene. How could avarice hope to find a resting place in the minds of those nursed amidst such objects? How could slavery expect to find its votaries resident amidst such fortresses? The tyrant could not dare to add these horrors of nature to those already revelling in his breast. A slave who shrinks before the frown of a despot, could not stand erect amidst these awful monuments of a power that mocks at human prowess. Upon this occasion, it seemed as if the sun threw its proudest ray upon these rocks; they had seen, might hope to see, men worthy of gazing upon that nature which, lifting unappalled its head amidst the thundering clouds, had snatched their weapon from their grasp, and had thrown it at its feet, while, with its snowy head, it struck in defiance the arching canopy of heaven. I was thus engaged in thought, which but served to increase my indignation at the conduct of men, who sacrificed to personal interest the safety of their country, when I was suddenly struck with the sound of a voice, which I shall never, never forget. In unison with my feelings at that moment, the notes sometimes broke out into the wildest tones of defiance; at others, suddenly sinking, they seemed uncertain and soothing. I dared not look around; I felt as if entranced, and I imagined I heard the voice of these mountains, mocking the invaders, then sinking into despondence. Gradually the voice approached,—I could distinguish words.—I heard footsteps. I suddenly turned round, and beheld a figure; I cannot describe it to you. Arrayed in a dress foreign to these mountains, her white drapery, breathed on by the wanton breeze, now betrayed the delicate form of her limbs,—now hid them from my sight. Her dark eye seemed exultingly to gaze upon my native rocks, while the wild notes of defiance played upon her lips. She suddenly saw me, and was silent. She looked around, as if for some one; and I then perceived, at a little distance, a man worn down more by grief than by age. I approached, and re-assured her. She blushed, and in that language which, in its very sound, breathes love, told me that she did not understand me. I could not answer; but, gazing on her, I seemed to be fascinated by her words. The old man approached, and we soon entered into conversation. I spoke Italian fluently; her surprize and pleasure cannot be painted, when she heard me address her father in her native language. I walked by her side, and I was often so lost in thought, that I was obliged to answer, by an unmeaning yes or no, the questions of the old man. Our conversation at last turned upon Switzerland; he seemed to be perfectly conversant with its situation. She entered with enthusiasm into its cause, and asked me, why I was idling amidst these valleys, when my country called me to the post of danger. These simple words from her lips caused an emotion in my breast that drew the blood to my cheeks. She thought of me. I at once promised to join my countrymen tomorrow. She then told me, that orders had arrived at the neighbouring towns for an instant levy to join the army of d'Erlach, which it was expected would be immediately brought into action.

'I was yet walking by her side, when we arrived at Lauterbrunnen. At the gate of a small cottage, after having asked me to take some refreshment, which I declined, they bade me farewell. There was a carriage waiting at the door. The thought rushed upon my mind that I might never see her again. I know not by what impulse, but, ignorant of the forms of the world, I summoned courage, at the moment of parting, to ask of her a ribbond with which she was playing; that, as I said, I might wear it in remembrance of her who had made me decide upon joining the patriots. Blushing, she looked at her father, who smiled consent, and she bound round my arm the scarf which she had worn during the morning. I have often heard that song again; I have often seen that form; and many are the years I have worn that scarf:—they have been years of misery and grief. Memory has no moment to look back to between the present and that happy day. Yet, for such another moment of enthusiasm I would undergo all my miseries afresh. I revert to it as the Arab, in the midst of the rising sands, turns to his visions of the green speck upon the desert's sandy ocean; amidst dangers, that is his hope; in anguish, that is his refuge. That moment seemed to bestow upon me the happiness which my fancy had so long pictured in the future. But every moment since has only served to weave closer round me the meshes of that net, which has shut me out from joy. I then, however, felt as if time no longer weighed upon me; and I was grieved, when arriving at my father's door, I found that the joys of hours had passed as those of a minute.

'I found my sister in tears; Berchtold, with his grey locks hiding the hands covering his face. Hearing my footsteps, my aged father rose, and taking me in his arms, with tears in his eyes, he told me, that he could no longer take upon himself to hinder me from joining my countrymen in the sacred cause of independence. He bade me take leave of my sister, and, while my courage remained, to surmount the pang of bidding her farewell. He told me, that he had caused my sister to prepare every thing for a parting, which he feared was to be our last. He embraced me, and rushed out of the house. My sister's eyes, wet with tears, now turned upon me, anxious to show the same resolution as my father had displayed, she hastened my departure. She gave me my gun and powder flask,—bound round my waist more than half the savings of Berchtold; and kissing me, bade me farewell. Bewildered by the rapidity of my different emotions, I hurried to the side of the lake, looked once more up the steep mountain, on the ascent of which Beatenberg raised its white cottages, and, turning the point of land which encroached upon the lake, I was soon wafted, in company with many others, towards the town of Thun. I did not heed the white sails hurrying along the blue rippling waves. I could not gaze upon the rich cultivated scenery of the lake. My mind was straying midst those wild glaciers, that once had been my horror,—which to-day had shewn me the unknown. Why does fate cause the approaches of misery to be decked with all the show of promised happiness? From this moment begins my eventful history; till now I had only been in the hands of the foul fiends that have tormented me, as plastic clay, which they formed in that manner, best fitted to contain the miseries they were preparing to pour upon it. You may think I have rested too much upon my early years, which passed without action; but those years saw deposited in my breast the seeds which have brought me to the state of apathy and misery you witness. That vision has proved to me the harbinger of more woes than it promised pleasures, and that scarf, which you see is yet bound round my heart, has felt it beat more violently through anguish, than it did even through hope, at the moment it first encircled my arm. My life till now had passed in dreams. I had not known the rude blast of worldly interests; I had been unconscious of the activity of the bad passions, and had only viewed man in the shape of my foster-father, breaking by his presence the shackles of grief that restrained the energies of his children, as the sun destroys the icy bonds that bind the vital powers of the spring. In the cause of charity and virtue, I had seen employed those powers and that activity which, exerted in a less degree, have often excited the admiration of the multitude, and concealed follies, nay, crimes, from even the philosopher in that halo of fame they bring around them. The earliest impressions, I received, were those from my foster-mother's tales, and they have not left me even at present; how much less, when but entering on manhood. I had so often gazed upon my mother's picture, which my sister wore round her neck from her earliest infancy, that, while sitting by her tomb, it seemed as if her image had haunted me in my sleep, for I frequently found myself arguing as if I had had actual proof of the existence of beings superior to ourselves.

'The evening had closed before I arrived at Thun. The town was crowded with the peasantry of the neighbouring mountains; there were fires throughout the streets, around which stood the aged and the boy, the mother and the virgin. They were all come to offer their arms in defence of their country. I approached the town-house; the door was crowded with petitioners, who were attempting to induce the sentinel to give them precedence in the enrolment of their names. I stood for some time watching the earnestness with which the aged laid hold of their very weakness and uselessness, as a reason why they should be preferred in the cause of death; while the young, elate with the hopes of youth, showing their sinewy limbs, appealed to their expectations of victory from their strength, as a reason why they should first be put upon the lists for battle. Their arms were more various than their ages; an iron wedge, sharpened and fastened to the end of a stick, served some as the substitute for a hatchet; burnt stakes and the chamois hunter's rifle mingled with the scythe rounded into a sabre, and the sickle straightened to a sword. While thus silently gazing upon the scene, a magistrate, a friend of Berchtold, going to his post, recognized me, and approaching, led me through a private entrance into the council chamber. My proffered services were immediately accepted, and I was directly ordered to put myself at the head of those villagers, who could be found in the town belonging to Berchtold's parish, avoiding, however, as much as possible the burthening myself with the infirm and women. I received orders to reach Berne in the shortest possible time, and to depart with the earliest dawn. I went out into the streets, a great part of the peasants had retired under the arcades which are on each side of the streets of Thun; they there formed one promiscuous mass, in which it was impossible to distinguish between man and woman. All was silent, save the dead sound of heavy footsteps and the hoarse voice of individuals like myself, treading amidst these sleepers, and calling out the name of that place, whose inhabitants they sought. The night was damp and dark, there was no light in the heavens, and often as I went, I stumbled over the body of some unseen person, who, uttering a note of impatience, again turned himself to sleep. Imitating the example of the others, I called out the name of Beatenberg at every step, and soon mustered almost the whole population of Berchtold's parish. I had a painful task, the old pointed to their children, and with tears in their aged eyes, asked me if I intended to hinder them from setting the example to their children, of dying for their native soil. The women, pointing to their lovers, would take no refusal; they seemed determined to witness their conduct on the day of battle, and see if they were worthy of the love they claimed. I spoke separately to the young men, and advised them to steal from their companions and meet me at a certain hour about a mile from the town.

'They retired to rest, and I laid myself down in the street to sleep; I was soon lost to all external objects, and I again saw hovering at my side, her, who had seemed in the morning but a vision. She smiled upon me, again urged me by those words;—but suddenly it seemed as if the earth parted between us, and a huge chasm opened at my feet; we seemed to stretch our hands towards each other; I threw myself into the gulph, and awoke. Finding it but a dream, I again attempted to compose myself to sleep, but in vain; her image still stood before me, and the moment I rested upon it, the idea of my orphan state and her apparent affluence startled me. I had not asked her name. I knew nothing of her; her form, her face, her voice, and her words already began to appear to my memory as the recollections of an unsubstantial, supernatural vision; but at this moment my hand fell upon the scarf, which I had now bound round my chest. The touch roused me from my painful reveries, and hope pervaded my breast. I started from the ground convinced that she did exist, I fell upon my knees, and uttered aloud a prayer to the Divinity to make me worthy of her. Hardly had the words passed my lips, when a loud hoarse laugh sounded on my ear. It was but a drunkard laughing at some wild imagination of his own; but it made me shudder. I left the town; a heavy thick rain was falling, there was no wind, nothing seemed stirring, the shape of the distant mountains could be perceived by the white mass they presented on the dark canopy of night, every thing else was of one dead hue. I leant myself against the trunk of an old tree, and the dawn had, unperceived by me, risen in the east, when I found myself roused by the salutations of many of my comrades.

'I had in vain attempted to dissuade the old and the women from joining us; they were all with us at the appointed hour. I again as fruitlessly endeavoured to show them the embarrassment they would prove to our march; they would not listen, and I gave orders for the men to proceed.

In consequence of the exercise the peasants had been accustomed to in their native villages, I found no difficulty in forming them into something like a regular body. Towards night, as I had purposely pressed the march throughout the day, I was glad to perceive that the number of the old and infirm had much diminished. Next morning I again proceeded; it was with great difficulty that I could restrain myself and comrades from stopping to assist the women and old men who fell by the roadside through actual weakness and fatigue. Their cries imploring assistance from lovers, from sons, were heart-rending. I shut my ears and dared not listen. The nearer I approached Berne, the more deserted I found the country, all had flocked to the town or to the posts of danger. At last, with a body of two hundred men, not even yet entirely deserted by the women, I entered the capital. I read dismay and horror upon every face, even the peasantry, which here, as at Thun, crowded the streets, were silent; there were no signs of enthusiasm, but the glance of suspicion fell from every eye. Just as we were approaching the great place, we met a party of soldiers with their bayonets wet with blood. They seemed with hasty steps to be hurrying from a spot that brought something horrible to their mind. They did not speak, but we soon learnt that they were the murderers of Stetter and Ryhiner. They washed the blood of their countrymen from their weapons in the blood of their invaders, and at last bathed them with their own. Posterity may then spare their names the brand of infamy, for a momentary fit of rage against those they imagined traitors to their country.

'We were ordered immediately upon our arrival to reinforce the army at Frauenbrunnen, and were joined upon our departure by other militias, and by the venerable Steiguer, who had just thrown up the insignia of civil office in the determination of dying for his country. We arrived at a critical moment, the French having an advantage in cavalry and artillery, which the Swiss could not resist, were upon the point of surrounding the small army, the only impediment in their road to Berne. Steiguer immediately perceived the danger; ordering us to follow, he rushed forwards, and attacked the troops which, having already passed the right flank of General d'Erlach, were upon the point of gaining the road on his rear. The combat was obstinate, our chief attack was upon the artillery, with which the enemy was attempting to cross the road. Our women did not shrink, they rushed forward, threw themselves upon the wheels of the guns, and allowed themselves to be hewn to pieces ere they would quit their hold.

'The army under d'Erlach had in the meantime begun its retreat to Grauholtz. We found ourselves surrounded and engaged amidst the very carriages of our enemy's guns, which we had taken. By great exertions at last we formed ourselves again into a compact body, and suddenly, as if by one impulse, falling upon our knees, we offered a prayer to the God of battle. The enemy thinking we were about to throw down our arms, checked themselves for a moment; we arose; the officers placed themselves at the head of the column, which set up a loud shout, ran upon the foe, and bearing all opposition down, soon reached Urteren, where we made a momentary stand, and then reached Grauholtz.

'The troops were immediately employed in raising an abbatis in front. While the men were thus engaged, Erlach and Steiguer met; at the instigation of the latter, the general came forward, and thanked my troop for the intrepidity it had shown during the whole combat. I was particularly noticed by them, and received from the aged general a medal he wore round his neck, as a token of his country's gratitude. "I have seen," he said, "the sun rise today upon freemen; I shall not see it set upon my countrymen. Our country is lost; it cannot thank its sons; let me, therefore, who have directed its last efforts for freedom, acknowledge the few hours' respite you have obtained to its fate, by presenting you with this mark of honour, which I obtained from a free nation." The loud roar of cannon burst upon our ears; he left me. I stood for a moment still; in one hand I held the medal, with the other I pressed the scarf of my unknown friend closer to my heart. Again we fought, but again their numbers enabled them to turn our flank, and, in spite of the strength of our position, we were obliged to retreat. One more struggle at the gates of Berne, and all was lost. The slaughter was horrible. Determined to sell my life as dear as I could, I rushed into the thickest of the fight; but my peasants followed me; they snatched me from danger, and bore me struggling through the town. I reproached them with having deprived me of an honourable death; one approached with aged steps; looking me in the face, he merely mentioned the name of Berchtold. I understood him; and, leaving Berne, we turned our steps towards Thun.

'Unfortunately, the slaughter by the enemy's sword was not the only horror that attended the dispersion of our troops. The peasants and soldiers never, in their legendary tales, having heard of a defeat accompanied by a retreat, on their native soil, imputed the whole to the treachery of their officers. The French had from the very beginning spread papers to this purport amongst them. As we proceeded, we therefore found the bodies of many of their officers hacked to pieces by the infuriate stragglers. Upon our arrival at Musingen, we found General d'Erlach in the hands of some of these men, who had determined to convey him to Berne. With him was his wife, who had accompanied him in his flight, and a young officer, whom I had remarked earnestly engaged in looking at my scarf, at the moment I was receiving the general's thanks at Grauholtz. I remonstrated with the soldiers, but in vain. I gradually, however, contrived to approach the general, and, when I thought myself sufficiently near to shield him, drawing my sword, I called upon the Beatenbergers to assist me, and instantly attacked them. The young officer, possessing himself in the struggle of a sword, was soon by my side. The peasants joined us; we drove the soldiers through the village; but in the meanwhile some stragglers issued from the houses, and striking the defenceless old man with their hatchets, left him for dead in the arms of his wife. When I returned, I found him apparently reviving through her care; it was only for a moment, he could not speak; it appeared, however, as if he recognised me, for he pressed my hand, and turned his closing eyes, first on his wife, then towards me. Thinking he recommended her to my care, I promised that I would protect her to the utmost of my power; his eye glistened, and he expired.

'At this moment I again heard the cries of the soldiers. As there was an unfrequented path over the mountains from this place towards Hoestetten, whence the young officer might easily get to Lucerne, I advised him to pursue it, and get immediately out of the canton of Berne. We parted. Gathering my peasants together, I directly set off with Madame Erlach in the cart towards Thun. She did not shriek or weep, she seemed stupified by the greatness of her loss, and, when arrived at the city, she without difficulty allowed herself to be taken from the body, and to be conveyed in a boat to Berchtold's, whence she retired in a short time to complete solitude, where she saw no one, and soon after died.

'I cannot paint to you the joy of Berchtold when he once more held me within his arms. My sister's tears flowed now as profusely as at our parting, but from a different cause. I had only been away a few days, yet the crowded events that took place in that short period made it appear as many weeks. The first spot I sought with my sister was my mother's grave. There I sat with her silently engaged in thought; after some time we began to converse, and as I had nothing hidden from her, I soon told the whole of my history from the morning of that day on which I had seen the unknown. She seemed disturbed, and upon my pressing her to explain to me what passed in her breast, she advised me to beware, for that it was probably one of the spirits of the Jungfrau's eternal frosts that had accosted me. I laughed at what I deemed her folly; but I soon perceived that there was something more on her mind than she was willing to confess. In vain I besought her to disclose it to me; she told me she durst not, and asked me as a favour not to speak to her any more on this subject. Alarmed, I knew not why, I looked at her with earnest attention. She could no longer bear it, but throwing herself into my arms, informed me that while I was away she had seen our mother, who had appeared to her, arrayed in mourning, announcing, that I was in the greatest danger, and that she must guard me, but that unless she wished to share my peril, she must conceal it from me. "Ernestus," my sister said, "I cannot obey, let your fate be mine, and I am content." Saying this, she again pressed me to her bosom, and wept. I was moved, I sat down by her side; bound in each other's arms, we gazed upon the green sod in silence, unwilling to disturb those thoughts which we knew must be the same in the breasts of both.

'Anxious to learn some tidings concerning the fate of my native country, I went every day to Thun. My indignation was excited by the recital of the cruelties and extortions of the French, and, when they dared to attempt disarming the inhabitants, determined not to submit to so base an insult, I was proscribed, and sought refuge amongst those mountains which had been the scenes of my prowess in the chase. I went and sat whole days by the rocks in the Wengern Alp, where I first saw that form which has since engrossed the whole of my thoughts. I made enquiries at Lauterbrunnen concerning the two strangers, but ineffectually; they had merely been there as other travellers, to view the sublime scenery of the mountains, and had not been heard of since. I remained a whole month amidst these rocks, only going to Beatenberg at night, when Berchtold and my sister would receive me, and supplying me with provisions for the ensuing days, tell me of all the insults that added to the shame of Switzerland. But at last they showed me the proclamation of Schwarenberg against the six eastern cantons. I immediately announced my determination to join them. Berchtold said nothing; my sister followed me out of the house, and begged to be permitted to accompany me. I refused, and upon her reminding me of her dream, told her, that, as it promised she should share my peril, it would prove impossible for me to go into any real danger without her, that therefore she need not follow me, or, if the fates decreed it, we should meet at that moment without any endeavours on our part to assist their fiat. I painted to her the horrors of the exterminating warfare that was carried on, and asserted that it was most likely not the peril of the sword in which she was to partake. In short, I forced her to promise me not to follow, by representing to her the misery Berchtold would undergo, if at once deprived of both of his adopted children. I led her back to the door, and left her in his arms.

'It is useless for me to give you an account of this campaign. It is recorded in history with even all the unsuccessful struggles for liberty, as one of those gleamings of that noble spirit in men, which, though generally hidden under the pressure of vice and corruption, at times bursts forth like the volcano's fire. I was taken prisoner, and could find no means of escaping, till the French, towards the end of June, after the restoration of Rapinat, became more lenient in their treatment of their prisoners, and less careful in their watch over them. I once more joined the Underwalders, and was again witness to the defeat of my country-men. I met the young officer I had saved from slaughter at Musingen. His name was Olivieri. We had no time for intercourse, always in action or on the march, we only saw one another in the field, where we often joined and tried to vie with each other in acts of daring and courage. We became at last noted in the army, and though only volunteers, we each soon found ourselves at the head of about ninety men, who always were ready to obey our commands.

'In the midst of our struggles in the Underwald, intelligence reached us of an insurrection having taken place in the upper Valais; it was deemed necessary by the leaders of our army to send them assistance, and thus cause a diversion in our favour. They proposed that one hun-dred men should be given to each of us, and that with this force we should be sent to aid the Valisians in their attempt. It was a hazardous undertaking, we had to cross upon the flanks of the enemy, and should be obliged, it was supposed, to pass through the Grimsel, which was in the possession of the French. When it was proposed, no one was found to volunteer; no Underwalder would leave his home in the hour of dan-ger. I had however remarked a number of Schweitzers, who had joined us singly, having left their dwellings, though not countenanced by their countrymen who were ranged on the other side, to partake in the dan-gers of the patriotic Underwalders. To these men we applied, and in a short time, two hundred men were selected. We kept almost upon the summit of the high ridge that joins the Furca from the Lake of Lucerne, and crossing the glaciers by rocks, that even in the chase of the chamois would have startled me, we arrived at Realp, and soon crossed into the Valais. At Obergesteln we learnt that some French troops had that very night crossed from the Grimsel, while the whole body of peasants were engaged in the lower part of the valley, amidst the fastnesses attempting to stop that force which was advancing by the bridge of Hochflue. They had committed great outrages, and had caused those, who were able, to fly behind the glaciers of the Rhone.

'Our undertaking now seemed desperate. The number of the French in the rear of our allies was greater than ours, and the end of the Valais through which we were to advance was flat and open, without any shel-ter, surrounded by steep mountains. Olivieri was however before me, we had each one hundred chosen men, and he seemed resolved on advanc-ing. Not knowing how to procure intelligence of the enemy, I immediate-ly offered to advance by myself and reconnoitre. As I well knew every part of this valley, I was certainly the fittest person in our body for such an undertaking; but my companion would not hear of ceding the post of danger to me; we were obliged to draw lots, and it fell upon him, and he departed.

'In the mean time the women, hearing of our arrival, came from their fastnesses, and joined us. They seized upon every thing which offered the semblance of a weapon, and resolved to follow us. As my companion did not return as soon as I expected, fearful of a surprise, I determined to advance, and, if possible, gain some of the passes before the enemy knew of our arrival. I, however, previously sent forward a young woman, to see if she could obtain any intelligence of Olivieri. I then ordered the men to follow in silence, and marching all the evening, we at last, towards night, reached the village of Blizingen, where the valley straightens, and becomes more inclosed and rocky. The river here runs through a deeply-cut channel, more resembling a ravine, than a common bed. As I knew there was but one path, and that very steep and dangerous, I ordered my men to rest upon their arms, while I went along the river's channel to learn something concerning the enemy, who I thought could not have advanced much farther. At last, being arrived opposite the village of Vietsch, I heard a great noise, and saw many lights; making no doubt but that these proceeded from the point where the enemy was stationed, I returned. I found my men asleep; arousing them I ascended at their head the steep sides of the mountain, and making them march parallel with the path, but much higher, I brought them above the village, and hid them in a wood of pines that stretches along the steep. I now no longer feared the superior numbers of the enemy, the ascent was so precipitous that we could not be attacked, except to great disadvantage, while we could either join the Valisians, or fall upon the foe with every prospect of victory.

'I determined once more to go and discover their exact position, giving the word that if I thought it a fit moment for an attack, I would fire my gun, and then sound my hunting horn, so that no mistake could occur from the firing of any drunken soldiers or guard. Wrapt up in my mantle I descended from the wood, and found the men lying securely asleep in the road between the houses. They were certainly all there; anxious to know something concerning my companion, I resolved, in spite of the risk, to awaken some straggler, and learn from him if any prisoner was amongst them. I accordingly approached one who, stretched along the edge of a precipice over the river, was sunk in a sleep that seemed that of the innocent. Putting my pistol to his breast, I awoke him. Alarmed, he was upon the point of calling out, when I threatened him with instant death. To my inquiries he answered, that a person had been surprised by some stragglers in the course of the day, and he added that he was then lying bound in a cottage in the very centre of the village, destined to be in the morning a butt for their muskets. It did not appear that his having been found armed had excited suspicion, as he was taken for a common peasant. Determined to save Olivieri, I knew not what to do with this sleeper, to shoot him would alarm the enemy, they might immediately dispatch my friend, and yet I could not leave this man to raise his comrades. I pushed him down the precipice, and directly entered the village. All were asleep, I found the cottage, there was a light in the window. I stole close to it, wrapping myself up in my mantle. I looked in; you may imagine my alarm when I saw two soldiers awake in conversation, while my friend, upon his back, was bound to a bench fastened to the floor. There were several soldiers at my feet, with their arms by their sides, a sudden thought struck me, I seized one of their guns and firing it, I instantly retreated to the other side of the cottage, where I had remarked a window close to the fatal bench. As I expected, the two soldiers went out to inquire about the report which they had heard; I took advantage of the few moments, leapt into the room by the window, roused Olivieri, who gazed upon me expecting death; I made a sign for silence, cut his bonds, and was again out of the cottage with my companion, when I heard the door open to admit the two soldiers. We hastened up the ascent, and when, amidst the rocks I fired my own fowling piece, and blew a national air upon my horn. Before the enemy, alarmed by the two soldiers, who missed their prisoner, could form, we were amongst them, and morn had hardly dawned before we had cut to pieces the whole of this detachment. I could have induced the men to give quarter, but the women were outrageous, they followed our soldiers, and dispatched the wounded, whom their more merciful companions had spared, while they excited the Schweitzers to slaughter even those who threw up their arms; none were saved. The Valisians who were making head against this body, hearing the report of so many guns, did not know what to believe; they however approached, and when they heard the Swiss war cry of liberty, they immediately joined us. Their joy cannot be expressed by words; Olivieri and myself had in the mean time met, and his thanks were profuse; but what was my sorrow to find that the young woman had been seized and bayoneted in cold blood, because she would not acknowledge the right of the French to a superiority over her nation; she had pretended not to know my companion, and thus avoided betraying us, by not being confronted with him.

'We had gained a victory, but it only served to delay the subjection of this noble peasantry; they were obliged to come at last to a capitulation. We could not be included in it; the French asserted that the Schweitzers were deserters. We therefore determined to attempt once more a passage over the most unfrequented Alps. To avoid the Grimsel, where the French might pass to interrupt our passage, we crossed at once into the valley of Formazza. Hidden in the day amidst the woods, or upon the tops of precipices, my few companions, for our numbers had been greatly diminished, journeyed in the night by a circuitous route into the Vadi Bedretto, and thence over the St. Gothard by the path we had come, towards the valley of Stantz. We had there expected to find our former companions yet struggling for life, if not for victory. We entered the valley, there was no living creature to be found, there was a silence unbroken by any sound of human labour, the hoarse ravens fluttered above us, as if they thought we also came to spread their banquet. We could find no one to guide us, no one even to tell us of our misfortune. Our imaginations pictured sufficient. The villages were burnt, the cattle lay slaughtered on the field, it seemed as if death, with one sweep of his scythe, had cut off the life of all. Creeping along the sides of the mountains, we approached Stantz, we expected to find the destroyers there; but when we were in sight, there was no town appearing. We found but sixteen straggling houses yet standing, all the rest were burnt; these also bore the Frenchmen's mark, they were billetted. We looked at one another in silence. The birds of prey were not disturbed by our presence, they continued feeding on the dead. While walking amidst these ruins, I at last heard the sound of a voice, it was the cry of sorrow. A mother had found words to call on heaven for strength to bear her individual grief, heedless of her country's death. I saw her amidst these ruins, her hands were tearing up the soil to give the last refuge her country could afford to her child,—a grave. She did not at first perceive me, when she did, her hand worked doubly quick, while, with her eyes fixed upon the corpse, her hurried lips uttered, "hold your hand, hold your hand for a moment, I shall soon be ready to follow." I dug her son's grave, and left her striking the sod as if she repented of having resigned the body to the earth.

'We assembled our few remaining companions, Olivieri and myself addressed them, we advised them to separate and seek singly a refuge in their homes. While yet speaking one of them brought before us a man, who seemed to have risen from the grave. His grey locks, thinly scattered on his head, were entangled, his eyes were sunk so deep within their sockets, that their lustre seemed the last glimmering of life before it sinks. He had sought death from the foes, and they, in mockery, had bade him live. They had fastened him to a table in the open air, with several days' provision within his reach, and had placed before his sight the corpses of his aged wife, his children, and grandchildren, all marked with the wanton infliction of their barbarous cruelty, not even excelled by the voracity of the vulture or beasts of prey. This wretched being told us that the Schweitzers had troops placed the whole length of the other side of the lake, to hinder the fugitives from this valley escaping. Upon this intelligence our men became dejected; the thoughts of dying ingloriously by the hands of their treacherous countrymen, weighed upon their mind. They spoke some time amongst themselves, and then begged of us not to desert them, assuring us that if we enabled them to reach the upper part of Schweitz unbroken, they then could disperse to their families without danger. We could not refuse them. We ordered them to go along the shore, and see if they could find any boats; they soon got together more than enough to convey us over. But they had been observed by an individual, who had immediately put off in his skiff, and crossed to the other side. This rendered greater caution necessary, as he would undoubtedly inform the enemy of our neighbourhood. We offered to take the old man with us; he refused; determined, not even in ruin, to desert those spots which had seen his birth, and infancy, and manhood, he returned to the bodies of his children, threw himself upon them, apparently resolved to breathe his last sigh in defending these mangled remnants from further insult: all that we could do was to lay a fresh stock of provisions by his side.

'Hoping to find the enemy unprepared, upon some point or other, we immediately entered our boats. They however watched us, and at the moment of our landing, appeared before us in a body so numerous, that it seemed impossible to escape. We formed our men in the very water into a wedge, and taking a gun and bayonet ourselves, we led them against the foes, determined either to cut our way through, or to fall upon the field of battle. After repeated charges we at last succeeded, but our numbers were reduced to fifty, and several were wounded. We mustered upon the very spot where the liberty of Switzerland had been sworn to by the three patriots; it was the valley of Brunnen. Fortunately the Schweitzers did not pursue us. Travelling night and day, we at last gained the higher parts of the canton, whence my companions came. We separated, and it was a proud moment when they brought their wives and children to thank us as the preservers of their husbands and fathers. Olivieri and myself were now alone amongst the mountains, as a reward was set upon our heads, and as we here depended entirely upon the fidelity of many who had shunned our cause, we determined to depart and seek some other refuge. My friend knew not where to go, being ignorant, as he said, where his family was; he having left it privately, while travelling, to join the Swiss. He however determined to go into the Austrian dominions, and there seek for information. We parted with mutual protestations of friendship, and a promise from him of letting me know by means of Berchtold, when he had found safety. We had had little communication; I therefore scarcely knew more than that Olivieri was not his family name, and that he was an Italian. I had often remarked his eyes to be fixed upon my scarf, but his delicacy preventing him from speaking upon a subject, he perceived I was not willing to converse on, was the cause of our parting without further communication. He was indeed the brother of that object, which had never deserted my thoughts, which, sleeping and waking, my lips had often called upon. No night passed, though dangers surrounded me on every side, without her image rising to cheer for a moment my wearied heart; but the dreams always ended unhappily. It seemed as if the fates were determined to embitter even those moments, in which I was engaged in a noble cause, thus to prepare my mind for those pangs which follow guilt. You may think I rest too much upon these instants of my life; but I dread to narrate my miseries; the recalling to memory anguish and grief racks my heart; but I have begun, and you shall hear the whole.

'Knowing the country well, and being acquainted with every pass, I found no difficulty in reaching the neighbourhood of Beatenberg, and I was soon locked in my sister's arms. Berchtold and Julia's anxiety about me had been great, they had heard by report of my being in action, and had seen in the papers the immense reward offered for my person. Seeing me safe they could not contain their joy; but morning came, and I was obliged to depart into the mountains, for who could be trusted? Treachery and avarice had proved at last the master passions in many breasts, though they had at first worn the mask of the noblest virtues. Promising to be back at night, I flew to the Wengern Alp, and there again visited the spot, which now began to appear sacred to my mind. At night I returned to the pastor's cottage; I only found my sister there, he was gone to Thun. Leaving the house, Julia led me to our mother's grave, and again begged of me to be cautious, for constantly while I had been absent the same admonition had been given. It did not seem to her to relate to a personal danger; it was a vague threat, that seemed the more terrific, because it could not be decidedly represented to the mind. She then begged of me to relate the dangers I had undergone; I gave her a minute account of the whole.

'Amongst other things which she mentioned to me, was the arrival of a stranger, who had taken up his abode at Interlaken, and who excited the wonder of his neighbours by the account his servants gave of his riches, and by their intimation of his having communication with an evil spirit. The source of his riches was unknown. Many were the tales related concerning him, and if but half were true, she said, he must certainly be possessed of a wonderful power. He was old and apparently wretched. His only daughter accompanied him, her beauty was as much the subject of conversation, as the riches of her father. These were the only rumours my sister had heard, for they had only arrived a few days before. I wish that I had never known more. I did not laugh at the idea of the supernatural part of the report. We were both too strongly imbued with the tales of our foster-mother not to attach some credit to them. My sister's dreams, in which our mother visited her, my own which always portended misfortune, had enforced upon our minds the belief of the interference of superior beings.

'For several nights I returned, but Berchtold was yet, as we imagined, at Thun. My sister and myself left entirely to ourselves, again talked over the feats of Olivieri, and she often asked me to repeat them, seeming with pleasure to rest upon every circumstance regarding him. Foolishly, I also took a pleasure in relating them, for though we had been constantly rivals, there was a frankness, a heedless daring about him, that excited admiration, at the same time, that the warmth of his expressions called forth a reciprocal feeling of love. I knew not then how to discover the sting protruding from the rich scales of the snake. We conversed upon our mother, and my enquiries were numerous about her person, her voice. I cannot explain it, but I wished even from Julia's dreams to aid the representation I had formed from her portrait of a being, who seemed even after life, to feel an interest in my fate. In the locket, there was a melancholy look about her dark blue eyes, that was rendered heavenly, by the soft smile playing upon her open lip. I had gazed upon it so often, that I had her image before me, even when far from home, but it was only distinct in the face, which appeared to be gazing on heaven, with the consciousness of having obtained a prayer for me. Since my sister's dreams, it seemed as if I knew a mother's care, and I often sighed, to think, that though thus thoughtful of me even in heaven, she did not think me worthy of enjoying her smile.

'One morning I left my sister, and retired to the wild borders of the Brientz lake. The sun rose, and with its glittering ray painted on the water, the reflected images of the wild rocks upon the other side. There is a point which juts into the lake, and on it are the ruins of an old church; I did not feel inclined to exert myself to reach a more distant spot, but I laid myself down by an arching gateway, round which the ivy clustered, as if by its tenacious grasp, it would hold together the monuments of another age, upon which the breath of time was acting with a destructive power, unheeded by man. I seemed to feel this breath of time acting upon me as upon these works of man, the wild joys of youth seemed sunk into the melancholy uniform feeling attendant upon age, when all joy is passed, all hope extinguished by the consciousness of the presence of death. I gazed upon the mists as they rolled slowly along the hills, veiling successively the various beauties of the banks, and watched the cloud's shadow, depriving the lake of its glittering sheen. I rested upon their passing powers, but did not notice, that the glow of the bright sun invariably returned upon the spots, before darkened by a shadow. The peasants' barge, and the light skiff, passed rapidly before me, but unheeded they passed in silence, for it appeared, as if, even they sympathized in my grief. It was mid-day, I rose to shelter myself from the sun's ray, and sought that side of the point towards Interlaken. There was a small light skiff upon the water, and in it was a female figure. It was at some distance, it gradually approached; my heart fluttered, my breathing became difficult, my eyes were fixed upon a form I seemed to recognise. Her face was not lit up, as I had seen it, by all the fire of her indignant eye; carried along by her small latin sail, she approached. Her eye was gazing upon the rippling wave, cut by her prow, it seemed as if joy did not dwell there, her eye-lash veiled its splendour, while her black locks curling on the breeze, floated playfully around. Her breast at times would heave as if the sorrow in her bosom was loath to grieve her, but she seemed unwilling it should go, for she rested upon it. I stood intently gazing, it seemed as if my least motion would have at once destroyed an illusion. The current brought her heedless close to the shore, and the boat struck the bank; she looked around and saw me. It was plain she recognised me, for her eyes fixed upon her scarf. To paint to you, the varying expressions of that eye, and the varied colour of that cheek, is impossible. With slow hesitating steps she approached, our eyes did not dare to meet, and I stood by her for some moments in silence; at last with a trembling voice, she asked me if my name were not Ernestus Berchtold? "If you own that name, fly instantly, you have been betrayed, and the blood-suckers are already, at Interlaken upon their way to Berchtold, do not go there to-night." I could hardly acknowledge my name, I was so moved by her voice; she offered to convey me to the other side of the lake, if I thought myself safer there. Unconscious of what I was doing, I entered her boat, and taking the oars, tried by violent exertions to rouse myself; we did not speak; when upon the other side, I landed. Farewell fell from her lips, and it seemed as if the echoes mocking me, repeated farewell. I stood still, watching her as entering the current of the Aar, she was gradually borne down towards Interlaken; even when she had passed the bridge, I gazed, and seemed to see a white speck, that I imagined was her.

'I turned away, and towards evening found myself upon the same spot on which I had first seen her. Again, she had appeared. At first, she had guided me into the path of honour, this day she ensured my safety. Was she then a vision? I asked myself. Was it my guardian angel, who invested that form? I did not think of pursuing my route to any place of greater safety, it seemed as if this spot where my protector had appeared, was secure, I laid me down beneath the rock, that had witnessed her presence, and offering up a prayer to heaven, I gave way to all the visions my imagination offered. She had recognised me, she knew my name, my rank, and still felt an interest in my safety. If you have ever known, what it is to be in love, you may judge what my feelings were, if not, my words are useless, I hardly slept the whole night.

'Next day I roamed restless over the Alpine heights around, I did not heed the horrors or the beauties of these solitudes. The cataract fell by my side, and yet I heard it not, wherever the valley wound, thither I followed; but as evening threw its stillness over nature, ere the light canopy of heaven was darkened, I found myself upon the covered bridge of Interlaken, I had forgotten my danger. The open spaces between the beams supporting the roof, enabled me to see the different houses which skirt the river's side. Mine eyes however gazed upon that one, in which I had heard, the new inhabitants of this neighbourhood had taken up their abode. I had imagined my unknown was the beautiful daughter I had heard of from my sister; and I had not long been upon my station, when I saw her come forth, supporting upon her arm the feeble steps of the old man I had seen with her upon the Wengern Alp. Her eyes, fixed upon his languid face, seemed anxiously to be watching the features of her invalid father. There was a bush not far from the door beneath the wide-spreading canopy of a lofty elm; she placed him there, and I saw reflected on her face, the smile which beamed upon the old man's, as he gazed upon the setting sun. I watched her slightest action, her every glance, it seemed as if her words soothed the pains of sickness, and lightened the languor attendant upon an invalid's inactivity. Oh, if that smile had fallen upon myself, as it then fell upon her father, if I had only felt its cheering influence without that burning passion it has excited in this breast; but I must not anticipate my narration. The sun sunk behind the mountains, she carefully shielded her sire from the damp. I watched her retiring steps, heard the door close after her, and at last turned away.

'Intending to depart again to some retired spot, I was advancing, when I perceived that there was some one at the end of the bridge apparently watching me, and then retiring as if to look up the road. Alarmed, I seized my hunting knife and approached him: seeing me advance, he came towards me, it was the servant of Berchtold. He had seen me from a neighbouring height, and anxious, as he said, for my safety, had immediately followed me, and finding me on the bridge, had several times spoken to me without my paying the least attention; perceiving at last how I was engaged in contemplating the beautiful object before me, he had contented himself with guarding the entrance to the bridge. I enquired about the French soldiers, he turned pale, but at that moment I hardly noticed it; he told me that they had been watching Berchtold's house during the whole of the night, apparently aware of my being in the habit of going there every evening. He informed me that there were only two remaining, whom he had supplied so abundantly with wine, that if I chose to venture towards the cottage, he would inform Berchtold and my sister where they could meet me, while he engaged the attention of my pursuers. How easily I was deceived; I have since known the value of men's professions; then I was young and confident in virtue. Berchtold and my sister met me, but there were other soldiers in the neighbour-hood; those the servant led to a pass by which I must descend on my return. It was but another instance of that venal boasted honour which so much stains the Swiss patriotic history.

'In the mean time I learnt from Berchtold that he had walked to Berne, hoping to cause my sentence of outlawry to be cancelled; that the French employers had lulled him with hope until he had been rash enough to acknowledge my being in this neighbourhood; when they would listen to him no longer, but sent the soldiers I have mentioned. Even Ochs, who had formerly been his school-fellow, had laughed when he reproached him for so vile a breach of confidence. I spoke with my sister apart, and informed her of my discovery, she was surprised, and seemed downcast; but Berchtold, who had gone to listen, and reported all silent, joining us, we could not proceed in our conversation. I em-braced them, and had begun to descend the steep, when I heard myself challenged; having my gun with me, I fired, and the challenger fell; but one leapt upon my back, it was my own servant, and I was surrounded. I struck upon every side, but it was in vain: determined, however, to be revenged, I threw myself upon the ground with the traitor; as we turned, I succeeded in getting him undermost, and plunged my hunting-knife up to the hilt in his chest. He groaned and died. I surrendered.

'I was hurried to Interlaken, put into a boat, and before the dawn of day, was locked in the prisons of Thun. I expected to be immediately taken out and shot. I was not, however, disturbed till night, when I was awakened from a sound sleep, and, guarded by a company of soldiers, was ordered to be conveyed to the castle of Chillon, upon the lake of Geneva. Entering into conversation with the soldier who marched by my side, I heard from him that Berchtold and my sister had in vain applied for admission to my dungeon, upon hearing of my misfortune; that the reason I was removed at this late hour arose from the magistrate's fear-ing a rescue by the people, who once or twice in the day had seemed, by their tumultuous meeting, inclined to force the prison of him whom they called their only remaining patriot. From him I first learnt that my name was in every mouth; that there were romantic tales printed about me, and spread over all the country in spite of the police which endeavoured to suppress them. I did not feel any vain exultation at this; I was too near death; but I certainly experienced some satisfaction in the thought, that for Louisa,—that—that was her name. For years locked up within my breast, it has not passed my lips. I have not dared to utter that name, not even whisper it to my own ear; but it has been deeply engraven here. It is now a spell that conjures up horrid thoughts; once it did not.

'But I must command myself. I had not visited this part of Switzerland yet, though beautiful, and perhaps richer than any I had seen, it passed unobserved before my eyes. The simple villagers, hearing my name, came round the inns at which we stopped, and looked upon me in silence. Mothers brought their children to me to kiss, as if my kiss could call down a blessing, or inspire heroism. I crossed the Dent de Jamanu, and soon saw the castle once the prison of Bonniva, now destined to be my own.

'The draw-bridge was up, and the sentinels were parading as if they esteemed the castle of importance. Upon my name being mentioned the bridge was lowered, and I soon heard the clash of the chains employed in raising it after me. It seemed to be accompanied by a voice that bade hope to leave me. The rude stare of the soldiers, and the bustling scene of the officers, running to and fro, did not tend to relieve the sorrow that weighed upon me. I had dared danger in the chase upon the Alps; death in battle; yet here the thoughts of leaving all, oppressed me. I did not think of the pain of parting with existence; but Berchtold, my sister, the vision of the Wengern Alp, all seemed to press upon my imagination with eyes, that, by their look, seemed to denote a breaking heart. My head fell upon my breast, while, with folded arms, I walked along the vaulted passage. I was searched, all was taken from me, my knife, the little money I had. The rude jailor already had his hand upon the scarf, retaining it with a firm grasp, I looked at him, and seeing his daughter close by his side,—"if that child," I said, "should be far—far from thee, and thou couldst not hope to see her but in heaven, couldst thou part with the only relic of her memory?" He looked upon his child, and let go his hold.

'I was taken into a room where several officers were deliberating concerning me. I had stood before them some time, when one asked me my name. "Ernestus Berchtold" was my answer. "It is the traitor;" fell from the lips of one. I looked upon him; he could not stand my glance, but sunk into silence. They were considering whether they should lead me to instant execution, or whether I should be confined till the pleasure of the government at Berne should be known, as it was thought that they might wish to make a more public exhibition of the punishment of him they so gratuitously called a traitor. I was respited by one voice, and was instantly ordered to my dungeon.

'To descend into the prison, which is below the level of the water, it is necessary to go down a narrow circular staircase. While descending it, we were stopped by that child upon whom I had rested my appeal to the jailor; to pass her we were obliged to go singly; when I came close to her, I felt something pressed into my hand, while at the same time she made a sign with her finger for silence. I put her present into my breast and followed her father, who was before me, while the others were at my back. I entered a long vault, its floor was the solid rock, and its high roof was supported by seven thick massy pillars. The waves of the lake dashed sullenly against the walls above my head, and the feeble light that pierced the high windows only showed me the damp black sides of this prison. There were the steps of a prisoner marked during a long imprisonment upon the very rock; I still heard the noise of bolts, but did not heed it, till I arrived at a narrow cell, partitioned off from the greater dungeon, which I had not perceived in the general obscurity. Into this narrow space I was forced to enter. It was not sufficiently long for me to lie down at full length, and the barred grating, which, far above my reach, was intended in mockery to represent a window, received no reflected light from the dark floor of Bonniva's prison. I heard the doors fastened one after another.

'Beneath the slowly sounding wave I was cut off from humanity; the monotonous dashing against the castle's base alone broke the dread silence; it seemed like the loud note of the moments in nature's last hour. My spirits fled, and I leant against the stones to which I was chained, with hands clasped, and my eyes painfully straining, as if they sought at least to see the real horrors of my dwelling. Fatigued by my long journey over the steep Jamanu, I sought to sit and sleep, but the damp floor for a long time kept my racking mind awake to all the torments of thought, while it hoped for a momentary oblivion of woe.

'At last I sunk into repose, and it was not until late the next morning that I awoke, but I awoke refreshed; I had seen the constant attendant upon my dreams, and I soon lost myself in thought upon her various appearances. The waves above me seemed silenced to a calm, and the sun's powerful meridian ray reflected upon the various sides of the greater vault, penetrated, though in a feeble glimmer, my solitary cell. Gradually stealing upon my ear, I heard a distant voice, which in melancholy notes seemed to sympathize with my sorrows. I listened; it approached; the measured strokes of an oar interrupted the heavenly strain; suddenly breaking into livelier notes it sung of hope; the voice was, they were Italian words, it was my vision's voice. It gradually sunk away into indistinct sounds. I seemed another being, hope breathed upon my heart, and Louisa wore the semblance of that enchanter; oh that I had died, that she had left me to myself to die! it was not the will of heaven. Again I heard the splashing sound of the oar, and again that voice sounded on my ear; it was no longer the thrilling notes of an air, but in slow recitative it bade me hope, it told me that a boat should be stationed at two or three stone throws distance from the castle, ready at all times to receive me if I could manage to get out, and that in the mean time endeavours were making at Berne, to gain a repeal of the sentence passed upon me. Again the song of hope sounded in my cell, losing itself gradually in the distance, it at last left me with nothing human within hearing.

'I now remembered the child's present; feeling in my breast, it proved to be a file and a knife; I instantly began to work at the wall, dividing me from the great dungeon; while thus busily employed I heard the bolts of the vault withdrawn; my jailor entered, he spoke not, but threw me my pittance of bread, and laid down my pitcher of water. Hardly was he gone, when I resumed my work, the dampness of my cell aided me. The mortar was soft, and the wall built of small stones; when therefore I had scraped the mortar away from the crevices, I did not find any difficulty in forcing them out. One by one I tore away many, and I had already almost pierced the wall, when, fearful of penetrating entirely through, lest the jailor might next day detect my attempt, I managed to replace most of the rubbish in its situation, and to push the rest into a corner. I now began with my file to cut the chain that surrounded my waist. The jailor came next morning, and told me, that at the dawn of the ensuing day I was to be conveyed to Berne. This gave me additional strength, the hopes of liberty, of seeing Louisa, spurred me on, and in a few moments I was free from my chains. With what impatience I waited for the night. It came; I forced a passage through the wall, and I found myself in the great vault without a manacle. The moon's ray seemed with a smile to seek the ground on which I trod, for its cold beams pierced the grated apertures above, and illumined some dreary spots. I was not yet free, the window was high above my reach; but I did not despair, taking the whole length of the dungeon to give me power, I leapt, and caught with my hands at one of the bars. I raised myself, and resting my knee upon the shelving sill, I immediately began to employ my file, and the rusty bars soon gave way to my arm.

'I paused a moment, the cool fresh air of the night, no longer poisoned by the noxious vapours of the subterranean dungeon, played amidst my hair; I seemed to inhale life. The moon's ray, decked with one glittering streak of light the whole breadth of the wide lake; it seemed the path of hope. Not far distant was a barge; in three or four hours my murderers would be at my prison door. The ground was covered with snow even to the water's edge; I leapt into the lake, and being a good swimmer I reached the boat numbed by the cold, I had hardly the strength to raise myself into it. There was no one to be found; there were some coarse provisions, a peasant's habit, and a letter; it had no direction, "if safe," it said, "proceed to Milan, you will hear of us there. Your sister is well, Berchtold ill, but do not go to him, he knows we are attempting to save you, and he shall immediately be informed of your escape. The daughter of Olivieri's father." It was now that I learnt that Olivieri was the brother of Louisa Doni. It was now explained why he so attentively examined my scarf.

'I could not resolve on leaving Switzerland without seeing Berchtold, there was a western breeze, I hoisted the latin sail, and in a few minutes I was free from immediate danger, and on my way towards Beatenberg. It was necessary that I should keep amongst the mountains, and I only dared approach the most solitary chalets. They were generally deserted, and it was with difficulty that I procured sufficient to support nature during the three days I was upon my way. Arriving at Œschi, I took a boat from the side of the lake, and crossing, was soon at the foot of the steep, on which stands Beatenberg. The stillness of the night was broken by the sound of voices chaunting, which, stealing down the mountain, sunk upon the wave. Alarmed I knew not why, I rushed up the path; before the church porch, around the great cross that stood upon the green sward, knelt Berchtold's parishioners arrayed in white. Though the red glare of the pine torch fell upon their faces, it did not allow me to distinguish any one. Breathless I stood incapable of motion. The chaunt ended, the minister of peace arose, it was not Berchtold; "he's dead," I cried, and rushed forward; alarmed, the peasants rose, they recognized me and were silent; my sister took my hand and bade me pray for him who had died. Incapable of any longer bearing the anxiety attendant upon my fate, I knew not what I did, I knelt, I heard the solemn chaunt sing Berchtold's requiem, and could not join it. The earth closed over him, and the minister led me to my former home.

'I was inconsolable, they talked to me of ensuring my safety; I was deaf to their remonstrances, and only listened to grief; my sister was left alone with me. She wept with me, and ere it was dawn, had persuaded me to depart. She told me that Louisa had been with her, had made her promise to join her, in case of Berchtold's death, so that I need not be under any anxiety on her account. She informed me that Louisa had walked with her over my haunts, had enquired after every minutest circumstance about me. My sister said, she thought she loved me. I could listen to no more, embracing her, I issued forth, visited my mother's and Berchtold's grave, and soon lost sight of Beatenberg.

'Louisa loved me! it was too true, if that love had fallen upon any one else it would have proved a blessing. On me; you see my withered lineaments, my sunken eye, my feeble step, think you, a common curse could thus blast the bloom of life? Berchtold was but the first victim to my love. My love has left me, a scattered pine amidst this desolate scene, but first it has destroyed all who were bound to me, my love has proved,—but I must preserve my strength,—I have horrors to relate,—going through the Simplon, then a road only passable by mules or on foot, I soon arrived at Milan.

'I was in safety, the city was in possession of the Austrians. I had hardly rested at the inn, at which I took up my abode and was making enquiries, in hopes of discovering the Donis, when Olivieri entered. We flew into one another's arms, he answered none of my enquiries, but leading me to his carriage, we arrived through the corso at a palace close to the gates. We got out, I knew not whither he was leading me, the doors of the saloon were thrown open, and I found myself in the presence of his father, his sister. The old man advanced, and taking my hand, which hung by my side, he thanked me for having twice saved the life of his son. I knew not what to say; conscious I owed my life to Louisa's interference, I could not find words to thank her. The father at last led me towards his daughter, and bade her attempt to thank me. Her eyes turned upon me, suffused with blushes she had some words upon her lips, when I forced myself to stop her. "Do not mock me, what do I owe to you? my life is nothing, when compared to that thirst of honour, you inspired in my breast." Again, she blushed and was silent. At that moment, another carriage arrived, it was my sister attended by two faithful domestics of my friend; locked in my arms, she was at last taken thence to be clasped in those of my preserver.

'After taking some refreshment, the father led me into another room, he there told me that Berchtold's last request was, that he should supply his place, and take my sister and myself to him, as his children. As he spoke, he showed me at the same time, the last lines which my foster-father had written a few moments before he died. They contained our history as far as he was acquainted with it; in them he bade me trust always in God, and recommended me to bow under that dispensation, which had made me an outcast on my native soil, and not to murmur at the will of him, who had deprived me of the feeble support a Swiss pastor could afford against the pressure of events, since he had raised me up a protector, so much more powerful in the father of him whose life I had saved. Doni took me by the hand, and perceiving the tear trembling in my eye, he begged of me to let him supply the place of Berchtold. He called me son; Louisa's father could not call me so in vain, I fell upon his neck, but could not speak.

Ernestus Berchtold – Part Three

'I HAD already undergone more than falls to the lot of most men in this valley of miseries; but I was not allowed repose; from this moment my heart was torn piece-meal, by fiends each more horrible than the other. Not many days had elapsed since Julia's death, when Olivieri's father received an anonymous warning to prepare himself for the worst news. The letter was dated Strasburgh. Next day he read in another letter, that his son, under an assumed name, had been taken with several others of a band of robbers, who had for a long time infested the banks of the Rhine. Doni had now become aged and infirm, he was not capable of undergoing the fatigues of a long journey, yet it was hardly possible to hinder him from setting off, to attempt saving his only son. He blessed me when I insisted upon performing that office. "You have twice saved his life in the field of honour, may you be as successful in snatching him from the death of infamy." He gave me unlimited power, and rushed into his daughter's apartment to seek there for the comfort all else seemed to deny him.

'I departed, travelled night and day, I saw Switzerland again, but did not even notice it, my mind was anxious, was alarmed; it seemed as if heaven wished by repeated inflictions of its bitterest curses, to humble to the dust the family circle of my protector. I was so rash, that for a moment I dared to question Providence. So weak is all mortal knowledge; misery is but the fruit of vice, virtue never feels the world's infamy; there is a heavenly beam of certainty in the merciful justice of their God that enables the just to look upon all the inflictions of this life, but as the most lenient atonement due to a tender, though offended father, for those weaknesses belonging even to our nature.

'I arrived at Strasburgh; its fretted spire, rising high above the houses, upon the far extended plain, for a long time marked the bourne to which I was tending, while the winding road that forms the approach, seemed to mock my endeavours to reach it. Justice had been summary, there had not even been a regular trial, but a court martial had been summoned, and instantly had condemned the prisoners to death. A respite had however been granted for a few days, in consequence of the hopes entertained of inducing some individual to betray the secret retreats of their comrades. I immediately proceeded to the prison and asked admission. Application being made to the governor, and it being evident that I was not one of the gang, I obtained it. I entered; bolt after bolt slowly sounded as they were forced from their rusty clasps, and I found myself in a low gallery, the damp was slowly falling in measured drops from the arched vault above, and the coldness of the chilly air made me shiver. The jailor bore a torch before me; its red light at last rested upon the strong fastenings to a narrow door. I gave him money, and seizing the torch, entered.

'Upon a little straw, covering a few loose stones in a corner, lay a form, which seemed reckless of all. The light of the torch did not cause it to move, its hands were upon its face, clenched; its whole posture was strained, as if by the convulsive stiffening of its limbs it would harden itself against the inflictions of the mind. I could not speak; thrice I strove to utter the name of Olivieri, and thrice it stuck in my throat. "Speak, I can listen to my fate," Olivieri at last said in a hurried voice, "Death they say silences all voices, if it can silence that which echoes through the chambers of my breast, scaring oblivion and repose, I shall be content to die, though on the wheel, waiting, when all my limbs are crushed, for that repose the iron bar may give." He did not move, but seemed to mutter this, addressing himself as much as me. "Olivieri," at last fell trembling from my lips. He with one exertion stood erect; his eyeballs straining in their sockets, seemed to seek the horrid certainty they knew would blast them. Berchtold appeared before him. He threw himself upon the straw, and with a hand clenching with furious grasp his long black hair, he seemed to force his head upon the ground, fearing his eyes should again turn upon me. I sate upon the stones at his side, laid my hand upon him, bade him be comforted. He shrunk as if my touch froze him. I told him of my hopes of obtaining his release, of the wealth I could employ in bribing his judges. He looked up; "You talk to me of mercy; Julia was seduced by me." "I know it," I replied, "it is your father, who acts by me, I am but my benefactor's agent. For him I am to attempt to save his son." "His son?" he echoed in a faltering voice, "true, I was his son." I in vain asked him for information on which to proceed; he would give me none. I left him.

'I applied to the court which had passed his sentence. I saw the members who had composed it in private. They gave me an account of the desperate gang to which he had belonged, and painted in horrid colours the devastations they had committed in the French territory. It appeared that Olivieri had put himself at the head of these outlaws, and had with the most daring rashness and carelessness of life, always eluded the numbers that often seemed to surround him. I made those who appeared favourable to my pleading great presents, under the pretence of enabling them to aid the furtherance of my objects. Amongst the others, the governor seemed to have the most influence. I gave him immense sums, which he promised to expend for the prisoner's advantage. The next day was appointed for the execution. I had not seen Olivieri again, I was anxious not to encourage too much his hopes of life, while all seemed uncertain. I called early in the morning, upon the governor; I saw him. He raised my expectations very high, he said, that if I could but find the slightest pretence for a respite, that it was determined to grant it. "If I were to judge by your riches, he and yourself must be of higher rank than you pretend." I had concealed both our names. "Now, if you can but show that some one of influence is interested in his fate, we will admit of an appeal." Rashly I was induced to utter the names of Olivieri Doni, and Ernestus Berchtold. I was surprised at seeing the man before me turn of a most deadly pale. His limbs seemed to fail him, but he in an instant recovered himself; his voice alone betrayed an emotion I could not understand. He assured me that he would instantly occupy himself about it, and I left him. An hour afterwards I received a note from him saying, that I should prepare a carriage and post horses upon the bridge, and as the clock struck the first hour of the morning, that I should present myself at the prison door, where I should meet my friend. That this had been thought the best means of allowing his escape. Passports were enclosed, which would allow us to pass the bridge, and we should then be in safety. I immediately prepared every thing, anxious for the arrival of the moment when I was again to save the brother of Louisa.

Towards evening, restless, I issued out. I wandered up and down that part of the main street, which, covered by arcades, brought to my recollection the towns of my native country. Memory was rapidly crowded with the images of infancy, while the evening tints, and the stillness of nature soon enabled me to abstract myself entirely from the surrounding objects. I at last found myself in the cathedral. There was no one there, even devotion seemed for a while to have laid aside its pomp to enjoy the balmy freshness of an April evening. I had at last advanced into the most obscure part of the aisle; when turning round, a light figure dressed in the singular vestment of the neighbouring peasantry, caught my eye. Her step was hurried, and her head moved anxiously as if seeming to shun observation. Thinking that my presence might be painful, I was retiring, when she beckoned to me. I stood still, and she was immediately by my side. She hastily addressed me. "You are a friend of Olivieri Doni's, you perceive from my knowing his name, that I am in his confidence. He once professed love to me, he has probably done so to many more, who are now like me ashamed of their name; but even if I told it you, it would be useless. Hoping to be of service, and anxious to hear of him who still possesses my affection, though he has broken the peace of her, who loves him; but I deserve it, for I am guilty, he cannot love guilt; I am so lowered, that I was not ashamed to gain my object, by seeking one of the prison guard. I have just left him intoxicated. From him I learnt, while he was blabbing all, that he was called upon to perform a service this night in the course of his duty, that he disliked. I gained from him that he was to belong to a party, who were to lurk in one of the streets and seize my lover and yourself, at the moment you thought yourselves secure of freedom, for that the police were anxious to take you, who, they suspected belonged to the same gang, and therefore had resolved to arrest you, while engaged in aiding the escape of your friend, which alone will ensure your condemnation." I was astonished, could I then be so shamefully betrayed? I immediately remembered the sudden emotion of him, who had promised so much, when he heard our names, and it flashed upon my mind, that I had a faint recollection of his name as being that of an officer in the French troops opposed to us in the Underwald, who having been placed in a post of importance, had been surprized by Olivieri and myself, and had been, in consequence of his precipitate flight, broken and disgraced. It was now nearly dark, I could not think of deserting Olivieri without still attempting his rescue. The girl's information might be false. I spoke with her, she appeared sincere; I offered her money, she refused it; my case was desperate, I determined to confide in her, I got her to lead me to the neighbourhood of the prison, and show me all the turnings and secret cuts through the different streets. I soon gained a perfect idea of the plan of this part of the town, and I began to hope in consequence of the intricacy and number of turnings in this neighbourhood that I might elude the ambush, if I could at any point break through the guards. I did not entirely open my plan to my guide, but asked her if she knew of any certain place of refuge, whither I could retreat in case of need. She led me and showed me her apartment, it was miserable, but there was an air of neatness about it that seemed, in contradiction with the poverty, visible in every article. "If you can arrive here without being observed, you are safe."

To avoid suspicion, I immediately left her and returned to my hotel, which was close to the river. The hour approached, I armed myself with a sabre and a pair of pistols, and hiding under my large Italian cloak another sword and pair of fire arms, I sauntered negligently out of the inn door, and calling my servant, I told him in a loud voice to take care the horses were ready, as I intended to set off the moment I had fixed on. This I did to blind any one, who might be watching my motions. Then turning down some of the most abrupt windings, I first went whither I had learnt the different parties were to be placed. By means of keeping close to a shaded part of the walls of the streets, which being lit by a single reverberating lamp1 suspended in the middle between the houses, were rather dark, I could approach very near them without being perceived. I discovered one point which I thought weaker than the rest, for the number of the men seemed smaller, the silence being greater. I then returned, entered the main street leading to the prison, and soon found myself at its gate, without meeting any one. The high narrow windowed walls, were suddenly illuminated by the moon bursting in all its splendour from behind a cloud, and high above my reach I perceived some one watching me, he retreated and I heard the gates open. I could not perceive who was there, for the hollow opening was in the dark shadow thrown over it by a salient buttress. My heart beat violently. It might not be Olivieri, a person was pushed out, I heard the words, "I am free," spoken in a voice that denoted the despair within. I approached, it was Olivieri. Throwing off my mantle, I stood before him; he did not notice me, though the moon's ray was full upon us. I roused him, thrust the sword and pistols into his hand, and bade him follow me. "We are not safe, we must baffle the traitors yet," said I, "be firm, we have escaped greater perils than these, follow me." His broken voice, merely answered, "To death."

'I hastened towards the point I thought the weakest. A shrill whistle sounded at our back, and we found ourselves surrounded. The first who approached, were dead at our feet. They retreated before us, we had broken their circle and were already free towards the street down which it was necessary to turn. "Now to the right," I cried to my companion. A shot struck him and he fell; I rushed to the spot hoping that he might rise. I struck on every side determined not to leave him in their hands, their numbers increased, but at the same time I heard a trampling of feet at my back; desperate, I rushed forward; a female shriek struck my ear, and at the same time I found myself joined by about twenty men. Their blows told, we caused the town-guard to retreat, I could not again find Olivieri's body. I rushed along the streets, and was soon at the young woman's door. I heard voices; alarmed, I listened, they were evidently from their conversation trying to console some one. I knocked, a female voice immediately exclaimed, "'Tis he," and the door was opened. I entered, Olivieri was extended upon a couch, attempting to write a few lines; he had just finished. Around him were many men in a strange uncouth garb. They were his former companions, who having received the same intelligence from the girl as myself, had resolved to attempt a rescue, and had stolen singly into the town. Olivieri gave me what he had written, it was to his father; his pale face was turned towards me, his feeble arm could hardly support its own weight. "Berchtold, I have not deserved the risking yourself for me; can, can you forgive me dying." "I do," was my answer, and I held his extended hand. He threw himself upon his bed, and in a stifled voice, "There is another, whose forgiveness I do not ask, but tell, oh! tell her, it was her shame that has damned me, that made me desperate, damned me." "She's dead, she too would have forgiven you; she died speaking of you, but not cursing you." His limbs were instantly relaxed, and moved no more.

'We were now aroused by the entry of another robber, the soldiers were approaching, I begged of them not to leave the body of my Louisa's brother to their insults; they lifted it from the couch, and placed it in a recess so artfully contrived, that it bid defiance to the most accurate search, and they promised me they would return and bury it. We took the young woman with us, and separating, we singly hastened to a spot by the river's side, where we hoped to find boats. Ten only reached it, we entered a small wherry. The town was in such confusion that the necessary orders had not been sent to the different boundaries. We let the boat float down the stream, and soon found ourselves beyond the fortifications. We landed on the German side, and presently reached one of the dwellings of the freebooters. I now learnt that it was this same girl, who had written the anonymous letter to her lover's father. I offered her a considerable sum of money, again offered to secure her an independence, she refused it all, and insisted upon remaining with those men amongst whom she had first known Olivieri. I remained with them a considerable time, anxious to see the body of my former friend secure against any insult, and before I left them, aided by the daring of these men, who managed to enter the town and take the body from its secret hiding place, I had the satisfaction of consigning him to the earth. I gave them all the loose money remaining with me, secure upon my letters of credit of having more than enough to convey me whither I liked.

'I reached Inspruck, not deeming myself safe in any part of the French territory, I determined to remain here, and I wrote to Doni merely mentioning that I had been unsuccessful, and telling him where I had stopped. I thought it best not to tell him more for fear of my letter being intercepted, and hoping that when I saw him I should be able to break the fatal news to him. My last hope was vain, for all the papers and public prints contained a full account of the daring attempt I had made to save a robber from the ignominious sentence of the law. Our real names were also mentioned, and at the same time that many rested upon the courage, they pretended had been shown in this attempt, many took advantage of the connection of our names with a gang of robbers to throw discredit upon our former conduct in the cause of Switzerland. It was soon known through my banker, at Inspruck, that I was the notorious Ernestus Berchtold, and I was surrounded by people, who were glad to seek some refuge from their ennui, in gazing upon one, whose name seemed to have something like romance attached to it.

'Count Doni arrived, Louisa too, though weak and feeble, still in better health than when I had last seen her, accompanied him. She had been forced to exert herself to support her father under his anxiety for his son, and then under the severe blow of seeing his own name in all the prints, known to all as the father of Olivieri, "a captain of banditti." The spring had given her the requisite strength, and I was glad, after so long an absence, to see her once more sitting by my side with renovated life. I could not take my eyes from her, and I rested upon her face so long, that I gradually forced myself to hope that her hectic flush was but her natural colour. We were constantly together, and tried in each other's presence to forget the griefs that weighed upon us both. I had given the last lines of my former friend to his father. He had read them in his own room, and though when we next met I remarked that his eye turned upon me wet with tears, as he evidently did not intimate the least inclination to expose to me what his son had written, I did not seek to learn the substance of Olivieri's note; though I was anxious to learn whether he had disclosed his conduct towards Julia. We never after mentioned his name, and we tried to keep the thoughts of his melancholy fate out of our minds, by resting upon our hopes of Louisa's welfare.

'Count Wilhelm, whom I have before mentioned, found us on his way to his native country; hearing of our being at the same hotel, he sent in his name to my friend. Day after day he remained at Inspruck. The whole of the evening was spent with us in our apartment, and he seemed to seek more and more the means of showing attentions to Louisa. At first I was not disturbed by them, but at last I became fretful and irritable, for it appeared as if Louisa took a pleasure in his conversation. I had heard so much of his power of attaching women, that it seemed impossible for her to resist him. Every thing he did, though the most simple action, was perverted in my mind, to a covert sneer at my poverty and insignificance. I often answered him abruptly, and even insulted him. Louisa's meek eye turned upon me, but it seemed to have lost its influence. I one night found him by her side, he seemed to be earnestly pleading, he had hold of her hand, and she smiled. Stung to the quick by so slight a circumstance, I turned furiously away and retreated to my chamber. Had Berchtold taught me to command my passions, had he but shown me as models for my conduct, men, in the privacy of life, I might have escaped much. It is vain to rest upon it. I had thought that Louisa's influence over my mind, would have hindered me ever again losing myself, hurried away by any passion. But here Louisa's form arose in all the hideousness of jealousy's distorting mirror! I was mad. My clenched fist struck the table, I could not command myself. I remained some time in this state, when turning my eyes towards my bureau, I perceived an almanack; I seized it in mockery; I counted up the days since she had told me she loved me. I was suddenly struck, it was the 28th day of the month, it was a combination of seven. It seemed as if by one exertion I might free myself from doubt, and be at once lost in the horrible certainty, or be for ever blest in the knowledge of Louisa's heart.

'I did not reflect; the hour struck; I seized my lamp, and rushing out was already close to the apartment of Doni, when wavering on the wick the flame suddenly sunk and expired. Yet nothing around was dark, it seemed as if I was surrounded by a mist formed by a dazzling light, too dazzling to allow me to view the objects round. I was a moment startled, but undismayed I strove to rush forward, my feet were bound to the floor. I strove but in vain to move. Gradually the light cleared, and gradually the features of that face, which I had so often gazed upon in my imagination, my mother's, appeared distinctly before me. Her form was majestic, but in her eye there was a softness, which was not even destroyed by the severity of her feeling. "Ernestus," were her words, "heaven has decreed at my prayer, that this crime shall be spared to you, you shall not act ungratefully."—She seemed to vanish with an expression of sorrow upon her face, as if she were not allowed to continue, and felt the horror that burst upon me in consequence of the ignorance in which I was left. My senses forsook me, and the dawn of day had already pierced the thick clouds before I recovered.

'I did not return to my room, I went into the open air, my thoughts were hurried; baffled, I was not subdued; jealousy still was not banished, I did not rest upon my mother's apparition, so strongly had the idea of Louisa's infidelity taken hold of me. While walking amidst the intricate windings of a public garden, I heard voices near me. One was Count Wilhelm, I heard him boasting of the favours of some lady, whom another thought loved him, and he suddenly presented himself before me; I grossly insulted him. He took a pleasure in torturing me with his pretended concern at my mistress's kindness to another. I struck him, we fought and he fell severely wounded. I stood by him and he was amply revenged. He told me that he had seen me entering the preceding evening, that being at that moment engaged in speaking about me, and Louisa having expressed her wish that I might be received into the Austrian service, he was offering his interest to forward my views, and that knowing how easily I was irritated, he had purposely taken her hand. He advised me to fly, I was obliged to do so for I was no longer safe where I was.

'Louisa was then innocent. I cursed that fate which seemed to hang about me, always shielding me from death. I had fought in battle, but never yet had received the slightest wound: I had escaped from prison while the axe was falling. My rashness seemed to be incapable of hurting me; for there was a shield around me, that snatched me from peril. I was preserved from worse than death. Even this last act could not divide me from Louisa. She loved me indeed. Alarmed at seeing my antagonist brought in wounded, she did not shriek; she did not give herself up to loud and weak lamentations; but conscious, that probably my life depended upon the event of his wound, she sacrificed herself entirely to the care of the invalid. With unremitting attention she watched by his bedside. But when he was declared free from danger, then the cold hand of strengthened disease made itself felt. She was obliged again to return to her sick chamber. But first she begged her father to inform me of the favourable result. I returned. Doni met me on the stairs,—embraced me; but no joy was visible on his face. He announced to me the dangerous state in which Louisa lay, but did not reproach me; she had forbidden it. I was introduced into her room. Consumption was ruining her system; she was faint and weak; her continued cough and the marked colour on her cheek, but too well denoted the power it had acquired. I could not even ask her how she felt; but the tears fell down my cheek on the moist hand that held mine. She allowed me to stay with her. Talked to me of that power, whose pleasure it was to strengthen the weak and console the wretched, she said that he had soothed the agony of death's visible approach, and until she saw me, that she had found relief in the thought of the short time we should be separated. But now she saw my grief, she was sorry I should be left alone, even for those few moments, without a being, to whom I was attached; that she again wished for life, if amidst all its miseries she could but hope for the power of consoling me through these inflictions. In fine, she did not speak of herself, but of me—of the wretch who had gradually broken the weak threads which bound her pure soul to life. Count Wilhelm perfectly recovered, left us. I had seen him, and as the only atonement in my power, had acknowledged my folly, and had begged he would pardon it, though it had been so severely felt by him. He returned a vague answer, and I saw him no more.

'Doni's interest was great; his wealth insured him friends, active in bringing back to their neighbourhood one whose riches fell in beneficent showers upon all. By their influence, he soon obtained a pardon for my resistance to the civil authorities in behalf of Olivieri, and I was granted permission to return to any part of the French territory. As the cold Alpine air seemed to hasten the rapid steps of his daughter's decline, he determined upon having her conveyed again to the borders of the Lago Maggiore, which had seemed last year to have possessed such renovating powers. We departed, and soon found ourselves fixed in our abode. Nature wore the same aspect as the year before. Palanza, with its white walls and glittering columns shone as brilliantly in the sun's ray;

the smile of heaven seemed to play upon the fairy islets of the Boromei, and the rich woods of Belgirato reflected in the blue surface of the water, seemed to put the beauty of this in competition with the sublimity of the wild rocks of the upper part of this long lake. But Louisa's health had faded. She could hardly hope, if the disease continued its hasty steps to see these scenes again. But still that fairy enchanter, hope, acted upon me, and as each day she gained some slight addition to her strength, I pictured to myself years of happiness united with her I had long so ardently loved. She would not undeceive me, but left me the illusion. She was again able to enjoy the freshness of the air, and to walk out, amidst the varying scenery around. I supported her, and felt the light pressure of her feeble form resting upon my arm. She would stop, and draw some reflections on the bounty of God, even while in pain, from the various pictures before her; always attempting to turn my mind towards those thoughts, which she well knew could alone give me consolation, and a resting place in this vale of miseries. But still she seemed to recover strength. I entreated her to hope, and not to give way to such desponding thoughts. Her father, who was deceived as well as myself, begged of her to console herself; talked to her when alone of me, and spoke of his hopes of seeing us united, of her forming the only prop to his old age, and that I, how could he say it? was alone worthy in his estimation of receiving from a father's hand so great a treasure.

'Unwilling to grieve her father, she yielded to my importunities, promised to be mine, if upon a certain day her acquired strength had not given signs of decay. You may imagine with what anxiety, with what hopes I watched each intervening moment. Every cold breeze made me shudder; every cloud that veiled the sun's ray caused me pain. I counted her breathings: whenever she moved, watched the firmness of her step. The day arrived. She was not weaker, but had seemed to find renewed energy in the thought of being mine. She was mine. I cannot paint to you the delirious state of mind, in which the next months passed over my head. I had a right to protect. I was something to that being; but I will not rest upon these feverish moments, you may imagine them; Louisa was mine—Louisa mine! But heaven had not smiled upon our union—no, no. It was but the anger of a God veiled under the brightest hues. Louisa was my,—but I must relate the whole. Her health, as the winter approached declined again, and we returned to Milan. We lived with her father.

'To engage my wife's attention, I resolved upon fitting up a part of the palace anew for our private use. Every thing was ordered, when it occurred to her that the best ornament we could add would be the portrait of her father. I had recovered from my sister our mother's locket, and shewing it to Louisa, we determined upon having it copied and hung opposite the Count's. To give Doni, as we thought an agreeable surprize, we determined upon having them privately executed, and placed in their situation without his cognizance. I sought for a painter, and spent whole mornings with him at his eazel, directing him how to paint my mother. I described to him, as well as I could, her appearance to me at Inspruck, and pretending that I had seen her in a dream, I insisted upon his representing her in such a situation. He executed it, and by the magic effect of his pencil, excited a most extraordinary impression of awe in my breast, whenever I turned my eyes upon the picture. She seemed starting from the canvass; the outline of her figure was lost in the blaze of light, and her face, meek amidst splendour, severe, though with features naturally mild, seemed speaking those words I had heard. I took Louisa to see it; she felt the same awe as myself, though she could not assign a reason for it, but she continued gazing, till I perceived her eyes wet with tears.

'The pictures were privately introduced into the house. We had succeeded in keeping them secret from Doni. In a few days was Louisa's birth day, we resolved therefore to make him our guest upon that occasion in our new apartment. We invited several of our most intimate friends. Every thing passed in gaiety. At last, all the company were gone, and we remained alone. We then, taking him each by one hand, led him into what we intended should be our private sitting room, telling him he should then see our best friends, the one in heaven, the other on earth. The door was opened; directly before him was his own portrait; he seemed surprized and pleased; he turned round; I had hardly announced to him that the one he then saw was my mother's, when he fell. Alarmed we raised him. "Your mother! did you say, your mother?" He threw himself upon the floor, and called upon God to free him from the consciousness of horror like to his. We knelt by him close together; he saw us, raised his aged hands, and with a fluttering voice bade us, if we dreaded heaven's most dreadful curse, to separate. But again he fell to the ground, crying, "It is too late, too late, the crime is consummated." We raised him, he turned hastily away, for he was opposite the portrait, and besought us to take him thence. We led him to his chamber; he motioned us to leave him.

'We retired in silence, we knew not what to understand; was it merely the greater effect of that portrait's power which had been exerted over us. We could not hope it, we were lost in conjectures. Louisa's health was so much broken that I was alarmed for the effects it might have upon her, and, therefore, strove to turn her mind from the subject; but in vain. She did not sleep the whole night, the anxiety concerning her father would not allow her to seek forgetfulness even for a moment. The effect may be imagined upon so weak a constitution. Her father refused to see us for several days, and each day I saw the mind acting upon my wife's health with alarming rapidity. When this reached the ears of her father, he could no longer resist our importunities, he saw us; but the sight of his haggard and wild countenance did not restore Louisa. He had evidently been engaged in writing. We pressed him to explain his conduct. He replied, I knew not what I wished to learn. "It will blast you, as it has done your friend. You must learn it, but it shall be when I am in the grave, and before him who has thus punished my crime; then, then, I may intercede for you, if I myself am sufficiently purified by suffering. He may hear a father's, though it be a criminal's, prayer." His words seemed almost incoherent, he at times called me son, but then with hurried impatience he corrected himself; he asked me whence I got that portrait, I put the locket into his hands. "'Twas mine, I gave it," he hurried, pressed it to his breast, and bade us leave him. We did; he saw us daily, but in silence; he seemed absorbed in one thought, and to that he could not give utterance. He took little, too little, nourishment; but always occupied in writing; he seemed but to find strength for that; when we saw him, he was hardly capable of motion. His task was at last finished. We had been with him as usual, when we were suddenly recalled. He was dying; he bade us kneel down by his side, he blessed us. He took the papers from his table, and putting them into my hands, he bade me read them when he was in the grave, and know the horrors that awaited me; he commanded us to trust in God's mercy, and he sunk, blessing us, upon his couch, breathed no more.

'I bore my Louisa from this scene, she was from this moment confined to her bed. I saw the Count laid in the vault of his ancestors, and then returned to my wife's chamber, whence I never issued till I had no longer a wife. It was evident that all art was unavailing. It was the undermining of a constitution, not by a common bodily disease, but by the griefs of a heart that had never lately found a moment's respite from the most bitter inflictions. Yet, even at this moment, she seemed to forget herself, in her attempts to console me. She alone broke the silence around; I sat in mute despair; I saw Louisa before me, and I was to be left isolated, scathed by divine anger, without consolation. She held my hand, spoke to me of another world; for a moment her words would even subdue my grief, and let me feel as if that hope were enough. At last, seeing the silent sorrow that was preying confined within my breast, she sought to rouse me, bade me read those papers; I did in a luckless moment; only hinted at the horrible mystery unfolded there, and saw the last convulsive throe I was destined to witness in any bound to me by love. I cannot tell you more; read that damning tale, and then you may know what I dare, nay, dare not rest upon. My history is quickly ended. I was dragged from the now lifeless Louisa; but I stole from my guards in the night, gained an entrance into the room, where death showed, as if boasting his beauteous victim, dressed in pomp. The wax tapers seemed to burn dimly, as if in unison with the solemn scene; the black walls, the felted ground, the corpse stretched out, arrayed in white, the stillness visible upon that beauteous face, stilled even the tumult in my breast. She did not seem dead but asleep, I had held her in my arms, upon my breast, looking as she then looked, I gazed upon her for moments, it seemed as if I believed the still appearance wronged my senses. I was about to press her to my heart, my lips were approaching hers, but I started; there were two flies already revelling on those lips, and she could not chase them. I hurried away, I could not remain any longer there. I followed her bier also, and I saw my dearest, my last bond to this earth deposited there, where peace seemed to invite me too. Religion, Louisa's words, however, had not lost all influence, I resisted that will, which would have led me to immolate myself a victim to the manes of those my love had slain. The hopes of a futurity, of Louisa in heaven, upheld me. I retired first to Beatenberg, there in the former house of Berchtold, I spent some time: it was too near the first scenes of memory. I left them and came hither; here, amidst these rocks, bound to me by no memory of the past, I spend the few hours allotted me by heaven, in penance; here each day, my prayer is offered up, that in mercy I might be taken to Louisa. My life has been a life of anguish, of vice, of crime; but still amidst these there have been moments, there has been a being, which, if life could be renewed, would cause me to dare all again, once more to go through those few moments. Often in my dreams I see that form, but now, if when in this mortal life her beauty could not be described, how can I now, that her form, her face, are decked with the smile of him, who glories in the glory of his children. When she now appears in my dreams, there is no longer that hideous chasm opening between us; she is always decked as if for another bridal day, and I awake confident in that day's approach without guilt.

'But leave me, depart to-morrow upon your intended journey, if that you stay, who knows but the curse which has attended me through life may yet be acting, and may fall upon you as well as all others whom I have loved. These papers will explain to you what I have withheld, the life of Doni. If that you return this way, you may find me dead. Drop not a tear over my grave, I shall be with Louisa. Farewell, but depart knowing that there exists a consolation, which man cannot take from you, which misfortune cannot destroy, the belief in a future state, in the mercy of a redeeming God. It is there I find refuge.

The Life of Count Filibero Doni

'The family to which I belong is one of the most noble in Lombardy; but I, being the son of the younger branch, did not enjoy many of those advantages which belong to high rank. I was sent at a very early age to a college of Jesuits, and soon distinguished myself so much, that all the allurements the society was in the habit of holding out to young men of promise, were employed to attach me to this community. I had, however, been educated amongst the mountains; and having been nursed by an old retainer of the family, I had conceived so high an idea of the importance and consequence attached to nobility, that I could not resolve upon putting on a dress, which bound me to forego all those advantages and pleasures, the early associations excited by my nurse, had taught me to believe, belonged to the entry of a nobleman into that very world, my venerable master endeavoured, in vain, to persuade me, was every thing horrible. In the mountains, a son of even the lateral descendants from the Lord, is always looked up to with so much respect and veneration by the poor inhabitants of these districts, that it is no wonder if I was deceived. When the religious began to flatter and distinguish me above my companions, as I was not conscious of any exertion in the acquisition of that mental superiority about which they talked, I attributed their attentions to the respect they felt for one of such exalted rank, as I imagined myself born to, having been left also for the whole of the time with the men, without having paid a single visit to my family, the distant memory of what I had seen at home, appeared to me in contrast with the plain life of my superiors, as something magnificent and passing comparison. My parents, hearing of the talents of their son, were anxious for his entry into an order, whose influence they well knew could be profitable in the greatest degree, not only to the individual, but to the whole of his family. When, therefore, they found that their son was determined not to bind himself by any bond which should hinder him from enjoying, what his imagination had pictured; they thought the best plan in such a case was to allow me to view nearer, that misery which attends nobility devoid of riches. I was accordingly sent for home.

'I arrived—I was astonished at not being led to one of those numerous palaces I met on my way to my father's, in the streets of Milan. My guide and myself came at last into the Corso; I began to reconcile myself, seeing the end of the city before me nothing but palaces on both sides; when suddenly, we turned down a narrow street, and I came to the gate of an obscure house. I did not speak, but my feelings were hurt. I ascended a narrow staircase, and I found myself in the presence of my mother. She was lying on a couch covered with leather, dressed in all the dirty tawdry of one who glories in the past; she was playing with a dog with one hand, while the other was stretched over an earthenware brazier. A dirty servant, slip shod, with hair which had apparently never been touched by a comb, led me into the room, and announced me. My mother did not even move, she was too busily engaged by her puppy to notice me. At last, tired of seeing only the same jumps, turning round in the act of stretching her weary limbs, she saw my figure; imagining it to be that of her son, she addressed herself to me. "Ah, Filiberto, so you are really come home to load your parents with your expences, when you might have become a jesuit with every prospect of power. Well, we shall see how your father will bear it. For my part I will not sacrifice any more first representations for your follies. I had already engaged a box at the Scala, with the money I had spared from our very food; when your father, hearing of it, went and sold the tickets because you were expected." These were the first words, I remember, my mother spoke to me. I cannot describe to you the various feelings they excited in my breast. I could not believe this to be my mother. I did not answer her; but engaged in thought, I sat down, and soon lost sight of the white cold walls and brick floor, in the bitterness of my imaginations. My father entered, throwing off his huge great coat, which, placed upon his shoulders, covered both his body and the clay vessel containing the heated charcoal; he embraced me, and seemed really pleased to see me.

'I spent a miserable day, for it was the very one on which a new opera was to be brought out, and all the usual companions of my mother, having, by intrigue and what not, secured places, she was left alone without even her cavalier servente, in the company of her husband and son: this was insupportable, and she did nothing the whole evening but vent her bad emper upon me, sneering at my foolish ideas of rank. My father, who seemed accustomed to these scenes, quietly took his seat in a retired part of the room, and with his great coat confining the warm air arising from his scaldino around his body, soon fell asleep. The servant came in after the Caffè, and spinning at my mother's side, for a time diverted her attention from me, by joining with the complete appearance of an equal in all that mean criticism of their neighbours, which is esteemed the more witty according to its ill-nature. I was at last glad to go to bed. You may imagine what was the bed room of the son, when the receiving room of the Padrona was such as I have described.

'As I passed by a door upon the staircase, I saw two heads put out to look at me; they were my sisters; I cannot describe to you the sensation I felt, when I found no one had thought it necessary to bring them to see their brother, or even to mention them to him. I found them dressed in the most coarse clothes, and I had hardly been there a few minutes, before they began recounting to me the hardships and privations they had lately undergone in consequence of the anxiety of my mother to secure a box at the opera for this night. It is useless to paint more scenes of this nature; my mother was vain, and spent even what should have been given to feeding her children, in the most distant imitation of the rich, to whom she had the honour of being allied, and who condescended to laugh at her for her pains. My father loved quiet above all things; his income was small, very incompetent to supply the foolish vanity of my mother, he was therefore always in debt, and even obliged to be a mean hanger on upon the elder branch of the family.

'Next day I went with my father to visit the head of our family, and I there saw what my imagination had represented to me. The numerous servants seemed bustling about, as if their wills were too rapid for their limbs. The rich liveries, which were almost reflected in the burnished floors of marble and precious woods, the porphyry columns, the fresco paintings, and the silken coverings to even the footstools astonished me. I followed in silence the officious servant, who seemed amazed at my astonishment at that splendour, in which he had always bustled, though but the son of a cowherd. We were conducted into the boudoir of our relation. He was at his toilette, every thing breathed effeminacy, all was luxurious, the delicately coloured curtains let in the enfeebled light of the noon day. When I entered I could hardly distinguish the objects around, for coming from rooms illuminated by all the powers of the sun, my eyes could not feel the weaker impressions of this veiled obscurity. My relation struck with the astonishment I displayed at such magnificence, amused himself with calling forth signs of wonder from me. I was invited to stay with him, and I accordingly went from my mother's, who was glad to get rid of the inconvenience arising from the addition I caused to be made to the daily expences, at the same time that she was proud of having to talk about the notice I had excited at the Palazzo Doni. My relation conducted me every where. I was introduced by him to the casino of the nobles, and was always in his box at the theatre of La Scala. He advised me to attach myself to an old countess, whose cavalier servente was just dead. I did so, and soon had the honour of carrying her shawl, and whispering in her ear even to the exclusion of her superannuated husband, at all the places of public resort.

'I was now initiated into all the magic enjoyments of wealth and splendour. Without any riches or merit of my own, I enjoyed all the luxuries, which were not a little heightened by the visits I paid my father's house, where I saw poverty in its most appalling state, accompanied by pretensions to rank. I was intoxicated. The Countess had several daughters, these I seldom saw, though they were approaching rapidly to womanhood. It however happened, that soon after I had obtained a footing in her house, that a birthday of her eldest child occurred. She resolved upon celebrating it by a little ball, chiefly composed of the immediate connections of the family. I was admitted by virtue of my office. I had never before been in a ball-room. The splendid chandeliers, the gay dresses, and the beautiful women, surrounding me on every side, raised a scene before me, which even my most vivid fancy had never imagined.

'I could not dance, I was therefore a mere spectator; but I was not idle, I had never been accustomed to see unmarried females, for they are not admitted into the society to which I belonged. There appeared a charm about them I could not define; they fixed my attention, and as each moved in the light dance, with all the agility and grace attendant upon youth, while their retreating looks seemed to denote a fear that they excited observation; I attempted in vain to discover what fascinated me. My heart beat violently, it seemed as if I had never before witnessed beauty. Towards the end of the evening, a party of foreigners entered; they had come to reside in Milan; with them was a young lady. She entered into the dances. She had not the light airy step of her companions, she had not the same brilliancy of eye, but there was something so powerful in her meek glance, in her measured graceful step, that enchained the senses. From that moment I could gaze upon no one else. She alone seemed to be moving, she alone seemed to be the object worthy of attention. I was yet gazing upon her, when the Countess called me to join her party at tre sette. I accompanied her, but it was in vain for me to attempt fixing my mind upon the cards before me. I saw nothing but that figure which had been that moment before my sight. I made blunders that called forth impatient exclamations from my partners, and I was at last allowed to rise upon the plea of a headache. I instantly entered the other room, but she was gone.

'She had however left her image in my breast. For several days I did not see her again, but at last she began to appear in public, for being a foreigner, her parents did not confine her as is customary amongst Italians. I often left the Countess in the Theatre, and placing myself in the pit, near the box in which she was, watched her slightest motion. There was a melancholy look about her that seemed to indicate an acquaintance with grief, that was extraordinary in so young a person. Her dark blue eye was seldom unveiled; her long modest eyelashes generally hid their splendour, and her silence, and her uninterested glance, added a charm to her figure I cannot describe. Her goodness and charity were spoken of by all, her beauty was not envied or denied by her own, while her gentle manners and winning smile, seemed to gain the heart of all the other sex. I accompanied the Countess to her house. I sat by her, but could not speak with her. It seemed as if the emotion in my breast, stifled the words I was about to utter. She however noticed me, and her parents in repeating their compliments to the lady I accompanied, included me in a general invitation to the house.

'As it was not the custom for ladies of rank to rise until a late hour, I had a great part of the day upon my own hands. I used generally to lounge about, and sometimes go to the Ambrosian Library, in quest of something to engage my attention. One morning I was there as usual, and I found the Ernachs there. Matilda was with them, they were just then occupied in viewing the manuscript of Virgil, with Petrarch's annotations. When the Cicerone pointed out the last note of this latter poet, in which he speaks of his love to Laura, I could not help remarking, a momentary emotion which passed across the face of Matilda. Her mother also observed it, and immediately taking her arm, accompanied her into the room containing pictures of several of the greatest masters. I followed them, and entered into conversation by pointing out the heads of the Milanese Raphael, which one cannot examine without feeling a stillness come over our senses foreign to our nature. There is so much beauty and heavenly quiet about them, that they indeed resemble representations of a poet's dream. Before we parted, I was accepted as the guide to the curiosities, which they had not yet seen, and my office was to begin the next day.

'It is useless to describe to you the gradual steps of love. I at last neglected the attentions due to the Countess, while sitting by the side of Matilda. At last, no longer capable of enduring the feelings within my bosom, I confessed my love to the object I adored. She was not angry, nor did she seem surprised; but in a voice that betrayed inward agitation, she begged of me to lay aside all hopes of gaining her hand, and conjured me not to mention it to her father. I was confused and abashed. I retired and returned to the palace, where I confined myself to my chamber. Not having appeared for several days in society, and enquiries being made concerning me, I was soon sought for by my kind relation. He seemed so anxious about the ill health, which he imagined was the cause of my absence from those gaieties in which I always seemed to delight, that I was induced to lay open to him the whole of my heart. He tried to administer consolation, but could not succeed; my vanity was mortified, and reflecting upon my poverty, I had imagined that I was despised for some richer rival. He seemed to know Matilda better, told me he could not believe it, but I dwelt so much upon the subject, that he saw it was useless to oppose my opinion any longer. He attempted to induce me to accompany him into society, but I refused, and for some days remained alone in my chamber.

'Sick with all the splendour around, which seemed to mock me, I determined in spite of the expected reproaches of my mother, to return to my father's house, where by long confinement I fell ill. My kind relation hearing of this came to me, and tried to represent to me the folly of my conduct; but disappointed love and mortified vanity, did not allow me to listen. Seeing me thus haunted by the idea of riches, he generously offered to advance me a considerable sum, and to give me letters to a friend at Alexandria, where I might he thought employ my capital to the greatest advantage in commercial speculations. I thanked him, and accepted his kind offer. I soon left Milan, determined never to return till those riches were mine, which should enable me to assert a rank equal to any in my native city. I arrived at Alexandria, and was soon engaged in mercantile speculations, with an eagerness that caused all my transactions to appear more like the ventures of a desperate gambler than the secure projects of a merchant. I found several Europeans established in this city, chiefly engaged in the commerce of grain.

'Amongst the rest, there was one who seemed to form a particular attachment to me; he was several years older than myself, and was noted amongst us for a certain avoidance of pleasure which did not appear natural to his years. He was always engaged, when not occupied in his business, either in reading or in a solitary ramble through the burnt neighbourhood of this ruined town. I was the only person he sought; he seemed to place his confidence in me, and made many enquiries, at first vaguely, concerning those I had known at Milan. Happening to name the Ernachs, his face immediately became anxious, and his questions evidently bore a stamp of interest they had not before shown. This excited my attention and caused me to make more particular enquiries concerning him. Little was known; he was a German, and it was thought he had been disappointed in love. He perceived the attention I began to show him, and one evening when we were alone, he told me that he had at first been induced to seek my society, from a letter he had received from Matilda. "You must have perceived the interest, with which I listened to your account of the family of the Ernachs; know that I love Matilda, that I have reason to believe my affection is returned, but that owing to my poverty, I have never dared to confess even to her the feelings of love I bear within my breast. We were together from earliest infancy, all our pleasures were in common, and though, when I grew to manhood, I no longer dared to use the familiarity of my earlier years with her, who began to vest the charms of woman, still we partook in the pleasures of each other's occupations. Many things we studied together. I read the lighter authors of literature to her while she was engaged in those occupations attendant, in our country, upon every female member of a family. I at last opened Petrarch, and read those sonnets in which love is so delicately pourtrayed. You cannot conceive my emotions, when I perceived that she felt them as I did myself, and that she often raised her modest eyes, while a blush mantled her cheek, to gaze upon me, while my trembling voice seemed not to be reading the sentiments of another, but speaking the feelings of my own breast. We seemed, indeed, not to want to comment upon what we were both sensible expressed only those truths which echoed in the breasts of both. When, however, I retired, I always upbraided myself for thus exposing, though indirectly, that love, of which I had no reason to think her parents would approve, for I had no profession, and was not born to riches. When, however, I saw her, and she again asked for the author whose delicate pencil only traced the most fading hues of love, I again read. We were thus engaged, when we were interrupted by her mother, who had stood unperceived some time watching the emotions but too visible in our countenances. She did not then speak, but taking another opportunity, when I was alone with her, she gently intimated, that I had not acted honourably in thus engaging the attention of Matilda to such poetry, as was but too powerful a seducer of the mind. I was but too conscious of it. I acknowledged my error, and promised to take no further occasion of thus acting upon her daughter's susceptible heart. She placed entire confidence in me, and was not deceived. I applied to my father, who, at my desire, sent me hither to push my fortune, and I have succeeded as well as I expected."

'How shall I convey to you an idea of what passed in my mind? Before me stood the unconscious cause of my being rejected by Matilda. He had told me, he loved her, that she loved him. I was silent when he ended, I could not rouse myself to speak to him; he, thinking that his narration had tired me, made an apology, to which I could only answer by monosyllables; he retired and left me to my own thoughts. It was evident Matilda preferred another. My feelings may be imagined,—cannot be described. It seemed as if some demon actuated me, I fell upon my knees, and dared even to call God to witness my vow of obtaining the object of my affections, in spite of all obstacles. It seemed as if I felt more at peace after having thus resolved upon not yielding even to him she loved, the possession I ambitioned.

'I sought Huldebrand, for so was my rival called, determined to worm into his confidence, and gain the whole of his secret. I told him not to impute my abstraction on the former evening to any thing but my mind being engaged in thought upon a circumstance, which I noticed at Milan, and which was now fully explained. I then mentioned to him the emotion I had noticed in Matilda's countenance, while listening to the memorial of Petrarch with regard to the duration of his love. This immediately secured his attention, and I soon learnt many circumstances with regard to their early years; and I became convinced, that there was really no engagement between them.

'In the mean time my speculations, which had been begun rashly, had for the greater part turned out badly, and I found myself with a capital considerably diminished. Huldebrand who could not remain ignorant of my losses proposed to me, as I seemed ignorant of the best means of securing a profitable commerce, to join him. I did so; but growing tired of the slow advantages to be obtained by the regular channels, I at last induced him to join me in a speculation that seemed to promise a certain and at the same time immense profit. We ventured, and lost all we risked. My loss did not grieve me much, for it had reduced my Matilda's favoured lover to the same want as myself. He was not however dismayed, nor did he reproach me, but immediately exerting himself to recover all that remained of our property, he proposed, that we should join some Armenians, who were about to leave Alexandria and penetrate into the interior of Asia, in hopes of finding some opportunity of bettering our small fortunes. I consented, and we accompanied them.

'We entered Persia, and travelled even into India. We soon found our capitals rapidly increasing, for, imitating the Armenians, we bought upon several occasions precious stones, which we resold almost immediately greatly to our advantage. It is, in no way necessary for me to give an account of these countries, towards the understanding the fatality that attended my life. I travelled through them careless about the scenery or inhabitants; the whole of my attention was engaged in my endeavours to acquire wealth. Matilda stood constantly before me as the bride of Huldebrand, and my father's house always appeared in contrast with the palace of the head of our family. I soon entered into the spirit of the traffic I was engaged in, and restrained as I was by Huldebrand's steadiness, we rapidly indeed accumulated an immense sum, which we carried always with us in precious stones.

'I had been particularly struck by the venerable appearance of one of our companions, he was aged, his head was white with the numbered years that had passed since his birth. This was the more remarkable from the contrast it offered with the jet black hair and beards of his countrymen. He was never engaged in their occupations, he never seemed to be concerned in any mercantile transaction, yet he seemed to be careless of his money, which he gave profusely to all. He seemed to delight in the society of strangers, and therefore sought ours; but Huldebrand not speaking his language did not gain the same hold of his affections as myself, he indeed treated me completely as his son, and often directed me in the conduct of our concerns; his advice was always advantageous.

'This stranger seemed to look upon me as his pupil, and he gradually turned my mind to the objects around me. But he did not improve my heart by the opening of my mind. He was himself extremely rich; when therefore he held forth upon the happiness of contented poverty, I thought he was but a mere visionary, imagining the Arabian delights of a sandy desert, while shaded by the canopying foliage of a grove, and surrounded by all the riches of a cultivated country. I looked around, and I saw the genius and the ideot both equally subservient to the will of the wealthy. I saw virtue trodden under foot, and vice, that monster in rags in the cottage, adored as a goddess in the temples of the gaudy palace. Wherever I went, it seemed as if gold, in the bustling of the whole of life, had the same effect as a few aspers thrown amidst the obstreperous crowd that immediately leaves off its hideous yell in haste to scramble for the miserable gain. Riches were a thirst upon me. I could not believe that Matilda or Ernach, her father, could resist the splendour of wealth. But Huldebrand was with me, half our common property was his. He loved,—was beloved. Whenever I looked upon him, my heart did not beat quicker; it seemed for a moment to pause, as if his sight blasted its vital action, but it beat again with redoubled violence, when Matilda's image rose upon my mind, and my former vow was again repeated.

'Though my appetite for riches was not sated, it was gratified; our speculations had been constantly doubling our capital, and we had already left the banks of the Euphrates, turning our steps towards Europe, when we gradually entered the vast desert that spreads its subtle sands from the Red Sea, almost to the Mediterranean. Having all our wealth about us in jewels and gold, we were anxious about our safety. Every night the cry of the watchful sentinel bidding us be upon the alert, while it called to the roaming Arab to depart, sounded on my waking ears, and often I arose in painful anxiety, to gaze upon the far spread horizon, lost sometimes in the misty light of the bright moon. I envied the sound sleep of the poor camel-driver, who lay extended by the animal entrusted to his care, as heedless of my wealth, as the brute about the fate of his burden. At last the ground seemed to acquire firmness to the foot, and the camel already began to browze upon the solitary stunted plants that here and there spread their parched growth to the no longer beneficent ray of an eastern sun. I thought myself secure, night came, and I was standing by my open tent, for I could not rest; I was gazing upon a long line which bounded the horizon, with a thin dark streak, indicating the palm boundary to our toilsome pilgrimages; there were slight clouds flitting before the moon, and as their shadows fled over the vast expanse, my heart beat quicker, for each, as it approached from the horizon, seemed to my hurried imagination, as the dark shadow formed by an Arab troop; one followed the other, always bearing deceit with it. At last from the long line of palms, a black speck seemed to move with great rapidity; I could trace no cloud upon the heavens, which could throw its dark shadow upon this track; I breathless called a sentinel, the alarm was given, but we were surrounded; I went about like a madman, encouraged the men to fight,—fought. The circle was gradually straightened round us; the men fell by the distant arrows at first, but the work of death was not slower, when the sword clashed against sword, and the robber's foot trod upon his antagonist's. I struggled, my riches were lost; while yet struggling amidst our very tents, I heard the old Armenian cry for help, he was combating with a young Arabian, who had thrown him to the ground. I rushed forward, bade the robber defend himself; we fought, I succeeded in disarming him, and was upon the point of thrusting my sword through his body, when he begged of me to spare his life, promising that both the Armenian and myself should be safe. I saw all resistance was at an end, I gave him back his weapon, and approached the old man who was wounded. He took my hand, thanked me for my attempt to save him, but he thought his wound was mortal; he bade me at the same time console myself for the loss of my accumulated wealth, saying that he would, ere he died, make me ample amends.

'Our lives, at the intercession of the Arab I had spared, who proved to be a man of rank amongst the robbers, were granted us. He conveyed the Armenian to his own tent, and I anxiously placed myself by the old man's side, watching, with the agitation of a desperate gambler, every various expression of his countenance; it was my last stake. Huldebrand I knew was not killed, but had been given, as part of the booty, to one of the robbers, in hopes of his ransoming himself, but he was ruined like myself, had lost every thing; I was however, if not deceived, to obtain riches as abundantly as before. Matilda might then be mine; I made no further enquiries about him who had partaken the vicissitudes of commerce and of life with me, who had been almost beggared by my rashness, and whose steadiness had enabled me to recover every thing, and to gain wealth. I sat by the old man; every sound that fell from his lips, seemed the announcement of his bequest, but he was silent on that subject.

'Five days elapsed, at last the sixth was passing, and his strength was evidently rapidly failing, his breath became hurried, and his eyes began to take that lustre, which seems to be the last exertion of the departing soul; he then spoke, "I wished," he said, "that my life had been spared but a short time longer, I could then have bestowed wealth upon you, without the conditions that may now startle you. Know, but how dare I tell it? you may look upon me with horror, and while I am wishing to bless you, may turn away from me. I have a power that is supposed to bring the curse of the Almighty upon it; I can,—I have the power of raising a spirit from the vast abyss, and make him lay at my feet, the infinite wealth enclosed within the earth's recesses. But if you would listen to one aged, who has borne this blasting power from early youth, you would refuse the dangerous gift. For there is a condition necessarily bound to that power, which will undoubtedly quell your ardent longing even for riches." It was in vain that he addressed me thus, Matilda and wealth connected rose to my imagination. I pressed him to explain himself. He did. He told me that either I could only call for a certain sum at a time, and that at each time, some human domestic infliction, worse than the preceding, would fall upon me, or that, I at once, could gain unlimited power, and constant domestic prosperity, on the condition of giving myself up for ever to the will of a malignant being. He had chosen the first, had called but once for the exertion of the demon's power, but his happiness had been withered by that once. I did not hesitate, I laughed in my own mind at domestic happiness, I had lived only in Italy, and in the East, I begged of him to disclose his secret; he did. I bound myself to the first condition.

'I impatiently rose, I left the old man upon his dying couch, and re-treated to my own tent. I raised the spirit, his hideous form might have appalled a stronger heart than mine. I trembled, but his mocking laugh subdued my fears, and bending my knee, I acknowledged him as my superior through life. I cannot describe the scene, I could not without recording some part of the spells by which I raised this monster, and he has but too fully proved his power for me to be willing to put the least clue into the hands of any one which might bring the curse I have felt upon him. Besides riches, I gained other powers, but these are not connected with yours and my Louisa's fate, I shall not speak of them.

'I returned to the sick man's tent, the Armenian was dead. I did not feel sorry, how could I at that moment; I was exultant, my wealth was so enormous, I did not see a possibility of spending it. The next day the robbers buried my benefactor in the burning sands. I proposed a ransom for myself to the Arab, he insisted upon my accepting my freedom. I did, and we eat together; no longer fearing treachery, I made him a present to an enormous amount. He was surprized, but did not make even the smallest enquiry.

'I roamed about the encampment, for I was desirous of seeing these robbers in their native barren plain. While wandering about their black tents, I heard a voice of pain issuing from one of the most miserable. It was Huldebrand, he was calling, in the delirium of a fever, for a drop of water to allay his thirst. The well was close to me. The tent was open, no one was near, he was extended upon the sandy floor, with hardly any clothes to defend him from its hot touch. I, even I, could not resist this appeal, I seized a vessel lying by his side, and drew it from the well full. I was turning towards him, when suddenly his tones altered, he seemed to press his breast, while in the softest words he addressed some one. I approached, he was imagining Matilda stood by him. The words sounded on my ear,—"I know, Matilda, that you love me." The pitcher fell upon the sand, and the water was drank up by the burning dust, and I turned away with a raging heart, from the dying Huldebrand.

'I instantly determined upon leaving the spot. The noble Arab escorted me to the utmost boundary of the desert, and I was safe from danger. I hired camels and horses, and proceeded to Aleppo, spreading every where that I was a merchant, who had been very successful in my speculations. This was easy to me, for I could refer to people with whom I had had transactions, and my name was known. I hastened to Italy, and soon reached Milan, I entered with all the pomp of riches; I will not describe my entry, it was foolishly splendid, nor will I attempt to paint to you the daily display I made of some new folly; they were produced by the intoxication of a madman. Matilda, for she held no less a powerful influence over me than my avarice, was the object of the whole. I found her health much decayed, she had not heard of Huldebrand for more than two years. Yet there was perhaps a greater charm in that pale cheek and languid eye, than I had found in the delicate colouring of the one, or the splendour of the other. If I could gain her love now, it would, indeed, be an ample compensation for her former rejection. I began by spreading the report of her lover's death, though I was not certain of the fact, yet I thought, at any rate, that he could not re-appear so soon as not to allow me time to accomplish my end. I then went to her father's, and in the course of the conversation announced it.

'Matilda was inconsolable, but she took pleasure in my society, for I could talk to her of Huldebrand, I related indifferent particulars concerning him, the eagerness with which she listened reached my heart; I determined, however, to endure even these pangs, rather than lose the opportunities afforded me of sitting by her side. As in the course of narration, I introduced the relation of actions in which I had been his benefactor, she blessed me for it. I felt like a baffled demon. I gradually began to talk of myself. I sounded the father and mother with regard to a marriage; obtained their full consent and approbation. They gradually broke it to their daughter. She wondered at my seeking for a widowed heart; insisted upon my taking some months to consider of it, while she herself fulfilled the term of mourning she thought due to her lover's memory. I was anxious, and fearful of Huldebrand's appearance. I pressed my suit with earnestness; my relations, her father, her mother, used all the arts of persuasion to induce her to anticipate the day. She did, and we were married.

'It now seemed as if I could dare the world. I had Matilda, had wealth, the only objects my mind had ever rested upon were mine. I had two children, Louisa and Olivieri. You cannot imagine the splendour in which I lived. Where could the mortal be found who had greater supposed sources of happiness than mine? yet I was miserable; Matilda was mine, my wife, but her affections still rested upon the image of my rival. I doated upon her; it seemed as if the price of guilt I had paid bound her the more to me, as if she were to form the only happiness I was to know, and she did not love me. She differed entirely from my countrywomen; she enjoyed her domestic circle, she was modest; and while she stood amongst the abandoned wantons, who formed the only society around her, she stood erect, as if she were sent by Heaven to show deluded men the beauties of the virtues they despised.

'I had not enjoyed the society of my wife more than three years, when my momentary happiness was blasted. Matilda came home one day, as I imagined, from the Corso, flurried and violently agitated. She threw herself upon the sofa, and lost in thought, she did not perceive that I was near her. She drew from her breast a note: I could see over her shoulder; it struck me that it was Huldebrand's hand-writing. She seemed to look upon it as if she could not believe her eyes. She viewed it, her hands fell, and the movement of the eyelids over the fixed eyes seemed to denote the belief in a deceit of the senses. Her breath was still, her cheek pale, she did not move. I unavoidably discovered myself; she turned, looked at me, and the tears bursting from her eyes, rolled down her cheeks, as she rushed out of the room. I dared not follow her. Huldebrand might be stalking in my very house, might be close to me, his words of reproach might be already in the air, prepared to damn me with their sound. I should be proved in the world's face, a liar, a wretch without a spark of generosity, of gratitude, in Matilda's face—I hid myself in my chamber, for the consciousness of my guilt caused me at first to wish for concealment. But the thought of my rival roused me; was it not possible to remove him? I rushed out of my room, and was upon the point of going through the great gate, when I perceived a figure descending the staircase, wrapt closely in a large mantle. It was a woman—it was Matilda. Her hurried step and anxious glances thrown around caused me to watch her. She went out into the street, I followed her; there was an obstacle near the theatre, she cleared it, but I lost her in the crowd of carriages. In vain I tried every opening leading to the theatre, I could not recover a trace of her. At last I was obliged to lean exhausted against the wall, and Ernach, her father, coming from the theatre, discovered me. Perceiving my agitation at sight of him, he insisted upon escorting me home. He attempted to lead me to explain to him the cause of my trembling limbs, which weighed upon his arm. He did not know that he sought to know my shame; I insisted upon his leaving me, and I at last fell exhausted upon a chair in my saloon.

'I know not how long I had remained in this situation by myself; I at last heard Matilda's light step ascending the staircase. I did not move, my eyes remained still gazing on the ground when she entered. At sight of me she started, but she commanded herself—approached me with a faultering step. I attempted to clasp her to my bosom, as if—I know not what passed in my mind. She retreated. "You have a right to know where I have been in this clandestine manner." I hid my face with my hands, I was conscious she had been to see Huldebrand. She had been with him, she would say no more. I threw myself at her feet, she turned away. "I can no longer even esteem you," were the last words she said, when she left me.

'She went out several times in the course of next day; once I attempted to follow her. She perceived me at the door: "Filiberto," she said, "seek not to pursue my steps, I am but active in the cause of virtue. Retire and leave me. You must be aware of what hangs over your head. Would that heaven may grant I could avert it from my husband, my children's father." I was left in a state of mind that bordered upon phrenzy. I rushed out of the house, and turning my steps another way, I did not return towards my home till night. When I did return, I found every thing in the greatest confusion. There was a carriage with posthorses at the gate. The moment I approached, my valet came to me to tell me of my shame. Matilda had been seen leaving Milan, with a gentleman in her company. I jumped into the carriage, and followed upon the road they were reported to have taken.

'I did not speak during the whole time; I did not listen, though my servant, having entered with me, was telling me more of the circumstances. Night and day I travelled in pursuit. I seemed to be gaining on them. I at last overtook them just as I was entering a village in Savoy. They were upon the point of leaving it. I sprung out of my carriage, and with the speed of a demoniac I ran after them. In my furious haste, I fell. I did not attempt to rise, but instantly fired; my wife's shriek was heard: they, however, drove on. When my carriage with fresh horses overtook me, my servant tried to raise me, I had dislocated my ancle. Blood, my servant told me, could be traced upon the road, as if it had fallen from my wife's carriage. I could but look upon myself as Matilda's murderer, the shriek was her's. My emotions and feelings were so violent and various it would be impossible to portray them. The demon's power was upon me, and his curse proved a bitter one.

'I was conveyed home, where I was for a long time delirious; I became calm but not less miserable. My attendants then gave me a letter, which had been found upon my wife's dressing table, after my departure in chase of her. She was innocent, she had not fled with Huldebrand, but with her father. Huldebrand had upon that condition agreed to conceal my crime, my shame. She had left her home, her children; had sacrificed her own to shield my name from infamy. I did not at this intelligence relapse into the violent ravings I had undergone. I sunk into a state of apathy, whence nothing could rouse me. I refused even to see my children, and hardly ever leaving my chamber, I spent the night and day with short intervals to self-reproach in combating inflictions of the mind more dreadful than any corporeal penance of the holy anchorite.

'Many years had thus passed, I had not once seen my children, not even heard of them, for I would speak with no one. I at last saw them by accident. You know Olivieri's violent character. He had constantly enquired after me, always baffled by the servants in his wish of seeing me; he at last seized his opportunity, but Louisa had watched him, and they both appeared in my sight struggling with one another; for she was trying to hinder his disturbing me. If Matilda herself had stood before me she could not have affected me more; for Louisa, though her features are different, her eye dark, has the expression that gave such power to her mother's looks, playing upon her face. She at last, no longer capable of resisting her brother, threw herself at my feet, and earnestly begged me not to be offended with her dear Olivieri. I took her to my arms. From that moment I was aroused. I could not leave my daughter, but gave up all my time to the education of my children; but I brought another curse upon my head, for I neglected Olivieri; except in his literary studies I did not assist him, his mind was allowed to be biassed by any one who chose to trouble themselves with acting upon him. Louisa on the contrary was my constant companion, she rewarded my care. You know her, if ever a wretch like me might have hope, it must be in the prayers such a being can offer up for me to the throne of heaven. After some time I proposed journeying through the different countries of Europe, to show my children the different peculiarities of nations. We had already entered Switzerland when my son left me. I had been accustomed to his often quitting me for days together, and hardly noticed his departure. Louisa and myself proceeded to the different spots remarkable for their beauty or sublimity. On the Wengern Alp we saw you. We soon after heard daily of the feats of Ernestus Berchtold and Olivieri. I don't know why, but the thought of the chamois hunter we had seen being this Ernestus, first struck my daughter, and I soon joined in the belief. A letter from Olivieri appointed Interlaken as the place of meeting; we went there. Events in which you were concerned brought us again to Milan.

'The immense riches I had obtained from the spirit under my command, though much diminished, were yet more than sufficient to maintain us in sufficient splendour, not to fear any thing like a competition. But Olivieri and yourself were gamblers. Louisa forced me again to risk an infliction equally severe as the last, for your sake. I could not resist her prayers for you. I again called the spirit from his immortal haunts, and Olivieri's infamy was the consequence. Your debts had proved so enormous, that in my attempt at saving him from an ignominious death, I was again obliged, though I knew the horrible powers of the demon, to call upon him. I did so. He announced to me that I had exhausted my spells, and that after this infliction, as nothing round me would remain, on which he could breathe his pestilential breath, he would no longer obey my summons. I called upon him to take back his gold, he laughed and left me. I had no suspicion of Olivieri's seduction of your sister; when therefore his letter was put into my hands, you may imagine how your noble conduct affected me. I did not speak of it, for what could a father say? Must I even acknowledge it to you, I sometimes rested upon it with a feeling of consolation, for I hoped, that crime of my son's might be the infliction upon his father, meant by the demon as passing all others. Louisa I thought might then be spared, and you two might at least be happy.

'But you married; I dreamt of happiness, on Louisa's birth-day accompanied you to your room, and the demon's threat I found had indeed been fulfilled. Your mother's portrait was Matilda's. Olivieri had seduced, you married a daughter of Matilda, of Matilda's husband, and I was the murderer of her father.'

About the Author

To the popular imagination, paranoid schizophrenics hear the Devil instructing us to commit murder, or we crowd mental institutions believing we are Jesus Christ Himself. My mental condition has coloured my creativity in a variety of different ways. Many writers will often encounter their "characters" actively participating in the stories they are writing. This "inner-voice" instructing the writing process can be unsettling to nascent writers. For an author with my condition, the voices are audible and very, very communicative.

My voices, however, are not those of the characters I am writing, but of pseudonymous co-writers, actively and audibly participating in the writing process. Each of my books has a very different and unique co-writer. Ophelia T'Wat, the co-writer of *The Marquis de Sade's Wettest Midummer Night's Dream Conceivable*, is a 21 year-old college student who is stripping her way through college. The co-author of Satan's Study Bible: The Four Gospels is far more a nefarious personality, Satan himself, but instead of instructing me to murder, he wanted nothing more than a Study Bible written from his own point-of-view. Satan's Preacher Man manifested more as a dreamlike past life experience. And finally, the granddaddy of them all, God and His Only Begotten Son Jesus Christ spoke to me audibly and through dreams instructing and inspiring The Holy Bible Trilogy and its Next Testament.

But can a novelist, who was diagnosed schizophrenic as a teenager, actually hear the Voice of God tell him to continue the Word of God? As a dutiful Catholic, I sought the intersession of a priest for exorcism from demonic forces. He instructed me to see a psychiatrist to alleviate my hallucinations. I am caught in a spiritual conundrum, would I rather be a Prophet of God or crazy?

Over decades of constant psychoanalysis, I have come to peace with my rather unique creativity. I have embraced the quirks that come with my writer's voice, or voices as it were. I hope you, the Reader, can appreciate and enjoy my collaborations with my voices.

This is a major contributing factor to both the Pale Student of the Unhallowed Arts and his Creation/Creature haunting Mary as a hallucinogenic phantasm. Authors often describe to lay readers that their characters 'speak' to them, specifically telling the author what they are going to say and do. Readers are aghast at the idea that a creation of the author's brain can override the author's own intentions with 'their' story. But it is not the author's story, it is the characters. The Pale Student and the Creation/Creature may be products of Mary's imagination, but they are a real to the author (and reader) as if they were flesh and blood. It is a shocking experience for the nascent author when their characters 'speak' to them, often saying, 'No! This is my story now. I shall relate it the way I wish!.'

If writing is as schizophrenic an experience as I allege, then what about an author who is a diagnosed schizophrenic? When I said earlier that 'pseudonymous co-writers, actively and audibly participat[e] in the writing process', I was not exaggerating. I, more often than not, hear my characters speaking to me over my left shoulder while I type on a MacBook. It *is* like they are a co-writer looking over my shoulder saying, 'No. No. Say this.'

To me my characters are co-writers ,and I have, in the past, given them co-writing credits, like I did with Abigail K.C. Sterling, the co-author of *Alistair Strange & the Fan Friction*. She deserves the credit as much, if not more so, than I do.